Praise for *My L[...]*

"A dark and irresistible debut."

—*People*

"The thriller we're most excited to stay up with all night."

—*Entertainment Weekly*

"Side effects of reading this include sleepless nights and awkward looks from strangers on the subway due to your horrified expression."

—*Cosmopolitan*

"Think *Dexter* but sexier."

—theSkimm

"Will shock even the savviest suspense readers."

—*Real Simple*

"A new twist on the genre."

—Refinery29

"If you read one book this year, make it *My Lovely Wife*."   —Betches

"Wow! *My Lovely Wife* is a stunner—full of twists, well-drawn characters, and riveting suspense."

—#1 *New York Times* bestselling author Harlan Coben

"Clever. Manipulative. Dark. Disturbing. What more can you ask for?"   —Jane Corry, national bestselling author of *My Husband's Wife*

"An assured and deliciously engrossing debut. You'll surely devour *My Lovely Wife,* but it will linger long after you've reached the last page."

—Sarah Pinborough, *New York Times* bestselling
author of *Behind Her Eyes*

"You'll never look at your neighbors the same. I couldn't pull myself away from this story. . . . Make sure you clear your schedule before you pick it up. Absolutely unputdownable."

—Liv Constantine, *USA Today* bestselling
author of *The Last Mrs. Parrish*

"A wicked, delicious tale of secrets, relationships, and the lengths to which some will go to keep the magic alive." —CrimeReads

"[A] dark, disturbing exploration of family, marriage, and murderous compulsions." —*The Washington Post*

"You might want to read this one during the daytime." —*Woman's Day*

"Mark our words: *My Lovely Wife* will be one of the most shocking and suspenseful thrillers you'll read all year." —HelloGiggles

"A knockout. . . . An effortless page turner." —*Publishers Weekly*

"It's a remarkable achievement, full stop." —Shelf Awareness

"Do you hear me screaming and/or the sound of my hefty exhale? This novel is a JOURNEY. I was invested from the very first unsettling page." —Elite Daily

"Truly horrifying in the most delicious way. Samantha Downing sucks you in with a great story, pitch-perfect prose, and disturbingly dead-on insights into the dark side of human nature. I hope I never meet her in a dark alley."
—Nick Petrie, national bestselling author of *The Drifter*

"A fantastic foray into what we know—and what we do not—about those closest to us. Intricately plotted, fascinating characters—I loved it!"
—Heather Graham, *New York Times* bestselling author of *Fade to Black*

My Lovely Wife

SAMANTHA DOWNING

BERKLEY
New York

BERKLEY
An imprint of Penguin Random House LLC
penguinrandomhouse.com

Copyright © 2019 by Samantha Downing
Readers Guide copyright © 2020 by Samantha Downing
Excerpt from *He Started It* copyright © 2020 by Samantha Downing
Penguin Random House supports copyright. Copyright fuels creativity, encourages diverse
voices, promotes free speech, and creates a vibrant culture. Thank you for buying an
authorized edition of this book and for complying with copyright laws by not reproducing,
scanning, or distributing any part of it in any form without permission. You are supporting
writers and allowing Penguin Random House to continue to publish books for every reader.

BERKLEY and the BERKLEY & B colophon are registered trademarks of
Penguin Random House LLC.

Second Berkley trade paperback ISBN: 9780593637753

The Library of Congress has catalogued the Berkley hardcover edition of this book as follows:

Names: Downing, Samantha, author.
Title: My lovely wife / Samantha Downing.
Description: First edition. | New York: Berkley, 2019.
Identifiers: LCCN 2018016347 | ISBN 9780451491725 (hardcover) |
ISBN 9780451491749 (ebook)
Subjects: | GSAFD: Suspense fiction.
Classification: LCC PS3604.O9457 M9 2019 | DDC 813/.6—dc23
LC record available at https://lccn.loc.gov/2018016347

Berkley hardcover edition / March 2019
First Berkley trade paperback edition / March 2020
Second Berkley trade paperback edition / February 2023

Printed in the United States of America
1st Printing

Book design by Tiffany Estreicher

One

SHE IS LOOKING at me. Her blue eyes are glassy, they flicker down to her drink and back up. I look at my own drink and can feel her watching, wondering if I'm as interested as she is. I glance over and smile to show her I am. She smiles back. Most of her lipstick is gone, now a reddish smear on the rim of her glass. I walk over and take the seat next to her.

She fluffs her hair. It is unremarkable in both color and length. Her lips move, she says hello, and her eyes are brighter. They look backlit.

Physically, I appeal to her the same way I would appeal to most women in this bar. I am thirty-nine, in excellent shape with a full head of hair and a deep set of dimples, and my suit fits better than any glove. That's why she looked at me, why she smiled, why she is happy I have come over to join her. I am the man she has in mind.

I slide my phone across the bar toward her. It displays a message.

Hello. My name is Tobias.

She reads it and crinkles her brow, looking back and forth between the phone and me. I type another message.

I am deaf.

Her eyebrows shoot up, she covers her mouth with one hand, and the pink rises on her skin. Embarrassment looks the same on everyone.

She shakes her head at me. Sorry, so sorry. She did not know.

Of course you didn't. How could you?

She smiles. It is not quite whole.

I am no longer the picture in her head, no longer the man she imagined, but now she isn't sure what to do.

She picks up my phone and types back.

I'm Petra.

A pleasure to meet you, Petra. You are Russian?

My parents were.

I nod and smile. She nods and smiles. I can see her mind churning.

She would rather not stay with me. She wants to go find a man who can hear her laugh and does not have to type out his words.

At the same time, her conscience tells her not to discriminate. Petra does not want to be the shallow woman who refuses a man because he is deaf. She doesn't want to turn me down the way so many others have.

Or so she assumes.

Her internal battle is like a three-act play unfolding before my eyes, and I know how it ends. At least most of the time.

She stays.

Her first question is about my hearing, or lack of it. Yes, I have been deaf from birth. No, I have never heard anything—not a laugh, not a voice, not a puppy barking or a plane overhead.

Petra gives me a sad face. She does not realize this is patronizing, and I don't tell her, because she is trying. Because she stays.

She asks if I can read lips. I nod. She starts to talk.

"When I was twelve, I broke my leg in two places. Bike accident." Her mouth moves in the most exaggerated, grotesque way. "Anyway, I had to wear a cast that went from my foot all the way up to my thigh." She stops, draws a line across her thigh in case I have trouble understanding. I don't, but I appreciate the attempt. And the thigh.

She continues. "I couldn't walk at all for six weeks. At school, I had to use a wheelchair, because the cast was too heavy for crutches."

I smile, half imagining little Petra with a big cast. Half imagining where this sad story is heading.

"I'm not saying I know what it's like to live in a wheelchair, or to have any permanent disability. I just always feel like . . . well, it feels like I've had a small taste of what it would be like, you know?"

I nod.

She smiles with relief, afraid her story might have offended me.

I type:

You are very sensitive.

She shrugs. Beams at the compliment.

We have another drink.

I tell her a story that has nothing to do with being deaf. I tell her about my childhood pet, a frog named Sherman. He was a bullfrog who sat on the biggest rock in the pond and hogged all the flies. I never tried to catch Sherman; I would just watch him, and sometimes he watched me, too. We liked to sit together, and I started calling him my pet.

"What happened to him?" Petra asks.

I shrug.

One day the rock was empty. Never saw him again.

Petra says this is sad. I tell her it isn't. Sad would've been finding his dead body and being forced to bury him. I never had to do that. I just imagined he went to a bigger pond with more flies.

She likes this and tells me so.

I do not tell her everything about Sherman. For instance, he had a long tongue that darted around so fast I could hardly see it, but I always wanted to grab it. I used to sit by the pond and wonder how bad of a thought that was. How terrible was it to try and grab a frog's tongue? And would it hurt him? If he died, would it be murder? I never tried to grab his tongue and probably couldn't have anyway, but I thought about it. And that made me feel like I wasn't a good friend to Sherman.

Petra tells me about her cat, Lionel, who is named after her child-hood cat, also named Lionel. I tell her that's funny, but I'm not sure it is. She shows me pictures. Lionel is a tuxedo cat, with a face divided between black and white. He is too stark to be cute.

She continues to talk and shifts to her work. She brands products and companies, and she says it's both the easiest and the most difficult thing. Difficult in the beginning, because it's so hard to get anyone to remember anything, but as more people start to recognize a brand, it becomes easy.

"At some point, it doesn't even matter what we're selling. The brand becomes more important than the product." She points to my phone and asks if I bought it because of the name or because I like the phone.

Both?

She smiles. "See. You aren't even sure."

I guess not.

"What do you do?"

Accountant.

She nods. It is the least exciting profession in the world, but it is solid, stable, and something a deaf guy can easily do. Numbers don't speak with a voice.

The bartender comes over. He is neat and clean, college-aged. Petra takes charge of the ordering, and it is because I am deaf. Women always think I need to be taken care of. They like to do things for me because they think I am weak.

Petra secures us two more drinks and a fresh bowl of snacks, and she smiles like she is proud of herself. It makes me laugh. Silently, but still a laugh.

She leans toward me and puts her hand on my arm. Leaves it there. She has forgotten I am not her ideal man, and our progression is now predictable. It's not long before we go to her place. The decision is easier than it should be, though not because I find her particularly attractive. It is the choice. She gives me the power to decide, and right now I am a man who says yes.

Petra lives downtown, close to the bar, in the middle of all the big branding signs. Her place is not as neat as I'd expected. There is clutter everywhere: papers and clothes and dishes. It makes me think she loses her keys a lot.

"Lionel is around here somewhere. Hiding, probably."

I don't look for that stark cat.

She flits around, dropping her bag in one place and removing her shoes in another. Two glasses appear, filled with red wine, and she leads me into the bedroom. She turns to face me, smiling. Petra has become more attractive—even her plain hair seems to sparkle. It is the alcohol, yes, but it's also her happiness. I get the feeling she has not been this happy in a while, and I'm not sure why. Petra is attractive enough.

She presses up against me, her body warm, her breath soaked in wine. She takes the glass out of my hand and puts it down.

I do not finish drinking it until much later, when we are in the dark and the only light is from my phone. We type back and forth, making fun of ourselves and the fact that we do not know each other.

I ask:

Favorite color?

Lime green. Ice cream?

Bubble gum.

Bubble gum? The blue stuff?

Yes.

Who says that?

What's your favorite?

French vanilla. Pizza topping?

Ham.

We're done here.

Are we?

Wait, are we still talking about pizza?

We are not talking about pizza.

Afterward, she dozes off first. I think about leaving, then about staying, and the idea bounces around so long I doze off.

When I wake up, it's still dark. I slip out of the bed without waking Petra. She is sleeping facedown, one leg askew and her hair spread out on the pillow. I cannot decide if I really like her or not, so I don't decide at all. I do not have to.

On the nightstand, her earrings. They are made of colored glass, a swirl of blue shades, and they look like her eyes. After getting dressed, I slip the earrings into my pocket. I take them to remind myself not to do this again. I almost believe it will work.

I walk toward the front door without looking back.

"Are you really deaf?"

She says it out loud, to my back.

I hear her because I am not deaf.

And I keep moving.

I pretend I don't hear her, go straight to the door and shut it behind me, then continue until I am out of her building, down the block, and around the corner. It is only then that I stop and wonder how she figured it out. I must have slipped.

Two

MY NAME IS not Tobias. I use that name only when I want some-one to remember me. In this case, the bartender. I introduced myself and typed out my name when I first walked in and ordered a drink. He will remember me. He will remember that Tobias is the deaf man who left the bar with a woman he just met. The name was for his benefit, not Petra's. She will remember me anyway, because how many deaf guys could she have slept with?

And if I hadn't made a mistake, I would have been an odd footnote in her sexual history. But now she will remember me as the "fake deaf guy" or the "possibly fake deaf guy."

The more I think about it, the more I wonder if I slipped twice. Maybe I froze when she asked if I was deaf. It's possible, because that's what people do when they hear something unexpected. And if I did, she probably saw it. She probably knows I lied.

On the drive back home, everything is uncomfortable. My car seat feels scratchy, and it hurts my back. Everything on the radio is too loud, almost like everyone is screeching. But I can't blame that all on Petra. I have been irritable for a while now.

At home, all is quiet. My wife, Millicent, is still in bed. I have been married to her for fifteen years, and she does not call me Tobias. We have two kids; Rory is fourteen, and Jenna is one year younger.

Our bedroom is dark, but I can just about see the shape of Millicent under the bedcovers. I take off my shoes and tiptoe toward the bathroom.

"Well?"

Millicent sounds wide-awake.

I half turn and see the shadow of her propped up on an elbow. There it is again. The choice. From Millicent, a rarity.

"No," I say.

"No?"

"She isn't right."

The air between us freezes. It doesn't thaw until Millicent exhales and lays her head back down.

SHE GETS UP before I do. By the time I walk into the kitchen, Millicent is organizing breakfast, school lunches, the day, our lives.

I know I should tell her about Petra. Not about the sex—I wouldn't tell my wife about that. But I should tell her that I made a mistake and that Petra is right for us. I should do it because it's a risk to leave Petra out there.

Instead, I say nothing.

Millicent looks at me, her disappointment hitting like a physical force. Her eyes are green, many shades of green, and they look like camouflage.

They are nothing like Petra's. Millicent and Petra have nothing in common, except they've both slept with me. Or some version of me.

The kids tumble down the stairs, already yelling at each other, fighting over who said what about so-and-so at school yesterday. They are dressed and ready for school, just as I am dressed for work in my tennis whites. I am not and never have been an accountant.

While my kids are in school and my wife is selling houses, I am outside on the court, in the sun, teaching people how to play tennis. Most of my clients are middle-aged and out of shape, with too much money and time. Occasionally, I am hired by parents who believe their child is a prodigy, a champion, a future role model. So far, they have all been wrong.

But before I can leave to teach anyone anything, Millicent makes us all sit together for at least five minutes. She calls it breakfast.

Jenna rolls her eyes, taps her feet, anxious to get her phone back. No phones are allowed at the table. Rory is calmer than his sister. He makes the most of our five minutes by eating as much as possible, then stuffing his pockets with whatever doesn't fit in his mouth.

Millicent sits across from me, a cup of coffee perched at her lips. She is dressed for work in a skirt, blouse, and heels, and her red hair is pulled back. The morning sun makes it look like copper. We are the same age, but she looks better—always has. She is the woman I should not have been able to get.

My daughter taps my arm in a pattern, like the beat to a song, and she continues until I pay attention to her. Jenna does not look like her mother. Her eyes, her hair, and the shape of her face come from me, and sometimes this makes me sad. Other times not.

"Dad, can you take me to get new shoes today?" she says. She is smiling, because she knows I will say yes.

"Yes," I say.

Millicent kicks me under the table. "Those shoes are a month old," she says to Jenna.

"But they're too tight now."

Not even my wife can argue with that.

Rory asks if he can go play his video game for a few minutes before school.

"No," Millicent says.

He looks at me. I should say no, but now I can't, not after I said yes to his sister. He knows this, because Rory is the smart one. He is also the one who looks like Millicent.

"Go ahead," I say.

He races off.

Millicent slams down her coffee cup.

Jenna picks up her phone.

We are done with breakfast.

Before getting up from the table, Millicent glares at me. She looks exactly like my wife and, at the same time, nothing like her.

I FIRST SAW Millicent in an airport. I was twenty-two and on my way back from Cambodia, where I had spent the summer with three friends. We got high every day and drunk every night, and we never shaved. I left the country as a clean-cut kid from the suburbs and returned as a shaggy, bearded man with a deep tan and some great stories. None compare to Millicent.

I was on a layover, my first back in the country. I went through customs and was heading to the domestic terminal when I saw her. Millicent was sitting in an empty gate area, alone, with her feet propped up on her suitcase. She was staring out of the floor-to-ceiling windows overlooking the tarmac. Her red hair was knotted into a loose bun, and she was wearing a T-shirt, jeans, and sneakers. I stopped to watch her as she watched the planes.

It was the way she looked out the window.

I had done the same thing when I set off on my trip. My dream had been to travel, to see places like Thailand and Cambodia and Vietnam, and I did. Now I was back on familiar ground, back to where I had grown up, but my parents were gone. Although I am not sure they were ever really there. Not for me.

When I returned, my dream of traveling had been fulfilled but not replaced with another. Not until I saw Millicent. She looked like she was just beginning her own dream. In that moment, I wanted to be a part of it.

At the time, I didn't think of all this. I came up with it later, when I tried to explain to her or anyone else why I found her so attractive.

But back then, I continued to my next gate. After traveling for twenty hours with still more to go, I couldn't even muster up the energy to speak to her. All I could do was admire.

It turned out we were on the same flight. I took it as a sign.

She had a window seat, and mine was in the center of the middle row. It took a little convincing, some flirting with a flight attendant and a twenty-dollar bill, to get my seat moved next to Millicent. She did not look up when I sat down.

By the time the drink cart came by, I had come up with a plan. I would order whatever she ordered, and, because I had already decided she was special, I could not imagine her ordering anything as mundane as water. It would be something more unusual, like pineapple juice with ice, and when I ordered the same thing we would have a moment of symmetry, symbiosis, serendipity—it didn't matter what.

Given how long it had been since I had slept, this plan sounded plausible in my head right up until Millicent told the flight attendant thanks but no thanks. She did not want a drink.

I said the same thing. It didn't have the effect I wanted.

But when Millicent turned to the flight attendant, I saw her eyes for the first time. The color reminded me of the lush, open fields I had seen all over Cambodia. They were not nearly as dark as they look now.

She went back to staring out the window. I went back to staring at her while pretending I wasn't.

I told myself I was an idiot and I should just talk to her.

I told myself there was something wrong with me, because normal people didn't act like this over a girl they had never seen before.

I told myself not to be a stalker.

I told myself she was too beautiful for me.

With thirty minutes left on the flight, I spoke.

"Hi."

She turned. Stared. "Hi."

I think that's when I stopped holding my breath.

Years passed before I asked why she kept staring out the windows, both in the airport and on the plane. She said it was because she had never flown before. The only thing she had been dreaming about was a safe landing.

Three

PETRA WAS NUMBER one on the list, but now that she's been eliminated I move on to the next, a young woman named Naomi George. I haven't spoken to her yet.

In the evening, I drive to the Lancaster Hotel. Naomi works as a front desk clerk at the Lancaster, one of those old-world places that survives because of its past glory. The building is huge and so grand in decor it could never be built today. It would be too expensive to do right and too cheesy if done wrong.

The front of the hotel has glass doors and side panels, offering a good view of the front desk. Naomi stands behind it wearing the Lancaster uniform, a blue skirt and jacket, both trimmed in gold braid, and a crisp white blouse. She has long dark hair, and the freckles on her nose make her look younger than she is. Naomi is twenty-seven. She probably still gets carded in bars but is not as innocent as she looks.

Late at night, I have seen her get a little too friendly with more than one male guest. They have all been alone, older, and well dressed, and she doesn't always leave the hotel when her shift ends. Either

Naomi has been making extra money on the side or she has aspirational one-night stands.

Because of social media, I know that her favorite food is sushi but she won't eat red meat. In high school, she played volleyball and had a boyfriend named Adam. Now he is referred to as The Cretin. Her last boyfriend, Jason, moved away three months ago, and she has been single ever since. Naomi has been thinking about getting a pet, probably a cat, but she hasn't yet. She has more than a thousand online friends, but from what I can tell, Naomi has just two close friends. Three at the most.

I'm still not sure she is the one. I need to know more.

Millicent is tired of waiting.

Last night, I found Millicent in our bathroom, standing in front of the mirror, taking off her makeup. She was wearing jeans and a T-shirt proclaiming her the mother of a seventh-grade honor student. Jenna, not Rory.

"What was wrong with her?" she asked. Millicent does not use Petra's name because she does not have to. I know who she means.

"She just wasn't the one."

Millicent didn't look at me in the mirror. She smoothed lotion on her face. "That's the second one you've eliminated."

"She has to be right. You know that."

She snapped the lid of her lotion bottle closed. I went to the bedroom and sat down to take off my shoes. The day had been long and needed to end, but Millicent wouldn't let it. She followed me into the bedroom and stood over me.

"Are you sure you still want to do this?" she asked.

"Yes."

I was too busy feeling guilty about sleeping with another woman to show much enthusiasm. It had hit me in the afternoon, when I saw a little old couple; they had to be at least ninety years old, and they held hands as they walked down the street. Couples like that didn't cheat on each other. I looked up at Millicent and wished I could make us become like that.

Millicent knelt in front of me and placed a hand on top of my knee. "We need to do this."

Her eyes flickered, the warmth from her hand spreading as it inched up my leg. "You're right," I said. "We do need this."

She leaned closer and kissed me long and deep. It made me feel guiltier. And it made me want to do whatever will make her happy.

LESS THAN TWENTY-FOUR hours later, I am sitting in front of the Lancaster Hotel. Naomi's shift does not end until eleven, and I cannot just sit outside the hotel for the next three hours. Instead of going home, I get something to eat and then sit in a bar. It's a convenient place to go when there is nowhere else.

The place I have chosen is half-full, mostly with men who are alone. It's not as nice as the bar I was in with Petra. The cocktails cost half as much, and anyone wearing a suit has already loosened their tie. The wood floor is patterned with scrapes from the barstools, and watermark rings decorate the bar. This is a place for drinkers, by drinkers, a place where everyone is too inebriated for details.

I order a beer and watch a baseball game on one screen and the news on another.

Bottom of the third, two outs. Rain tomorrow, maybe, but then again it might be sunny. It is always sunny here in Woodview, Florida, a so-called enclave from the real world. In about an hour, we can be at the ocean, in a state park, or at one of the biggest amusement parks in the world. We always say how lucky we are to live here in central Florida, especially those of us who live in the Hidden Oaks subdivision. The Oaks are an enclave from the enclave.

Top of the fourth inning, one out. Still two more hours until Naomi's shift ends and I can follow her.

And then, Lindsay.

Her smiling face stares at me from the TV screen.

Lindsay, with her narrow brown eyes and straight blond hair, her outdoorsy tan and big white teeth.

She went missing a year ago. For a week, she was a blip on the news, and then the story was gone. Without any close family to keep her on TV, no one paid attention. Lindsay wasn't a missing child; she wasn't defenseless. She was a grown woman, and in less than seven days she was forgotten.

Not by me. I still remember her laugh. It was infectious enough to make me laugh along with her. Seeing her again makes me remember how much I liked her.

Four

I FIRST SPOKE TO Lindsay while on a hike. One Saturday morning, I followed her to the hilly trails just outside town. She started on one trail, I started on another, and an hour later we ran into each other.

When she saw me, Lindsay nodded and said hello in a way that did not invite further conversation. I waved and mouthed hello. Unconsciously, she gave me an odd look, and I handed her my phone to introduce myself.

Sorry, that probably looked strange! Hello, my name is Tobias. I am deaf.

I watched her guard drop.

She introduced herself, we talked, and then we sat down to drink some water and she offered me a snack. Pixy Stix. She had a handful of them.

Lindsay rolled her eyes at herself. "That's terrible, right? Eating sugar while exercising? But I love them."

So do I.

It was the truth. I hadn't eaten Pixy Stix since I was a kid, but I loved them.

She told me about herself, about the job, house, and hobbies I already knew about. I told her the same stories I told all of them. As the morning sun rose, we decided to finish our hike together. We were silent most of the way, and I liked it. My life was almost never silent.

She declined my invitation to lunch, but we did exchange numbers. I gave her the number to the phone I use when I am Tobias.

Lindsay texted me once, a few days after the hike. Hearing from her made me smile.

It was great to meet you last week, hope we can hike together sometime.

We did.

A different trail the second time, farther north and near Indian Lake State Forest. She brought the Pixy Stix again; I brought a blanket. We stopped to rest in an area where the sun was blocked by heavy foliage. As we sat down, I smiled at her, and it was real.

"You're cute," she said.

No, you're the cute one.

She texted a few days later, and I ignored it. By then, Millicent and I had agreed that Lindsay was the one.

Now, a year later, Lindsay is back on TV. They found her.

I GO STRAIGHT home from the bar. Millicent is already there, sitting on the front porch. She is still dressed in work clothes, and her patent leather pumps match the color of her skin. She says they make her legs look longer, and I agree. I always notice when she is wearing them, even now.

After working all day and then being cooped up in the car watching Naomi, I realize how badly I need a shower. But Millicent doesn't even turn up her nose when I sit down next to her. Before I can speak, she does.

"It's not a problem."

"Are you sure?" I ask.

"Positive."

I do not know if this is true. We were supposed to take care of Lindsay together, but it didn't work out that way. And I don't have any options to argue with.

"I don't understand how—"

"It's not a problem," she says again. She points up, gesturing to the second floor of our house. The kids are home. I want to ask more, but I can't.

"We have to wait on the next one," I say. "We shouldn't do anything now."

She does not answer.

"Millicent?"

"I heard you."

I want to ask her if she understands, but I know she does. She just doesn't like it. She is upset Lindsay has been found now, right when we were planning another. It's like she has become addicted.

She is not the only one.

WHEN I MET Millicent on the plane, it wasn't love at first sight. Not for her. It wasn't even mild interest. After saying hello, she looked away and continued staring out the window. I was right back where I'd started. I leaned back on the headrest, closed my eyes, and berated myself for not having the courage to say more.

"Excuse me."

My eyes flew open.

She was looking at me, her green eyes huge, forehead wrinkled.

"Are you okay?" she said.

I nodded.

"Are you sure?"

"I'm sure. I don't understand why you're—"

"Because you're knocking your head against this." She pointed to the headrest. "You're shaking the seat."

I hadn't even realized I was doing it. I thought all that mental berating was just that: mental. "I'm sorry."

"So you're okay?"

I recovered enough to realize the girl I had been staring at was now talking to me. She even looked concerned.

I smiled. "I'm okay, really. I was just—"

"Beating yourself up. I do the same thing."

"About what?"

She shrugged. "Lots of things."

I felt an urge to know everything that made this girl beat her head in frustration, but the landing gear had just dropped and we didn't have time. "Tell me one," I said.

She considered my question, even putting her index finger up to her lips. I bit back another smile, not just because it was cute but because I had her attention.

After the plane landed, she answered.

"Assholes," she said. "Assholes on planes who hit on me when all I want is to be left alone."

Without thinking, without even realizing she was talking about me, I said, "I can protect you from them."

She stared at me, stunned. When she realized I was serious, she burst out laughing.

When I realized why she was laughing, I did the same thing.

By the time we walked up the jet bridge, we had not only introduced ourselves; we had exchanged phone numbers.

Before walking away, she said, "How?"

"How what?"

"How would you protect me from all those assholes on planes?"

"I would force them into the center seat, hog the armrests, and give them paper cuts with the emergency information card."

She laughed again, longer and harder than she had before. I'm still not tired of hearing her laugh.

That conversation became part of us. The first Christmas we spent together, I gave her a huge box, big enough to fit a giant TV, all wrapped up and tied with a bow. The only thing inside was an emergency information card.

Every Christmas since, we have tried to come up with the most creative reference to our inside joke. Once, I gave her an underseat life jacket. Another time, she redecorated our tree with drop-down oxygen masks.

Whenever I get on a plane and see that emergency card, I still smile.

The strange thing is, if I had to pick a moment, the exact moment everything went into motion and brought us to where we are now, I would have to say it was because of a paper cut.

It happened when Rory was eight years old. He had friends but not too many, a middle-of-the-road kid on the popularity scale, so it came as a surprise when a boy named Hunter gave Rory a paper cut. On purpose. They had been arguing about which superhero was strongest, when Hunter got mad and cut Rory. The cut was in the crease between the thumb and index finger of his right hand. It was painful enough to make Rory scream.

Hunter was sent home for the day, and Rory went to see the nurse, who bandaged his hand and gave him a sugar-free lollipop. The pain had already been forgotten.

That night, after the kids were asleep, Millicent and I talked about the paper cut. We were in bed. She had just closed her laptop, and I turned off the TV. School had just started, and Millicent's summer tan hadn't completely faded. She didn't play tennis, but she loved to swim.

Millicent picked up my hand and rubbed the thin stretch of skin between my thumb and index finger. "Have you ever had a cut here?"

"No. You?"

"Yes. Hurt like hell."

"How did it happen?"

"Holly."

I knew very little about Holly. Millicent almost never talked about her older sister. "She cut you?" I asked.

"We were making collages of all our favorite things, and we cut pictures out of magazines and pasted them all on big pieces of construction paper. Holly and I reached for the same piece at the same time, and"—she shrugged—"I got cut."

"Did you scream?"

"I don't remember. But I cried."

I picked up her hand and kissed the long-healed cut. "What favorite things?" I asked.

"What?"

"You said you cut out pictures of your favorite things. What were they?"

"Oh no," she said, taking her hand back and turning out the light. "You're not going to turn this into another crazy Christmas thing."

"You don't like our crazy Christmas thing?"

"I love it. But we don't need another."

I knew we didn't. I was trying to avoid the subject of Holly, because Millicent didn't like to talk about her. That's why I asked about her favorite things.

I should have asked about Holly.

Five

LINDSAY DOMINATES THE news. She is the only one who has been found, and the first surprise is where her body is found.

The last time I saw Lindsay, we were in the middle of nowhere. Millicent and I had taken her deep into the swamp near a nature preserve, hoping the wildlife would find her before any people did. Lindsay was still alive, and we were supposed to kill her together. That was the plan.

That was the point.

It didn't happen, because of Jenna. We had arranged for both kids to spend the night with friends; Rory was with a friend playing video games, and we had dropped Jenna off at a slumber party with half a dozen twelve-year-old girls. When Millicent's phone went off, it sounded like a kitten. That was Jenna's ring. Millicent answered before the second meow.

"Jenna? What's wrong?"

I watched Millicent listen, my heart beating a little faster with each nod of her head.

Lindsay was lying on the ground, her tanned legs sprawled out on the dirt. The drug we'd knocked her out with was wearing off, and she had started to move a little.

"Honey, can you pass the phone to Mrs. Sheehan?" Millicent said.

More nodding.

When Millicent spoke again, her voice had changed. "I understand. Thank you so much. I'll be right there." She hung up.

"What—"

"Jenna's sick. A stomach flu or maybe food poisoning. She's been in the bathroom for the past hour." Before I could answer, she said, "I'll go."

I shook my head. "I'll do it."

Millicent didn't protest. She looked down at Lindsay and back at me. "But—"

"I'll do it," I said. "I'll pick up Jenna and take her home."

"I can take care of her." Millicent was looking down at Lindsay. She was not talking about our daughter.

"Of course you can." I never had a doubt. I was just disappointed I had to miss it.

When I arrived at the Sheehans, Jenna was still sick. On the way home, I pulled over twice so she could throw up. I sat up with her most of the night.

Millicent returned home just before dawn. I didn't ask if she had moved Lindsay, because I assumed she had buried her in that deserted area. I have no idea how she ended up in room number 18 at the Moonlite Motor Inn.

The Moonlite closed when the new highway was built more than twenty years ago. The motel was abandoned and left to the elements, rodents, transients, and drug addicts. No one paid attention to it, because no one had to drive by it. Lindsay was found by some teenagers, who called the police.

The motel is a single strip of a building, one story, with rooms lining both sides. Room 18 is on the back side, in the corner and not visible from the road. As I watch aerial video of the motel on TV, I try to imagine Millicent driving around the back of the Moonlite and parking, getting out of the car, opening the trunk.

Dragging Lindsay across the ground.

I wonder if she is strong enough to do that. Lindsay was quite muscular from all those outdoor sports. Maybe Millicent used something to transport Lindsay. A cart, something with wheels. She is smart enough to do something like that.

The reporter is young and earnest; he speaks as if every word is important. He tells me that Lindsay had been wrapped in plastic, shoved into the closet, and covered with a blanket. The teenagers discovered her because they had been playing a drunken game of hide-and-seek. I don't know how long she has been in the closet, but the reporter does say Lindsay's body was initially identified with dental records. The DNA tests are pending. The police could not use fingerprints, because Lindsay's had been filed off.

I try not to imagine how Millicent did this, or that she did it at all, but it becomes the only thing I *can* imagine.

The images in my mind stay there. Still frames of Lindsay's smiling face, of her white teeth. Of my wife filing away Lindsay's fingertips. Of her dragging Lindsay's body into a motel room and shoving her in the closet. These all flash through my mind throughout the day, the evening, and as I try to go to sleep.

Millicent, however, looks normal. She looks the same when she gets home from work and throws together a salad, when she takes off her makeup, when she works on her computer before going to sleep. If she has been listening to the news, it doesn't show. A half dozen times, I start to ask her why or how Lindsay got into that motel.

I don't. Because all I can think about is why I have to ask. Why she didn't tell me.

The next day, she calls me in the middle of the afternoon, and the question is on the tip of my tongue. I am also starting to wonder if there is anything else I don't know.

"Remember," she says. "We have dinner with the Prestons tonight."

"I remember."

I do not remember. She knows this and tells me the name of the restaurant without my asking.

"Seven o'clock," she says.

"I'll meet you there."

ANDY AND TRISTA Preston bought their house from Millicent. Although Andy is a few years older than me, I've known him forever. He grew up in Hidden Oaks, we went to the same schools, and our parents knew one another. Now he works at a software firm, making enough money to take tennis lessons every day, but he doesn't—that's why he has a paunch.

But his wife takes lessons. Trista also grew up around here, but she's from the other part of Woodview, not the Oaks. We meet twice a week, and she spends the rest of her time working at an art gallery. Together, the Prestons make twice what we do.

Millicent knows how much all of her clients make, and most earn more than us. I have to admit that this bothers me more than it bothers her. Millicent thinks it's because she makes more money than I do. She's wrong. It's because Andy makes more money than I do, though I do not tell her that. She is not from the Oaks; she doesn't understand what it's like to grow up here and then end up working here.

Our dinner is at an upscale restaurant where everyone eats salad, chicken, or salmon, and drinks red wine. Andy and Trista drink the whole bottle. Millicent doesn't really drink and hates it when I do. I don't drink around her.

"I envy you," Trista says to me. "I would love to have your job and be outside all day. I love playing tennis."

Andy laughs. His cheeks are red. "But you work in an art gallery. It's practically the same thing."

"Being outside all day and working outside all day are two different things," I say. "I'd love to sit around on the beach all day, doing nothing."

Trista scrunches up her pert nose. "I think that would be boring, just lying around like that. I'd rather be doing something."

I want to tell her that taking a tennis lesson and teaching them are two different things. At work, the great outdoors is the last thing on my mind. Most of my time is spent trying to teach tennis to people who would rather be on their phone, watching TV, getting drunk, or eating. I don't need even one finger to count the number of people who really want to play tennis, much less exercise. Trista is one of them. She doesn't really love tennis; she loves to look good.

But I keep my mouth shut, because that's what friends do. We don't point out each other's faults unless asked.

The talk shifts to Andy's work, and I tune it out, catching only key words, because I am distracted by the sound of silverware. Every time Millicent cuts a piece of grilled chicken, I think about her killing Lindsay.

"Attention," Andy says. "That's the only thing software companies care about. How can we get your attention, and how can we keep it? How can we make you sit in front of your computer all day?"

I roll my eyes. When Andy drinks, he tends to pontificate. Or lecture.

"Come on," he says. "Answer the question. What keeps you in front of the computer?"

"Cat videos," I say.

Trista giggles.

"Don't be a dick," Andy says.

"Sex," Millicent says. "It has to be either sex or violence."

"Or both," I say.

"Actually, it doesn't have to contain sex," says Andy. "Not actual sex. What's necessary is the promise of sex. Or violence. Or both. And a story line—you have to have a story line. Doesn't matter if it's real or fake or who's telling it. You just need people to care what happens next."

"And how do you do that?" Millicent asks.

He smiles and draws an invisible circle with his index finger. "Sex and violence."

"That goes for everything, though. Even the news is built on sex and violence," I say.

"The whole world turns on sex and violence," says Andy. He draws the circle with his finger again and turns to me. "You know that—you're from here."

"I do know." Officially, the Oaks is one of the safest communities in the state. That's because all the violence is behind closed doors.

"I know that, too," Trista says to her husband. "Woodview isn't that different."

It is, but Andy doesn't argue. Instead, he leans over and gives his wife a peck on the lips. As their lips touch, she touches his cheek with her palm.

I am jealous.

Jealous of their simple conversations. Jealous of their heavy drinking. Jealous of their simple foreplay and the sex they will have tonight.

"I think we all get it," I say.

Andy winks at me. I glance over at Millicent, who is staring at her food. She thinks public displays of affection are distasteful.

When the check arrives, both Millicent and Trista leave the table and go to the restroom. Andy grabs the check before I can.

"Don't bother protesting. I got it," he says, looking over the bill. "You guys are cheap dates anyway. No alcohol."

I shrug. "So we don't drink much."

Andy shakes his head and smiles.

"What?" I say.

"If I had known you were going to end up such a boring family man, I would've made you stay in Cambodia a lot longer."

I roll my eyes. "Now you're the one being a dick," I say.

"That's what I'm here for."

Before I can respond, our wives return to the table and we stop talking about drinking. And about the check.

The four of us walk out together and say our goodbyes in the parking lot. Trista says she will see me at her next lesson. Andy says he'll start soon. Trista is behind him rolling her eyes and smiling. They drive off, leaving Millicent and me alone. We have two cars, because we met at the restaurant.

She turns to me. Under the streetlights, she looks as old as I've ever seen her. "You okay?" she says.

I shrug. "I'm okay." I do not have any other option.

"You worry too much," she says, staring out over the sea of cars. "Everything is fine."

"I hope so."

"Trust me." Millicent reaches out and slips her hand into mine. Squeezes it.

I nod and get into my car, but I don't go straight home. Instead, I drive by the Lancaster Hotel.

Naomi is behind the front desk. Her dark hair falls loose around her shoulders, and although I can't see the freckles on her nose, I think I can. I am relieved to see her, to know that she is still working behind the front desk and probably still engaging in her extracurricular activities. There is no reason for me to think anything has happened to her, because we have agreed to wait. Checking on Naomi is irrational, but I do it anyway.

This is not the first time I have been irrational. Ever since they found Lindsay, I have not slept well. I wake up in the middle of the night, my heart pounding, and it is always about some irrational thing. Did I lock the front door? Are those bills paid? Did I remember to do all the little things I am supposed to do so the house won't burn down or get taken by the bank, and the car won't crash because the brakes weren't checked on time?

All these little things keep my mind off Lindsay. And the fact that I cannot do anything about her now.

Six

SATURDAY MORNING, JENNA'S soccer game. I am alone because Millicent has to show a house. Saturday is the biggest day of the week for both real estate and tennis lessons. It is also the biggest day of the week for our kids' activities. Millicent and I trade off Saturdays with the kids, and the last time we were all together was more than a year ago, when Rory went to the finals in a preteen golf tournament. He is playing golf now—I dropped him off early this morning before his sister's game started—and he is at the same club where I teach tennis. He plays golf because it is not tennis, and I hate that just as much as he wants me to.

So far, Jenna has not displayed any of the same rebelliousness. She does not try to be difficult. Jenna does something because she wants to, not because it will make someone else angry, and I admire that quality in her. She also smiles a lot, which makes me smile back and then give her everything she wants. I have no idea what I am missing, and because I can't figure it out, Jenna scares the hell out of me.

Soccer is not my game. I learned the rules only when Jenna started to play, so I am not much help. I cannot tell her what to do or how to do better, like I could if she played tennis. It's only by some stroke of luck that she plays goalie, so at least I know her job is keep the other team from scoring. Beyond that, all I can do is encourage her.

"You can do it!"

"Nice job!"

"Great effort!"

I often wonder if I am embarrassing her. I think so, but I do it anyway, because my only other option is to watch her games in silence. That seems cruel. I would rather be embarrassing. When she blocks the ball from going in the net, I lose my mind. She smiles but waves her hand, telling me to shut up. In these moments, I do not think about anything but my daughter and her soccer game.

Millicent interrupts by sending a text.

Don't worry.

This is all she says.

On the field, the kids are yelling. The other team tries to score, and my daughter has to block the ball again. She misses.

Jenna turns around, her back to me, hands on hips. I want to tell her it's no big thing, everyone makes mistakes, but that would be exactly the wrong thing. All parents say that, and all kids hate it. I did.

Jenna looks straight down at the grass. A teammate walks up and pats her on the shoulder, says something. Jenna nods and smiles, and I wonder what her teammate said. I think it is the same thing I would've said, but it meant more.

Play resumes. I look back down at my phone. Millicent has not said anything else.

I pull up the news and gasp.

The medical examiner's report states that Lindsay has been dead only a few weeks.

Somewhere, somehow, Millicent kept her alive for almost a year.

* * *

I HAVE AN urge to run. To where, I don't know. It doesn't matter. To do what, I have no idea. I just want to run anywhere.

But I cannot leave Jenna here, alone at a soccer game with no one to cheer for her. I cannot leave my daughter. Or my son.

When Jenna's game is over, I pick Rory up at the club and the three of us have our usual post-sport pizza followed by frozen yogurt. It is difficult for me to stay with the conversation. They notice, because they are my kids—they see me every day and know when something is wrong. This makes me wonder what they think about Millicent.

Except she never looks like anything is wrong. For the past year, she has been calm, even for her. She'd mentioned finding the next woman a month ago.

Everything falls into place. She didn't mention the next one until after she had killed Lindsay.

For me, the past year had been filled with work, the kids' activities, chores around the house, arguing about bills, and getting the car washed. Nothing stood out. No single event, day, memory, was anything I would remember twenty, thirty, or forty years from now. Jenna's soccer team almost went to the city finals but didn't. Millicent had another good year at work. Gas prices went up and then down, a local election came and went, and my favorite dry cleaner went out of business and I had to find another.

Or maybe the dry cleaner closed two years ago. It all runs together.

During the same time, Millicent had been keeping Lindsay alive. Holding her captive.

The images running through my mind range from disturbing to barbaric. I envision the kinds of things I have heard about in the news, when women are found after years of being held captive by some deranged man. I have never heard of a woman doing this. And as a man, I cannot imagine doing this myself.

I leave the kids at home and drive to the open house where Millicent is working. It's just a few blocks from ours; the drive takes minutes. Two cars are out front, hers and one other, an SUV.

I wait.

Twenty minutes later, she comes out of the house with a couple younger than us. The woman is wide-eyed. The man is smiling. As Millicent shakes their hand, she sees me out of the corner of her eye. I can feel her green eyes land on me, but she does not pause, does not break her fluid movement.

The couple walk back to their car. Millicent stays in front of the house, watching them go. She is wearing navy blue today, a slim skirt and heels, and a pin-striped blouse. Her red hair is straight and cut sharp at her jawline. It was much longer when we met and has grown shorter each year, as if she were committed to cutting off half an inch at regular intervals. It would not surprise me to learn that this is exactly what she has done. I am not sure anything about Millicent would surprise me now.

She waits until the SUV is gone before turning to me. I get out of my car and walk up to the house.

"You're upset," she says.

I stare at her.

She motions to the house. "Let's go inside."

We go in. The entryway is huge, the ceilings more than twenty feet high. New construction, just like ours, only this one is even bigger. Everything is open and airy, and it all leads to the great room, which is where we go.

"What did you do to her? For a year, what did you do?"

Millicent shakes her head. Her hair swings back and forth. "We can't discuss this now."

"We have to—"

"Not here. I have an appointment."

She walks away from me, and I follow.

* * *

A FEW MONTHS after we married, Millicent got pregnant. It was a surprise in some ways, because we'd talked about waiting, but not completely. We were not always careful about using protection. We had discussed various methods of birth control but always came back to condoms. Millicent did not like taking anything with hormones. They all made her too emotional.

When Millicent was late, we both suspected she was pregnant. We confirmed it with a test at home and one at the doctor's office. Later that night, I could not sleep. We sat up for a long time, sitting on our secondhand couch in our run-down rented house. I curled up next to her, my head on her stomach, and I started worrying about everything.

"What if we screw it up?" I said.

"We won't."

"We need money. How are we going—"

"We'll manage."

"I don't want to just manage. I want to prosper. I want—"

"We will."

I raised my head to look at her. "Why are you so sure?"

"Why are you so unsure?"

"I'm not," I said. "I'm just—"

"Worried."

"Yes."

She sighed and gently pushed my head back down to her stomach. "Stop being silly," she said. "We'll be fine. We'll be better than fine."

Minutes earlier, I had felt more like a child than a soon-to-be father.

She made me stronger.

We have come a long way from those early days when we had no money. I had gone back to school to get my MBA, but I was halfway through when she got pregnant. We needed money, so I withdrew from the program and returned to what I know best: tennis. It was my one talent, the thing I could do better than anyone else I grew up with.

The tennis court was where I shone. Not bright enough to go pro, but bright enough to start offering private lessons.

When I met Millicent, she had just finished a year of real estate classes and was studying to take the test. Once she passed, it took a while for her to start selling, but she did, even while pregnant, even when the kids were babies. And she was right—we made it work. We are better than fine. And as far as I know, we have not screwed up the kids yet.

Seven

Now, as we stand in that empty house she is trying to sell, Millicent does not make me feel stronger. She makes me feel scared.

"It's not okay," I say. "None of this is okay."

She raises one eyebrow. That used to be cute. "Now you're growing a conscience?"

"I always had—"

"No. I don't think you did."

She is right again. I have never had a conscience when I'm trying to make her happy.

"What did you do to her?" I ask.

"It doesn't matter. She's gone."

"Not anymore."

"You worry too much. We're fine."

The doorbell rings.

"Work calls," she says.

I walk with her to the door. She introduces me, tells them about my tennis skills. They are as young as the last couple and just as clueless.

I head home and drive right by our house.

First, I go to the Lancaster. Naomi is there, behind the counter, with many hours left on her shift.

Next, I go by the country club. I think about distracting myself by hanging out in the clubhouse, chatting with some of my clients while watching sports. Again, I don't stop.

A number of other places run through my mind: a bar, a park, the library, a movie. I burn through almost half a tank of gas driving around, trying to pick a destination, before I head toward the inevitable.

Home.

It is where I always go.

When I open the door, I hear the sounds of my life. My family. The only real one I ever had.

Rory is playing a video game, electronic gunshots ringing through the house. Jenna is on the phone, talking, texting, and setting the table. The smell of dinner wafts throughout the great room, chicken and garlic and something with cinnamon. Millicent is behind the counter, putting it all together, and she always hums to herself while fixing meals. Her song choice is usually something ridiculous—a show tune, an aria, the latest pop music—and that's another inside joke of ours.

She looks up and smiles, and it is real. I see it in her eyes.

We all sit down and eat together. Jenna entertains her mother and bores her brother with a play-by-play of her soccer game. Rory brags about his golf score, which today was better than anyone else under sixteen. On most days, our meals are like this. They are boisterous and loud, filled with tales of the day and the ease of us, we who have lived together forever.

I wonder how many times we did this while Lindsay was being held captive.

When I get into bed, I am surprised that hours have passed since I last thought about Lindsay, about the police, about what Millicent and I have done. Home, and all that goes with it, is that powerful to me.

My childhood was not the same. While I did grow up in a two-parent family in our nice Hidden Oaks house, with two cars, good schools, and a lot of extracurricular activities, we did not eat meals together like my own family does. And if we did happen to all eat at the same time, we ignored one another. My father read the paper, my mother stared off into space, and I ate as quickly as possible.

They showed up to watch me play tennis only if I was in a tournament and even then, only if I made it to the last round. Neither of my parents would have given up a Saturday for anything. Home was a place to sleep, a place to hold my stuff, a place to leave as soon as possible. And I did. I left the country as soon as I could. It was impossible to imagine an entire life of feeling like a disappointment.

Though I am not sure it was me, not personally. If I had to guess, I was the one who was supposed to fix their marriage. After spending years thinking about it, running through my whole childhood again and again, I have come to the conclusion that my parents had me to try and fix their marriage. It didn't work. And their disappointment became my failure.

I returned to Hidden Oaks only because my parents passed away. It was a freak accident, impossible to prevent or predict. They were driving down the highway, and a tire flew off a car ahead of them. It smashed through the front windshield of my father's luxury sedan, and they both died. Gone, just like that. Still together, still undoubtedly miserable.

I never saw their bodies. The police said I wouldn't want to.

It turned out my parents had far less money than they pretended to, so I came home to a house buried in mortgages and just enough money to pay an estate lawyer to settle everything and get rid of it. My parents weren't even who I thought they were; they were frauds. They couldn't afford to live in Hidden Oaks; they just pretended they could. I had no family left and didn't know what one was.

Millicent built ours. I say it was her because it couldn't have been me. I had no idea how to build a home or even how to get everyone together for a meal. She did. The first time Rory sat in a high chair, she pushed him up to the table, and we've been having meals together ever since. Despite the rising complaints from our growing kids, we still eat together.

When Millicent was pregnant with Jenna, she created our family rules. I called them Millicent's Commandments.

Breakfast and dinner together, always.
No toys or phones at the table.
Allowances must be earned by doing chores around the house.
We will have movie night once a week.
Sugar will be limited to fruit, not fruit juice, and special occasions.
All food will be organic, as money allows.
Physical activity and exercise are encouraged. No, they're mandatory.
Homework must be done before TV or video games.

The list made me laugh. She glared at me when I did laugh, though, so I stopped. By then, I knew the difference between when she was pretending to be mad and when her anger was genuine.

One by one, Millicent instituted her rules. Instead of turning the house into a prison, she gave the family structure. Both our kids play sports. They aren't given money unless they work for it. We all sit down and watch a movie together once a week. They eat mostly organic and very few sugary foods. Their homework is always done by the time I get home from work. This is all because of Millicent.

The same Millicent who kept Lindsay alive for a year while doing god knows what to her.

I STILL CANNOT sleep. I get up and check on the kids. Rory is spread out on his bed, the covers thrown everywhere. When he turned fourteen, he no longer wanted dinosaurs painted on the walls. We redid the room, repainted it, refinished the furniture, and now it has one dark wall and three beige ones, a smattering of rock band posters, a dark stain on all the wooden furniture, and blackout curtains for when he sleeps. It looks like a child's idea of an adult room. My son is becoming a teenager.

Jenna's room is still orange. She has been obsessed with the color almost since birth. I think it comes from the color of Millicent's hair. Jenna's hair is like mine, dark brown with no sign of red. She has posters of female soccer players on her walls, along with a few musical groups and a male actor or two. I don't know who they are, but whenever they are on TV, Jenna and her friends squeal. Now that she has reached the mature age of thirteen, all her dolls have been stuffed into her closet. She is into fashion, jewelry, and makeup she is not allowed to wear yet, along with a few stuffed animals and video games.

I walk around the house, checking all the doors and windows. I even go into the garage, looking for signs of rodents or bugs or water damage. I go out into the backyard and check the side gate. I do the same in the front yard, and then I go around the house again, relocking all the doors.

Millicent used to do this, especially after Rory was born. We were living in the run-down rental, and every night she walked around locking all the doors and windows. She would sit down for a few minutes, then get up and do it all over again.

"This isn't a dangerous neighborhood," I told her. "No one is going to break in."

"I know." She got up again.

Eventually, I decided to follow her. I fell in lockstep behind her and mimicked every move she made. First, I got the glare, the real one.

When I still didn't stop, she slapped me.

"You're not funny," she said.

I was too stunned to speak. I had never been slapped by a woman. I hadn't even been spanked, not even playfully. But since I had just mocked my wife, I threw up my hands and apologized.

"You're only sorry because you got slapped," Millicent said. She whipped around, went into the bedroom, and locked the door.

I spent the night thinking she was going to leave me. She was going to take my son and just go, because I had ruined everything. Extreme, yes. But Millicent does not put up with shit, period. Once, when we were dating, I said I would call her at a certain time, and I didn't. She didn't speak to me for more than a week. Wouldn't even pick up the phone.

She came back to me that time. But I had no doubt that if I pissed Millicent off enough, she would just leave. And one time she did.

Rory was one and a half, Jenna was six months old, and Millicent and I spent all day, every day, juggling the kids and our jobs. One day, I woke up, exhausted again, and realized I was twenty-seven years old with a wife, two kids, and a brand-new mortgage.

All I wanted was a break. A temporary reprieve from all that responsibility. I went out with the guys, and I got so drunk they had to carry me into the house. When I woke up the next day, Millicent was gone.

She did not answer her phone. She was not at her office. Her parents said she was not with them. Millicent had only a few close friends, and none had heard from her. She had vanished, and she had taken my kids with her.

After three or four days, I was calling her phone every hour. I e-mailed, I texted, I became the most insane version of myself I had ever been. It wasn't because I was worried about her. I knew she was fine, and I knew my children were fine. I went crazy because I thought she, they, were gone forever.

Eight days went by. Then she was back.

I had fallen asleep late, sprawled out on the unmade bed littered with pizza boxes and assorted plates, cups and random food packages. I woke up to a garbage-free bed and the smell of pancakes.

Millicent was in the kitchen, making breakfast. Rory was at the table, in his high chair, and Jenna was in her bassinet. Millicent turned to me and smiled. It was real.

"Perfect timing," she said. "Breakfast is just about ready."

I ran over to Rory and picked him up, holding him high in the air until he squealed. I kissed Jenna, who stared up at me with her dark eyes. I sat down at the table, afraid to speak. Afraid I was in a dream, and I didn't want to wake up.

Millicent brought a full stack of pancakes over to the table. As she set them down, she leaned in close, so that her mouth was right next to my ear, and she whispered, "We won't come back a second time."

I have spent our entire marriage with no choice but to believe her. Yet I still slept with Petra.

And the other one.

Eight

WHEN I GET home from work, Millicent and the kids are there. Rory is lying on the couch, playing a video game. Millicent is standing over him, hands on hips, her face hard-set. Behind her, Jenna is moving her phone back and forth, trying to take a selfie in front of the window. The TV screen casts a glow over all of them. For a second, they are frozen, a portrait of modern life.

Millicent's glare shifts from Rory to me. Her eyes are the darkest of green.

"Do you know," she says, "what our son did today?"

Rory's baseball cap is pulled down low over his eyes and face. It doesn't completely hide his smirk.

"What did our son do today?" I ask.

"Tell your father what you did."

Jenna answers for him. "He cheated on a test with his phone."

"Go to your room," Millicent says.

My daughter walks out. She giggles all the way up the stairs and slams her bedroom door.

"Rory," I say, "what happened?"

Silence.

"Answer your father."

I do not like it when Millicent tells our son how to act toward me, but I say nothing.

Millicent snatches the game controller out of Rory's hand. He sighs and finally speaks.

"It's not like I'm going to be a botanist. If I ever need to know about photosynthesis, I'll look it up, the same way I did today." He looks at me, eyes wide, silently saying, "Right?"

I want to agree, because he is kind of right. But I'm the father.

"He's been suspended for three days," Millicent says. "He's lucky he wasn't kicked out."

If they kicked him out of private school, he would be placed in a public school. I do not remind Millicent of this while she is doling out our son's punishment.

". . . no phone, no video games, no Internet. You come straight home after school, and, don't worry, I'll check."

She whips around and clicks down the hall to the garage. She is wearing her flesh-colored heels.

After I hear her car start, I sit down next to my son. He has Millicent's red hair, but his green eyes are lighter. Open.

"Why?"

He shrugs. "It was just easier."

I get it. Sometimes it's just easier to go along with things. It's easier than breaking it all up and starting from scratch.

"You can't cheat," I say.

"But you do."

"What are you talking about?"

"I hear you sneak out."

He is right. I have been sneaking out in the night because I cannot sleep. "Sometimes I go for a drive."

Rory snickers. "Do I look like a moron?"

"No."

"Dad, I saw you sneak back into the house wearing a suit. Who puts on a suit to go out for a drive?"

I haven't worn a suit since I was with Petra.

"You know I spend a lot of evenings at the club. Networking is part of the job."

"Networking." He says this with no small amount of irony.

"I am not cheating on your mother," I say. And it's almost true.

"You're a liar."

I start to tell Rory I'm not, but realize this is useless. I start to deny that I am cheating, but realize it's also useless. My son is too smart.

I wish I could explain it to him, but I can't. So I become the hypocrite.

"We aren't talking about me," I say.

He rolls his eyes, says nothing.

"And I never cheated in school. I mean, what if one day the zombie apocalypse arrives and you escape to an island to start a whole new civilization and you have to grow plants? Don't you think photosynthesis would be a helpful thing to know?"

"I really appreciate the effort there, Dad. Especially the zombie apocalypse and all. But let me save you some time." He pulls something out of his pocket and sets it down in front of me.

The shiny blue glass makes my jaw drop. One of Petra's earrings.

"Jenna doesn't have pierced ears," he says. "And Mom would never wear something this tacky."

He is right. Millicent wears diamond stud earrings. Real diamonds, not glass.

"Not much to say now, I guess," Rory says.

Two for two. I have nothing to say.

"Don't worry. Jenna doesn't know about your side chick." The smirk is back. "Yet."

It takes a second for me to realize my son is trying to blackmail me. With evidence.

I am impressed, because he is so clever, and petrified, because the last thing I want is for my children, especially my daughter, to grow up with an asshole cheat for a father. This is the kind of thing experts say to avoid. They say it will affect her relationships with men forever. I have seen daytime TV.

Jenna cannot know, cannot even suspect what Rory believes is true. Anything must be better than that.

I turn to Rory. "What do you want?"

"The new *Bloody Hell* game."

"Your mother banned those from the house."

"I know."

If I disagree, he will tell Jenna I am cheating on their mother. He will do exactly what he threatens.

If I agree, my fourteen-year-old son will have succeeded in blackmailing me.

I feel like I should have seen this coming. Should have seen it the day he was born. He was so quiet at first everyone thought he was dead. When he finally did cry, it was so loud it made my ears ring.

Or maybe I should have seen it the day his sister was born and he made just as much noise, not to announce his arrival but to announce his lack of attention.

Then there was the time Jenna and Rory went trick-or-treating together, and he convinced her all the mini candy bars had been poisoned by the psycho who worked at our local superstore. The psycho was a big lumberjack of a man, gentle as a hamster, but he scared children without even trying. Jenna believed her brother and dumped out all the allegedly poisoned candy. Neither Millicent nor I knew what happened, not until Jenna had nightmares for a week and we found a pile of mini candy bar wrappers in Rory's room.

So now, while I am in the midst of being blackmailed by my son,

I can look back and say I should have known he would do this. But before this moment, I didn't have a clue.

"Answer me one question," I say to him.

"Okay."

"How long have you known about this?" I am careful not to use the word *cheat*. As if it matters.

"A few months. The first time, I went down to the garage early in the morning to get my soccer ball. Your car wasn't there. Then I just started paying attention."

I nod. "I'll buy your game tomorrow. Don't let your mother see it."

"I won't. Don't let her see you sneaking back in, either."

"I won't be doing that anymore."

He smiles as he picks up the earring and puts it back into his pocket. Rory doesn't believe me but is smart enough to keep his mouth shut when he's ahead.

I SHOULD TELL Millicent about our son. I think about this during dinner while Jenna does her best to make fun of Rory without getting caught. I think about it after dinner, as Millicent takes Rory's phone away for the night. I even think about it when it's just my wife and me, in our bedroom, going through our nightly routine. This is when I should tell her what our son is up to, but I don't.

I don't tell her because it will create more questions than I can answer.

It has been just two weeks since I spent the night with Petra. I think about her only in the middle of the night, when I am already awake and can't go back to sleep. That's when I wonder what I did to give myself away. What made her ask if I was really deaf? Did I react to a sound, did I look at her eyes instead of her mouth when she was talking, or did I pay too much attention to the sounds she made in bed? I don't know. I don't know if I will ever act deaf again, but this still keeps me up at night. It has become a loose thread I have to pull.

Rory's blackmail is the same. Another mistake. Like I'd slipped and should not have let my son figure out I was sneaking out at night. Millicent would not like that.

So I don't say anything. Rory and Petra are both secrets that I do not tell my wife. Maybe because she has her own, more than I thought she did. Rory and Petra are also both risks, each in their own way, and still my mouth stays shut.

I do not want her to know how badly I've screwed up.

Nine

I T DIDN'T START out as something bad. I still believe that.

Three years ago, late one Saturday afternoon in October, I was in the front yard with Rory and Jenna. They were still young enough to be around me without getting embarrassed, and the three of us were putting up Halloween decorations. The holiday was almost their favorite, second only to Christmas, and every year we blanketed the house in cobwebs, spiders, skeletons, and witches. If we could have afforded animatronics, we would have used those as well.

Millicent came home from showing a house. Dressed in her work clothes, she stood on the front walk and smiled, admiring our work. The kids said they were hungry. With a big, overdramatic roll of her eyes, Millicent said she would go put some sandwiches together. She was smiling when she said that. I think we all were.

Things weren't perfect, however. The house we were decorating was new to us—we had been living there only six months—and the mortgage was huge. Millicent was under a lot of pressure to sell more houses. I was under the same pressure; at times, I even thought about getting a second job.

We also had ongoing issues with Millicent's mother. Her father had passed away two years earlier. Then her mother had been diagnosed with Alzheimer's and had begun the long, slow decline that came with it. We had spent a long time looking for a live-in nurse. The first two didn't work out, because neither met Millicent's standards. The third one was working out, at least so far.

Our family had its problems—lots of them—but on that day, we were all smiling, right up until Millicent screamed.

I ran inside, the kids right at my heels. I made it to the kitchen just in time to see Millicent throw her phone across the room. It crashed against the wall, breaking into pieces, making a mark. She buried her face in her hands and started to cry.

Jenna screamed.

Rory picked up the pieces of the broken phone.

I put my arms around Millicent as her body shook with sobs.

The two most horrific things went through my mind.

Someone was dead. Maybe her mother. Maybe a friend.

Or someone was dying. A terminal disease. Maybe it was one of the kids. Maybe it was my wife.

It had to be one of the two. Nothing else warranted this kind of response. Not money or a job or even the loss of a pet we didn't even have. Someone had to be dead or soon would be.

It came as a shock to learn it was neither. No one was dead, no one was dying. In fact, it was the opposite.

A FEW MONTHS after we started dating, Millicent and I had what we called Trivia Night. We bought pizza and wine and brought it to her tiny apartment. The living room was so small she just had a love seat and a coffee table, so we sat on the floor. She lit some candles, arranged the pepperoni slices on real dishes, and poured the wine into champagne glasses, because that was all she had.

We spent the whole night asking questions. No boundaries, nothing was off-limits—we'd planned it that way. The first questions were pretty tame; we were still too sober to talk about sex, so we talked about everything else. Movies, music, favorite foods, favorite colors. I even asked if she had any allergies. She does. Eye drops.

"Eye drops?" I said.

She nodded, taking another sip of wine. "The kind that get rid of the redness. They make my eyes swell up until I can hardly see."

"Like Rocky."

"Exactly like Rocky. I figured it out when I was sixteen and got stoned. Tried to hide it from my parents and ended up at the hospital."

"Aha," I said. "So you were a bad girl?"

She shrugged. "What about you? Any allergies?"

"Only to women not named Millicent."

I winked to show her I was kidding. She kicked my foot and rolled her eyes. Eventually, we became intoxicated enough to ask the good questions. Most revolved around sex and old relationships.

I grew tired of hearing about her ex-boyfriend, so I asked about her family. I knew where she was from and that her parents were still married, but that was about it. She had never mentioned siblings.

"Do you have any brothers or sisters?"

We were pretty intoxicated by then, or at least I was, and I kept playing with the wax that had dripped off the candle in front of us. It had pooled onto the little dish below, and I squished it between my fingers, rolling it into a ball and then flattening it out again. Millicent watched me instead of answering my question.

"Hello?" I said.

She took a sip of wine. "A sister. Holly."

"Older or younger?"

"She was older. Now she's gone."

I dropped the wax and reached over, placing my hand on hers, clasping it against her champagne glass. "I'm so sorry," I said.

"It's okay."

I waited to see if she would say anything else. When she didn't, I asked, "How did it happen?"

She leaned back against the wall behind her. The alcohol and candlelight made everything flicker, including her red hair. For a split second, it looked like hot embers were falling away from it.

She turned away as she spoke. "She was fifteen, two years older than me. Holly wanted to drive more than anything else in the world. Couldn't wait to get her license. Then one day our parents were out. They had used Dad's car and left Mom's. Holly said we should take it out. Just around the block—she said she'd go real slow." Millicent turned to me and shrugged. "She didn't. And she died."

"Oh my god. I'm so sorry."

"It's okay. Holly was my sister, but she was . . . not a nice person. She never was."

I wanted to ask more, and I could have, because it was Trivia Night, but I didn't. Instead, I asked about the first time she got drunk.

Holly didn't come up again until I went to dinner at their parents' house. I had met them once before, at a restaurant when they were in town, but this time we drove the three hours to their house. Millicent's parents lived in a large house up north, near the Georgia border, in the middle of nothing. Her father, Stan, had invented a fishing lure, had it patented, and then sold it to a sporting goods company. They weren't rich, but they also didn't have to work. Stan now spent his time bird-watching, fly-fishing, and carving wooden birdhouses. Millicent's mother, Abby, used to be a teacher, and when she wasn't tending to the herb garden, she wrote an educational blog. They were a bit like hippies except they grew cilantro instead of weed.

Millicent looked like her father, right down to the multihued eyes, but her personality was like her mother's. Abby was even more organized than Millicent.

I didn't see the picture until dinner was over. I helped clear the table and carried my dishes into the kitchen. The picture was on the windowsill above the sink; it was just a tiny thing half-hidden behind a plant. The red hair in the photo caught my eye. When I picked it up to look at it, I realized it was Millicent and her sister, Holly. Up until that moment, I hadn't noticed the lack of photos throughout the house. There were pictures of Millicent's parents, and of Millicent, but this was the only one of Holly.

"Don't let her see that."

I looked up. Millicent's mother stood in front of me. Her warm brown eyes almost looked as if they were pleading.

"Do you know what happened to Holly?"

"Yes. Millicent told me."

"Then you know it upsets her." She took the picture out of my hand and put it back behind the plant. "We take the pictures down when she comes over. Millicent doesn't like to be reminded of her."

"The accident upsets her. Losing Holly like that must have been difficult."

She gave me an odd look.

I didn't understand that look until the day the phone rang and Millicent screamed.

Ten

THE BOX FOR *Bloody Hell VII* is so graphic it is covered with a big yellow warning sticker. On the back, there is a red warning sticker about the game itself.

I am not sure this is something that should be in my house.

I buy it anyway.

Rory, still on his three-day suspension from school, is at home. His mother took Rory's computer, changed the Internet password, and tried to disconnect the cable TV but gave up halfway through. Rory is on the couch in the living room, channel surfing.

I throw the game on the couch next to him.

"Thanks," he says. "But your attitude could use an adjustment."

"Don't."

He smirks and grabs the game, peeling the yellow warning sticker off the front. The picture underneath shows dozens of bodies piled up on top of one another. An ugly horned creature, presumably the devil, stands on top of them.

Rory looks up at me, his green eyes lit up. He asks where the game system is. I hesitate, then point to the glass hutch in the dining room. "Behind the silver tray. Don't break anything."

"I won't."

"And put it back."

"I will."

"You aren't going to cheat again, are you?" I say.

He rolls his eyes. "Like father, like son."

We are interrupted by the TV. A breaking-news announcement interrupts a daytime talk show.

The local news logo appears. It is followed by that young, earnest reporter following Lindsay's story. His name is Josh, and I have been watching him every day since Lindsay's body was found. Today, he looks a little tired, but his eyes are wild.

The police department has finally revealed how Lindsay was killed.

"*We're here tonight with Dr. Johannes Rollins, the former medical examiner of DeKalb County, Georgia,*" Josh says. "*Thanks for joining us, Dr. Rollins.*"

"*Of course.*" Dr. Rollins looks older than everyone I know put together and reminds me of Santa Claus, except the clothes are wrong. He is wearing a plaid button-up with a plain blue tie.

"*Dr. Rollins, you've seen today's police statement. Given your expertise, what can you tell us about it?*"

"*She was strangled.*"

"*Yes, yes. It says that right here. Asphyxia due to ligature strangulation.*" Dr. Rollins nods. "*That's what I said. She was strangled.*"

"*Anything else you can tell us?*"

"*She lost consciousness in seconds and died in minutes.*"

Josh waits to see if Dr. Rollins has anything else to say. He does not. "*Okay then. Thank you very much, Dr. Rollins. We really appreciate your time.*" The camera zooms in on Josh, and he takes a breath. His official report is always followed by an unofficial report, because Josh is ambitious and seems to have sources everywhere.

"*That isn't all we have. As always, News 9 has more information than anyone else, and you won't find it in the police statement or on any other station. My sources tell me that the marks on Lindsay's neck indicate she was probably strangled with a chain. The killer stood behind her and held the chain against her windpipe until she was dead."*

"Cool," Rory says.

I feel too sick to admonish him, because I am imagining his mother, my wife, as the murderer Josh is describing.

It's all very clear in my mind, in part because I know, or knew, both women. I can see the look of horror on Lindsay's face. I can also see Millicent's face, although the expression keeps changing. She is horrified, she is relieved, she is orgasmic. She is smiling.

Rory starts setting up his video game.

"You okay?" he says.

"I'm fine."

He doesn't answer. *Bloody Hell VII* is booting up.

I leave, because I have to get to a tennis lesson. I have canceled far too many recently.

Down the road, at the club, a middle-aged woman is waiting for me. She has straight dark hair, a deep tan, and an accent. Kekona is Hawaiian. When she gets frustrated, she curses in pidgin.

Kekona is a retired widow, which means she has a lot of time to pay attention to what everyone else is doing. And she gossips about it. Because of Kekona, I know who is sleeping with whom, which couples are breaking up, who is pregnant, and which kids are getting into trouble. Sometimes, it is more than I want to know. Sometimes, I just want to teach tennis.

Today, I learn one of Rory's teachers may be having an affair with a student's father. It is disturbing, but at least she isn't having an affair with the student. She also has news about the McAllister divorce, which has been going on for more than a year now, along with a new rumor about a possible reconciliation. She is quick to label that one as "probably unreliable, but you never know."

Thirty minutes into our one-hour lesson, she mentions Lindsay.

This is unusual, because Lindsay was not found within our little community of Hidden Oaks, nor was she a member of the country club. Lindsay lived, worked, and was found twenty miles away, which is outside Kekona's gossip zone. Most of the time she stays inside the Oaks, deep within its gates, where she lives in one of the largest houses. She lives less than a block away from where I grew up, and I know Kekona's house well. Or I used to. My first girlfriend lived there.

"There's something weird about this girl in the motel," Kekona says.

"Isn't there something weird about all murders?"

"Not really. Murder is almost a national pastime. But then again, normal girls don't just show up dead in abandoned motels."

Kekona says what I've been thinking all along.

The motel still baffles me. I don't understand why Millicent didn't bury her or take Lindsay's body a hundred miles out to the woods, or anywhere but here, near where we live, in a building where she was sure to be found eventually. It doesn't make sense.

Not unless Millicent wants to get caught.

"Normal girls?" I say to Kekona. "What's a normal girl?"

"You know, not a drug addict or a prostitute. Not someone who lives on the fringe. This girl was normal. She had a job and an apartment and, presumably, paid her taxes. Normal."

"Do you watch a lot of those police shows?"

Kekona shrugs. "Sure, who doesn't?"

Millicent doesn't. But she does read the books.

I send my wife a text:

We need a date night.

Millicent and I haven't had a real date night in more than ten years. The phrase is our code, because at some point we sat down and came up with a code. *Date night* means we need to talk about our extracurricular activities. A real conversation, not just whispers in the dark.

*　*　*

BETWEEN THE TEXT and date night, there is Rory's suspension. He has been at home alone all day, and in Millicent's fantasies her son has been reading a book to improve his mind. Instead, he has been playing his new video game, courtesy of me. There is no sign of it when I walk in the door. Rory is setting the table in silence.

He looks up at me and winks. For the first time, I do not like the person my son is becoming. And it's my fault.

I go upstairs to take a quick shower before dinner. When I come back down, Jenna has appeared. She is making fun of Rory.

"Everyone was talking about you today," she says. Jenna types into her phone while she talks. She always does this. "They said you're so stupid you had to look up the spelling of your own name. That's why you were cheating."

"Ha ha," Rory says.

"They said you're too stupid to be older than me."

Rory rolls his eyes.

Millicent is in the kitchen. She has changed out of her work clothes and is now wearing yoga pants, a long sweatshirt, and striped socks. Her hair is piled on top of her head, secured with a giant clip. She smiles and holds out a bowl of salad for me to put on the table.

The kids continue to bicker as she and I put the food out.

"You're so stupid," Jenna says. "They say I got all the brains in the family."

"You sure didn't get any beauty," Rory says.

"Mom!"

"Enough," Millicent says. She sits down at the table.

Rory and Jenna shut up. They put their napkins on their laps.

It is all so normal.

When we are done eating, Millicent asks Jenna and me if we will take care of the dishes. She wants to go over Rory's schoolwork with him to make sure he got it all done today.

I see the panic in his eyes.

It is going to be a long evening for Rory; I can hear it from the kitchen as Jenna and I clean up. I rinse, she stacks the dishwasher, and we talk a little.

Jenna babbles about soccer, going into details I cannot possibly understand. Not for the first time, I wonder if I should become more involved and volunteer to be an assistant coach or something. Then I remember I just don't have the time.

She keeps talking, and my mind wanders to Millicent. To our date night.

When the dishes are done and Rory is out of excuses, everything winds down for the night. Rory goes to his room to do the homework he didn't do earlier. Jenna chats and talks and texts all at the same time. When it is time to go to bed, Millicent takes both of their computers. She takes them every night at bedtime so they won't stay up and chat with strangers on the Internet after we've gone to bed. I think there are strangers on the Internet at all hours, but I do not argue with her about this.

Once the kids are in bed, Millicent and I go to the garage for our date night.

Eleven

WE SIT IN Millicent's car. She drives the nicer one, a luxury model crossover, because she often drives clients around while showing them houses. The leather seats are comfortable, it's roomy, and with the doors shut, the kids can't eavesdrop.

My hand rests between us, on the center console, and she puts hers on top of it.

"You're nervous," she says.

"You aren't?"

"They won't find anything that leads to us."

"How can you be sure? Did you think they'd find her?"

She shrugs. "Maybe I didn't care."

It feels like what I know could fit in my hand and everything I don't know would fill the house. I have so many questions but don't want to know the answers.

"The others have never been found," I say. "Why Lindsay?"

"Lindsay." She says the name slowly. It makes me think back to when we first found her. We did that together: We looked, we chose, I was a part of every decision.

After I went hiking with Lindsay a second time, I told Millicent she was the one. That was when we first devised the code, our special date night, except we didn't meet in the garage. While a neighbor watched the kids for a little while, Millicent and I went out for frozen yogurt. She got vanilla, I got butter pecan, and we walked through the mall, where everything was closed except the movie theater. We stopped in front of an upscale kitchen store and stared at the window display. It was one of Millicent's favorite stores.

"So," she said, "tell me."

I glanced around. The closest people were at least a hundred yards away, in line to buy movie tickets. Still, I lowered my voice. "I think she's perfect."

Millicent raised her eyebrows, looking surprised. And happy. "Really?"

"If we're going to do it, then yes. She's the one." She wasn't the only one; she was the third. Lindsay was different because she was a stranger we chose from the Internet. We picked her out of a million other options. The first two we didn't pick at all. They had come to us.

Millicent ate a spoonful of vanilla yogurt and licked the spoon. "You think we should, then? We should do it?"

Something in her eyes made me look away. On occasion, Millicent makes me feel like I cannot breathe. It happened right then, as we stood in the mall deciding Lindsay's fate. I looked away from Millicent and into the closed kitchen store. All that new and sparkly equipment stared back at me, mocking me with its unattainability. We could not afford everything we wanted. Not that anyone could, but it still bothered me.

"Yes," I said to Millicent. "We should definitely do it."

She leaned over and gave me a cold vanilla kiss.

We never said anything about holding Lindsay captive.

Now, we are sitting in the garage having another date night. No frozen yogurt, just a small bag of pretzels I have in the glove compartment. I offer them to Millicent, and she turns up her nose.

I get back to the reason we are sitting in the car. "You must have known Lindsay would be found—"

"I did."

"But why? Why would you want her to be found?"

She looks out the car window to the stacks of plastic tubs filled with old toys and Christmas decorations. When she turns back to me, her head is cocked to the side and she is half smiling. "Because it's our anniversary."

"Our anniversary was five months ago."

"Not that one."

I think, not wanting to screw this up, because I'm supposed to know. I'm supposed to remember these things.

All at once, I do. "We picked Lindsay a year ago. We decided."

Millicent beams. "Yes. A year to the day that she was found."

I stare at her. It still doesn't make sense. "Why would you want—"

"Have you heard of Owen Riley?" she says.

"What?"

"Owen Riley. Do you know who he is?"

The name is not familiar at first. Then I remember. "You mean Owen Oliver? The serial killer?"

"That's what you called him?"

"Owen Oliver Riley. We used to just say Owen Oliver."

"So you know what he did?"

"Of course I know. You couldn't live here and not know."

She smiles at me, and, as sometimes happens, I am lost. "It's not just our anniversary—it's Owen's," she says.

I think back, scouring my mind for events that happened when I was barely an adult. Owen Oliver showed up the summer after I graduated from high school. No one paid attention when one woman disappeared, and no one paid attention when the second woman disappeared. They noticed when one was found dead.

I remember being in a bar with a fake ID, surrounded by friends the same age. We drank cheap beer and cheaper liquor as we watched the first body being uncovered. Nothing ever happened in Woodview. Certainly nothing like the murder of a nice woman named Callie who worked as a clothing store manager. She was found inside an abandoned rest stop off the interstate. A trucker found her body.

At first, it was just the gruesome murder of one woman. I spent that summer watching, riveted, as the news and the police and the community tried to come up with a motive.

"A drifter" became the acceptable answer. Everyone felt better believing the killer wasn't a resident, even if it meant this outsider kidnapped Callie and kept her alive for months before killing her. We believed it anyway. Even I did.

When it happened a second time, we all felt betrayed. It had to be one of us.

No one knew it was Owen Oliver Riley. Not yet. We just called him the Woodview Killer.

Nine dead women later, he was caught. Owen Oliver Riley was a thirtysomething man with strawlike blond hair, blue eyes, and the beginning of a paunch around the middle. He drove a silver sedan, hung out at a sports bar, and volunteered at his church. People knew him, had spoken to him, had sold him goods and services, and waved to him as he passed. I stared at his picture on the TV, thinking that couldn't be him. He looked so normal. And he was, except that he had killed nine women.

Owen Oliver was initially charged with one murder; the rest of the charges were pending, due to lack of evidence. Bail was denied. Owen Oliver stayed in jail for three weeks, right up until he was released on a technicality. The warrant for his DNA sample had not been signed at the time the police swabbed the inside of his cheek. Even his court-appointed lawyer could drive a truck through that discrepancy. And he did.

With the DNA thrown out, the police had nothing. They were still scrambling for evidence when Owen Oliver walked out of jail. He was so normal-looking he blended right back in with society and disappeared.

When he went free, I was overseas and I still heard about it. That was one of the few times I heard from my parents before they died. When they did, I returned home but had no plans to stay, until I met Millicent. Back when she first agreed to go out with me, I assumed it was because she was new and didn't know anyone else.

Sometimes, I still think that.

By then, Owen Oliver was long gone. But every year, on the anniversary of the day he was released, his face is back on the news. Over the years, Owen grew to be our local monster, boogeyman, serial killer. Eventually he became a myth, too large for life.

"It must be seventeen years since he last killed someone," I say.

"Eighteen, actually. Eighteen years ago this month, his last victim disappeared."

I shake my head, trying to put the pieces together in my head. As always, Millicent does it for me.

"Remember when Lindsay first disappeared? When people were looking for her?" she says.

"Of course."

"So what do you think will happen when another one goes missing? Like one of the women on our list."

One by one, the loose ends start to come together. If another woman disappears, the police will start to think we have a serial killer. Millicent has resurrected Owen to blame our work on him.

She is setting up our future.

"That's why you kept Lindsay alive for so long," I say. "You were copying him."

Millicent nods. "Yes."

"And he strangled his victims, didn't he?"

"Yes."

I exhale. It is both physical and psychological. "It was all a setup."

"Of course it was. When the police start looking, and they will, they're going to look for Owen."

"But why wouldn't you tell me? For a *year*?"

"I wanted to surprise you," she says. "For our anniversary."

I stare at her. My lovely wife.

"It's demented," I say.

She raises an eyebrow at me. Before she can speak, I put my finger against her lips.

"And it's brilliant," I say.

Millicent leans in and kisses me on the tip of my nose. Her breath smells like the dessert we had tonight. Not vanilla this time. Chocolate ice cream and cherries.

She slides over the center console, straddling me in the passenger seat. As she pulls off her sweatshirt, the clip in her hair comes loose and her hair tumbles out. She looks down at me, her eyes dark as a swamp.

"You didn't think we were going to stop, did you?" she asks.

No. We can't stop now.

I don't even want to.

Twelve

W HEN IT STARTED, it was about Holly. And it was because we had to.

On that brisk fall day when the phone rang, our world shattered. The phone call had been about Holly. She was going to be released from a psychiatric hospital.

I was not hearing right. That's how I felt when Millicent first told me her sister had not died in an accident at the age of fifteen. She had been committed to a psychiatric hospital.

It was late that Saturday night, after the kids had been calmed down and fed, and had gone to sleep. Millicent and I sat in our living room, on the new couch we were still paying off on the credit card, and she told me the real story of Holly.

The first time was the paper cut. I already knew that story, about how they had been making collages of their favorite things.

"She did it on purpose," Millicent said. "She grabbed my hand and sliced it with the paper. Right there." She pointed to the spot between her thumb and index finger. "She convinced our parents it was an accident."

A month passed, and six-year-old Millicent had almost forgotten about it. Until it happened again. She and Holly were in Holly's room, playing in what they called the Purple Pit. Millicent and her sister had created their own little world, using dolls, stuffed animals, and plastic model horses, and they called it the Purple Pit. The name referred to the color of Holly's room. Hers was lavender, and Millicent's was yellow.

While they were in the Pit, Holly cut her again. This time she used a sharp piece of plastic she had broken off another toy.

The cut was on Millicent's leg, down near her ankle. She screamed as the blood trickled onto the rug. Holly stared at it until their mother came into the room. Then she started to cry right along with Millicent.

The incident was dismissed as another accident.

Over the next couple of years, Millicent suffered a number of other accidents. Her father thought she was clumsy. Her mother told her to be careful.

Holly laughed at her.

The more Millicent told me, the more horrified I became. Some of what I had seen now made sense.

The bite on her arm, blamed on the dog. Two small discolored marks that never went away.

A broken finger slammed in the door. It was still a little bent.

That tiny chip on her front bottom tooth, from when she tripped and fell into the doorjamb.

The long, deep cut in her calf from broken glass in the street. The scar is still visible, a tan stripe almost six inches long.

The list went on for what seemed like hours. And as they got older, it got worse.

When Millicent was ten, Holly pushed her down the stairs. Millicent broke her arm. Six months later, Holly crashed into Millicent with her bike. After that, she fell out of a tree in the backyard.

Her parents believed they were all accidents. Or they saw what they wanted to see. No parent wants to believe their child is a monster.

Part of me could understand that. Nothing would make me believe Rory or Jenna could act like that. It just isn't possible, isn't feasible. And I was sure Millicent's parents felt the same way about Holly.

That didn't make me any less angry. As I sat and listened to what Millicent had endured growing up, I could not reason away the rage.

The treatment—no, the torture—continued into their early teens. By then, Millicent had long given up trying to be nice to her sister in the hopes she would stop. Instead, she tried to hurt Holly back.

The first and only time she tried to hurt Holly was when they were both in middle school. When the day was over, they headed out front with the rest of the children, to the line of parents waiting to pick up their kids. They walked together, side by side, and Millicent stuck out her foot.

Holly fell flat on the ground.

The whole thing happened in a second but was seen by half the school. Kids laughed, teachers rushed to help, and, inside, Millicent smiled to herself.

"It sounds sick," Millicent said. "But I really thought it was over. I thought hurting her would make her stop hurting me."

She was wrong.

Hours later, Millicent woke up in the middle of the night. Her wrists were bound and tied to her headboard. Holly was in the process of tying a gag around Millicent's mouth.

Holly didn't say a word to her. She just sat in the corner, staring at Millicent until the sun came up. Just before their parents woke up, Holly untied her and took the gag out of her mouth.

"Don't ever try to hurt me again," she said. "Next time I'll kill you."

Millicent didn't. She continued to take the abuse while searching for a way to prove she wasn't clumsy and she wasn't hurting herself by accident. Holly was too smart to get caught on camera, too clever to get caught by anyone.

To this day, Millicent is convinced it would have continued if it hadn't been for the car.

The car accident she told me about did happen. Holly was fifteen, Millicent was thirteen, and Holly did decide to take their mom's car out for a spin. She ordered Millicent to come along for the ride, then purposely drove into a fence, passenger side first.

It would have been written off as an accident if not for the video.

Two separate security cameras recorded the accident. The first showed the car driving straight down the street when a sudden turn right made it plow into a fence. The second video showed the driver's side of the car. Holly was behind the wheel, and it looked like she turned the wheel on purpose.

The police interviewed her and decided the accident was no accident.

After many interviews with Millicent, Holly, and their parents, they came to realize something was very wrong with Holly. They also believed she was trying to kill her little sister.

Rather than have their daughter charged with attempted murder, Millicent's parents agreed to put her in long-term psychiatric hospitalization. Her doctors kept her there.

Twenty-three years later, she was released.

Holly was the first.

AFTER OUR DATE night, I research Owen Oliver Riley. If our plan is to resurrect our local boogeyman, then I need to brush up on the facts, specifically the types of women he targeted. I don't remember much about that. What I remember is that he scared the hell out of every woman in the area, which made it either very easy or very hard to meet a woman. They'd either looked at me like I might be the Woodview Killer or they evaluated my chances of fighting him off.

These were girls around my age at the time, between eighteen and twenty, although it looks like Owen Oliver wouldn't have given them a second glance. He liked them a bit older, between the ages of twenty-five and thirty-five.

Blond or brunette—it didn't matter. Owen Oliver had no prefer-
ence.

He had others, though. The women were on the shorter side; none
was taller than five-three. Easier to move them. And much easier for
Millicent.

They all lived alone.

Many worked at night. One was even a prostitute.

Owen's final requirement was the one that gave him away. At one
time or another, all of his victims had been patients at Saint Mary's
Memorial Hospital. Sometimes, the work had gone back years. One
had her tonsils out at Saint Mary's; another had pneumonia and spent
two days on an IV. Owen had worked in the billing department. He
knew everything about their procedures, as well as their age, marital
status, and address.

Saint Mary's was the one thing tying the victims together. For a
long time, that was overlooked, because everyone goes to Saint Mary's.
It's the only large hospital in our area. The second-closest is still an
hour away.

I skip past most of the details about what he did to his victims
while they were held captive. Too much information I don't need, too
many mental images I do not want.

The only one that catches my eye is the fingerprints. Owen had
filed them off all his victims. Millicent had done the same to Lindsay.

Next, I scroll through pictures of the women he killed. They were
young, bright, and happy. This is how victim pictures always look. No
one wants to see a picture of a somber young woman, even if she's
dead.

I notice a few more things. All of the women were quite plain.
They didn't wear a lot of makeup or stylish clothes. Most looked simple: ordinary hair, jeans and T-shirts, no dark lipstick, and no painted
nails. Lindsay fit this profile, and she fit Owen's height requirement.

Naomi was more simple than glamorous, but she was too tall.

Up until now, I have never chosen a woman based on this kind of profile. My criteria revolved around how many people would be looking for her, how quickly the police would be notified, and how much time they would put into finding a grown woman.

Everything else was arbitrary. I chose Lindsay because she fit all the important criteria, and because Millicent would not get off my back about choosing the next one.

Petra was different. Because I slept with her, or because she suspected I wasn't deaf. Maybe both. She is still out there, still a risk, but she doesn't fit our new profile at all. Petra is too tall and far too glamorous; she wears skirts and heels, and even her toenails were painted red.

I need to find another one. Our fourth.

That was how Owen Oliver worked. He always took his next victim after the last one was found.

As I scour through social media sites, I can feel my adrenaline start to surge. It's not quite a rush, not yet, but it will be. Millicent and I will bring back Owen together.

And I'm looking forward to it.

Thirteen

WE DIDN'T PICK the first two women. Lindsay was the first one we chose, and we found her on social media. But that was when we didn't have a profile or a height requirement. Most don't put their physical statistics on social media, and there are no categories for exact height or weight or eye color. This makes my preliminary search for number four difficult.

I do find one place that lists height: dating websites. But a brief search through a few of them is uninspiring. The next day, I ask Millicent to meet me for a midday break. We grab a cup of coffee and sit in the park across the street. The day is a beautiful one, the sky an unbroken blue and not too much humidity in the air, and the park is close enough to use the coffee shop's Internet.

I explain our new profile requirements and show her what I've found online. She pages through the women on the dating site and then looks at me.

"They all seem so . . ." She shakes her head as her voice trails off.

"Fake?"

"Yes. Like they're trying to be who men want instead of who they are."

I point to one, who says her hobbies are windsurfing and beach parties. "And they might have too many friends."

"Some do, I'm sure."

She continues to page through profiles, her brow furrowed. "We can't pick from a dating site."

I say nothing, and she looks up at me. I am smiling.

"What?" she says.

"I have another idea."

She relaxes, no longer worried, and raises one eyebrow. "Do you now?"

"I do."

"Tell me."

I glance across the park, my eyes finally settling on a woman sitting on another bench and reading a book. I point. "What about her?"

Millicent looks over, studies the woman, and smiles. "You want to look for someone in the real world."

"To start, yes. So we find someone that fits the physical profile. Then we'll research online to make sure she'll work."

Millicent's eyes turn to me. They are so bright. She places her hand on mine. Her touch spreads throughout my whole body; it feels like I am being recharged. Even my brain hums.

She nods, and the corners of her mouth turn up as she starts to smile. All I can think about is kissing her. About throwing her down in the middle of the park and ripping off her clothes.

"I knew there was a reason I married you," Millicent finally says.

"Because I'm unbelievably brilliant?"

"And humble."

"Not too bad-looking, either," I say.

"If we do this right," she says, "the police will never even think to look for a couple. We'll be free to do whatever we want."

Something about that makes me even more excited. The world is filled with things I can't do and can't afford, from houses to cars to kitchen equipment, but this, *this*, is how we can be free. This is the one thing that is ours, that we control. Thanks to Millicent.

"Yes," I say to her.

"Yes to what?"

"Yes to everything."

I DRIVE TO the SunRail station and take the train to Altamonte Springs, the opposite direction from where Petra lives. Technically, the town is outside Woodview, but it was still part of Owen's original hunting grounds.

Women are everywhere. Young, old, tall, short, thin, heavy. They are on every street, in every store, around every corner. I don't see the men, only the women, and it has always been this way. When I was young, I couldn't imagine choosing only one. Not with so many available.

Obviously, that was before Millicent.

I'm the one who is different. I still evaluate all women, just not the same way. I do not see them as possible partners, lovers, or conquests. I evaluate them based on whether or not they will fit Owen's profile. I size each one up first based on height, then on makeup and clothes.

I watch a young woman leave a Laundromat and go upstairs, to the apartment above it. From where I am standing, I am not sure if she is too tall.

A second woman exits an office building. She is quite short but annoyingly brisk, and I watch as she gets into a car that is nicer than mine. I am not sure I could get close to that one.

I see a woman at a coffee shop and sit at the table behind her. She is on a laptop, scrolling through sites that fall into two categories: politics and food. I know a smidge about both and wonder what kind of conversation we would have. This makes me curious enough to watch as she leaves, and then trail after her to get a license plate number.

I continue down the sidewalk until I see a small woman who is also a meter maid. She is writing a ticket. Her nails are cut short; so is her hair. I cannot see her eyes because of her sunglasses, but she isn't wearing lipstick.

I pass by her close enough to read her name tag.

A. Parson.

Maybe her, maybe not. I haven't decided yet. When she isn't looking, I take a couple of pictures.

LATER THAT NIGHT, Millicent is lying in bed and studying a spreadsheet on her computer. The kids are asleep, or should be. If nothing else, they're silent. That might be the most we can hope for these days.

I slide into bed next to Millicent. "Hey there," I say.

"Hey." She scoots over to make room, though our bed is more than big enough.

"I went shopping today."

"Jesus, I hope you didn't spend any money. I'm looking at our budget right now, and we don't have any extra. Not after the washer had to be replaced."

I smile. "Not that kind of shopping." I place my phone in front of her, with a picture of A. Parson on the front.

"Oh," Millicent says. She zooms in on the picture and squints at it. "What kind of uniform is that?"

"Meter maid."

"I certainly wouldn't mind getting a little revenge on one of those."

"Me neither." We laugh together. "And she fits Owen's profile."

"Indeed she does." Millicent closes her computer and turns her whole body to me. "Nice work."

"Thank you."

We kiss, and all our budget problems melt away.

Fourteen

A T FIRST, NOTHING about it was sexy. It was petrifying.

Holly was supposed to be the end, not the beginning. The day after she was released from the hospital, Millicent opened the front door to find Holly on the porch. She slammed the door in her sister's face.

Holly wrote a letter and put it in our mailbox. Millicent did not answer it.

She called. Millicent stopped answering the phone.

When I contacted the psychiatric hospital, they wouldn't tell me anything.

Holly started showing up in public, staying at least a hundred feet away, but she was everywhere. At the grocery store when Millicent went shopping. In the parking lot at the mall. Across the street when we went out to dinner.

She never stayed anywhere long enough for us to call the police. And every time we tried to take Holly's picture for proof, she turned, walked away, or moved to create a blur.

Millicent would not tell her mother. The Alzheimer's was already making her forget who Holly was, and Millicent wanted to keep it that way.

Online, I researched the stalker laws and made a list of every time Holly had showed up so far. When I showed it to Millicent, she told me it was useless.

"That won't help," she said.

"But if we—"

"I know the stalker laws. She hasn't broken them, and she won't. Holly is too smart for that."

"We have to do something," I said.

Millicent stared at my notebook and shook her head. "I don't think you understand. She made my childhood hell."

"I know she did."

"Then you should know a list isn't going to help."

I wanted to go to the police and tell them what was happening to us, but the only physical evidence we had was the letter Holly put in the mailbox. It was not threatening. As Millicent said, Holly was too smart for that.

M,

Don't you think we should talk? I do.

H.

Instead of going to the police, I went to see Holly. I told her to leave Millicent and my family alone.

She didn't. The next time I saw her, she was in my house.

It was on a Tuesday, around lunchtime, and I was at the club finishing up a lesson and thinking about what to eat. My phone dinged three times in a row, all texts from Millicent.

911

Get home NOW

Holly

This was less than a week after I paid Holly a visit.

I didn't pause to text Millicent back. When I arrived home, Millicent met me at the door. Her eyes were wet, tears threatening to slide down her cheeks. My wife does not cry over every little thing.

"What the hell—"

Before I could finish, she grabbed my hand and led me into the family room. Holly was at the far end, sitting on the couch. As soon as she saw me, she stood up.

"Holly was here when I got home," Millicent said. Her voice shook.

"What?" Holly said.

"Right here, right in our family room."

"No, it wasn't like that—"

"I forgot my camera," Millicent said. "I was supposed to photograph the Sullivan place today, so I came home and she was just here."

"Wait—"

"I found her *sitting on our couch*." The tears finally came, in force, and Millicent covered her face with her hands. I put my arm around her.

Holly looked like a normal thirtysomething woman dressed in jeans, a T-shirt, and sandals. Her short red hair had been slicked back, and she wore bright lipstick. Holly took a deep breath and held up both hands as if to show me they were empty. "Hold on. That's not—"

"Stop lying," Millicent screamed. "You're always lying."

"I'm not lying!"

"Wait," I said, stepping forward. "Let's all just calm down."

"Yes," Holly said. "Let's do that."

"No, I'm not going to calm down." Millicent pointed to the window in the corner, facing the side of the house. The curtain was pulled shut, but glass was scattered on the floor. "That's how she got in. She broke a window to get into our home."

"I did not!"

"Then how did you get in?"

"I didn't—"

"Holly, stop. Just stop. You're not going to fool my husband the way you fooled Mom and Dad."

Millicent was right about that.

"Oh my god," Holly said. She clasped her hands on her head and closed her eyes, as if trying to block out the world. "Ohmygodohmygodohmygod."

Millicent took a step back.

I stepped forward. "Holly," I said. "Are you okay?"

She didn't stop. It was like she couldn't even hear me. When she smacked the side of her head with an open hand, I glanced back at Millicent. She was staring at Holly and looked too scared to move. Millicent had frozen.

I raised my voice. "Holly."

Her head jerked up.

She dropped her hands.

Holly's face had contorted into something angry, something almost feral. It felt like I was seeing what Millicent was so afraid of.

"You should have died in that accident," she said to Millicent. It sounded like a growl.

Millicent moved closer, using me as a shield, and she gripped my arm. I half turned to tell her to call the police, but she spoke first. Her voice was barely a whisper. "Thank god the kids aren't here to see this."

The kids. A picture of them flashed in my mind. I saw Rory and Jenna in the room instead of us. I felt their fear as this insane woman confronted them.

"Holly," I said.

She couldn't hear me. She couldn't hear anyone. Her eyes were fixed on Millicent, who was trying to hide behind me.

"You bitch," Holly said.

She lunged toward me.

Toward Millicent.

In that moment, I did not make a decision. I did not run through the options in my mind, weighing the pros and cons, using logic to arrive at the best possible course of action. If I had gone through all that, Holly would still be alive.

Instead, I did not think, did not decide. What I did next came from somewhere much deeper. It was biology, self-preservation. Instinct.

Holly was a threat to my family, so she was a threat to me. I reached for the closest thing. It was right next to me, leaning against the wall.

A tennis racket.

Fifteen

A FEW DAYS PASS before someone on TV asks about Owen Oliver Riley.

Josh, my earnest, young Josh, brought up the serial killer's name during a press conference. Ever since Lindsay was found, the police have been holding press conferences at least every other day. They are held in the late afternoon so the highlights can be replayed on the evening news.

Josh's question will be today's highlight.

"Has it occurred to you that Owen Oliver Riley is back?"

The lead detective, a balding man in his fifties, did not look surprised at the question.

Josh is far too young to remember any details about Owen Oliver, but he is an intelligent, ambitious reporter, capable of surfing the Internet at light speed. He just needed someone to give him a starting point.

For this, I went back to some of the most famous serial killers. Several communicated with the press, sometimes even the police, and that was long before e-mail was invented. But given how easy it was to track anything electronic, I decided against using e-mail. I went old-school.

Owen never wrote letters to anyone, so all I had to do was create something just plausible enough to be real. After several attempts, from long to short, poetic to rambling, I ended up with a single line:

It's good to be home.

—Owen

I wore surgical gloves while handling the paper, envelope, and stamp. When it was sealed and ready to go, I spritzed the envelope with a cheap drugstore cologne. It smelled like a musky cowboy.

That was just to mess with Josh.

Then I drove across town and dropped it in a mailbox. Three days later, Josh brought up Owen at the press conference but not the letter. Maybe Josh is keeping this to himself, or maybe the police have asked him not to mention it.

For now, I am content to wait and see, because there is something else I need to do. Last night, I was out watching Annabelle Parson's apartment. Finally. The meter maid who'd caught my eye was more difficult to find than the others. For Lindsay and Petra, all I had to do was look up their names on the Internet. Annabelle was smarter than that, no doubt to hide herself from all those angry people who got a parking ticket from her. To find out where she lived, I had to follow her home one evening. It was a little annoying.

Last night, I waited outside her apartment to see if she would return home alone or if she was seeing someone. Around midnight, I received a text from my son.

Out again? It's going to cost you.

What do you want?

You mean, how much do I want?

This time he doesn't want another video game. He wants cash.

The next day, I meet him at home after work. He is already on the couch, channel surfing, texting, and playing a game. Millicent is not home yet. Jenna is upstairs.

I sit down next to him.

He glances up, eyebrows raised.

This is a mistake. I should have told Millicent everything. We could have sat down with both Rory and Jenna, and explained that nothing is going on.

Dad just likes to take long drives in the middle of the night. Occasionally while wearing a suit.

I hand Rory the cash.

He is so busy counting the money he isn't paying attention to the TV, where they are replaying press conference highlights on the news. Rory is oblivious to the real reason his father is out at night. All he has to do is look up.

WE HAVE TACOS for dinner, made with leftover chicken, and they are delicious. My wife is a good cook and insists on making dinner every night, but the quicker she throws something together, the better it seems to be.

I don't tell her that.

Dessert is peach slices sprinkled with brown sugar, and we each get one snickerdoodle cookie. Rory is the first to roll his eyes, though Jenna is right there with him. Millicent has always been stingy with dessert.

We all eat it differently. Jenna licks the brown sugar off her peaches, then eats the cookie and finishes the rest of the peaches. Rory eats the cookie first, then the peaches, although it's all sort of a blur, because he inhales everything so fast. Millicent alternates between the fruit and the cookie, a bite of one and then a bite of the other. I mash the peaches and cookie together and eat it all with a spoon.

Tomorrow is our movie night, and we discuss what we will watch. Last week, it was a talking animal movie. Rory always groans at first, but he loves those as much as anyone. Both of the kids like sports movies, so we pick one about a baseball youth league trying to make it to the world championships. We vote on this like it's a serious election, and *Batter Up* wins by a landslide.

"I'll be home by five thirty," I say.

"Dinner at six," says Millicent.

"Are we done here?" Rory asks.

"Who's Owen Oliver Riley?" Jenna says.

Everything stops.

Millicent and I look at Jenna.

"Where did you hear that?" Millicent says.

"TV."

"Owen is a horrible man who hurt people," I say. "But he can never hurt you."

"Oh."

"Don't worry about Owen."

"But why are they talking about him?" Jenna asks.

"Because of that dead girl," Rory says.

"Woman," I say. "Dead woman."

"Oh. Her." Jenna shrugs and looks over at her phone. "So are we done?"

Millicent nods, and they pick up their phones, clearing the table while texting. I rinse off the dishes, Jenna helps put them in the dishwasher, and Millicent gets rid of whatever is left of the tacos.

WHILE WE GET ready for bed, Millicent turns on the local news. She watches the press conference highlights and then turns to me. Saying nothing, she asks if I had something to do with it.

I shrug.

She raises an eyebrow.

I wink at her.

She smiles.

Sometimes, we do not have to say anything.

We weren't always like this. In the beginning, we spent entire nights talking, just like all young couples do when they fall in love. I told her all my stories. Couldn't get them out fast enough, because I had finally found someone who thought they were fascinating. Who thought I was fascinating.

Eventually, she knew all my old stories, so we traded only new ones. I texted her in the middle of the day to tell her the smallest things. She would send me a funny picture depicting how her day was going. I had never known someone so well, nor shared my life so completely with another. This continued until we got married, even afterward when Millicent was pregnant with Rory.

I still remember the first thing I didn't tell her. The first thing of any importance, I mean. It was the car. We had two; hers was the newer one, and mine was a beat-up old truck that held all my tennis equipment. When Millicent was eight months pregnant, my truck broke down. It needed a thousand dollars in repairs, and we didn't have the money. Any money we did have had been squirreled away, bit by bit, to afford a crib and a stroller and the mountains of diapers we were going to need.

I didn't want to upset her, didn't want to make her worry, so I made a choice. I told her the truck broke down but not how much it would cost. To pay for the repairs, I opened a new credit card only in my name.

It took more than a year to pay it off, and I never told Millicent. I never told her about the rest of the charges, either.

That was the first big thing, but we both stopped talking about the small things. We had a baby, then another, and her days became more exhausting than funny. She no longer recounted every little thing, nor did I tell her all the details about my clients.

We both stopped asking, stopping sharing the minutiae, and instead we stuck to the highlights. We still do.

Sometimes a smile and a wink is all we need.

Sixteen

WITHIN TWENTY-FOUR HOURS, Owen Oliver Riley is everywhere. His face is all over our local news and websites. My clients want to talk about him. Those who aren't from here want more details. Those who are from here have not decided if he's really back. Kekona, the local gossip, is in the middle on both counts.

Though she was born in Hawaii, she has been living here long enough to know all our legends, myths, and infamous residents. She doesn't believe Owen Oliver is back. Not for one second.

We are on the court, and Kekona is working on her serve. Again. She thinks if she can just serve one ace after another, she doesn't need to play the rest of the game. In theory, she is right. In reality, no one can do that. Not unless her opponent is a five-year-old.

"Owen could go anywhere to kill women, but they think he's back here?" she says.

"If by 'they' you mean the police, then no, they haven't said anything about Owen Oliver. It was just some reporter's question."

"Pfft."

"I'm not sure what that means."

"It means that's ridiculous. Owen got away once. He has no reason to come back."

I shrug. "Because it's home?"

Kekona rolls her dark eyes. "Life is not a horror movie."

She is not the only one who feels this way. Anyone who didn't live through it the first time thinks it would be ridiculous for him to come back. They see this as Kekona does, like a choice that makes no rational sense.

But those who did live here, and are old enough to remember, believe Owen has returned home. Especially the women.

They remember what it was like to be scared whenever they were alone, indoors or out, because Owen snatched his victims from almost anywhere. Two disappeared from inside their own homes. One was in a library, another in a park, and at least three had been in parking lots. Two of these had been caught on security video. The footage was old and grainy; Owen looked like a big blur dressed in dark clothes and wearing a baseball cap. The videos have been on the news all day, all over again.

Today, I have a tennis lesson with Trista, Andy's wife, but as I walk through the clubhouse I see her in the sports bar. She is watching the news on one of the big screens. Like her husband, she is in her early forties and couldn't pass for younger. The ends of her hair are too blond, her eyes are always rimmed in black, and she has a deep, disturbingly natural tan. She is alone and drinking red wine at one o'clock in the afternoon. The bottle sits on the table.

I guess we are not having a lesson today.

From a distance, I watch her, unsure if I should get involved. Sometimes, my clients tell me more than I want to know. I'm like the hairdresser of exercise.

But I have to admit, it can also be interesting.

I walk up to Trista. "Hey."

She waves and points to an empty chair, never taking her eyes off the TV screen. I have seen her drink plenty of times at parties and dinners, but I've never seen her like this.

At the commercial break, she turns to me. "I'm canceling our lesson today," she says.

"Thanks for letting me know."

She smiles, but it doesn't make her look happy. It occurs to me that she might be upset with Andy. Maybe he has done something wrong, and I don't want to get in the middle of it. I start to get up from the chair when she speaks.

"Do you remember what it was like back then?" she says, pointing at the TV. "When he was killing?"

"Owen?"

"Who else?"

"Of course. Everyone from here remembers." I shrug and sit back down. "Did you ever go to The Hatch? A bunch of us used to drink there on Saturday nights, and all the TVs were tuned into the news. I think that's where I—"

She takes a deep breath. "I knew him."

"Who?"

"Owen Oliver. I knew him." Trista picks up the bottle and refills her glass.

"You never told me that before."

She rolls her eyes. "Not exactly something to be proud of. Especially because I dated him."

"No way."

"I'm serious."

My jaw drops. Not an exaggeration. "Does Andy know this?"

"No. And don't even think about telling him."

I shake my head. No way would I tell him. I am not about to be the bearer of that news. "But how did you—"

"First, have some of this." Trista pushes the bottle of wine toward me. "You're going to need it."

TRISTA WAS RIGHT. The wine dulled the horror of the story she told.

She met Owen Oliver when he was in his early thirties. She was a decade younger with a degree in art history and a job at a collections agency. That was how they met. Owen worked in billing at Saint Mary's. When the bills weren't paid, they were turned over to the collections agency.

"It was a scum job," she said. Her voice slurred from the wine. "I called sick people and demanded money from them. So that was me. Scum. All day, I felt like a scummy person who did scummy things."

Owen told her she wasn't. They first spoke about someone named Leann, who owed the hospital more than $10,000. After calling Leann seventeen times, Trista had become convinced the number was wrong. The only person to answer the phone was a man who sounded about ninety and had an obvious case of dementia. Leann was a twenty-eight-year-old woman who lived alone. Trista called over to the billing department of Saint Mary's to check the phone number. She wasn't supposed to contact the hospital directly, but she did it anyway. Owen had answered the phone.

"Of course I had the right number. Owen told me Leann was an actress." Trista heaved a big sigh. "I was so embarrassed I didn't even ask how he knew that."

They talked. She liked his voice, he liked her laugh, and they agreed to meet. Trista dated Owen for six months.

"We both liked to eat and drink, and would rather watch sports than play them. Except sex. We had a lot of sex. Good but not great. Not earth-shattering. But"—Trista held up a finger and waved it around—"he did make earth-shattering cinnamon rolls. Made them from scratch, too. Rolled out the dough, spread melted butter over it, and then added this cinnamon-and-sugar mixture . . ." For a second, she stared at nothing. She was slow to come back. "Anyway. The cinnamon rolls were good. There was nothing wrong with the cinnamon rolls. There wasn't really anything wrong with Owen, either. Except he was a medical billing clerk."

Trista looked down at the table and smiled. Not a real smile—one that is filled with loathing and aimed at herself. She lifted her head and looked me full in the eye. "I broke up with him because I was never going to marry a thirty-three-year-old medical billing clerk. There was no chance in hell. And if that makes me a snob, so be it, but hell if I was going to be poor my whole life." She threw up her hands, surrendering to whatever insults I may have wanted to sling at her.

I said nothing. Instead, I lifted my glass, we toasted, and we drank. Trista talked about Owen Oliver Riley for almost two hours.

He watched sports. Hockey was one of his favorites, although the closest professional team is hundreds of miles away. Owen always wore jeans. Always, unless he was in the shower, in bed, or near a pool. But he couldn't swim. Trista suspected he was afraid of the water.

He lived in a house on the north side of town, the same area Millicent and I lived when we first got married. The north side isn't a bad area, but it is older and more run-down than the southeastern side, where Hidden Oaks is located. Owen had inherited the house when his mother died, and Trista described it as "cute enough, but almost a shack." This wasn't surprising. A lot of houses on the north side are small cottages with porches, elaborate woodwork, and little dormer windows. Inside, most are outdated and falling apart. Owen's was no exception.

The heater didn't work, the bedroom window was jammed, and the carpet was an obnoxious shade of teal. The bathroom did have a claw-foot tub, which Trista liked, but the faucet dripped and drove her crazy. If she spent the night, she shut the door to the bathroom; otherwise, she would hear the drip down the hall. When they ate at Owen's, they used his mother's dishes, with a yellow floral pattern around the edge.

After a while, Trista was too drunk and tired to continue, so I had a driver at the club take her home. I told her if she wanted to talk more about Owen, I would be happy to listen. It was the truth.

She'd provided me with exactly what I needed for the second letter to Josh.

Seventeen

PLANS HAVE NEVER been my thing. Not even my trip overseas was planned. I got a call from a friend, and a week later I met up with him at the Orlando airport. When I realized I would never be good enough to play tennis professionally, I didn't have a plan. The day Millicent told me she was pregnant with Rory, I had no plan to raise a child. When she got pregnant with Jenna, I still didn't have one. Only the secret I have with Millicent makes me plan.

My game is tennis, not chess. I play, and teach, singles tennis, and usually that is all I see: two sides of the net, two opposing forces, one goal. It isn't complicated. Yet here I am, designing a plan involving multiple people, like I have something to prove.

The current version of my plan involves three people: Owen, Josh, and Annabelle. Millicent makes it four, and I could even include Trista. Or at least the information Trista gave me.

First, I'll send another letter to Josh. Not only will it include details about Owen's real life—specifically his mother's home—but it will also include the date when another woman will disappear.

This is risky, I know. Maybe even unnecessary. But in one fell swoop, it accomplishes our goal. Yes, Owen is back. Yes, he is responsible for Lindsay and for the next one. No guessing games, no back-and-forth between the police and the media, wondering if he is really back or if there is a copycat. The information Trista gave me will prove to them it's Owen. No one will have a doubt when the next one disappears.

It will be Annabelle Parson, though I don't include her name.

The downside is that the entire police department will be waiting for a woman to disappear that night, and they will be searching for her as soon as someone reports her missing.

The upside is that Annabelle has very few friends. No one is going to report her missing until she doesn't show up for work. It would be easy enough to give us a two-day lead.

We'll still have to figure out how to snatch Annabelle without being seen by anyone, including a camera, on a night when everyone is expecting a woman to disappear. And while the police are looking for Owen, they will completely miss Millicent.

The plan is so simple it could be brilliant.

I go through it again, starting with the letter to Josh and ending with the disappearance of Annabelle. Along the way, I see a hundred holes, loose ends, and potential problems.

This is why I do not plan. It's exhausting. Which is also why I do it. I try to put the plan together before telling Millicent about it. Even after all these years, I still want to impress her.

And it's been a while. Impressing Millicent wasn't easy when she was young. Now, it's almost impossible.

Our relationship is not one-sided, though. There have been plenty of times she has tried to impress me. Millicent was trying to impress me when she decorated our Christmas tree with the oxygen masks. On our fifth anniversary, she put on the same lingerie she wore on our wedding night. And for our tenth anniversary, she planned a little vacation.

With two kids and a bigger house on our wish list, we had no money for a vacation or even a nice dinner. Millicent found a way.

First, she showed up at the tennis courts. Millicent never comes to the tennis courts. If she comes to the club at all, it's to swim or have lunch with someone, so when she walked onto the court, I thought something was wrong. My wife just wanted to kidnap me.

Millicent drove us out to the middle of nowhere, stopped, and pointed to the woods.

"Walk," she said.

I did.

A couple hundred yards from the road, we came to a clearing. A tent was already set up, right next to a stone fire pit. A little picnic table was set with plastic plates, glasses, and thick candles.

Millicent took me camping. She is not the outdoorsy type, but, for one night, she pretended to be.

The bugs were a problem, because she forgot bug spray. The candles were covered, but they kept getting blown out, and she didn't think to bring extra water for cleaning dishes or brushing teeth. None of that mattered. We sat in front of our fire pit and ate warmed-up soup, drank cheap beer, and had even cheaper sex. We talked about the future, which looked much different than before, because of the kids. Not bad different, just priority different.

We avoided talking about the things we used to want but could no longer have.

Sometime after midnight, we fell asleep. I hadn't been up that late since Christmas Eve, when we had to stay up to put out Santa's presents.

The next morning when I stepped out of the tent, Millicent was just standing there, hands clasped over her mouth. Our camp had been ransacked.

Everything was overturned, tossed around, cleaned out. The food had been taken or ripped open, and our extra clothes were strewn across the ground.

"Scavengers," I said. "Probably raccoons."

She didn't answer. She was too pissed off to answer.

Millicent started gathering up what was left of our things.

"We still have some coffee," I said, holding up a little jar of instant. "We could make some—"

"I don't think those were raccoons."

I stared at her as she collected what was left of a backpack. "Then what—"

"People destroyed our camp. Not animals."

"What makes you say that?"

She pointed to where we had slept. "They didn't touch the tent."

"Maybe they just wanted the food. Maybe they didn't care—"

"Or maybe they were people."

I stopped arguing. We trudged out of the woods and back to the car.

To this day, if that camping trip comes up, she talks about the horrible people who ransacked our things. I still think it was done by some animal, not people, but I don't argue. Millicent sees a motive behind everything.

But what I remember most about that trip is different. The important thing was that Millicent planned the trip to impress me.

ANNABELLE PARSON HAS never called in sick or late, she has never taken more than two vacation days in a row, and she always fills in when someone is sick. That means she does not have a boyfriend. Anyone who does will occasionally call in late. Couples also take real vacations, especially couples who don't have kids, and Annabelle doesn't. To top it all off, like the perfect cherry on a sundae, Annabelle has been named "Meter Maid of the Month" five times and is featured on the county website.

I show all of this to Millicent, who looks through everything and says, "You're right. She's perfect."

"I'm also working on the next letter to Josh, but I'm not going to show you."

"You're not?"

"I want it to be a surprise."

She smiles a little. "I trust you."

This is the best news I have heard all week.

I start watching Annabelle the way I watched the others. Due diligence and all.

Today I take the train back out to where she works, just to switch things up in case she recognizes my car. It is impossible to follow her when she is working. Annabelle uses a county-issued ATV to drive around, looking for expired meters and illegal parkers. She stops and starts at random times.

For a while, I sit in a coffee shop on the main thoroughfare. Every twenty to thirty minutes, she passes by to check the meters. While waiting, I draft my next Owen Oliver letter. I work under the assumption that this one will be so convincing it will become public. Josh, and the station he works for, won't be able to resist.

Just the mention of Owen's return is getting everyone worked up. Local stations are replaying old news clips, retrospectives, and profiles. Owen has been on the cover of the paper for the past few days. Rory and his friends have already turned Owen's name into a verb ("I'll Owen Oliver your ass.") and the local women's group is lobbying for Lindsay's murder to be declared a hate crime.

I try to imagine how it would escalate if the rumor was confirmed. Or even if people thought it was confirmed. That's all we really need. Belief. If I can make the police believe it, they won't be looking for anyone but Owen.

Millicent may have started this, but I can bring it home. She will be so impressed.

Eighteen

IF IT HADN'T been for Robin, none of this would have happened. We didn't look for her; she hadn't been chosen the way Lindsay was. Robin changed everything by knocking on our door.

It happened on a Tuesday. I had just walked into the house. It was lunchtime, no one was home, and I had a couple of hours before my next lesson. This was almost a year after Holly, and life had returned to normal. Her body was long gone, wasting away in a swamp. Millicent and I did not talk about her. I no longer waited for the police sirens. My heart had stopped thumping every time the phone or doorbell rang. I was not on guard when I opened the door.

The woman on the porch was young, early twenties, wearing tight jeans and a shirt with a ripped neck. Her nails were red, her lipstick was pink, and her long hair was the color of a roasted chestnut.

Behind her, a little red car was parked on the street. The car was an old one, close to a classic but not quite. Minutes before, I had seen it at a stop sign not far from the house. She had honked, but I'd had no idea she was honking at me.

"Can I help you?" I said.

She cocked her head, looking at me sideways, and smiled. "I thought it was you."

"Excuse me?"

"You're Holly's friend."

Her name made me jolt, like I had stuck my finger in a light socket. "Holly?"

"I saw you with her."

"I think you've mistaken me for someone else."

She had not, of course. Now I recognized her.

When the hospital released Holly, one of the doctors helped arrange for her to work at a grocery store. Holly stocked shelves part-time. That's where I had gone to tell her to stay away from us, where I had confronted her about scaring our family.

I never meant for it to get out of hand.

I went on a Monday morning, when the store was slow and everything was being restocked. Holly was in one of the aisles, filling a shelf with boxes of granola bars, and she was alone. As I walked down the aisle toward her, she turned toward me. Her clear green eyes were startling.

Holly put her hands on her hips and stared at me until I stood right next to her.

"Yes?" she said.

"I don't think we've formally met." I stuck out my hand and waited for her to shake it. Eventually, she did.

I told her I was sorry we had to meet this way—that in another place, at another time, perhaps we would be like family. But right now, it wasn't possible, because her behavior was scaring my wife and kids. My kids had never done anything to her. They did not deserve this. "I'm asking you," I said. "Can you please leave my family alone?"

She laughed at me.

Holly laughed until tears sprang from the corners of her eyes, and she laughed some more. The longer it went on, the more humiliated I started to feel. That may have made her laugh harder. I started to understand how she made Millicent feel, and it made me angry.

"You bitch," I said.

She stopped laughing. Her eyes almost glowed with rage. "Get out."

"What if I don't? What if I stay here and make your life miserable?" My voice was much louder than it should have been.

"Get out."

"Stay away from my family."

Holly stared at me, still as a statue. She did not budge then, and she never did.

I turned around to leave, feeling a bit helpless. I could not reason with Holly, could not make her understand.

Robin was at the end of the aisle, watching everything.

She also worked at the store. She was wearing the same yellow shirt and green apron. I saw her, walked right past her, and I may have nodded at her. Or maybe I didn't. But she was there, she had seen me, and now she was standing at my door.

"I'm not wrong," she said. "You were the one I saw that day."

I did not pause. "I'm sorry—you've got the wrong person." I shut the door.

She knocked again.

I ignored it.

Robin's voice came through the door. "You know she's gone, right? Didn't even pick up her last check."

I opened the door. "Look, I'm really sorry about your friend, but I have no idea—"

"I got it, I got it. Wrong guy. Wasn't you. Now that I know who you are, I'll just let the police sort it all out."

She turned around and started to leave.

I did not let her.

No one knew Holly was missing. No one was looking for her, and I didn't want them to start. Millicent and I were not experts in forensics or DNA or anything of the sort. Anyone who looked too deep was bound to find all our mistakes.

I asked if Robin wanted to come inside and talk. She hesitated at first. She took out her phone and kept it in her hand as she walked into the house. We went to the kitchen. I offered her a drink; she said no. Instead, she grabbed an orange from the table and started peeling it. Without admitting a thing, without even introducing myself, I asked her what happened. She started to talk about the grocery store, about Holly, and about herself.

She gave me a history of how she came to work at the grocery store, when she met Holly, and how they had become friends. I got up from the table and went to the refrigerator to get a soda. While the door was open, I sent a quick text to Millicent. I used the same language she had used when Holly was in the house.

911 Get home NOW

It felt like hours passed before her car pulled up. By then, Robin was asking what we should do to resolve our current situation. She did not want justice for her dear old friend Holly. She wanted money, and lots of it.

"I figure this can be a win-win for both of us," she said. The front door opened, and Robin's head spun around. "Who's that?"

"My wife," I said.

Millicent appeared in the doorway, breathing hard, like she had been running. She was dressed for work in a skirt, blouse, and heels. Her jacket was open; she hadn't bothered to button it. She looked from me to Robin and back again.

"This is Robin," I said. "She used to work with a woman named Holly."

Millicent raised an eyebrow at Robin, who nodded.

"That's right. And I saw your husband talking to her. He called her a bitch."

The eyebrow turned to me.

I said nothing.

Millicent took off her jacket and slung it over a chair. "Robin," she said, walking into the kitchen, "why don't you tell me everything that happened?"

Robin smirked at me and started to talk, beginning with when I walked into the grocery store.

Behind me, Millicent was rummaging around in the kitchen. I could not see what she was doing. I heard her heels click against the floor as she came back to us. Robin gave her an odd look but kept talking.

I did not see the waffle iron in Millicent's hand until I heard the crack of Robin's skull. She hit the floor with a thud.

Millicent killed Robin the same way I had killed Holly. No hesitation. All instinct.

And it was sexy.

Nineteen

THE CALL COMES as I leave the club, on my way out to check on Annabelle. Millicent is on the phone, telling me our daughter is sick.

"I picked her up from school."

"Fever?" I ask.

"No. What's your schedule?"

"I can come home now."

All thoughts of Annabelle vanish. I turn the car around.

At home, Millicent is pacing around the foyer while talking on the phone. The TV is on in the family room, where Jenna is on the sectional couch, cocooned in blankets, her head resting on a stack of pillows. On the end table, a glass of ginger ale, a stack of plain crackers, and a big bowl just in case.

I sit down on the couch next to her. "Mom says you're sick."

She nods. Pouts. "Yeah."

"Not faking?"

"No." Jenna smiles a little.

I know she isn't faking it. Jenna hates being sick.

In kindergarten, she had pneumonia and missed a month of school. She wasn't sick enough to be in the hospital, but she was sick enough to remember it all. So does Millicent. Sometimes she acts like Jenna is five all over again. It's a bit much now that Jenna is thirteen, but I don't argue. I worry about Jenna, too.

"Watch with me." Jenna points to the TV.

I take off my shoes and put up my feet. We watch a game show, yelling out the answers before they are revealed.

Millicent's heels click across the floor. She walks over and stands in front of the TV.

Jenna hits the mute button.

"How are we? Are we good?" asks Millicent.

Jenna nods. "We're good."

Millicent turns to me. "How long can you stay?"

"All afternoon."

"I'll call you later."

Millicent walks over to Jenna and feels her forehead, first with her hand and then with her lips. "Still no fever. Call if you need anything."

Her heels click back down the hall. Jenna keeps the TV muted until after the front door closes. We go back to watching the game show. At the commercial break, Jenna mutes the TV again.

"Are you okay?" she says.

"Me? I'm not the one who's sick."

"That's not what I mean."

I know it's not. "I'm fine. Just busy."

"Too busy."

"Yeah. Too busy."

She doesn't ask again.

Millicent calls twice, first interrupting a talk show and then a teenage soap opera. Rory gets home around three, and, after some initial grumbling, he joins our TV marathon.

At five o'clock, I become a father again.

"Homework," I say.

"I'm sick," Jenna says.

"Rory, homework."

"You're just now remembering I go to school?"

"Homework," I say again. "You know the rules."

He rolls his eyes and heads upstairs.

I should have said something earlier. It wasn't because I forgot; it was because I couldn't remember the last time I spent time alone with my kids.

Millicent gets home forty-five minutes later. She is brisk with her hellos and then a flurry in the kitchen, getting dinner in the oven before she even changes her clothes. The energy in the house is different when she is here. Everything goes up a notch because expectations are higher.

Tonight, we all eat chicken noodle soup, and no one complains. It's what we do when someone is sick.

Other rules are relaxed as well. Since Jenna is set up on the couch, Millicent decides that's where everyone will eat. We all sit in front of the TV with our plates on tray tables. By then, Millicent has changed into sweats, and Rory claims he has finished his homework. We watch a new sitcom that's terrible, followed by a mediocre police show, and for a couple of hours everything feels normal.

After the kids go to bed, Millicent and I straighten up the family room. Although I have been lying around on a couch all day, I feel exhausted. I sit down at the kitchen table and rub my eyes.

"Did you miss a lot today?" Millicent asks.

She is talking about my real job, which I would have missed anyway, because I had planned on watching Annabelle.

I shrug.

She comes up behind me and starts to rub my shoulders. It feels good.

"I should be rubbing *your* shoulders," I say. "You're the one who worked all day."

"Taking care of a sick child is more stressful."

Millicent is right, though Jenna was more under the weather than sick. "She'll be fine," I say.

"Of course she will."

She keeps rubbing. After a minute, she says, "How is everything else?"

"Your surprise is almost ready."

"Good."

"It will be."

Millicent stops rubbing my shoulders. "That sounds like a promise."

"Maybe it is."

She takes me by the hand and leads me up to our bedroom.

AFTER ROBIN, WE didn't talk about her. And we didn't talk about Holly. Millicent and I went back to our lives, our work, our children. The idea of Lindsay—of a third—started a year and a half ago. I didn't know it at the time, could not imagine choosing, stalking, and killing a woman. It was just a little thing that happened at the mall.

I was there with Millicent, just us. We were buying Christmas presents for the kids. Money was more of a problem than usual. Millicent had been waiting for two houses to close, but both were on hold due to financing issues. A week before Christmas, and we had no presents, no cash, and not much left on the credit cards. We lowered our holiday budget three times. I wasn't happy about it. We didn't just have to buy presents for the kids; we also had to buy gifts for our friends, colleagues, and clients.

At the mall, Millicent kept saying no. Everything I picked up was too expensive.

"We're going to look cheap," I said.

"You're being dramatic."

"I grew up around these people."

Millicent rolled her eyes. "This again?"

"What does that mean?"

"Nothing. Never mind."

I put my hand on her arm. She was wearing a long-sleeved shirt but no jacket, because even in December our temperatures were around sixty. "No, what did you mean by that?"

"I mean you're always going on about 'these people.' Hidden Oaks people. You insult them but then brag about being one of them."

"I do not."

Millicent did not answer. She was looking at a shelf of candlesticks.

"I don't do that," I said.

"What do you think of these?" She held up a pair made of silver. Or something that looked like silver.

I turned up my nose.

She slammed the candlesticks back on the shelf.

I was already irritated. The fatigue hit next. Recently, all we talked about was money. I was tired of hearing we didn't have it, I couldn't buy it, I had to pick something cheaper. I couldn't even get my kids what they wanted for Christmas.

Millicent kept talking, going on and on about the budget and bank accounts. I tuned her out. I couldn't listen to it anymore, couldn't think about it—and I needed a distraction.

By chance, one walked right by. Her hair was the color of a roasted chestnut.

"Hello?" Millicent snapped her fingers in front of my face.

"I'm here."

"Are you sure? Because—"

"She looked kind of like Robin," I said. "Holly's friend."

Millicent turned around and watched the woman disappear into the crowd. When she turned back around, she had one eyebrow raised. "You think so?"

"Yes."

"How odd."

It was odd. So was the feeling I got when I replayed Robin's murder in my head. Every time I did, I thought about how fantastic that day was, how we came together and did what needed to be done to protect ourselves. To protect our family. It was amazing.

And so very sexy.

I started telling my wife just that.

Twenty

ANNABELLE'S WORK SCHEDULE never changes. Monday through Friday, from eight until five, she hands out parking tickets, calls for tow trucks, and gets yelled at for doing her job. People curse at her, make rude gestures, and call her names. Annabelle keeps her cool, but I wonder how she does it. Does she really not care, or does she get help from a substance or two? I wonder what the addiction rate is for meter maids.

Her evenings are not as easy. She is a single woman who likes to go out, but not too much, and as a meter maid, she doesn't make much money. On Wednesdays, she has dinner with her parents, but other than that, her nights have no set pattern. If I had to pick a night she goes out more often than the others, it's Friday.

Two weeks from now will be Friday the 13th. It doesn't get more ridiculously perfect than that. On Friday the 13th, Annabelle will disappear.

I am finally able to put together Owen's second letter to Josh. It is typed, like the first, only much longer.

Dear Josh,

I am not sure you believe it is me. Or maybe you do but the police don't. I am not a copycat or an imposter. It's me, the same Owen Oliver Riley who used to live at 4233 Cedar Crest Drive, in that little old house with the obnoxious carpet. I didn't put that in, by the way. That was my mother's bad choice.

I feel like what we have here is a lack of trust. Completely understandable, given that no one has seen me or spoken to me. Well, except Lindsay. She saw a lot of me. And we spoke many, many times during the year she was mine.

But now I'm alone and you don't believe me. So I'll make you a promise. Two weeks from now, another woman will disappear. I'll even tell you the exact date: Friday the 13th. Cheesy, right? Oh yes, it is. It's also easy to remember.

And Josh, you may not trust me now, but you'll learn that I always keep my word.

—Owen

Josh will have the letter by Tuesday. Once again, I spritz it with the musky cowboy cologne before mailing it. The letter will first be examined by the police, and who knows how many discussions must take place until they decide to go public with it. Or at least the part about Friday the 13th.

In the meantime, back to my real life. I've canceled too many lessons over the past few weeks. My work schedule is now packed all day, every day, in addition to all the little things that must get done. Picking up the kids, dropping them off, quick runs to the store for whatever we are missing. Burying myself in the minutiae makes my life feel normal. It almost makes that nervous twitch I always feel go away. And if Millicent didn't keep looking at me, asking so many questions with her eyes, it might have.

Her answers arrive on Thursday evening.

Millicent and I are at the country club, attending a retirement party for someone on the board. Soirees at the club are garish to the point of vulgar. The food is rich, the wine is heavy, and everyone congratulates everyone else on their success.

We go because we should; networking is part of both our jobs. We even have a system. After walking in together, we separate. I go left, she goes right, and we make our way around the room and meet again in the middle. We switch sides, separate again, and come together back at the entrance.

Millicent is wearing a bright yellow gown; with her red hair, she looks like a flame. From my side of the room, I catch glimpses of her as she moves within the crowd, that yellow dress never far from my eye. I see her laugh, smile, show concern or delight. When her lips move, I try to guess what she is saying. She carries a glass of champagne but never drinks it. No one has ever noticed.

Tonight, her eyes are the lightest I've seen in a long time, like a brand-new leaf under the sun. They shift up to mine. Millicent sees that I am staring at her.

She winks.

I exhale and move on with my own networking.

Andy and Trista are here, both with full glasses of wine. Andy pats his stomach and says he really needs to start working out or something, which he does. Trista doesn't say much, but she looks at me a little too long. She must remember our conversation about Owen, or at least parts of it.

Kekona is also at the party. She is with a young man, her latest escort, and she doesn't bother to introduce him. Instead, she talks about everyone else—who looks good and who doesn't, who has had work done and who needs it. As one of the wealthiest members of the club, Kekona can say anything she wants and people will still accept her.

Beth, a waitress at the club, passes by with a tray of drinks and offers me one. Her Alabama accent sticks out and makes her always sound perky.

I shake my head. "Not tonight."

"'Kay," she says.

I move on to a newer couple, the Rhineharts. Lizzie and Max just moved into Hidden Oaks. My wife sold them their house, and I met them once. Max is a golfer, but Lizzie says she used to play tennis. She thinks she should get back into it. Her husband tires of the topic and changes it to marketing, which is his business. Max thinks he can do great things for the Hidden Oaks Country Club, although he hasn't officially been hired by anyone.

I move on, telling Lizzie to call if she wants to play tennis again. She promises she will.

Millicent and I meet at the halfway mark. Her glass of champagne is still full. She pours half of it into a plant.

"You okay?" she says.

"I'm fine."

"Another round, then?"

"Let's do it."

We separate a second time, and I move through the other side of the room, greeting everyone I haven't seen yet. It feels like I am moving in circles, because I am.

The announcement comes before the eleven o'clock news. I don't know who saw it first or who mentioned it, but I do see people pulling out their phones. Too many of them, all at once.

A woman next to me whispers, "It's him."

And then I know.

Someone turns on the TV screens in the bar. We are surrounded by Josh, who is in the middle of his shining moment. He doesn't look quite as young tonight, and it might be the glasses. They're new.

"I received this letter earlier in the week. After discussing it with both the police and the owner of the station, we decided that in the interest of public safety, we had no choice but to put it on the air."

A shot of the letter appears on the screen. We all follow along, reading the typed words as Josh says them out loud. When he gets to the part about a woman disappearing on Friday the 13th, a collective gasp erupts from the party guests.

I look around and find the yellow dress.

Millicent is looking at me, a half smile on her lips and one eyebrow raised, as if she is asking me a question.

I wink.

"Brilliant," she says. "You are brilliant."

Millicent is lying on the bed, naked, the yellow gown thrown over a chair.

"You think everyone believes it now?" I know they do. I want her to say it.

"Of course they do. They all believe it."

I am standing at the foot of the bed, also naked, smiling, and feeling like I captured the flag.

Millicent stretches her arms up, grabbing on to the headboard.

I fall back onto the bed next to her. "They're all going to be looking for Owen."

"Yes."

"They won't see anything else."

Millicent touches me on the nose. "Because of you."

"Stop."

"It's true."

I shake my head. "We have to stop gloating."

"Tomorrow."

The next few days are as good as it ever was. The way Millicent smiles at me lifts my heart. I even stand up straighter.

She feels it, too. The day after the party, she sends me a text signed Penny. It is the only nickname I ever had for her. I haven't used it in years.

I first came up with it while we were on a date, before we were officially a couple but after we had slept together. Neither of us had much money, so many of our dates were simple. We took long walks, went to bargain matinees, and took advantage of happy hour buffets. Occasionally, we got more creative. On this particular night, we drove twenty miles to eat cheap pizza and play video games at an old-fashioned arcade. I beat her at the sports games, but she kicked my ass in anything involving guns.

Across the street from the arcade, there was a small park and a fountain. She took out a penny, made a wish, and tossed it in. We watched it sink to the bottom, settling on top of so many others. The water was so clear I could still see the words at the bottom of the coin.

One Cent.

"That's what I should call you," I said. "Penny."

"Penny?"

"Milli*cent*."

"Oh god."

"Plus you have red hair," I said.

"Penny? Are you serious?"

I smiled. "Penny."

She shook her head at me.

I was in love, fully and undoubtedly, but I hadn't said the words out loud. Instead, I called her Penny. Eventually, we said the real words and I stopped calling her Penny. Now, she has brought it back, and I don't want to let it go.

Twenty-one

MONDAY THE 9TH, Annabelle is at work. The day is beautiful—plenty of sunshine but not too hot. Almost brisk. Annabelle has parked her car at the end of the block and walks down the street, scanning license plates and checking meters. Her short hair sticks out from under the cap she wears to shade her eyes. She wears one earbud in her right ear, the white cord snaking down her chest, through her shirt, and into the right front pocket of her pants. Her blue uniform is decidedly unisex.

I watch from down the block, waiting. When she reaches the green car, she starts punching the buttons on her handheld scanner.

I sprint down the block, stopping a few feet away from her. I hold up my hands as if telling her to wait.

Annabelle looks at me like I'm crazy.

I pull out my phone, type, and hand it to her.

Sorry, didn't mean to startle you! My name is Tobias. I am deaf.

She reads it. Her shoulders relax, and she nods.

I point to the car and then to me.

She points to the expired meter.

I clasp my hands together below my chin, as if I'm begging. Or praying.

She laughs. Annabelle has a nice laugh.

I smile, showing her my dimples.

Annabelle wags her finger at me.

I hand her my phone.

Promise I'll never do it again . . .

She sighs.

I've won. The green car does not get a ticket.

It's not even my car.

I am not even sure why I spoke to Annabelle. This time, I didn't have to; I don't need to know more about her life or where she lives or who might be waiting for her. I already have the answers, but I did it anyway. All part of my process for choosing.

On Wednesday, I will see her again. She doesn't know it.

OWEN'S PICTURE IS everywhere. The computer experts have aged him up, theorizing about what he looks like now. They even consider how he might disguise himself. I am bombarded by these pictures; they are all over the news, in the paper, on the Internet. Flyers are taped to telephone poles. Owen with a beard, a mustache, dark hair, bald, fat, and thin. Owen with long hair and short, sunglasses and contacts, with sideburns and a goatee. Owen looked like everyman and no man.

I did this.

Well, Millicent did it. Or started it. But I did it, too.

I have not achieved much—certainly nothing out of the ordinary—but because of me, everyone is looking for Owen Oliver Riley.

I always wanted to be more than above average.

First, it was tennis. My father played, my mother pretended to, and at the age of seven I hit my first tennis ball. It was the first sport I was interested in, so they hired a coach, bought me my first racket, and sent me on my way. Within a few years, I was the best young player at the club. I still didn't get their attention, not the way I wanted, but that only made me better. I had no idea how much anger I had until I hit that little yellow ball.

I wasn't average then, wasn't a disappointment to anyone but my parents. I was better than everyone else, right up until I wasn't. Then I didn't know how to be average anymore, so I went overseas, away from my parents, in search of a place where I could be better than average, better than a disappointment. With Millicent, I am.

It's terrible to say, but my life has been so much better since my parents died.

And since Millicent came into my life. She makes me feel better than everyone. She is so impressed with my letter. In bed, she talks about it.

"I wish I could cut it out and paste it on the fridge."

I laugh and rub her leg. It is slung over mine in that lazy way. "The kids might think it's weird."

"They wouldn't even notice."

She is right. Our refrigerator is a mishmash of pictures, taped and mounted and pasted together into a family album of sorts. The details are so blurred nothing stands out. "You're right," I say. "They wouldn't."

Millicent rolls over and puts her face close to mine. She whispers, "I have a secret."

My heart jumps a little, and not in a good way. "What?" I say. Not a whisper.

"I watched her."

"Her?

"Annabelle." She mouths the name, not making a sound. My heart relaxes a little. We did this last time; we watched Lindsay and reported back.

"And?" I say.

"She's going to look perfect on TV."

The lights in our room are off, but it's not pitch-black. Our bedroom is on the second floor and faces the front. The light from a street lamp glows around the edges of the curtains. I have stared at it many times since we have moved into this house. The square of golden light seems so unnatural.

"Penny," I say.

She laughs. "What?"

"I love you."

"And I love you."

I close my eyes.

Sometimes, I say it first; other times, she does. I like that, because it feels even. But she said it first. Originally, I mean. She was the first to say she loved me.

It took three months. Three months from the time we met on the plane to the moment she said she loved me. I'd loved her for at least two and half months of the three I had known her, but I didn't say it. Not until she did. When it happened, we were literally up a tree. We were young, broke, and in search of something to do, so we climbed a tree.

As expected, Woodview does have trees. We have a park full of giant oak trees, perfect for climbing. But on that day, Millicent and I were up a maple tree. I should have known that when Millicent said she wanted to climb a tree, she would pick one that required trespassing.

The tree was on private property, in front of a house set a few hundred yards back. The only thing between the road and the front door was a flat green lawn and that giant maple tree.

It was the middle of August, the height of summer heat, and we stared at the tree from inside my air-conditioned car. We had parked down the block, a spot with a good view of everything, and we waited for all the lights in the house to go off. Just one was left, upstairs on the right. Millicent clutched my hand, as if she were on edge.

"You really want to climb that tree?" I said.

She turned to me, her eyes shining. "Don't you?"

"I never thought about it before."

"And now?"

"Now, I really want to climb that damn tree."

She smiled. I smiled. The light finally went out.

I turned the key, shutting down the air-conditioning. The inside of the car immediately felt hotter. Millicent got out first. She held the handle as she closed the door behind her, making as little noise as possible. I got out and did the same thing.

I stared down at the maple tree, which suddenly felt too open, too exposed, and I wondered if the punishment for trespassing included jail time.

Millicent took off running. She bolted across the street, over the lawn, and she disappeared behind the trunk of the tree. If she made a sound, I didn't hear it.

I ran the same path. My feet felt heavy, plodding, as if every step were booming through the neighborhood. I kept running until I got to Millicent. As I reached the tree, she pulled me against her and kissed me. Hard. I had to catch my breath when it was over.

"Ready to climb?" she said.

Before I could answer, she had hoisted herself up using a large burl. From there, she reached up to grab the lowest branch, and then climbed higher. I watched, waiting for a light in the house to turn on. Or waiting for her to fall so I could catch her. Neither happened.

"Come on," she whispered.

Millicent was sitting on a high branch and looking down at me. The moonlight turned her into an outline of herself. I could see her long hair swinging in the breeze, and her feet dangling on either side of the tree branch. Everything else looked like a shadow.

I climbed the tree, which was a lot harder than I expected, and again my grunts and pants sounded loud enough to wake anyone in a ten-mile radius. Still, the family in the house next to us continued to sleep. Their rooms stayed dark.

By the time I made it up to Millicent, I had broken out in a sweat. It was that hot. The air was thicker in the trees. It smelled of sweat and moss and bark.

Millicent grabbed my T-shirt, pulling me close to her, smothering my mouth with hers. I swear she tasted like maple syrup. She buried her face in my neck, as if she were trying to burrow into it, her breath hot against my skin.

"Hey," I said.

She lifted her head and looked at me. A damp strand of hair stuck to the side of her face.

"I love you," she said.

"I love you."

"Do you? Do you really?"

"Of course I do."

She put her hand against my cheek. "Promise."

"I promise."

Twenty-two

AUTOMATIC COFFEE MACHINES are one of the most convenient inventions ever. No baristas, no full-fat milk instead of 2 percent, no missing extra flavor shot. All I have to do is make my selections, choose the type of coffee, milk, flavor, and even the temperature, then hit the green GO button. Out comes my coffee. And it's cheap.

The downside is that these elaborate but simple machines are available only at gas station convenience stores. Real coffee shops don't have self-serve machines.

My favorite machine is at the EZ-Go store and gas station two miles from the Oaks. Even if I don't have the time, I go anyway. The cashier is a nice young woman named Jessica; she's the type who always smiles and has a nice word for everyone. Maybe she is part of why I drive the two miles to the EZ-Go. The point is, EZ-Go is part of my regular routine. And everyone has a routine.

Annabelle certainly does.

Every Wednesday night, she and her parents eat at the same Italian restaurant. My guess is that they order the same food, the same drinks, maybe even the same dessert. Dinner starts at six thirty and ends by eight. Annabelle walks, and it takes her eleven minutes to walk from the restaurant to her apartment, unless she stops at a store, gets a phone call, or runs into someone she knows. Like me.

While Annabelle is looking at her phone, I bump right into her.

She looks up at me in surprise. Then, recognition.

"Hi there," she says.

She is wearing more makeup than she does during the day. Her lipstick is darker, eyes outlined. Her short, cropped hair makes her face look even more attractive.

I take out my phone.

Well if it isn't the nicest meter maid in town ☺

She rolls her eyes. "How are you?"

I nod and point to her.

She gives me the thumbs-up.

What are you doing out alone? Don't you know there's a serial killer on the loose?

She smiles as she reads it. "I'm headed home right now."

Care for a drink first?

She hesitates.

I point to a bar down the street.

Annabelle looks at her watch. I am surprised when she says yes. She should say no, especially with the whole Owen Oliver thing, but Annabelle is even lonelier than I thought.

THE BARTENDER, ERIC, greets me with a wave. I have been here several times, always alone, always waiting for Annabelle to walk by on her way home from dinner with her parents. Eric knows me as Tobias.

I taught him all the sign language I know. He can spell out my name and my drink, gin and tonic.

Annabelle orders the same. "Heavy on the tonic," she says.

She does not trust me, and I do not blame her. I am just a guy who begged her not to give me a ticket. A probably very nice, nonthreatening deaf guy.

"So you know him?" Annabelle speaks to Eric while pointing at me.

"Sure, I know him. Tobias is a light drinker and a big tipper. He doesn't say much, though." He winks, letting her know he is kidding.

She laughs, and it is a nice sound. I start to picture being in bed with her. This makes me wonder how long it will take before she asks me to her place. I already know she will, and I know her place is not far. The power of knowing so much and choosing what will happen next—this is what I like.

"You're a tag team," she says, motioning to Eric and me. Annabelle is careful to face me when she speaks. She does not forget I am deaf.

After the first sip or two of our drinks, Eric fades to the other end of the bar. It is just Annabelle and me, and she tells me many of the things I know and some I don't. For example, I did not know that she had linguine with mushrooms tonight. But now I know this is what she eats on Wednesday nights.

I tell her my Tobias story. I am an accountant, divorced, no kids. I loved my wife very much, but we met in high school and married too soon. It happens.

Annabelle is a good listener and nods in all the right places.

What about you? Boyfriend?

She shakes her head. "I haven't had a boyfriend in a while."

I know it won't be long now. I expect that invite will come after drink number two and before number three.

Why don't you have a boyfriend?

The question is not just conversation. I am genuinely curious.

Annabelle shrugs. "I haven't met anyone?"

I shake my head.

Too generic.

It takes her a minute. I assume she is about to tell me her last boyfriend was an asshole. He cheated on her. He was always out with the guys. He was a selfish prick.

"My last boyfriend was killed," she says.

The shock almost makes me speak out loud.

That's horrible. How did it happen?

"Drunk driver."

I vaguely remember that Annabelle had posted something online about a fund-raiser against drunk driving. There was no indication it was personal.

I ask her more about him. His name was Ben, and Annabelle had met him through work. Ben had been a cop. He took night classes in criminal justice and wanted to work his way up to detective, then sergeant.

She no longer keeps his picture on her phone, because she didn't think it was healthy to stare at it.

This statement is so sad that I have to look away.

"Hey," says Annabelle. She taps me on the arm, telling me to look at her. "I'm sorry. This is all too serious."

No, it's okay. I asked.

"I'm tired of talking about me. What about you? Girlfriend?"

I shake my head no.

"Your turn. Why not?"

It's been hard to get back into dating. I was married for ten years.
And being deaf . . . it just makes things harder, I guess.

"Well, any woman that won't go out with you because you are deaf isn't worth it."

I smile. Her words are generic, but from her they sound genuine. It makes me wonder what she would say if I told her the truth.

Then I decide. I am not going to sleep with her.

Instead, I shift the conversation and we stop talking about ourselves. We talk about music, movies, current events. Nothing personal, just random talk that doesn't cause pain. When I stop flirting, so does she. The air between us changes.

Eric returns to our end of the bar and asks if we want another drink. Neither of us orders one.

She does not want me to walk her home. Understandable, but I insist that Eric call her a cab. She takes it, and I'm sure it's because of Owen Oliver. Before she leaves, I ask for her number. She gives it to me, and I give her the number to the disposable phone.

Annabelle thanks me for the drink with a handshake. It is both formal and endearing. I watch her walk out of the bar.

I will not text her. Of this I am sure.

I am also sure that Annabelle is not the one. She will not go missing on Friday night.

IT IS BECAUSE of her boyfriend. As soon as I heard the story, I knew it wouldn't be her.

Maybe because it would be too much tragedy for one young life. To lose a loved one in a violent crash only to be murdered.

None of this is fair. Our system of choosing her was developed, in part, by Owen, but how we did it was arbitrary. I just happened to see Annabelle that day. It could have been anyone.

Now, I am back at the Lancaster Hotel, watching Naomi. She is still a bit too tall for Owen's profile. I know her only through the computer and the glass doors of the Lancaster. I have never spoken to her, have never heard the sound of her voice.

I want to, though. I want to hear her laugh, to see how she acts after a drink or two. I want to know if she really has a thing for older men or if she just needs the money. I want to know if I like her, dislike her, or feel nothing for her. But I won't. I cannot take the chance that something will make me want to let her live.

So I do not go inside the hotel; I do not approach her. When her shift is over, I watch her leave. She has changed out of her uniform and into a pair of jeans and a T-shirt. She talks on the phone as she walks to her car, a tiny thing the color of a lime. At eleven fifteen on a Wednesday night, her only stop is at a fast-food drive-through. Minutes later, she is home, walking to her apartment, bag of food in one hand and uniform in the other. Naomi lives on the first floor of a quiet building that caters to people who don't make much money. The yard is overgrown, with thick bushes near her front door.

Perfect. We have lots of choices for Friday the 13th, from the hotel parking lot to Naomi's apartment building.

Now I just have to tell Millicent I've changed my mind.

Twenty-three

A T SIX IN the morning, the radio announcer's voice booms into my ear, and it's loud enough to make me jump. Millicent likes her clock radio. It is an old one, the kind with flip numbers and faux wood casing, and it annoys me to no end. The radio is her way of leaving the toilet seat up.

"Good morning. It's Thursday, October 12, and you've got one more day to lock up, ladies. Owen Oliver is coming to get one of you pretties—"

The radio goes silent. I open my eyes to see Millicent standing above me.

"Sorry," she says. "Forgot to turn it off."

She turns and walks back to the bathroom. Her red hair, cotton shorts, and tank top dissolve into a long dark ponytail and a blue uniform with gold trim.

I had been dreaming about Naomi when the alarm went off. She was behind the desk at the Lancaster, chatting with a man so old he wheezed when he spoke. Naomi threw her head back and laughed. It sounded like the cackle of a witch in a fairy tale. Then she turned to me and winked. The freckles across her nose started to bleed. I think I had been about to say something when the alarm went off.

Millicent lied; she did not forget to turn the alarm off. She is still a little upset with me. Not because we had to switch back to Naomi at the last minute, but because I made the decision without her.

Last night, we had another date night in the garage. She thought it was a last-minute planning session to run through everything before the big day. And originally it was, at least until I told her it couldn't be Annabelle.

"I don't understand," she said.

"I said we should switch back to Naomi."

"Naomi is too tall. She doesn't fit the profile."

"I know, but Annabelle is—"

"She's what?"

I made the decision to lie in a split second. "She started seeing someone."

"A boyfriend?"

"If he's not yet, he will be. He'll call the police right away." This is the type of scenario we prefer to avoid.

Millicent shook her head. She may have even cursed under her breath. "I can't believe we're just finding this out."

"We always watched her at work."

"Not always."

I let that go. This was not the time to question Millicent about what she hasn't told me. Not when I was lying.

"So," I said. "Naomi."

Millicent sighed. "Naomi."

We do not mention Annabelle again.

I DO NOT want to work, but I have no choice. My day is packed with back-to-back lessons, and when they are finally over I pick up the kids from school and take them to the dentist. By chance, their appointments have landed on Thursday the 12th. Millicent schedules their cleanings in advance, every six months on the dot.

As we walk into the office, Jenna and Rory play roshambo to see who goes first. It is one of the few times they speak in unison.

"Rock, paper, scissors, shoot."

Rory loses, Jenna gloats, and the bigger picture eludes them. Both still have to get their teeth cleaned.

In the waiting room, I check the news on my phone and am bombarded by pictures of Owen's previous victims. Our local paper put all of them on the front page, and all the pictures had been taken when they were smiling and alive. The message is not subtle. If you look like these women, tomorrow you will be at risk. Owen could be coming for you. There is no indication that anyone would be able to fight back or escape, and the only way to survive is to not get chosen. It is a little offensive, I think, that women are treated as if they are so helpless. The writer of this article has never met my wife.

After the dentist, ice cream. Millicent meets us for this bizarre family tradition. I was the one who started it, back when the kids were much younger and I wanted to make them stop crying at the dentist. The promise of ice cream worked, and now they won't let it go.

We all have our favorite. Millicent orders vanilla, I have chocolate, and Rory gets rocky road. Jenna is the experimental one. She always orders the special. Today, it is blueberry chocolate chip, and she loves it. I think it is disgusting.

Once everyone's teeth are tingling and our brains are frozen, we split up. Millicent takes the kids home, and I go back to work. On my way into the club, I run into Trista. She canceled our last lesson, and I've barely seen her since that drunken day she told me about her relationship with Owen Oliver. I am so grateful to her for that, but she doesn't know it. She doesn't know much of anything right now; she stares at me with the dead stare of a drunk, but it isn't because of alcohol. She is on pills—most likely painkillers, and a lot of them. I see it quite often at the country club.

But never from her.

"Hey." I reach out and touch her arm. "Are you okay?"

"Perfect." She says the word hard, like she's anything but.

"You don't look okay. Do you want me to call Andy?"

"No, I don't want you to call Andy."

I think I should, because I'd want to know if my wife was stoned up to her eyebrows. I reach for my phone.

Trista looks at me. "A woman is going to disappear tomorrow. And then she's going to die."

I want to tell her that maybe it won't happen, maybe they'll catch him, but I don't, because it's a lie. The police are not going to catch Millicent and me. They don't even know we exist.

"Yes," I say. "Someone is probably going to disappear."

"Owen's a bastard." Trista looks vacant but isn't. Beyond the pills is something that refuses to go numb. Something angry.

"Hey, stop that. You can't blame yourself for this asshole."

She snorts.

"You won't be alone tomorrow, will you?" I say this because I am genuinely worried about her. Everything Trista does hurts only herself.

"Andy will be home." She looks up at the TV, where they are showing footage from when Owen was arrested fifteen years ago. Trista shivers. "I have to go."

"Wait—let me give you a ride home."

"I'm not going home."

"Trista."

"I'll see you later. Tell Millicent I'll call her." She walks toward the women's locker room but then turns back. "Don't tell Andy, okay?"

I never told him about seeing Trista drunk, and didn't tell him about his wife's past with Owen Oliver. Another omission won't make the betrayal worse than it already is.

"I won't tell him," I say.

"Thank you."

She vanishes into the locker room, and I stare after her, wondering what we have done. Bringing back Owen has affected more than the police investigation.

My last client of the day also talks about it. He is a nice man with three daughters, and two are in Owen's target age group. All of them still live in the area. Two are single and live alone, and he is so worried he has offered to send them away for the weekend. He didn't live here when Owen was around the first time but has heard more than enough.

Despite the afternoon ice cream, dinner is still at six. Jenna says everyone at school has been talking about Owen all week. One of her friends has an older sister who is convinced that Owen is coming for her. Rory snickers at this and says it won't happen, that both are too ugly even for a serial killer. Jenna throws a dinner roll at her brother, and Millicent orders them to stop. They resort to calling each other names by mouthing them across the table.

"I said stop it."

Millicent does not like to repeat herself, so they stop. For a minute. Jenna flinches when Rory kicks her under the table. I am sure Millicent sees it, but she says nothing, because when dinner is over she announces an impromptu movie night. Sometimes when they fight too much, she makes them spend more time together. It is her way of making sure they work it out instead of going their separate ways.

They argue for twenty minutes about which movie to watch. Neither Millicent nor I interfere; in fact, we don't pay attention. We are in the kitchen, finishing up the dishes, when she asks if I am going back out tonight.

"Yes."

"Are you sure that's a good idea?"

"It's fine."

My tone is sharper than I mean it to be. Hearing about Owen all day not helped my stress level. Neither did seeing Trista. Something about her, about what she is doing to herself, bothers me.

Everything that happens tomorrow is because of me. I wrote the letter to Josh, I chose the date, I promised another woman would disappear. And I am the one who switched from Annabelle to Naomi just last night. I am the one who has to make sure she is right.

The flip of a quarter chooses our movie for the evening, and it is about a dolphin. Rory and Jenna sit together on the floor with a bowl of popcorn and do not throw it at each other. Millicent and I sit on the couch with our own popcorn. She spends more time looking at our kids than at the movie, and her eyes look ten shades lighter. They always do with the kids.

She stays like that until the movie is over and the kids trudge upstairs to bed, their banter light and filled with dolphins. I start to stand up when she puts her hand on my knee and squeezes it.

"You better get ready," she says.

She makes it sound like this is her idea, and it irritates me. "You're right," I say. "I need to get out of here."

"You okay?"

I look down at her, at my wife with the clear eyes that are so unlike Trista's. Everything about Millicent is the opposite of Andy's wife.

I smile, thankful I am not married to Trista.

Twenty-four

I HAD NOT INTENDED to wear my suit, because speaking to Naomi wasn't in the plan, but at the last minute I put on the one Millicent likes best. It is dark blue with a hand-stitched collar, and it cost too much. But since I have it, I might as well wear it.

As I stand in front of the mirror and put on my tie, Millicent appears behind me. She leans against the wall, arms crossed over her chest, and she watches me. I know she wants to ask, because I never wear this suit except with her. She bought it.

I continue with my tie, put on my shoes, collect my wallet, phone, and keys. My disposable phone is not in the house.

When I look up, she is still there, still in the same position.

"I guess I'm off," I say.

She nods.

I wait for her to say something, but she remains silent. I walk past her and down the stairs. As I reach the door to the garage, I hear him.

"Dad."

Rory is at the door to the kitchen with a glass of water. He holds up his other hand and rubs his thumb and forefinger together. More money.

He did not just happen to be in the kitchen. He was waiting for me.

I nod and walk out.

NAOMI IS AT the front desk, checking people in, answering the phone, troubleshooting for everyone who walks up with a problem. Tonight, I do not sit outside. I am in the lobby.

It is large and plush, with overstuffed furniture in dark colors and thick fabrics. Velvet curtains hang against the walls, trimmed in gold braid like the Lancaster uniforms. Fringe and tassels are everywhere.

I can hide in this lobby, hidden in the ornate decor, just another unknown guest working on my computer, having a drink, because I cannot sit in my hotel room for one more minute. This is almost the truth. I cannot sit in my car outside the hotel for one more minute. If Naomi is the one, I feel compelled to get a little bit closer.

But not to speak to her; I've decided not to do that. There is just no time. Not after the last-minute change. I am too stressed, too worried. Resurrecting Owen Oliver has become more complicated than I thought it would be. Maybe because of the media, maybe because of Trista, but it's also because my kids won't shut up about him.

This is so much different than Lindsay. It was just Millicent and me, no one else, not even on the periphery.

New Year's Eve, Millicent and I went to a party at the country club. Jenna was twelve, Rory a year older, and it was the first time we had left them alone on December 31. They had been ecstatic about it. So were we. Ringing in the New Year with adults hadn't happened since before the kids were born.

Less than a month earlier was when I saw that woman at the mall, the one who looked like Robin. Millicent and I had sex that night. Not the married, get-it-over-with kind of sex. It was the kind we had when we were first dating, when we couldn't get enough of each other. The great sex.

The next day, it was all over. The sex, the mood, the feeling. We went back to arguing about money—what we could and could not afford. That included the New Year's Eve gala.

It was a costume party. Millicent and I dressed up like we were from the 1920s, a gangster and his flapper girlfriend. My suit was pin-striped, and I wore shiny wingtips and a fedora. Millicent wore a shimmery violet dress with a feathered headband, and her lips were painted crimson.

I normally found costume parties depressing. They made me feel surrounded by people who dreamed of being anyone other than who they were.

That night, we were different. Not like the others, not like anyone else at that party. Millicent and I talked about doing it again. Killing a woman. We talked about what we would do to her. If we would do it. Why we would do it.

"What about her?" Millicent said, motioning to a woman whose breasts were so large they bordered on grotesque. They were fake, and we all knew it, because she had told everyone how much they had cost.

I shrugged. "We wouldn't be able to drown her."

"You're right about that."

"And her?" I said, nodding to a beachy blonde with a date as old as her grandpa.

Millicent smiled, her white teeth stark against her ruby lips. "Mercy killing. Judging by that tan, she'll get skin cancer anyway."

I stifled a laugh. Millicent giggled. We were being horrible, gossiping in the most twisted way, but it was all just talk. For most of the night, we spoke only to each other.

Given that it was our first big night out in a long time, I was prepared to stay out late, and even had an energy drink before leaving the house. But we didn't stay out late. By five minutes after midnight, we were on our way home.

By a quarter after, our 1920s costumes had been thrown off and discarded on our bedroom floor.

I had no idea if we were starting something or continuing it, but I didn't want it to end.

IN THE LOBBY of the Lancaster, I look at my watch, check my phone, and surf the Internet. It's all to pretend I'm not watching Naomi. She does not notice me. The night is much busier than normal, in part because the next day is Friday the 13th. People have come to town to see what Owen will do, who he will take and kill. Some of these people work for legitimate media sources; others are the kind who follow spectacles or events that can be recorded and loaded online.

A group of them sit near me in the lobby. They are college-aged kids who are looking to make money, and they speculate about how much money they can make. It's all based on how graphic their video is, although capturing the actual kidnapping of a woman would be the mother lode. Provided they hold the camera still.

When they finally leave, off to find likely places serial killers hang out, I can focus back on Naomi. I look for something to tell Millicent, something we can share. I want this to feel like it did before.

Naomi is smiling and has been all night. This is amazing, even admirable. Many of the people who approach the front desk are disgruntled or need something, yet she never fails to be kind. She smiles even when someone calls her an idiot.

I start to think she is some kind of Pollyanna, someone who is nice and happy no matter what. I don't like it. Millicent and I can't whisper in the dark about that.

Then I see it—the crack in Naomi's sugary-sweet persona. When one particularly rude guest turns his back, Naomi gives him the finger.

I smile.

Time to go home and tell Millicent.

Twenty-five

I WAKE UP TO silence. Dawn is an hour away, and the world is dark as velvet.

It is Saturday the 14th.

Millicent is not home yet.

Our decision to separate came late on Thursday night, after I returned home from the Lancaster. The plan was to keep Naomi alive for a while, just like Lindsay. It had to be done, because it's what Owen always did.

I just didn't like it. Didn't even want to see it.

Part of me knew I should, because it wasn't fair to make Millicent do it by herself. I tried to imagine what it would be like to lock Naomi up and keep her alive, feeding her, giving her water, and torturing her. It makes my stomach turn.

I don't think I can see that, up close and in person.

This keeps me from talking to Millicent about where she kept Lindsay and where she will keep Naomi. I've thought about asking her but never have. At times, I feel a little bad about it, but not bad enough. Most of the time, I'm just relieved.

"I can do it," Millicent said.

We were at home alone on Friday morning. The kids were already at school. We sat in the kitchen having another cup of coffee and discussing our plans.

"You shouldn't have to do it all yourself," I said.

"I did it before." Millicent stood up and carried her coffee mug over to the sink.

"Still," I said. My protests were weak, and I knew it. They made me feel better anyway.

"Still nothing," Millicent said. "I'll take care of it. You take care of that reporter."

"I will. Eventually, I'll have to contact him again."

"Exactly."

She turned to me and smiled, lit up by the morning sun coming through the window.

Our plan was set. It was the same plan we had used on Lindsay.

We had prepared every detail, the way Millicent always does. First, the drug. Lindsay, and now Naomi, had to be unconscious so we could take her to a deserted place. Turned out chloroform is not the miracle knockout drug the movies pretend it is. Our research led us to some dark and scary places on the Internet, where everything is available for a price. Electronic currency, an anonymous e-mail, and a private mailbox can get you anything, including a tranquilizer strong and quick enough to knock out a dinosaur.

Since we only had to knock out a 130-pound woman, we didn't need much.

Millicent bought a notebook computer that only we knew about. We used it for researching the drugs. Also to find Lindsay.

And Petra.

And Naomi.

On Friday night, we took Naomi together. Just as we had done with Lindsay.

In the parking lot behind the hotel, Millicent waved down Naomi as she was driving away. They were just beyond the security cameras.

I watched as Millicent bent down to the driver's-side window, talking fast as if she needed help because her car had broken down. Then I saw the telltale jerk of her arm when she injected Naomi with the drug. Millicent pushed Naomi's body to the side as she slipped into the driver's seat and drove away.

I followed, smiling. After so much searching and planning and talking, I loved watching it all play out.

WE SEPARATED IN the woods. I took Naomi's car and got rid of it while Millicent drove away in my car with our still-unconscious victim. By the time I made my way to Millicent's car, parked a block from the Lancaster, and then back home, it was after midnight. In Hidden Oaks, everyone's porch light was on, including ours.

The kids were not asleep. They were doing exactly what I would've done at their age: watching scary movies. Both were camped out in the living room with their phones and tablets and a pile of junk food. I joined them.

They thought I had been out patrolling the neighborhood, helping to protect Hidden Oaks from Owen Oliver. We have our own private security, but last night a group of residents decided to help be on the lookout. I just wasn't one of them.

The kids already knew Millicent wouldn't be home until morning. We told them she would be with a group of girlfriends who didn't want to be alone. Neither cared. I'm not sure Owen Oliver is real to them. He is the boogeyman on TV, the psycho in the movies. It doesn't occur to them that any woman—a teacher, a neighbor, or even their mother—could be at risk. My feelings about this are conflicted. I want my kids to feel safe. I also want them to know how dangerous the world is.

Still lying in bed, I start to wonder about where Millicent took Naomi, about what will happen to her. What may already be happening. To stop myself, I get up and turn on the TV. The sports channel. While listening to the baseball scores from yesterday, I make coffee.

The newspaper thumps against the front door, and I leave it there. Instead, I drink coffee and watch cartoons until the kids get up, then turn off the TV before they come downstairs. Rory is first to the kitchen. He grabs the remote and clicks on the news.

"So who got whacked?" He takes a bowl out of the cupboard and dumps cereal in it.

"Don't say whacked."

He rolls his eyes. "Okay, who got murdered?"

Jenna appears in the doorway. She looks back and forth between Rory and me. "Did it happen? Did Owen come back?"

Rory turns up the volume on the TV. The reporter they show is not Josh. It is a young blond woman who looks like Owen's type.

"Police tell us they won't know anything for a while. Given the concern about last night, they have received many calls about women who have not answered their phones or checked in with their families. We don't know if any of these women are actually missing, and it will likely be some time before the police have sorted everything out . . ."

"The police are idiots," Rory says. He turns to Jenna and pokes her arm. "Like you."

She rolls her eyes. "Whatever."

They stop talking about Owen. I do not hear his name again until we are in the car, on the way to Jenna's soccer game. During a break in the music, the radio announcer says the police have received more than a thousand calls from people claiming they saw Owen Oliver on Friday night.

Still no word from Millicent, though I lie to the kids and tell them she is having brunch with her friends. Neither seems to care.

At the game, I start checking my phone more often.

A few of the parents talk about the news, speculating about Owen and the Friday the 13th note and wondering if it was all a hoax. One of the fathers said it had to be, but the women were not so sure. When he laughed, a woman asked what was so funny about claiming someone would be killed on Friday the 13th.

I check my phone. Still nothing.

Jenna's team is up by one. I give her the thumbs-up. She smiles and rolls her eyes at the same time. It occurs to me that the thumbs-up sign is probably uncool.

Then I see her. She is behind Jenna, near the parking lot, and she is walking around the field. Her red hair is down, bouncing as she moves. She is wearing jeans, sneakers, and a T-shirt with a lion, the school mascot, on the front. She's always trying to look like all the other soccer moms, but she never succeeds. Millicent always stands out.

As she gets closer, she smiles. It is a big, wide smile that reaches to the depths of her eyes. Relief floods through my veins. Only then do I realize how nervous I have been. Silly. I know better than to doubt Millicent.

I reach out to her. She slides her arm around my waist and leans in to kiss me. Her lips are warm, and her breath smells like cinnamon and coffee.

"How's Jenna doing?" Millicent says, turning toward the field. I cannot stop looking at her.

"Winning by one."

"Perfect."

She slips away from me and says hello to some of the other parents. They chat about the game, about the beautiful weather, and, eventually, about Owen.

When the game is over, I have to go to work. It is Millicent's Saturday to take the kids out to lunch, and we have only a moment alone in the parking lot. The kids are in the car, buckled up and arguing. We stand together between our cars.

"Everything good?"

"Perfect," she says. "No problems at all."

We go our separate ways, and as I drive to the club, I feel more than happy. Buoyant, maybe. Like I'm floating.

AT THE CLUB, I have a rare Saturday lesson with Kekona, our Hidden Oaks gossip. I think she scheduled it because she wants to talk about

Owen, about what may have happened the night before, and our lesson confirms it. Owen is all she talks about.

"Fifty-three women. The news says fifty-three women were reported missing between last night and this morning." She shakes her head. Kekona's long dark hair is rolled up into a bun at the base of her neck.

"Owen did not kidnap fifty-three women last night," I say.

"No, he didn't. He may not have kidnapped anyone. But fifty-three families believe he did."

I nod, absorbing her words, wrapping my head around so much pain. I feel removed, as if it has nothing to do with me.

Twenty-six

WE WAIT FOR everyone else to figure out what happened. When the news is on, Millicent winks at me. When someone mentions Owen, I give her a look only she understands. It is our thing, the thing that separates us from everyone else.

I first felt it after Holly. Again after Robin, and then after Lindsay. After each woman, Millicent and I had a moment in which we were the only ones in the world. It felt the same as it did when we climbed that big tree. It feels that way now, after Naomi.

Millicent and I are wide-awake while everyone else is asleep.

BY MONDAY, THE police are down to two women. All the others have been found or have returned home. I hear this on the radio during the drive to work, and it surprises me. I had no idea it would take this long for everyone to realize who had gone missing. It almost makes me want to send another note to Josh, to let him know it was Naomi.

Almost. But the more time they spend trying to figure out who is missing means the less time they spend trying to find her. The police do not even know who to look for.

Halfway through the day, I get a call from the school principal. This is odd, because the school always calls Millicent first, but the principal says Millicent isn't answering her phone. She also tells me there has been an incident at the school and that I need to come down there right away. I ask if it's Rory.

"It's your daughter," she says. "We have an issue with Jenna."

When I arrive at the school, Jenna is sitting in the corner of the principal's office. Nell Granger has been at the school forever and has not changed a bit. She looks like a sweet old grandmother who would pinch your cheeks until they bruised.

Jenna is staring at the floor and does not look up.

Nell gestures for me to sit, and I do. Then I see the knife.

Six-inch blade, stainless steel. Carved wooden handle. It comes from our kitchen, and now it is on top of Nell's desk.

Nell taps her pink fingernail against the knife. "Your daughter brought this to school today."

"I don't understand," I say. And I am not sure I want to.

"A teacher saw it in her backpack when she was taking out a notebook."

Jenna sits against the wall, facing us, but her head is still down. She says nothing.

"Why would you bring this to school?" I ask.

She shakes her head. Says nothing.

Nell stands up and motions for me to follow. We walk out of the office, and she shuts the door behind us.

"Jenna hasn't said a word," Nell says. "I was hoping you, or your wife, could get her to tell us why she has the knife."

"I'd like to know myself."

"So this isn't something you've—"

"Jenna has never been violent," I say. "She doesn't play with knives."

"And yet . . ." Nell does not finish the sentence and does not have to.

I go back into the office alone. It does not look like Jenna has moved an inch. I move a chair closer to hers and sit down.

"Jenna," I say.

Nothing.

"Can you tell me about the knife?"

She shrugs. It's a start.

"Were you going to hurt someone?"

"No."

Her voice is strong, unwavering, and it startles me.

"Okay," I say. "If you didn't plan to hurt anyone, why would you bring a knife to school?"

She looks up. Her eyes do not look as strong as her voice. "To protect myself."

"Is someone bullying you?"

"No."

It is all I can do to stop myself from grabbing her by the shoulders and shaking the answers out of her. "Jenna, please tell me what happened. Did someone threaten you? Hurt you?"

"No. I just wanted . . ."

"Wanted what?"

"I didn't want him to hurt me."

"Who?"

She whispers his name. "Owen."

The punch to my gut is shocking. Painful. It never occurred to me that Jenna would be afraid of Owen.

I put my arms around her. "Owen is never going to hurt you. Not in a million years. A million trillion years."

She chuckles a little. "You're stupid."

"I know. But not about this. Not about Owen hurting you."

Jenna pulls back and looks at me, her eyes not quite as wide now. "That's why I brought the knife. I wasn't going to hurt anyone."

"I know."

She waits outside the door while I speak to Nell, who nods and half smiles as I explain Jenna's fear of Owen Oliver. I say he has been all over the news for a few weeks now; his face is all over the Internet, the TV, and even on flyers in front of the grocery store. "Something like this was probably inevitable," I say, pointing to the knife. "Now that I think about it, this doesn't surprise me at all. The media hasn't stopped talking about Owen since he came back."

Nell raises an eyebrow. "You think he's back?"

It feels like I am thirteen, covered in dirt and bruises, and a little blood at the corner of my mouth. My fight with Danny Turnbull had gone well, at least from my perspective, except I was sent to the principal's office. When I told my principal Danny had started the fight, she gave me the same look Nell Granger is giving me right now.

"I don't know if he's back," I say. "But obviously my daughter thinks he is."

"So she says."

"You have some reason to doubt her? Because I don't."

Nell shakes her head. "No, no reason. Jenna has always been a good kid." She doesn't say "so far," but she doesn't have to.

"Can I take her home now?"

"You can. But I have to keep the knife."

I do not argue.

Jenna has been excused for the rest of the day, so we have lunch. We go to a big chain restaurant that has a ten-page menu, with everything from a greasy breakfast to barbecued ribs and everything in between. We have been to this restaurant a hundred times, and Jenna always orders a grilled cheese-and-tomato sandwich or a club. Today, she orders a salad with dressing on the side, and no soda, just water.

When I ask if she is okay, Jenna says she is fine.

I want to talk to Millicent. I want to tell her about our daughter. But my wife is still not answering her phone.

She must be with Naomi. They are probably in some bunker or cement room, just like in the movies, and this is why she has not picked up the phone. It does not ring underground.

Or maybe she is just busy.

I send her a text, letting her know everything is fine, even though

I'm not sure it is. After sending it, I hear the familiar sound of a breaking-news alert.

On the other side of our booth, there is a bar area with multiple TVs, and Naomi stares back at me from all of them. She looks larger than life on the giant screens. The banner across the bottom reads:

LOCAL WOMAN STILL MISSING

"That's her, isn't it?" Jenna is also looking at the screens. "She's the one Owen took."

"They don't know for sure," I say.

"She's going to die, isn't she?"

I do not answer. Inside, I am smiling. At least half of me is.

The other half is worried about Jenna.

Twenty-seven

NAOMI. NAOMI WITH her hair down, with her hair up, with no makeup, and with her lips painted bubble gum pink. Naomi in her work uniform, in jeans, in a green satin bridesmaid dress. Naomi is everywhere, all over the TV and online and on everyone's lips. Within hours, her three friends have multiplied. Suddenly, everyone knows her, and they are more than happy to tell reporters all about their dear friend Naomi.

We are at home Monday night, and the TV is on. Millicent is here. She offers just a vague explanation of her afternoon absence. In return, I give her a vague explanation of what happened at Jenna's school. I make it sound much less alarming than it was.

"Basically, it was a big misunderstanding," I say.

Millicent shrugs. "You're sure?"

"I'm sure."

The news is on. Jenna is obsessed with it, but Rory is bored unless there is new information. He orders her to change the channel. She refuses.

I did not realize how Owen Oliver would affect our kids. Holly and Robin never had this kind of publicity. Now, they have been talking about Owen for weeks. Jenna may talk about Naomi forever.

This makes the good feelings I had start to fade.

I walk out to the backyard. In one corner, we have a large oak tree. The kids' old playset is in the other corner; it has been wasting away for years. I forgot it was even here, but now all I can see is how faded it is, how the plastic is cracked and it must be dangerous. I go back through the house, into the garage, and get my toolbox. It is important, even crucial, that I take the playset apart and get rid of it before someone gets hurt.

The bolts hold tight, even though they are big pieces of childproof plastic. I break one with the hammer.

"What are you doing?"

Millicent's voice does not startle me. In fact, I expect it. "What does it look like?"

"It looks like this could wait until tomorrow."

"But I want to do it now." I cannot hear her sighing, but I know she is. She stands behind me and watches me break another plastic bolt. "Are you going to watch me all night?" I say.

She goes back into the house. The sliding door slams shut.

Less than an hour later, I have worked up a sweat and made a pile of plastic. I leave the backyard looking worse than when I started.

No one is in the living room. I hear them upstairs; someone is in the bathroom, and someone else walks down the hall. I sit down in front of the TV. A sitcom is on, and the family is like mine, with two parents and two kids, but they are much funnier than we are. Their problems do not involve thirteen-year-old girls bringing knives to school or sons blackmailing their fathers.

During the commercial break, a preview of the news comes on, and I turn the channel to another show, and another, and I keep doing this until Millicent comes into the room and takes the remote away from me. She leans in close and hisses in my ear.

"Get your shit together. Now." She tosses the remote to the other side of the couch and walks out of the room.

* * *

IT MAY SEEM like I never stand up to Millicent, but that isn't true. It may not be often, but it's not unheard of. It happened once, at least, and I remember it well. It was important enough to stand up for.

Rory was six, Jenna was five, and Millicent and I were too busy to breathe. I had two jobs. In addition to giving private tennis lessons, I also worked at a health club. Millicent was trying to sell real estate. The kids were in two different schools—kindergarten and first grade—and one always had to be dropped off or picked up. We had two cars, but one always seemed to be broken. Still, we had food and a roof and all the necessities. Everything else was just a pain in the ass.

One day, a windfall. A weird thing I never saw coming. There had been a class-action lawsuit against a former employer of mine, from a job I had back in high school, and after ten-plus years it had finally settled. Maybe the class had been small, or maybe the lawyers were better than most, but my portion was $10,000. It was more than I'd ever had at one time.

Millicent and I sat at the kitchen table and stared at that check. The kids were in bed, the house was quiet, and for a while we dreamed of all the things we could do with it. A week in Hawaii or a month in the mountains. A trip to Europe. The engagement ring Millicent deserved. We had a glass of wine, and our dreams became more ridiculous. Custom-made clothes. A home theater system. Fancy chrome wheels for both of our old cars. Ten thousand dollars was not a vast fortune, but we pretended it was.

"Seriously, though," she said, finishing off the last of her wine. "The kids. College."

"Very prudent."

"We have to."

She was right. College was expensive, and it never hurt to save for it. Except it did hurt. It hurt us and our future, which could make everything better for all of us. "I have a better idea," I said.

"Better than our children's education?"

"Hear me out."

I suggested we use the money to invest in ourselves. In the years since we were first married and had our kids, our economic situation had not improved much. Neither had our careers. Millicent was stuck selling condos and lower-priced homes. The more experienced agents had all the higher-end listings and sales. My private lessons were held at the public tennis courts at the park, and the clients were not consistent. I proposed we do something about this.

At first, it sounded like one of our ridiculous dreams. The Christmas gala at the Hidden Oaks Country Club cost $2,500 a ticket. But the gala was not just another party; it was a ticket to people we would not meet anywhere else. A new generation lived in the Oaks. Most never knew my parents or me. These were the people who could afford private tennis lessons and expensive houses. *They* would pay for our children's education.

"Insane," Millicent said.

"You aren't listening."

"No." She brushed off my idea with a wave of her hand.

That made me dig in.

We fought for a week. She called me a child, and I told her she was shortsighted. She called me a social climber, and I told her she had no imagination. She stopped talking to me, and I slept on the couch. Still, I did not give up. She did.

Millicent claimed she was tired. I think she became curious. I think she wanted to see if I was right.

We spent half the money on tickets, and then bought a dress and shoes for her, a tuxedo and shoes for me, and a luxury rental car for the night. Millicent also got her hair, makeup, and nails done. By the time we paid the babysitter, not much of the money was left.

It was worth every penny. Six months after the gala, I was offered a job as the tennis pro at the club. Millicent met her first wealthy clients at that gala and started to move up in the real estate world. In one night, we had skipped a good five years of grinding our way up the ladder. It was like automatically leveling up in a video game.

We aren't wealthy, not like our clients, but that night moved us closer.

And to this day, Millicent knows that it is because of me. Because I decided what to do with that money. She is reminded of this every year when we go to the annual gala, although, to be honest, I am not sure she cares.

Twenty-eight

AT FIRST, IT was impressive that Rory had figured out a way to blackmail me. I can admit that. I was more annoyed with myself for getting caught than with him for catching me.

But now, he is starting to piss me off.

I am in his room. He is sitting at his desk. His computer is on, and Naomi is staring back at me. Forty-eight hours have passed since she was named as the only missing woman left. Her face is everywhere, all over the news and social media.

"Why are you looking at that?" I say, nodding to his computer.

"You're changing the subject."

He is right. I am avoiding the fact that he has just asked for hundreds of dollars to keep his mouth shut about my nonexistent affair. Or my one-night-stand, I should say, because I did sleep with Petra.

"How long are you going to keep this up?" I say.

"How long are you? I saw you sneak out just last week."

It's impossible to think of Rory as a child when he talks like this. Despite his floppy red hair and baggy clothes, he does not look like a fourteen-year-old. He looks like my equal.

"I'll make you a deal," I say. "I'll give you the money, and we both stop. You will never see me sneak out again."

"And if you do?"

"If I sneak out again, I'll give you double."

Rory's poker face falls apart when his eyebrows shoot up. He covers his surprise by rubbing his chin, pretending to think about my offer. "I'll be watching," he says.

"I know you will be."

He nods, thinks, and then says no to my offer. "I have another idea."

I am already shaking my head at him, pissed off. Before, I was on the verge, and now I am there. "I am not giving you any more—"

"I don't want money."

"Then what?"

"The next time you sneak out, I don't want money. I don't want anything," he says. "But I'm going to tell Jenna."

"You'd really tell your sister?"

He sighs. It is not one of those old-man sighs, filled with weariness and fatigue. This is a child's sigh, the kind that comes with a trembling lip. "Stop, Dad," he says. "Just stop cheating on Mom."

Now I am the one who is surprised. The full impact of what he has said spreads over me an inch at a time, until I have the whole picture.

He is a child. Adulthood is still years away, and he is not even close. Now, he looks younger than ever. He looks younger than he did the first time I lied to him, younger than the second and the third. He looks younger than he did the day I taught him how to hold a tennis racket and younger than the day he rejected it for golf. Rory looks younger than he did yesterday. He is still just a little boy.

This has never been about the money or the video games or even the blackmail.

This has all been about what he thinks I am doing. He thinks I am sneaking out to cheat on his mother. And he wants me to stop.

When I realize this, it feels like a shotgun blast to the stomach.

Or at least how I imagine that might feel. It is much stronger than a punch. I do not know what to say or how to say it.

I nod and offer my hand.

We shake on it.

I KEEP ALL of this from Millicent, just as I have all along. I don't even tell her that Rory has been reading about Naomi on the Internet. The kids see it all anyway. It's everywhere.

Josh is still covering the story and is on TV all day, for breaking news and on the evening reports. He is still very young and earnest, but now he looks tired and needs a haircut.

For the past two days, he has been traveling around with the police as they check rest stops. That was where Owen kept his victims, in an abandoned rest stop, where he had hollowed out the building and turned it into a bunker. The police have been searching all of them, along with any bunker type of building on the map. They have not found a thing.

Tonight, Josh is out on an empty road, behind him a fleet of police cars. He is bundled up in a jacket and a baseball cap, which makes him look even younger, and he says they are checking on another possible location. They have been searching farther and farther out, even way out east near Goethe State Park.

It is because Naomi is still alive.

Josh does not say that. The police do not say it, either. But everyone knows that if Owen is still alive, so is Naomi. He always keeps them alive, and he does awful things to them. Things they do not talk about on TV. Things I do not think about, because Millicent is doing them now.

Or I assume she is. I assume Naomi is still alive, though I have not asked and have no idea where Millicent would keep her. The police searches make me wonder.

The next morning, while I am backing out of the driveway, Millicent comes out of the house. She raises her hand, telling me to wait. I watch her walk from the door to my car. She is wearing a slim pair of slacks and a white blouse with tiny polka dots.

Millicent bends down at the window. Her face is so close to mine I can see the tiny lines in the corners of her eyes—not deep wrinkles but well on their way. When she places her hand on the edge of the door, I see scratches on her forearm. Like she has been playing with a cat.

She sees where I am looking and pulls down the sleeve. My eyes go up to hers. In the morning sun, they almost look like they used to.

"What?" I say.

She reaches into her pocket and pulls out a white envelope. "I thought this would be useful."

The envelope is sealed. "What's this?"

She winks. "For your next letter."

This tiny thing lifts my mood. I do not write letters, but Owen does.

"It will convince them," Millicent says.

"Whatever you say."

She puts her hand on my cheek and strokes it with her thumb. I think she is going to kiss me, but she doesn't, not out here in the driveway where any neighbor could see us. Instead, she walks back to the house as casually as she walked out, like she has just reminded me to pick up almond milk on the way home.

I slide my finger under the flap of the envelope and open the corner.

Inside, a lock of Naomi's hair.

Twenty-nine

DESPITE WHAT MILLICENT said, I go back and forth about the lock of Naomi's hair. I wonder if it will make things better or worse. Although Jenna is no longer carrying a knife, as far as I know, she also is not eating much. She picks at her food, swishing it around her plate. She does not say much at dinner. We have not heard any blow-by-blows of her soccer practices or school days.

I do not like this. I want my Jenna back, the one who smiles at me, the one who asks for something, so I can say yes. The only thing she asks for now is to be excused from the table.

If I send a letter to Josh, confirming that Naomi is Owen's victim, the search will only intensify. The police will go through every building within fifty miles to find her, and the media will cover every moment of it.

But perhaps it is worse to not send the letter. Perhaps it's worse to let everyone wonder if Owen has Naomi, maybe forever. Because then Jenna will learn that people can just disappear with no one ever finding them. It is the truth, but maybe she should not know that. Not yet, anyway.

Once again, Millicent is right. The lock of hair is useful.

I go through several drafts of the letter. The first is too elaborate; the second is still too long. The third is down to a paragraph. Then I realize Owen does not have to say anything.

The hair will say enough.

They will DNA-test it, and they will know it is Naomi's. All I have to do is wrap it up in a piece of paper and sign at the bottom.

—Owen

The final touch is the cheap cologne.

I dump the lock of hair onto my letter. Fifty strands, a hundred—I don't know how many, but they are a couple of inches long. At one end, the hair is frayed with slight differences in length. The other end was cut so straight I can almost hear the scissors snip.

I do not allow myself to think about it any further. I do not want to picture the look on Naomi's face when she sees the scissors, do not want to imagine the relief she feels when only her hair is cut.

Instead, I fold up the paper around the hair, put it into a new envelope, and use a sponge to seal the flap. I do not take my gloves off until the letter is in the mailbox.

As soon as I drop it in, I feel a surge of adrenaline.

WORK SHOULD BE an escape, but is not. Everyone is talking about Naomi, about Owen, about where she might be held and if she will ever be found. Kekona is in the clubhouse; she does not have a lesson but is there anyway, gossiping with a group of women who are all old enough to be Naomi's mother. The men sitting at the bar stare up at the screen, at the pretty missing woman they would have liked to meet. No one is saying anything about Naomi's activities at the Lancaster. She has become everyone's daughter, sister, the girl next door.

It is scary how fast this has happened.

The others were not like this—especially not Holly. No one ever looked for her, because she was never reported missing.

Millicent and I made that decision together. We never discussed it after Holly was gone; it never occurred to me. I was too busy thinking about not getting caught to wonder what came next. Days later, Millicent's mother called. Her Alzheimer's had not advanced to the point where she'd forgotten how many daughters she had. We never told her Holly had been released, but she knew anyway. She had called the hospital.

That evening, we had our first date night. We'd never had one before. We used to make fun of the term right up until it became useful.

When I told Millicent her mother had called, the expression on her face did not change. Dinner had just ended, the kids were watching TV, and we were still at the table. Veggie-burger patties piled with tomatoes and organic cheese, sweet-potato fries, and salad. I was still picking at the fries, dipping them in the spicy pseudomayonnaise.

"I thought this would happen," she said.

I glanced behind me, making sure the kids were not around. In those days, I jumped at my own shadow. I was not used to breaking the law, much less killing anyone, so every little sound meant we were getting caught. Each day, it felt like I had aged a year.

"We shouldn't talk about this here," I said.

"Of course. Later, when the kids are asleep."

Even that made me nervous. "We should go outside. Or in the garage. We can sit in the car or something."

"Perfect. It's a date."

Our first date night took place after eleven-year-old Rory and ten-year-old Jenna were asleep. Millicent left the door to the house cracked, just in case they needed us.

I assumed we would tell her mother we had not seen Holly. I was wrong.

"We can't tell her that she's missing," Millicent said. "They'll look for her."

"But she won't find—"

"No, she won't. But she won't stop looking until she can't remember to."

"So we lie to your mother? We tell her Holly is here and she's fine?"

She shook her head. Millicent was staring at the dashboard, lost in thought. Finally, she said, "There's no way around it."

I waited, afraid I would sound stupid again.

When Millicent said she wanted to pretend Holly was still alive, I remember thinking it would not work. After all we had done, and after all we had apparently gotten away with, this was the thing that would ruin us. We had not thought it through properly. We never even discussed it.

"It won't work," I said. "Eventually, she'll want to talk to her, see her. They'll come down or try to get hold of her . . ." I rambled on, listing all the reasons this could not work. We could not claim to be the only people who saw or spoke to Holly.

"I think Holly wants to get away," Millicent said. "Probably because of me, because I remind her of what she did and why she was put away."

I started to get it. "If it were me, and if I wanted a fresh start, I might even leave the country."

"I would definitely leave the country," she said.

"Would you send your mother an e-mail?"

"A letter. A long one, letting my mother know that I'm fine, that I just need some time to figure it all out."

She sent the letter almost a week after Holly died. Holly said she was going to Europe to heal, to find herself, to make her own way in the world, but she would check in regularly. Her mother responded, saying she understood. She even included a picture. It came from my phone, when I took a picture of Holly in front of the kids' school. The letter then came full circle when she showed it to Millicent during a visit.

When my mother-in-law passed away, she no longer remembered either of her daughters.

Thirty

I FIRST SEE THE report on my phone, while sitting in my car outside a coffee shop. I am in between home and work, on my way back to the club after dropping the kids off after school, and I stopped to get a cup of coffee. The breaking-news alert on my phone goes off.

OWEN MAKES CONTACT AGAIN

In the video, Josh talks about the latest note from Owen. For the first time in a while, he does not look tired. He is standing outside the police station. His cheeks are flushed pink, and his eyes are wide from excitement, not caffeine. After spending a week watching the police check empty rest stops and abandoned sheds, he looks like a new man.

A picture of the letter flashes on the screen. Owen's name is clearly visible.

"This note was not the only thing I received from the man who claims to be Owen Oliver Riley. Wrapped up inside this piece of paper was a lock of hair. We don't know who it belongs to. We don't even know if the hair be-

longs to a man or a woman. DNA testing is going on as we speak, but as soon as we know anything more, we will bring it to you first."

Josh brings in a young woman who says she is a friend of Naomi's, though again he points out that we do not know what happened to Naomi. The friend does not look familiar; I do not remember seeing her with Naomi in real life or online. This woman has a nasally voice that grates, and it feels like I am locked in my car with her. She claims that Naomi is "sweet but not cutesy, a great friend but also independent, smart but not a know-it-all," and I have no idea what any of that means.

She steps out of view. The camera pans over to Josh and then widens. A man is standing next to him. He is a big man, with a mustache that makes him look like a walrus. Josh says he is an assistant manager at the Lancaster Hotel and he worked with Naomi. Josh does not ask him to describe Naomi in one word, but he does.

"If I had to describe Naomi in one word, it would be 'kind.' She was kind to everyone, all the guests and all of her coworkers. Always willing to help. If a guest needed something up in his room and room service was busy, she volunteered. If someone was sick, she would cover for them. Never asked for anything. Not from me, anyway. Can't speak for everyone."

A knock on my car window makes me jump.

Trista.

I see her, and the reflection of her, on the glass. The last time I saw her, she was drugged into a near coma. As promised, I never told Andy.

Trista is smiling, motioning for me to roll down my window. When I do, she leans in to kiss me on the cheek. Her apricot-colored lipstick feels sticky.

"Well, hey there," I say.

She laughs. It makes her look younger, and so does the daisy-print visor on her head. "Sorry. I'm in a good mood."

"I can see that." I get out of the car and face her. Trista's eyes are clear, her pupils not too big or too small. Her skin is a faint shade of pink, like she spent yesterday on the beach. "You look great."

"I am great."

Relief hits, making me realize how stressed I've been about her. "I'm so happy to hear that. I've been worried about you."

"I left Andy," she says.

"Left him where?" I look behind her, thinking he is in the coffee shop. Really.

"No, I mean we aren't together anymore."

I cannot hide my shock. Andy and Trista married not long after Millicent and I did. We attended their wedding. Neither has ever hinted at trouble, not to me and not to Millicent. She would have said something.

"He didn't tell you?" Trista says.

"No."

"Well, I did it. I left him."

I want to tell her I'm sorry her marriage has broken up, because I am. Because they are my friends. But she looks so happy I don't say a word.

Trista rolls her eyes. "It's okay. You don't have to say anything. But you know what? I never really loved him. Not the way you love Millicent." She smiles, not embarrassed at all. "It's true. I married Andy because he ticked all the boxes. That sounds horrible, doesn't it? Go ahead, you can say it. I'm horrible."

"I never said you were horrible."

"But you're thinking it. You have to—you're Andy's friend."

"I'm your friend, too."

She shrugs. "The lessons have to stop. I am sorry about that, but I can't come to the club with Andy there."

"I get it."

"You really helped me, you know," she says. "That day we talked helped sort everything out."

The talk helped me as well. Because of Trista, I knew things about Owen I would not have otherwise known and was able to write a convincing letter to Josh. But this is not what she means.

"I didn't do anything," I say. Maybe to convince myself I did not break up my friend's marriage.

"If you hadn't listened like that, I would never have gone on and on about Owen. No one wants to hear all that. They just want him to be a monster."

"Isn't he?"

She thinks about this while sucking on her straw. "Yes. And no. Remember I told you that sex with Owen was good? Not great but good?"

I nod.

"Lie. It was great. It was fantastic, actually. Owen was, he was . . ." Her voice drifts off. She stares out over the parking lot outside the coffee shop, lost in a memory I cannot see. It feels awkward to just stare at her, but it would be even more awkward to speak, so I don't.

"I loved him," she says.

"Owen?"

She nods and then shakes her head. "That sounds terrible. I don't mean I'm going to run off and be with him or anything. Not that I would know where to find him. Oh god, that didn't come out right." She throws up her hands, giving up on the explanation. "I'm sorry. This is weird."

"No, it's . . ." I cannot think of another word.

"Weird."

I shrug. "Okay, it's weird." And horrible.

"Loving a monster isn't bad?"

"You didn't know when you fell in love with him, did you?"

"No."

"And you didn't fall in love with him *because* he was a monster, did you?"

Now she shrugs. Smiles. "How would I know?"

I have no answer.

Thirty-one

A CHURCH CALLED THE Fellowship of Hope has become a gathering place for anyone who wants to talk about Naomi, pray for her, or light a candle. It began with her friends and coworkers, perhaps started by that walrus-looking guy or the nasally girl, and now it has expanded to the wider community.

I have not been inside the church, but I have stopped by on my way home from work and watched the people go in and out. Some stay awhile; others, just a few minutes. I recognize a few of them from the club, and I bet none of them had met Naomi. These are not the people who hang out with hotel desk clerks.

Word gets back to Millicent, perhaps through one of her clients, and she decides our family should go to the church on Friday.

That evening, we are all in a rush. I get home late from a lesson and jump in the shower. Rory went to a friend's house after school, but he forgot the time, and Millicent drives over to pick him up. Jenna is getting ready in her room. We have no time for dinner at home, so we'll go out after our visit to the church. Millicent starts a group text about which restaurant we will go to. Rory wants Italian, Millicent wants Mexican, and I do not care.

When the car pulls into the garage, I call up to Jenna.

"Let's hit it," I say. Jenna always tells me I sound like such a dad when I say that.

Now, she says nothing.

"Jenna?"

When she doesn't answer the second time, I go upstairs and knock on her door. She keeps a small whiteboard on the door. It is decorated with rainbow-colored ribbons, and the words *No, Rory* are written in her bubbly handwriting.

Downstairs, the door to the garage opens and Millicent calls out. "Ready?"

"Almost," I say and knock on the door again.

Jenna does not answer.

"What's going on?" Millicent says.

The door is unlocked. I open it a few inches. "Jenna? Are you okay?"

"Yeah." A tiny sound. It comes from the bathroom.

In our home, no one has just a bedroom. We have suites, with a bathroom attached. Four bedrooms, four and half baths—this is how all homes are built in Hidden Oaks.

"Come on!" Rory yells.

Millicent is walking up the stairs.

I cross Jenna's bedroom, through the childhood toys and the clothes, shoes, and makeup of a blossoming teenager. The door to the bathroom is open. Just as I look inside, Millicent appears in the hallway outside Jenna's room.

"What is going on?" she says.

Jenna stands on the white tile floor with her feet surrounded by locks of dark hair. She looks at me, and her eyes seem larger than ever. Jenna has cut off all her hair. Shorn down to the scalp, no more than an inch long.

Behind me, Millicent gasps. She rushes past me, to Jenna, and holds her head with both hands. "What have you done?" she says.

Jenna stares back, unblinking.

I say nothing, though I know the answer. I know what Jenna has done. The realization makes me freeze; my body roots itself right into the persimmon-colored rug on Jenna's floor.

"What the . . ." Rory is in the room now, staring at his sister, at the hair on the bathroom floor.

Jenna turns to me and says, "Now he won't take me, will he?"

"Jesus," Rory says.

Not Jesus.

Owen.

WE DO NOT go to church. We do not go out at all.

"A doctor," Millicent says. "Our daughter needs a doctor."

"I know a doctor," I say. "He is a client."

"Call him. No, wait. Maybe we shouldn't use one of your clients? Maybe we don't want them to know?"

"Know what?"

"That our daughter needs help."

We stare at each other, having no idea what to do. Surreal does not cover it.

This is a new problem for us. An answer for everything can be found in child-rearing books. Millicent has them all. Physically sick, go to doctor. Not feeling well, go to bed. Faking it, go to school. Problem with another child, call their parents. Throwing a tantrum, give them a time-out.

Not this problem, though. The books do not say what to do when your child is afraid of a serial killer. Especially not one like this.

We are in our bedroom, our voices low. Jenna is downstairs on the couch, watching TV with a baseball cap on her head. Rory is with her. We have told him not to let his sister out of his sight. We also told him not to make fun. For once, he does as we say.

Millicent decides to call our family doctor. Dr. Barrow is not a client. He is just a family practitioner we have been seeing for years.

He treats our sore throats and tummy aches, checks for broken bones and concussions, but I do not think he can be helpful in this situation. He is a much older man who may or may not believe mental health is a real thing.

"It's late," I say to Millicent. "He won't answer."

"The service will call him. There's always a way to get hold of a doctor."

"Maybe we should—"

"I'm going to call," she says. "We have to do something."

"Yes. I suppose we do."

Millicent gives me a look as she picks up the phone. It is rare when I cannot decipher what her look means, but this is one of those times. If I had to guess, I would say it looks a bit like panic.

I go downstairs to check on Jenna. Both she and Rory are on the couch. They are watching TV while eating sandwiches with potato chips stuffed between the bread. Jenna looks up at me. I smile at her, trying to convey that everything is fine, that she is fine, that the world is fine and no one will hurt her. She looks away and takes another bite of her sandwich.

I have failed to convey anything.

Back upstairs, Millicent is on the phone. Her voice is too calm, too even, as she explains to an answering service that, yes, this is an emergency and, yes, she does need to speak with Dr. Barrow tonight. She hangs up, waits five minutes, and tries again.

Dr. Barrow finally calls back. Millicent sounds rushed as she explains what has happened, what our daughter has done. She cannot get the words out fast enough.

This is a crisis for her, for us, for our family. My part is in between.

Jenna, the one in crisis.

Millicent, the one doing something about it.

Rory, the one staying out of the way. Out of the line of fire.

Me, the one running up and down the stairs, checking on everyone and deciding on nothing. I am in the middle again.

Thirty-two

DR. BARROW RECOMMENDS a child psychologist, who agrees to meet us on Saturday for twice his usual fee. Everything in his office is beige, from carpet to ceiling, and it feels like we are in a bowl of oatmeal.

The psychologist specializes in this kind of thing, because it is a real thing, and he says Jenna does not feel safe. He suspects she has some kind of media-induced anxiety disorder, although the real name is irrelevant. So are the reasons she is acting out, which do not matter, because they do not make sense. Reason has no place here.

"You can explain that Jenna is safe until she repeats it in her sleep, but it won't make a difference."

Millicent sits in front of the doctor, as close as possible. She spent the night in Jenna's room, barely slept, and she looks like hell. I look about the same. Jenna slept fine last night. Cutting off her hair seemed to bring her peace. When I try to tell the doctor this, he holds up his hand.

"False."

"False," I say. I try to mimic his tone, but the arrogance is too much.

"The peace is likely temporary, until some other piece of news sets her off again," he says. He has spent the last hour with Jenna, part of the emergency Saturday morning session arranged by Dr. Barrow. We are the second part.

"What do we do?" Millicent says.

He has some ideas for how to make Jenna feel safe. First, twice-weekly appointments in his office. They are $200 apiece, no insurance accepted, cash or debit card only. Second, do everything you say you will do. Never let Jenna down. Never let her think you will not be there for her.

"But we don't," I say. "We always—"

"Always?" he says.

"At least ninety percent of the time," Millicent says. "Maybe ninety-five."

"Make it a hundred."

Millicent nods, as if she can wave a magic wand and this will happen.

"Last but certainly not least," he says. "Get her away from the media—from this serial killer, from all the stories about his victim. I realize I'm asking the impossible, especially in this day and age, but try to do it as much as possible. Don't watch the news at home. Don't discuss Owen or anything about him. Try to act as if he has nothing to do with your family."

"He doesn't," I say.

"Of course not."

We write the doctor a big check and leave. Jenna is in the waiting room. The TV on the wall is showing cartoons. She is staring at her phone.

Millicent frowns.

I smile and try my best. "Who wants breakfast?"

THE WEEKEND IS a flurry of meetings: with the whole family, with Jenna alone, with Rory alone, with both the kids, and with just Millicent. So many meetings with Millicent. By Sunday evening, we have a new set of rules, and they revolve around eliminating the news from our lives. All news programs are banned, as are newspapers. We will stream movies and avoid live TV as much as possible. No live radio. All of these are easy compared to the Internet. The kids use it for school, for fun, for communication.

Millicent tries anyway, beginning with the password. No one will be able to connect unless she does it herself.

Mutiny.

"Then I can't live here." Rory goes for broke with his opening statement.

Jenna nods, agreeing with her brother. A rare moment of solidarity.

I agree with the kids. Millicent has proposed something that is impractical, unworkable. Absurd.

But I say nothing.

Rory looks from me to his mother, sensing weakness. He lists all the reasons the password idea will not work, beginning with Millicent's long hours.

Jenna finally pipes up. "I'll fail English."

That does it.

English has been difficult for her this year. She has worked twice as hard at it to stay on the honor roll, and the idea of Jenna falling off it changes Millicent's mind. She downgrades to a lesser set of rules.

Parental controls, laptops moved to the family room, all news apps removed from phones. Psychological rather than practical, but we all get the point. I have no idea if Jenna will follow the new rules.

A hairdresser tries to shape what's left of Jenna's hair. Now that it's even, it does not look bad—just different. Millicent buys all sorts of hats and caps in case she wants to cover up. She lays them all out on the dining room table, and Jenna walks the length of it, trying on each one. At the end, she shrugs.

"They're nice," she says.

"Do you have a favorite?" Millicent asks.

Jenna shrugs again. "I'm not sure I need a hat."

Millicent's shoulders slump a little. She is more concerned about Jenna's hair than Jenna is. "Okay," she says, gathering up the hats. "I'll just leave them in your room."

Before bedtime, I go see Rory. He is on his bed reading a comic book. He slides it under a pillow, and I pretend not to see it.

"What?" he says. Irritation everywhere.

I sit down at his desk. Books, notebooks, empty chargers. A full bag of chips, and a drawing of something that looks half monster and half hero. "It's not fair," I say. "None of this is your fault, but you have to live with it anyway."

"Take one for the team. Got it."

"What do you think?" I say.

"About what?"

"Your sister."

He starts to say something. I can tell by those green eyes that he is going to be a smart-ass.

But he stops. Pauses. "I don't know," he says. "She's been a little obsessed with this thing."

"Owen."

"Yeah. Like, more obsessed than usual. You know how she gets."

He is referring to Jenna's ability to laser-focus on a topic, whether it be soccer or ribbons or ponies. Rory calls it obsession because he doesn't have it.

"How's she been at school?" I say.

"Fine, as far as I can tell. Still popular."

"Can you let me know if anything changes?"

He thinks, perhaps about asking for something in return. "Yeah," he says.

"And don't be too much of an asshole to her."

"But that's my job. I'm her brother." Rory is smiling.

"I know. Just don't be so good at it."

* * *

MILLICENT AND I are finally alone late Sunday night. I am exhausted. Worried. I dread the next story about Owen or Naomi or Lindsay.

Naomi. For the first time in two days, it occurs to me that Millicent has not left our side. She has been with Jenna, me, us, since Friday night. It makes me wonder where Naomi is, if she is still alive. She must have water. She would not survive without that.

I never wanted to think about where Naomi was, how she was restrained, what her surroundings were like. I forced myself not to think about it. Still, the images come. The ones I have heard about, the underground bunker or basement, the soundproof room in an otherwise normal home. Restraints—I think about these as well. Chains and cuffs, made of steel so they cannot be broken.

But it may not be like that. Maybe she is just locked in a room and free to roam around. It could be like a regular room with a bed, a dresser, a bathroom, maybe a refrigerator. Comfortable and clean. Not a chamber of horrors or torture or any of those things. Maybe she even has a TV.

Or not.

I turn to Millicent, who is sitting up in bed, on her tablet, researching children who are afraid of what they hear on TV.

Again, I think about asking her about Naomi. I want to know where and how Millicent is keeping her, but I am afraid of what I might do with that information.

I don't think I could control myself.

If I know where she is, I will go to see her. I will have to. What if it's the worst-case scenario? What if she is chained to a radiator in a basement somewhere, covered in dirt and bleeding from torture? Because if that's what I see, I'm not sure what I would do.

If I would kill her. If I would let her go.

So I do not ask.

Thirty-three

Bringing Owen back has served its purpose. No one doubts he is the one who kidnapped and killed Lindsay, the one who now has Naomi. Now it's time for him to fade away. The only way is to stop the news: No more letters, no more locks of hair. No more missing women. No more bodies.

We need an exit strategy. Jenna needs it.

At the club, they are still talking about Owen. I refuse. I get out of the clubhouse, away from the gossip, even away from Kekona. We still have two lessons a week, but she is at the club every day. I spend the whole day on the court, either with a client or waiting for the next one. After the past few weeks, and the past weekend, the day is almost too normal. Something has to break it up.

I have a lesson with a couple who has lived in Hidden Oaks since its inception. They are slow to move, but the fact that they can move at all is saying something.

When we are done, the three of us walk up to the pro shop together. I want to get a coffee and get a look at my schedule for the week. The shortest route to the pro shop is through the clubhouse, which is where I see Andy.

I have not seen him since before Trista left him. Back then, he looked like always: paunch around the middle, thinning hair, ruddy complexion from all that wine.

Now, he looks all wrong. He is leaning up against the bar, wearing sweatpants that look a hundred years old. His cotton Hidden Oaks shirt is brand-new, still creased in the folds, as if he just bought it from the pro shop and put it on. He is clean-shaven, but his hair looks unkempt. The drink in his hand is brown and pure—no mixer, no ice.

I walk up to him because he's my friend. Or he was until I started hiding things from him.

"Hey," I say.

He turns to me but doesn't look happy. "Well, if it isn't the pro. The tennis pro, I mean. Unless you're some other kind of pro."

"What's up?"

"Oh, I think you know what's up."

I shake my head. Shrug. Act like I have no idea what's going on. "You okay?"

"No, not really. But maybe you should ask my wife about that. You know her pretty well, right?"

Before he has a chance to say anything else, I take him by the arm. "Let's go get some air," I say. Thankfully, he does not protest. He does not say anything that could get me in trouble at work.

We walk through the clubhouse and out the front door. We stand in an arched walkway. Ivy crawls up and around and down the other side. In one direction, the pro shop. The parking lot is in the other.

I stop and face Andy. "Look, I don't know—"

"Are you sleeping with my wife?"

"Jesus. No."

He stares at me, unsure.

"Andy, I'd never sleep with your wife. Never."

His shoulders slump a little as the anger leaves him. He believes me. "But she's in love with someone else."

"It's not me." I have no intention of telling him who it is.

"But you see her all the time. Twice a week, right? She does take tennis lessons from you?"

"For a few years now. You know that. But she never mentioned having an affair."

Andy narrows his eyes at me. "Is that the truth?"

"How long have we known each other?"

"Since we were kids."

"And you think I'd be more loyal to Trista than to you?"

Andy throws up his hands. "I don't know. She was really upset about those missing girls. She won't watch the news anymore." He looks down and scuffs his foot against the faux cobblestone. "You swear you don't know anything?"

"I swear."

"All right. Sorry," he says.

"It's okay. You want to grab some lunch or something?" I do not mention getting a drink.

"Not right now. I'm going to go home."

"You sure?"

He nods and walks away. Andy does not go back into the club-house; he goes toward the parking lot. I start to tell him he cannot drive, but I don't. The valets will stop him. Liability and whatnot.

MY LESSONS CONTINUE. There is no news. No calls, no further disruptions. Not until I leave work and stop at the car wash on the way home.

I normally check my phone—the disposable—at least every other day, but I broke my own rule. Too much going on, too many other things to deal with.

The phone is hidden inside the spare tire in my trunk. At the car wash, I take everything out of the back so it can be vacuumed, grabbing the phone along with everything else. As the car goes through the wash, I turn on the phone. The new-message beep startles me. Both the sound and the phone are old-fashioned. It's not even a smartphone, just a prepaid phone that is heavier than it looks.

I bought it at a discount store years ago. It took me a while to decide. Not on the phone itself—back then all the prepaids looked the same. It took me a while to decide to get one in the first place. A nice saleswoman came along and asked if she could help. She looked too old to know a lot about electronics, but it turned out she knew everything. And she was so patient, so kind, and I asked one question after another. The answers did not matter. I did not care about the technical details. I was trying to decide if I wanted a second phone, the disposable kind, and I think I ended up with one because at some point it would have been rude not to buy something. I had taken up too much of her time.

I have had this thing ever since. Annabelle is just the latest entry.

I have not thought about her since deciding she would not be the one. There has been no reason to think about Annabelle, not until she called. Or texted, I mean. It does not do any good to call a deaf man.

Hey stranger, let's have a drink again soon. Oh, and it's Annabelle ☺

I have no idea when she sent the message. It does not arrive on my phone until I turn it on, but she could have sent it a week ago. At least a week has passed since I checked it.

I consider answering the text, at least to say I was not ignoring her on purpose.

My car is still being washed, so I scroll backward on the phone. Before the text from Annabelle, there is the one text from Lindsay. The one I ignored. It is now fifteen months old.

Had a great time the other day, Tobias. See you soon!

Tobias. He was never supposed to have a personality of his own. And he wasn't supposed to sleep with anyone.

Millicent and I came up with him together. It was on a rare cold night in Florida, where the temperatures dipped below forty degrees. Between hot cocoa and a pint of ice cream, Tobias was born.

"You can't really change how you look," she told me. "I mean, not without some kind of wig or paste-on beard."

"I'm not wearing a wig."

"So then you need something else."

I was the one who suggested pretending I was deaf. Just a few days before, I had taught a teenage kid who was deaf and we used cell phones to communicate. It stuck with me, so I suggested it.

"Brilliant," Millicent said. She kissed me just the way I like it.

Next, we discussed my name. It had to be memorable but not weird, traditional but not common. It came down to two: Tobias and Quentin. I wanted the latter because of the nickname. Quint was better than Toby.

We debated the pros and cons of both names. Millicent even pulled up the origins of them.

"Tobias comes from the Hebrew name Tobiah," she said, reading from the Internet. "Quentin comes from the Roman name Quintus."

I shrugged. Neither origin meant anything to me.

Millicent continued. "Quentin is from the Roman word for 'fifth.' Tobias is a biblical name."

"What did he do in the Bible?"

"Hang on." Millicent clicked and scrolled and said, "He slayed a demon to save Sarah and then he married her."

"I want to be Tobias," I said.

"Are you sure?"

"Who doesn't want to be the hero?"

That night, Tobias was born.

Not many people have met him—just a few bartenders and a few women. Not even Millicent has met him. Tobias is almost like my alter ego. He even has his own secrets.

I do not answer Annabelle's text asking me out for a drink. I shut off the phone and put it back in my trunk.

Thirty-four

CHRISTMAS, SIX YEARS ago. Rory was eight, Jenna was seven, and both had started asking why they had only one set of grandparents. I had never talked about my parents, never said anything about who they were or how they died. Their questions made me think about what I could say. What I should say.

One night, I went down to the kitchen, hoping that if I filled up my stomach it would make me sleepy enough to get past the insomnia. I ate leftover black bean casserole right out of the pan. Cold, but not half-bad. I was still eating when Millicent came into the kitchen. She grabbed a fork and sat down with me.

"What's going on?" she said. Millicent took a big bite of the casserole and stared at me, waiting. I never got up in the middle of the night to eat. She knew that.

"The kids are asking about my parents."

Millicent raised her eyebrows, said nothing.

"If I lie and tell them their grandparents were wonderful, they'll hate me if they find out the truth, right?"

"Probably."

"But they might hate me anyway."

"For a while," she said. "I think all kids go through a stage where everything will be our fault."

"How long does it last?"

She shrugged. "Twenty years?"

"I hope things are pretty quiet during that time."

I smiled. She smiled.

I could tell them my parents abused me. Mentally. Physically. Even sexually. I could say they beat me, tied me up, burned me with cigarette butts, and made me walk to school and back uphill both ways. They did not. I grew up in a nice home in a nice area, and no one touched me the wrong way. My parents were refined, polite people who could recite manners in their sleep.

They were also horrible, cold people who should not have become parents. They should have been smart enough to know a baby couldn't fix anything.

The final straw came when I went overseas. When I told them I wanted to take a break from college and travel, they gave me some money. I bought an open-ended ticket and a large backpack, and drank a few dozen shots. Andy and two other friends decided to join me, so we made a haphazard plan and set a date. I did not tell them, or tell anyone, that I was afraid.

A few hours before the flight, I was still packing, still trying to decide which T-shirts to bring or if I needed a heavy jacket. Excited, yes. I was dying to get out of Hidden Oaks. Dying to get away from my childhood bedroom, where the walls were painted to look like I was in the sky, surrounded by stars. I was tired of dreaming about what else was out there, and wanted to see it for myself.

I also had no idea what would happen. I had already failed at tennis, then again at getting into a good college. Middle-of-the-road tennis player, middle-of-the-road grades. What would happen if I was middle-of-the-road while on the road? No idea. But it had to be better than feeling like I should never have been born.

I'd hoped I would never return and never see those sky-painted walls again.

My parents did not drive me to the airport. A cab picked me up, because I was too embarrassed to ask for a ride from my friends and their parents. It was a Wednesday morning, my flight was early, and dawn had just started to break. My mother with her coffee cup, my father already dressed—all of us stood in the foyer, on the shiny tile, surrounded by mirrors. The vase on the center table was filled with orange chrysanthemums. The rising sun hit the crystal chandelier above us, making a rainbow on the stairway.

The cab honked. My mother kissed me on the cheek. My father shook my hand.

"Dad, I want—"

"Good luck," he said.

I could not remember what I was going to say, so I left. It was the last time I saw them.

IN THE END, I didn't lie to the kids. I said their grandparents died in a freak car accident and had been gone for many years.

I did not tell them everything, but it was close. That was because of Millicent. Together, we decided how much to say. To make it as official as possible, we called a family meeting. Rory and Jenna were so young. Maybe it wasn't fair, but we did it anyway.

We sat in the living room. Jenna was already in her yellow pajamas with the balloons all over them. She loved balloons, and Rory loved to pop them. Jenna's dark hair was cut to the chin, and she had bangs straight across her forehead. Her dark eyes peeked out from under them.

Rory was wearing a blue T-shirt and sweatpants. When he'd turned seven, he had declared himself too old for pajamas. Millicent and I decided we could live with that, and she stopped buying them.

It was hard to look at their tiny, trusting faces and tell them that sometimes people are better off not having kids.

"Not everyone should be a parent," I said. "Just like not everyone is nice."

Jenna was the first to speak. "I already know about strangers."

"Not everyone in your family is nice. Or was nice."

Scrunched-up faces. Confusion.

I spoke for ten minutes. That was all it took to tell my children their grandparents were not good parents.

The irony of what I had done hit me years later, after Holly and the others. Someday, Rory and Jenna might have a talk with their kids and say the same thing about Millicent and me.

Thirty-five

I HAD ASSUMED THE DNA testing on the lock of Naomi's hair would take longer than a week. Perhaps because it was always so fast on TV, I figured that their timing must be fake. That real DNA testing must take months. And apparently it does, but not for the preliminary tests. And not when the police are trying to find a woman who may still be alive.

The tests indicate there is more than a 99 percent chance the hair belongs to Naomi.

Kekona is the one who tells me all of this. Our regular tennis lesson becomes a class in forensics, because her new hobby is true-crime TV and documentaries. Missing and/or dead women are common on these shows.

"Always young, beautiful, and basically innocent," she says, ticking off the qualities one by one. She has a cup of coffee with her, and I do not think it is her first. "Although occasionally they have a case about a prostitute, as a cautionary tale."

"Then what?" I ask.

"What do you mean?"

"I mean, after this young, beautiful, and basically innocent woman goes missing, what happens?"

Kekona holds up both her hands, as if she is trying to quiet a loud audience. "Option one—the boyfriend, because he's jealous and possessive. Or the ex-boyfriend, because he's jealous and possessive."

"Was that all one option?"

"Yes. Pay attention. Option two is the stranger, or most likely a stranger. This is the psycho/stalker/sociopath/mentally ill/serial killer option. At least one of them, maybe more."

Kekona is not telling me anything new. I watch TV, too. But not the past day or so, because the news is still banned in our house. I missed Josh's report about the DNA results, and I make a mental note to look it up online.

"Possible outcomes?" Kekona says this as if I'd asked about them. I had not. "Death. Rape and death. Torture and rape and death."

Not much to say to that.

"Occasionally, one lives," she says.

"But not often."

Kekona shakes her head. "Not even in fiction."

We go back to playing tennis. Eventually, I have another question for her. "Why do you think it's so popular? The missing-woman story?"

"Because who can resist a damsel in distress?"

THE NEWS BAN in our house has always been a little fake, because all of us have the Internet on our phones. Everyone knows the DNA results. After dinner, Millicent brings me into the garage. An impromptu date night.

She wants to discuss the results with Jenna. It's been less than a week since the hair incident, but Jenna has seemed fine since then. Even happy. Millicent is worried about a relapse. Into what, I am not sure. I am starting to think Jenna is being proactive, not paranoid. Because who wants to be abducted by a psycho/stalker/sociopath/serial killer? Not my daughter.

As we sit in the car, Millicent describes her plan for how we should approach the topic. We do not want to upset her, but we do not want to ignore the news. We do not want to talk down to Jenna, but we cannot be her friend. We want to discuss but not lecture, to comfort but not baby. Millicent keeps using the word *we*, as if this plan is ours, not hers.

"How is she?" I say.

"Right now, she seems fine. But last week she seemed fine, and then—"

"I'm not talking about Jenna."

She tilts her head, confused. Annoyed. Then, clarity.

"We're talking about Naomi," she says.

"Is she still alive?"

"Yes."

I want to take that question back. I want to say something that makes Millicent laugh, that makes my adrenaline surge, that makes us both feel good.

My mind is blank.

We stare at each other, her eyes so dark they look like holes. I stare until I have to either stop or ask where Naomi is.

I look away.

Millicent exhales.

I follow her back into the house. In the family room, we sit down on the couch, where Jenna and Rory are watching TV. Rory is the first to notice that we are looking at them, not the TV. He does not stick around for the talk.

It goes well, I think. Jenna listens and nods and smiles. When Millicent asks if she has any questions, Jenna shakes her head. When I ask how she feels, she says fine.

"Are you scared?" Millicent says.

Jenna reaches up and touches her short hair. "No."

"Owen won't hurt you."

"I *know*."

The irritated tone is reassuring. She sounds normal and looks normal, except for her hair.

LATER, MILLICENT AND I are in our room. She is organizing, walking back and forth between the bedroom and the closet, putting some things away and taking out others. She fixes everything before bed so the mornings are easier. Frantic is not her thing. Nor is being late.

I watch. Her red hair is loose, messy, and she keeps brushing it back with one hand. She wears thermals, the nubby old-fashioned kind, and striped socks. Her nighttime clothes are the least-fashionable thing about her, and I have told her how dorky they are. But I do not say that tonight. Instead, I go down the hall and check on Jenna.

She is asleep, nestled between the orange sheets under the white comforter. Her face is relaxed, peaceful. Not afraid.

Back in our room, Millicent has just gotten into bed, and I get in beside her. She looks at me, and I think she is going to mention our earlier talk in the garage. Instead, she turns out the light, like it meant nothing.

I wait until her breathing slows, then get up and check on Jenna again.

The second time I get up, I do not bother going back to bed. Throughout the night, I check on her three more times. During the hours in between, I watch TV. Around two in the morning, I doze off while watching an old movie. When I wake up, I see Owen's face. A documentary about him is on TV.

Several of these shows have been made with varying levels of detail about Owen's crimes. I have managed to avoid them, just as I avoided reading about what Owen did to his victims. This time, I cannot, because I wake up at exactly the wrong time. Just as I see Owen's face on the screen, the show cuts away. The next thing I see is the room where he kept each one of his victims.

The video had been made for Owen's trial, which never happened.

It is fifteen years old and filmed with a handheld camera that shakes too much. Owen had gutted an abandoned rest stop, knocking down the wall between the men's and women's restrooms. The tiled floors might have been white but now were a greyish brown. One toilet remained, along with a sink, a mattress, and a table. Pipes ran up and down the cutout walls; they started deep in the ground and ran across the ceiling, down the other side, and back into the cement floor. They were the perfect size for handcuffs. A pair is still attached to one of the pipes.

The video jerks and zooms in on the floor. The blood was not visible in the wider angle. Now, I see a smattering of blood here, a few drops there. The red spots are everywhere, as if someone had flung a brush of red paint at the floor. The camera moves across the floor, into a corner. A larger amount of blood is smeared on the wall. It is down low, inches from the ground, as if whoever was bleeding had been crouched down.

The angle moves again, toward the mattress. I imagine Naomi lying on it.

I change the channel.

Thirty-six

Two days pass before I hear about Trista. Millicent is the one who tells me.

It is Saturday evening. Rory is upstairs, and Jenna is staying over at a friend's house. As soon as they are out of sight, I flop down on the couch and put my feet on the table. This is not allowed—not for me or the kids—but when Millicent sits down next to me, she does not mention it.

This makes me remove my feet without being asked. It is that weird. "What's wrong?" I say.

She puts her hand on mine, and now I'm worried. Panicked, even. "Millicent, just—"

"It's Trista," she says.

"Trista?"

"Her sister called me earlier. Andy is too upset to talk to anyone."

"Her sister? Why would her—"

"She committed suicide."

I shake my head as if my ears aren't working. As if she didn't just say Trista killed herself.

"I'm so sorry," Millicent says.

I realize this is real, and it knocks the wind out of me. "I don't understand."

"From what she said, neither does anyone else. Especially Andy."

"How?" I say.

"She hung herself on the shower rod."

"Oh god."

"I knew they were having problems, but I had no idea she was so upset."

Millicent has no idea what the real reason is, because I never told her about Trista, never mentioned she had dated Owen. And was still in love with him.

My dinner feels like it is burning a hole in my stomach. I run to the bathroom and throw it all up. Millicent is at the door, asking if I am okay. I say yes even as the dry heaving starts.

Too much food, I tell her.

She reaches down and checks my forehead; it is not warm. I sit down on the floor against the wall and wave my hand, letting her know I am fine.

She walks away. I close my eyes, listening to her in the kitchen, rummaging through the refrigerator. Hunting for whatever made me sick.

I want to tell her it is us. We have a daughter who brought a knife to school and has cut off all her hair. Now a woman is dead. Not Naomi, a different woman.

Because of Owen. Because of me. I wrote those letters to Josh.

Millicent runs back into the bathroom with a bottle of the pink medicine.

I chug it down and get sick all over again.

THE FUNERAL SERVICE is held at Alton's Funeral Parlor, the same place Lindsay's was held. I did not attend hers but read about it. Lindsay had a closed casket, because of what Millicent had done to her. Trista has an open casket.

Andy is still her husband, and he arranged everything. The room is large, and every chair is filled. I think Trista would have been pleased to know her funeral is standing room only. Everyone is here, dressed in their finest black clothing, either to pay their respects or to gawk. I am here because I am responsible.

Millicent is with me, though she still has no idea why Trista killed herself. Neither does anyone else. For days, people at the club have talked about the breakup of her marriage, depression, money problems. At any given moment, she could be a drug addict, an alcoholic, a nymphomaniac. She was pregnant, or had been, but lost the baby. Maybe she was dying anyway, a terminal disease or a brain tumor.

No one seemed to remember, or even know, she had dated Owen Oliver Riley some twenty years ago.

Her sister is at the service. She is a heavier, brunette version of Trista. She says Trista used to take care of her while their parents worked; she fixed dinner and did their laundry.

"We grew up on the other side of town. She didn't always live in Hidden Oaks."

It sounds like an insult. Trista's younger sister still lives on the other side of town.

She does not mention Andy.

Next is one of Trista's more recent friends. She is as thin and blond as Trista was, and she tells a long story about how Trista was always willing to listen, help, and pitch in whenever she could.

The last one to speak is Andy. He has cut his hair since the last time I saw him, and he is wearing a dark suit instead of sweatpants. He talks about how he met Trista. She was an unpaid intern at a museum, still looking for a job that used her art history degree. He was there attending a benefit, and their paths crossed in front of a sculpture. She told him all about it.

"I was enchanted. By her, by the way she spoke and what she said, and even the tone of her voice. I can't think of a better word. Trista was simply enchanting."

Andy breaks down as he says this. First tears, then sobs.

No one moves.

I look away. This makes me feel sick all over again.

Andy's brother walks up to him and whispers in his ear. Andy takes a deep breath and collects himself. He keeps talking. I do not listen. I am thinking about that word.

Enchanting.

When he is done, we have a chance to walk by the coffin, to say our final goodbyes to Trista. Just about everyone does. Only a few hang back. Millicent and I do not.

The coffin is made of wood so dark it is almost black, and the interior is pale peach. It is not as bad as it sounds. The color complements Trista's blond hair and that apricot lipstick. She looked good in that color, and I am glad someone knew to put it on her.

But her outfit is the opposite. It is a solid dark blue with long sleeves. A single strand of pearls hangs from her neck, and she has pearl studs in her ears. None of this looks like Trista. It looks like someone bought the outfit yesterday, because they thought she should be buried in something dignified instead of something she would have liked.

It upsets me, unnaturally so. I do not like to think of Trista spending eternity in an outfit she hates. I hope she is not looking down on this funeral.

"She looks beautiful," Millicent says.

If I could say something to Trista, I would tell her I am sorry. Sorry for the clothes, for asking her about Owen, for bringing Owen back.

I would also tell her that Andy is right. She was enchanting. I know this because I understand exactly what Andy meant.

Millicent is enchanting. This is exactly as I would describe her. She was enchanting when I met her, and she is enchanting now. And if she died and I had to speak at her funeral service, I would be just like Andy. If I had to describe how enchanting she was, at the same time knowing I would never be with her again, I would shake my fist at the sky. Or at whoever had ruined everything.

In Andy's case, it would be me. His friend.

Thirty-seven

THE MAN ON TV is overweight and unhealthy-looking, half-dead in his fifties. He has a soft, round gut, the beginning of jowls, and sprigs of grey hair around his head. I know the type. My clients are like him, or used to be.

Josh is interviewing him in front of the Lancaster Hotel. This man is the first to say, or even insinuate, that Naomi was anything other than the girl next door everyone says she was.

"I'm not saying she did something wrong," he says. "I just think if we're going to find her, we have to be honest about who she was."

He was a frequent guest at the Lancaster and came to town twice a month for work. He had spoken to Naomi several times, as well as to some of the other regulars. "Let's just say she didn't always keep things businesslike with some of the guests."

"Can you elaborate on that?" Josh says.

"I don't think I really need to do that. People are smart enough to figure it out on their own."

This is the first time anyone mentions Naomi's extracurricular activities. It is not the last.

Other coworkers come forward, claiming to know the truth about Naomi. She slept with a number of men. Some were guests at the hotel. No one mentioned money, just sex. She was not a prostitute. Naomi was a twenty-seven-year-old woman who'd had sex with more than one hotel guest.

The first of her lovers to come forward does not reveal his identity. On TV, he appears as a silhouette, and his voice is garbled.

"Were you ever a guest at the Lancaster Hotel?"

"Yes, I was."

"And did you know a front desk clerk named Naomi?"

"I did."

"And did you have sex with her?"

"I am ashamed to say that I did."

He goes on to say that Naomi was the aggressor. She is the one who came after him.

Another man comes forward. And another. More shadows, more garbles. All remain anonymous. None of the men who slept with Naomi will reveal themselves. It is not because they are married, because at least two are identified as single or divorced. They just do not want to admit that they were one of her men.

Or her conquests. Someone on TV calls them that.

At the club, the talk starts to change. People stop saying it is a travesty and a shame. Some even stop saying Owen is a monster. Instead, people start asking how Naomi could have prevented it. How she could have avoided being a victim.

Kekona is one of them. The stories about Naomi confirm her belief that trouble comes to people who look for it. And in her mind, sex counts as trouble.

On TV, they will not stop talking about Naomi's personal life. Josh is front and center on the story; everyone who comes forward goes to him first. The more I watch, the more mesmerized I become. Naomi is one person and then another in the blink of an eye.

The first time I have a chance to discuss it with Millicent is after we attend Jenna's latest appointment with her psychologist. We take her back to school, where she joins her friends to decorate the gym for an upcoming fund-raiser. Millicent then takes me back to the club, where my car is parked. She turns on the radio and the news blasts out of it. The announcer says that yet another man, who remains unnamed like the others, has claimed he slept with Naomi while staying at the Lancaster. That makes seven.

"Fantastic," Millicent says.

"Fantastic?"

"As long as they're talking about her, or Owen, we don't have anything to worry about."

I want to bring up Jenna and how this might be affecting her. While I would like nothing more than for my daughter to be a virgin for the rest of her life, even I can admit that is not healthy.

Millicent reaches over and squeezes my hand. "You were right to switch. Annabelle wouldn't have been the same."

This is true. It also makes me squeeze her hand back.

I GO UP to Jenna's room to say good night. She is lying on her bed, reading an actual book, because her laptop is downstairs. Her hair is a tiny bit longer now, and it is starting to look quite stylish, I think. She looks at me over the top of the book, asking without asking what I want.

I sit down on the edge of her bed.

"You want to talk, don't you?" she says.

"You're getting too smart for me."

Jenna narrows her eyes. "Why are you flattering me?"

"See? Too smart."

She sets down her book with a sigh. It makes me feel stupid, which is pretty common when I am around my children.

"How are you?" I say.

"Fine."

"Seriously. Talk to me."

She shrugs. "I'm okay."

"Do you like the doctor?"

"I guess."

"You're not still scared of Owen, are you?"

Another shrug.

For the past few weeks, our conversations have been like this. They used to be different. Jenna used to tell me about all her friends and teachers—what this one did or what that one said. She would babble on forever if I let her.

I even knew about her first crush. He sat in front of her in English, which was part of why English had become her most difficult subject.

Now, she will not say anything, and it's because of the psychologist. I think she is tired of talking.

I lean down and kiss her on the forehead. As I do, something flickers in the corner of my eye. Between the bed and the nightstand, underneath the mattress, something is sticking out. I recognize it from our kitchen.

My daughter has taken another kitchen knife and hidden it under her mattress.

I do not say anything.

Instead, I say good night and leave, closing the door without a sound. As I walk down the hall, I pass by Rory's room and hear him on the phone. I am about to go in and tell him to go to sleep, but then I hear him talking about Naomi.

It's impossible to keep the news blocked out of the house.

Thirty-eight

I HAVE KEPT A few things from Millicent. Like the broken-down truck from so many years ago. And Trista. I did not tell her Trista had dated Owen Oliver Riley. Never mentioned that was why she left Andy, why she committed suicide.

Petra. It would be silly now to mention Petra, the woman who suspected I was not deaf. No reason to bring her up.

And Rory. I have not mentioned Rory's blackmail, because that would lead back to Petra.

Then there is Crystal.

Millicent never wanted any help at the house; she did not trust that anyone would clean the way she wanted, nor did she want anyone raising her kids. The only time we did hire someone, it was to carpool the kids to and from school and to their various activities. That was a few years ago, when Millicent and I were both so busy at work we just could not get to everything without some help.

This was also right after Holly was killed. Before the rest.

Crystal was the one we hired to help drive the kids around. She was a nice young woman who was always on time and good with the kids. She worked for us until Millicent decided we didn't need her anymore.

But before that, she kissed me.

It was when Millicent was in Miami for a conference with a co-worker named Cooper. I never liked him.

For the three days Millicent was gone, Crystal was around more than usual. She picked the kids up from school and made dinner for them at the house. One afternoon, we found ourselves alone, and that's when it happened.

At lunchtime, I went home to eat, and she was there, alone, because the kids were at school. She made us a couple of sandwiches, and we ate together while chatting about her family. Nothing exciting, nothing out of the ordinary. Nothing that made me think she was flirting. After we finished eating, we bumped into each other as I went to the refrigerator and she headed for the sink.

She did not pull away.

Neither did I, to be honest. Maybe I wanted to see what she would do.

She kissed me.

I pulled away. At that point, I had never cheated on Millicent. I wasn't even thinking about it. I was thinking about Millicent in Miami with her male coworker.

Before I had a chance to say anything to Crystal, she apologized and left the room. I don't think we were ever alone again.

I considered telling Millicent right up to the moment I picked her up at the Orlando airport. I decided not to take the risk.

I am thinking about this because I don't think I'm the only one not being totally truthful. I think Millicent has been lying to me. The idea came to me when Jenna got sick. I had just arrived home from work, and I was late; we were supposed to go to a party thrown by an association of mortgage brokers. Millicent was rushing around, trying to get ready, Rory was playing video games, and Jenna was throwing up in the bathroom.

Millicent went to the party alone that night. I stayed home with Jenna.

We have taken Jenna to the doctor about her stomach once before. Our family doctor says I worry too much. Kids get upset stomachs all the time, he says. But now she has them more often, her stomach problems have gotten worse since Owen was brought back to life. This makes me think her fear of him is not getting better. It is making her physically sick.

I pulled up a calendar on my phone and tried to figure out how often she was getting sick. One of the first times it happened was the night we were with Lindsay, when I'd left Millicent alone with her to go be with Jenna.

Ever since Lindsay's body was found, I've wondered about that night, about what would have happened if Jenna had not been sick. Would we have gone ahead and killed Lindsay that night? Or would Millicent have told me she wanted to keep Lindsay alive?

And when did she take care of her? When she was supposed to be at work? How did she sell all those houses and still keep Lindsay alive for a year?

Too many questions I cannot answer. I have secrets. Why wouldn't she?

MY FIRST IDEA is stupid. I thought I could follow Millicent to find out what she is doing, maybe where she is keeping Naomi. But as soon as I think of following Millicent, I realize why it is impossible. She knows my car too well; she knows my license plate. She would spot me in a second.

Plus, I have to work. My job is flexible, not optional.

But I don't have to follow her, because technology can do it for me. Five minutes of research on the Internet tells me this works exactly like in the movies. I buy a GPS tracker with a magnetic case, press the power button, and stick it on the bottom of her car. All I have to do is log in to the app on my phone to see where her car is. The app also records the addresses where she stops, so I do not have to follow it in real time. The whole setup is unbelievably cheap, even with the fee for real-time information. Spying on someone has never been simpler.

I make it sound easy, and technically it is, but the real cost is to my psyche. And my marriage.

Even after I buy the device, I don't put it on right away. It stays in the trunk of my car, burning a hole in the back of my mind. I do not want to blow up my marriage and my family, which is what will happen if Millicent finds out I am spying on her.

I do not want to do it, but I want to know what she is doing.

When I get home from work, Millicent is already home and her car is in the garage. It takes only a second to attach it.

Later in the evening, it occurs to me that maybe there is a way for her to know there is a tracker on her car. All technology has counter-technology—at least I assume it does—so I spend an hour on my phone, looking up all the ways Millicent could find out what I have done. And I am right; she can find out. But first she would have to suspect she is being tracked.

I look over at her. She is sitting with Rory at the dining room table, and they are making flash cards for his history class. He has never been a great student, because, as his teachers say, he does not apply himself. Millicent agrees, and a few times a week she helps him do just that. No phones, no distractions, nothing but his homework and his mother. Not even I interrupt when Millicent is working with Rory.

After a few minutes, she feels me staring at her. She glances up and winks at me. I wink back.

Later that night, I remove the tracker from her car.

The next morning, I put it back on.

Thirty-nine

WHEN I WATCH someone in person, it feels intimate. They have no idea they are being watched, so they are not guarded or self-conscious. I get to know how they walk and move, their little tics and gestures. Sometimes, I can even tell what they will do next.

Using a tracker is much different, because I am not watching Millicent. I am watching a blue dot move around a map.

The app tells me where she goes—the address, latitude and longitude. I know how long she stays, how fast she drives, exactly how she parks. The app spits out charts and graphs that tell me how much time she spends driving, her average speed, and the average time at each location. I try to picture Millicent behind the wheel, dressed up for work, perhaps talking on the phone or listening to music. I wonder if she does something I don't know about. Maybe she sings when she is alone. Or talks to herself. I have never seen her do either one, but she must do something. Everyone does when they are alone.

On the first day, she drops the kids off at school and goes to the office. She works for a real estate agency but does not spend much time sitting at a desk. After that, she drives to Lark Circle, to a residential address in Hidden Oaks. Over the next eight or nine hours, she goes to eleven houses, all of which are for sale. I check them all. She picks up the kids, stops at the store, drives home.

The surprise is where she stopped to eat lunch. Instead of having a salad or a sandwich or even fast food, Millicent went to an ice-cream parlor.

For the rest of the afternoon, I wonder if she got a cone or a cup.

Our dinner is roast turkey with chorizo and sweet potatoes. Rory glosses over the grade on his history quiz by telling an exciting story about a kid who was caught smoking and made a run for it before anyone could identify him. Jenna had heard the same story, but a friend of a friend said the guy was the vice principal's son and that was why he ran.

"False," Rory says. "I heard it's Chet."

Jenna turns up her nose. "He's a jerk."

"Chet Allison?" Millicent says. "I sold the Allisons their house."

"No. Chet Madigan."

"You have two Chets at school?" she says.

"Three," Jenna says.

There is a lull in the conversation. I ponder the abundance of Chets while sneaking a look at Millicent's plate. She has a thick slice of turkey, a scoop of chorizo, and a tiny sweet potato. For her, it is a normal-size dinner. Dessert is fruit and gingersnap cookies. No ice cream.

All of a sudden, I find myself fascinated by my wife's eating habits. I wonder if her lunch always determines what we eat for dinner, dessert, or both.

I watch the blue dot again the next day.

Millicent drops off the kids, but I pick them up, and during that time she is at a house in the Willow Park gated community. Today, she goes to the office, but she does not stop for lunch. Again, she stays within a small radius, concentrated in the areas and subdivisions where she sells the most houses.

In contrast, the police have widened their search. At night, after

Millicent is asleep, I watch the news on my phone in the bathroom, because if I go into the garage, my son will think I am still cheating on his mother.

Josh now starts his reports with the number of days that have passed since Naomi has disappeared. He calls it "The Count," and it is at twenty-two. Twenty-two days have passed since Friday the 13th, and Josh is still following the police around to abandoned buildings, sheds, and bunkers. An expert says this is probably futile, because Owen is watching the news, and therefore Naomi would not be kept in an empty building, shed, or bunker. Besides, a woman can be held anywhere. A single room, a storage container. A closet.

The report is over in just a few minutes. It used to take up half the evening news. The story is starting to fade, because nothing new has happened and Naomi is no longer the girl next door. She is tainted. The viewers have grown restless.

And I have become mesmerized by the blue dot. In all my years of marriage, I have never wondered how much time it takes Millicent to show a house, or how long of a lunch she takes, or how many houses per day she sees. Now that I am tracking her, all of this has become intriguing.

I check the app every chance I get. Before and after tennis lessons, when I am in my car, in the clubhouse, in the locker room. There is no sign of Naomi. Millicent visits no unusual buildings or abandoned businesses, and the houses are all on the market. She goes to the store, to the school, and to the bank for a closing. After four days, I start to wonder if Naomi is already dead.

As disturbing as it is, I think this may be the best-case scenario.

If she is gone, never to be heard from or found, Owen may fade away with her. When he is gone from the news, it will be like he'd never come back.

Trista will still be gone. Nothing can be done about that. But Jenna will stop being scared. She will stop thinking about Owen Oliver.

Then, a year from now, Owen will be back on the news. The anniversary of the event will be marked with documentaries, specials, and dramatic re-creations, but there will be nothing new to report. We will hear about Naomi and the men in shadows with the garbled voices.

Once again, Owen will fade away. Naomi will go with him.

Jenna will be a year older and talking about boys. Her hair will be long again, and she will not have a knife under her mattress.

As the days go on, I start to think it is all happening. Naomi is no longer alive, and Millicent is not torturing her, not visiting her. The police still have nothing. Everything, all that we have done, will just fade away until everyone forgets.

With a smile, I watch the blue dot. Millicent goes home in the afternoon, drops the kids off, and then heads back out. She stops at a coffee shop, and I know she is getting a vanilla latte. Maybe with an extra shot, but it's hard to tell from just the dot on the map.

I am so busy watching Millicent that I miss the breaking news. A woman claims Owen Oliver Riley attacked her.

Forty

I FIRST HEAR ABOUT this woman when I'm at the EZ-Go. A TV screen is mounted above the soda machine, visible to everyone in the store, including in the security mirrors. The breaking-news banner is everywhere, but I pay no attention until Josh is on the screen. He says a woman has come forward to claim she was attacked by Owen Oliver Riley.

She doesn't appear on TV, not even in shadows. For now, she is just a report filed with the police. The text appears on the screen, and a female reporter reads it:

> On Tuesday night, I became Owen Oliver Riley's latest victim, but by the grace of God I got away from him. I am a hairdresser, and after work we all went across the street for a drink. Later that night, I was at a bar out on Mercer Road but I decided to leave, because I had to work the next day. This was right around 11 p.m., and I remember because someone said it and I thought I better get home soon, so I decided to leave. I was parked in the back lot, and it isn't even dark back there because of the lights, and the moon was real

bright—maybe it was a full moon, but I didn't check. It was light enough to walk by myself, so I did. Honestly, I didn't even think about Owen. He never crossed my mind.

I was a couple feet from my car when I felt a tug. Felt like my bag got caught on something, the strap. It wasn't hard, didn't scare me. I just stopped and tugged, and it was definitely caught on something. So I turned around.

He was just standing there, holding on to the strap of my bag. That's what it was caught on. Owen's hand.

I knew it was him, even though he had a cap pulled down so low it covered half his face. I could still see his mouth, though. His smile. Everyone knows that smile—it's all over the news because he smiled in that old mug shot, and that's how I know it was definitely him. And that's why I let go of the bag and ran.

Didn't get far before he tackled me. That's where I got all these scrapes, trying to get out from under him. But I couldn't, because he was just so strong, and every time I tried to move, his grip got tighter.

I'm only alive because of my phone. My brother called, and I knew it was him because of the ring. I personalize all my rings because I like to know who's calling, right? My brother's ring sounds like an explosion, because that's kind of what he's like—a big explosion. His life always seems to be blowing up, and when it does he calls me. But I can't complain anymore, because his life and that ring is why I'm still here. The exploding sound was so loud it made Owen jump. His head whipped around, and I think he believed something had really blown up.

I scrambled to get up and ran straight back to the bar, and he didn't follow me.

I don't think he realized nothing blew up. Maybe he still thinks something did.

That is the end of the statement, or at least the only part read on the news. The words disappear, and Josh is back. He is standing in the parking lot behind that bar on Mercer. I haven't been to that bar since I was about twenty. Back then, they were known for not carding.

Josh looks serious. Sad. He is getting better, because he no longer looks excited about something horrible. He calls the woman who got attacked Jane Doe.

"Excuse me."

An older woman brushes past me. I am still standing in the convenience store, right near the soda machine, staring up at the screen. The only other person watching is the guy at the register. It's not Jessica, the cashier I usually see. This guy has a bald head, which shines under the fluorescent lights.

He looks at me and shakes his head, as if to say, "Isn't it terrible? Isn't it a shame?"

I nod while buying my usual coffee and a bag of barbecue chips.

THIS IS WHAT living with Millicent has always been like. Life goes along like it's supposed to, an occasional bump in the road but otherwise a fairly smooth ride. And then suddenly the ground opens into a chasm wide enough to swallow everything. Sometimes, what's inside is good, even great; sometimes not.

It happened when she told me Holly was alive. It happened when she bashed Robin in the head with a waffle iron. And again when she resurrected Owen.

These are the giant events, where the chasm becomes wider than the earth itself. Not all have been quite that large. Sometimes, the chasm is just big enough to swallow me, like when she left with the kids and disappeared for eight days after I came home drunk.

And then there are the cracks. When the ground opens up, it causes cracks. Some are bigger than others, like Jenna having a knife under her mattress. Or Trista killing herself. They are all different sizes—long, short, a variety of widths—but they originate from the same chasm.

The first one cracked open on our wedding day.

Millicent and I got married at her parents' house in a field sur-rounded by cilantro, rosemary, and oregano. She wore a gauzy white dress that hung to her ankles, and she had a homemade wreath on her head, made of daffodils and lavender. I wore khakis rolled up to my ankles and a white button-up, left untucked, and both of us were barefoot. It was perfect, right up until it wasn't.

Eight people attended our wedding. The three guys I went overseas with were there, including Andy. Not Trista. They were dating but not married, and Andy wasn't ready to give her any ideas. Abby and Stan, Millicent's parents, were there, and so was a friend of Millicent's from high school. The last two were neighbors.

The ceremony was just that: an act, a ritual. Neither Millicent or I were religious; we were going to get legally married the following Monday at the Woodview City Hall. In the meantime, we pretended to marry, with Millicent's father playing the minister's role. Stan looked so official in a plaid shirt buttoned to the neck and his thin grey hair smoothed down with gel. He stood in front of their herb fields with a book in his hands. Not the Bible, just a book, and he almost said the right words.

"Ladies and gentlemen, this young man wants to marry my daugh-ter today, and I think he needs to prove himself." Stan pretended to give me the evil eye. "So make it good."

I had written and rewritten my vows a dozen times, knowing I would have to say them out loud. The other people did not bother me at all. I was nervous about saying them to Millicent. I took a deep breath.

"Millicent, I can't promise you the world. I can't promise I will buy you a big house or a fancy car or a giant diamond ring. I can't even promise we'll always have food on the table."

She stared at me, unblinking. In the bright sun, her eyes looked like crystals.

"I hope to give you all those things, but I have no idea if it will be possible. I do not know what will be in our future, but I do know we will be together. That's what I can promise you without hesitation, without any fear that I'd be lying. I will always be there for you, with you, next to you." I smiled a little, because I saw a little tear in her eye. "And hopefully, we'll be able to eat."

Eight people laughed. Millicent nodded.

"Well then," Stan said, turning to his daughter. "I guess it's your turn. Convince us this is the man for you."

Millicent raised her hand and pressed it against my cheek. She leaned in, put her lips right next to my ear, and whispered.

"Here we go."

Forty-one

A T DINNER, NO one mentions the news or Jane Doe. She is here with us, but we do not acknowledge her. Instead, we talk about a celebrity who has gone to rehab. Again.

We talk about a football game I did not see.

We talk about what to watch on movie night. Rory wants to watch a college-aged comedy, and Jenna prefers a romcom.

The only current event we discuss is a mall shooting in the next state over.

"Sicko," Rory says.

Jenna points at him with her fork. "You're the one who plays shooting games."

"The key word being 'game.'"

"But you like it."

"Shut up."

"You shut up."

"Enough," Millicent says.

Silence.

When dinner ends, they both go upstairs and retreat to their rooms.

Millicent and I stare at each other. She points to me, mouthing the words, "Was it you?"

She is asking if I am the one who attacked Jane Doe. I shake my head and point to the garage.

After the dishes are done and the kids are asleep, we go out and sit in the car. Millicent brings our leftover Halloween candy, and we share a bottle of sparkling water. She is wearing a bright blue shirt with short sleeves. I think it is new, because earlier in the day I watched her car stop at the mall.

"You had nothing to do with this woman?" she says.

"Absolutely not. I wouldn't do something like that without telling you." At least I don't think I would.

"I hope not."

"And I wouldn't do anything to make Jenna more afraid."

Millicent nods. "I should have known."

"Maybe Jane Doe is lying," I say.

"Possibly. Or maybe some random guy attacked her and she just thinks it was Owen. We don't know what she saw."

"There's a third option," I say.

"Is there?"

I unwrap a piece of chocolate, break it in two, and give her half. "What if he's really back?"

"Owen?"

"Sure. What if it was him?"

"It wasn't."

"How can you be so sure?"

"Because it would be stupid. Why would he come back right when everyone is looking for him?"

"Good point."

I AM BACK in the beige office, waiting for Jenna to finish with her psychologist. The doctor called after hearing about Jane Doe, saying he wanted an extra session. He is afraid this new attack will make

Jenna regress. I am not sure she has progressed enough to regress, but I take her anyway. Millicent says she is unable to make it, so I sit in the waiting room and watch her blue dot. My wife is at a house on Danner Drive; it is listed for just under half a million dollars.

Then she drives to a deli.

Sometimes, she goes out to lunch with clients, but I have never known her to take them to a deli.

Millicent is just a few minutes from the doctor's office, but she does not come here. She goes to a deli, and she is still there when the office door opens and Jenna comes out. My daughter looks neither happy nor sad, which is about the same as when she went in.

It is her turn to wait while I speak to the doctor. Dr. Beige. To me he is always Dr. Beige. The name is neither fair nor accurate, because only his office is beige; his personality is not. The doctor is a colorful, arrogant asshole. I have never met a doctor who is not.

"I'm glad I asked Jenna to come in," he says. "This new attack was quite a surprise."

Dr. Beige does not say Jenna was surprised, but it's what he means. This is how he gets around the doctor-patient confidentiality. "It certainly was a surprise," I say.

"The important thing is to let her know nothing has changed. That she's safe."

"She *is* safe."

"Of course."

We stare at each other.

"Have you noticed any changes in her behavior?" he says. "Any kind of change."

"Actually, I wanted to ask you something. Jenna has been having some issues with her stomach. Nausea."

"And this started when?"

"Not that long ago, and it's been getting worse. Is it possible these are connected?"

"Oh, absolutely. Mental stress can absolutely manifest into physical issues. Has there been anything else?"

I pretend to think about it and shake my head. "No, I don't think so."

I wonder if he can tell I am lying. No one knows about the knife under the bed.

Our talk is over when my phone vibrates. Millicent.

Sorry I couldn't make it, how did it go?

Her blue dot is just leaving the deli.

Jenna is in the waiting room, doodling in a notebook while watching a daytime talk show. Her short hair makes her eyes look huge, and she is wearing a long T-shirt with her jeans and sneakers. I tell her we are going to grab a bite before picking up her brother. She smiles.

Joe's Deli is a seven-minute drive by my watch. When I pull into the parking lot, Millicent is long gone. The deli has seen better days, perhaps because of the location. Joe's is in the older part of town, which has been losing the battle against the newer and shinier side.

Inside, it is bright enough to see the scratches on the counter and display case. The meats, cheeses, and premade salads look a little warped. We are the only ones in the deli, and it is silent until Jenna spins the display of potato chips, which creaks, perhaps from rust. A woman appears, as if she had been sitting down and suddenly stood up. She is plump and blond and looks tired, but when she smiles her whole face lights up.

"Welcome to Joe's," she says. "I'm Denise."

"Nice to meet you, Denise," I say. "We've never been here before. What's your specialty?"

She holds up a finger, telling me to wait, and disappears behind the counter. Her hand slips into one of the glass cases and she grabs a platter of sliced meat. She sets it down in front of us. "Sugar spice turkey. A little heat, a little sweet. Not too much of either."

I look at Jenna.

"Cool," she says.

We get two sandwiches, hers on seven-grain, and mine on a kaiser roll, both dressed with only lettuce and tomato. "You have to be able to taste the turkey," says the woman.

Joe's Deli has an outdoor patio on the side, not visible from the front parking lot. A few tables are scattered within a walled-in area; it is clean and neat, but without any character. After a minute, it does not matter, because the turkey is that good. Even Jenna is eating.

"Did you find this place online?" Jenna says.

"No. Why?"

"Seems like something you'd do. Search for weird sandwich places."

"It's not weird. It's good."

"Mom would hate it," she says. "It's not organic."

"Don't tell her we came here."

"You want me to lie?"

I ignore that. "What do you think about your doctor? Does he help?"

She shrugs. "I guess."

"Are you still scared?"

Jenna points. Through the side door of the deli, she has a view of the TV above the glass counter. The blond woman is sitting on a chair near the register, watching the news. The headline says that Jane Doe will hold a press conference tomorrow night.

Forty-two

MILLICENT AND I are standing in the empty parking lot of the Ferndale Mall. The only sound comes from the highway behind us. It is Friday night, and Jenna is at a slumber party while Rory is spending the night with a friend playing video games.

Jane Doe's press conference ended an hour ago. Millicent and I watched it at a popular restaurant and sports bar attached to the mall. The press conference was broadcast on every screen. The latest twist in our serial killer drama became a Friday night social, complete with chicken wings and beer. We watched it with another couple, the Rhineharts, who believed every word Jane Doe said.

Millicent is leaning against the car, arms folded over her chest, a stray hair blowing in the breeze. She always wears something appropriate for the occasion, even for this serious occasion at a sports bar. Her black jeans are paired with a T-shirt that reads WOODVIEW UNITY, a slogan that has popped up since Naomi's disappearance. Her hair is braided down her back, except for that one strand.

She shakes her head. "I don't like her," she says. "I don't like her story."

I think of Lindsay being held captive. Maybe Millicent hadn't liked her, either.

"It doesn't matter," I say.

"We don't know that."

"So what—"

"We just need to know more," she says.

"You aren't thinking—"

"I'm not thinking anything."

We stand in silence for a moment before Millicent turns and opens the door. I watch her get into the passenger side of my car. She shuts the door and looks over at me. I have not moved. I can almost hear her sigh as she opens the door and steps back out. She is wearing shoes with rubber heels, and they are silent as she walks to me.

Placing her palms against my chest, she looks up at me. "Hey," she says.

"Hey."

"You okay?"

I shrug.

"That means no," she says.

It is my turn to sigh. Or huff. Breathe hard. Something. "We've screwed up, you know," I say.

"Have we?"

"I think so."

"Tell me."

I don't know where to start; everything is so jumbled, and I do not want to mention the wrong thing. Like Petra, whom I have never mentioned. Or Rory's blackmail. She knows about Jenna, but not everything. Trista's suicide. The tracker on the car. Joe's Deli.

There is so much Millicent does not know. And still, I feel like there is so much more to discover.

"The Owen thing," I finally say. "It's out of control."

"I don't think so."

"What about Jenna?"

"I should have seen that coming."

Her response surprises me. It is not often she makes a mistake, let alone admits it. Because of this, I decide not to tell her what Dr. Beige said. It doesn't seem like a good time to tell her this whole thing is making Jenna physically sick.

We are hit by headlights as a car comes around the corner of the mall. As it comes closer, I see it is not a car at all. The security vehicles for the mall are golf carts, and this one is driven by a middle-aged woman. She stops and asks us if everything is all right.

Millicent waves to her. "Everything's fine. My husband and I are just discussing our son's grades."

"Oh, I understand that. Got three of my own."

"Then you get it."

The guard nods. She and my wife smile at each other as some motherly understanding passes between them.

"Best move along, though. The mall is closed."

"Thanks. We'll get going," Millicent says.

The guard waits as we get into the car and drive away. When we stop at a red light, Millicent puts her hand on my arm. "I was thinking we should enroll Jenna in a self-defense class. I think it would help her confidence."

"That's a good idea." And it is.

"I'll look into it tomorrow."

MILLICENT'S STOP AT Joe's Deli is not a one-time event. She goes again the next day, at lunchtime, and she stays for forty minutes before going to show another house. None of her other stops are out of the ordinary. She even looks at two different martial arts schools for Jenna and tells me about them after dinner, when we are alone in the bedroom.

"One of the schools teaches competitive tae kwon do. They have meets and teams, and compete for ribbons. But there's another one downtown for Krav Maga. It's a little more expensive but more geared toward self-defense."

"She could try out both, let her pick which one she likes."

Millicent comes over and kisses me on the nose. "You are so smart."

I roll my eyes. She giggles.

She does not mention the sandwich shop or the plump blond woman with the big smile. I try to think of a way to bring up what she ate for lunch without asking, "What did you have for lunch today?" out of the blue. But I am not as smart as Millicent says, because when I start rambling about how good my own lunch was, she does not reciprocate. She just nods and smiles while getting ready for bed, acting interested in my long monologue about a fictitious lunch. We go to bed without discussing Joe's Deli.

In the middle of the night, I get up and go down to the library. We call it the library because we filled it with shelves and books and a big mahogany desk, but the only thing we use it for is private phone calls. I have also started using it to surf the Internet in private.

Joe's Deli opened twenty-two years ago. The business has had two owners, not related to one another, and the deli has always been in the same building. Rented, not owned. No trouble other than a slip-and-fall lawsuit filed by a man who claimed the floor was wet. It was settled out of court. No other crime, lawsuits, or serious health code violations. Joe's Deli is exactly as it appears: a run-of-the-mill deli. The fact that it is so normal makes the whole thing suspicious. Millicent had no reason to go there once, let alone twice.

The satellite maps of the area show a freestanding building on what used to be a much busier road. Across the street, there is a small used-car lot. Next to that, a plumbing supply store, then a watch repair shop.

If she had stopped there only once, it could have been a fluke. An out-of-the-way place that someone had told her about and she decided to try but quickly realized it wasn't her kind of place. I would even be willing to believe she stopped because she was thirsty and Joe's was the only place around, even though it was miles from her usual area. I would believe just about any one-off reason for her to stop at Joe's. Except that two days later, she went back.

She has another reason for going to Joe's. At first, I think it's Naomi—perhaps she was being held in that area—but Millicent didn't stop anywhere else. There are no empty buildings or shuttered businesses in the area, no place she could walk to from the parking lot at Joe's.

It doesn't make any sense. Not unless she has developed a taste for unhealthy, nonorganic sandwiches.

And I know that hasn't happened.

Forty-three

AFTER HOLLY, IT never occurred to me there would be another. Not until Robin showed up at our door threatening to ruin everything unless I paid her.

After Robin, it never occurred to me there would be another. Not until I wanted to do it again.

The idea had been floating around for a while, first at the New Year's Eve party when Millicent and I talked about the other women. The conversation continued over the next few months, to the point that we looked up women online. The activity became our aphrodisiac.

We talked about how we would kill them and how we would get away with it, and those nights always ended with amazing sex. Wild sex. In every place we could, provided the kids weren't around. If they were in the house, we struggled to be quiet.

It was almost as if we were climbing a ladder. We joked about it, talked about it, picked out women, and planned it. Every time we escalated to one rung, we stepped up to another. Then someone suggested we do it for real. It was me.

I said it while we were in the kitchen. It was late morning, and we were naked on the cold tile. We had just found Lindsay online. Both of us agreed she was perfect.

"We should just do it," I said.

Millicent giggled. "I think we did just do it."

"Not that. Well, yes, that, but it's not what I meant."

"You meant we should kill Lindsay."

I paused. "Yes. Yes, I did."

Millicent looked at me with a mixture of surprise and something else. At the time, I wasn't sure. Now, I think it was interest. Or intrigue. But not revulsion. "Did I marry a psychopath?" she said.

I laughed. So did she.

The decision was made.

Millicent has never reminded me about that night, never said it was my idea. Never said it was my fault. But I know it is. If it weren't for me, there would be no Lindsay, no Naomi, and Owen would not be back. Our daughter would still have long, shiny hair, and she wouldn't have a knife under her mattress.

Or maybe it had been Millicent. Maybe she led me there all along.

I don't know anymore.

But a few days later, I am once again reminded of that decision. And the unintended consequences of it.

The martial arts studios let Jenna sit in on a beginners' class to see if she liked it. First, we went to tae kwon do. Half an hour later, Jenna shook her head at me and we left. She does not want to be in competitions, nor does she want to win ribbons and trophies. Jenna wants to fight off Owen.

The following afternoon we went to Krav Maga. Unlike tae kwon do, the Krav Maga school does not require uniforms or belts, which Jenna liked a lot better than the white gi everyone at tae kwon do had to wear. Jenna preferred to wear her sweatpants and T-shirt.

It never occurred to me that she would hurt the boy who was trying to teach her something, much less try to knock him out.

The whole thing happened so fast no one saw it. Not even me, and I had been watching Jenna from a row of chairs designated for parents.

One minute, they were both standing up and the boy was showing Jenna how to form a proper punch. The next minute, he fell to the floor and screamed in pain.

A few drops of blood hit the mat, and everyone lost their minds.

"What the—"

"How did—"

"Is that a rock?"

A mom in a turquoise jumper pointed to Jenna. "She did it. She hit him with a rock."

Pandemonium followed, along with a lot more screaming and big accusations.

It took a few hours to sort out, in part because the boy's mother arrived and started yelling about why no one had called an ambulance. That made someone call an ambulance. And the police.

Two uniformed officers showed up and asked what happened. The boy's mother pointed at Jenna and said, "She hit my son."

Understandably, the officers were confused, because we were in a Krav Maga studio where people get hit on a regular basis. They also thought it was a little funny that the boy was hit by a girl. The man who owned the studio did not think it was funny at all.

In the end, the boy was fine. The blood had come from a small cut on his lip and really was just a few drops. No one went to the hospital and no one got arrested, but Jenna and I were disinvited from the Krav Maga studio.

Throughout the course of the afternoon, the boy's mother vowed more than once that she would sue. And on top of everything else, I was forced to cancel several tennis lessons, and pissed off at least one client.

Once we were in the car, alone, I asked, "Why?"

Jenna stared out the window.

"You must have had a reason," I said.

She shrugged. "I don't know. Maybe to see if I could."

"Could hit that kid with a rock?"

"Could knock him out."

I do not point out the obvious. She did not knock him out. All she did was split his lip.

"Are you going to tell Mom?" Jenna said.

"Yes."

"Really?"

Actually, I had no idea. At that moment, I could not even look at Jenna.

She has never reminded me of Millicent. When Rory was born, he already had little tufts of red hair. Jenna was born bald. When her hair finally started growing in, it was the same color as mine: dark brown without a hint of red. Her eyes were the same as mine, too.

I was so disappointed.

It was not personal. It was not anything Jenna had done or hadn't done. I just wanted a little red-haired girl to match my boy and my wife with the flame-colored hair. This was the picture in my mind, the image I had when I thought about my family. The real Jenna did not fit, because she looked like my mother instead of her own.

The first time she ever reminded me of Millicent was when she hit that boy with a rock. She looked just like Millicent did when she hit Robin in our kitchen.

What I found sexy in my wife was horrifying in my daughter.

Forty-four

I T IS LATE at night. Millicent and I are in her office. She works for
Abbott Realty, a small pond of a business where she has been the
big fish for years. The office is in a strip mall, sandwiched between a
gym and a Chinese restaurant. Inside, it is empty and private, because
no one is looking for real estate at this hour. The downside is the glass
front, which means anyone can see inside. The open layout of the desks
provides no cover, so we leave the lights out and sit in the back. If the
circumstances were different, it might be romantic.

Millicent knows about Jenna. A friend told her before I could,
sending her into a rage. She called and yelled loud enough to make
my eardrum vibrate, because she said I should have called her when
we were still at the studio. She is right.

Now, Jenna is safe at home, asleep in her bed and not throwing
rocks. Not throwing up. Not cutting off what's left of her hair. Millicent is calm. She even brought dessert, a single chocolate éclair. She
cuts it in two, and the halves are perfectly even. I take a bite of mine
and she takes a bite of hers, and I wipe chocolate off her top lip.

"She's not okay," Millicent says.

"No."

"We need to talk to her doctor. I can call—"

"Is she like Holly?" I say.

Millicent sets down her éclair as if it's about to explode. "Like Holly?"

"Maybe it's the same thing. The same illness."

"No."

"But—"

"No. Holly started torturing bugs when she was two. Jenna is nothing like her."

By that comparison, she is right. Jenna screams whenever she sees a bug. She can't even kill a spider, let alone torture one. "Then it's our fault," I say. "We have to get rid of Owen."

"We've been trying to."

"I think the hunt for Naomi should end," I say. "We should let her be found."

"How will that help—"

"So we can get rid of Owen for good." When Millicent starts to point out the obvious, I hold up my hand. "I know, I know. Hard to get rid of someone that isn't even around, right?"

"That would be one way to put it."

"He was a great idea—I'm not denying it. But we've caused so many problems."

"So many?"

"Jenna. The people in this town. Women are really afraid." I am careful to omit what she doesn't know, like Trista.

Millicent nods. "I never meant to hurt Jenna."

"I know you didn't." I lean forward in my chair, closer to Millicent, so that she won't miss what I'm saying. "It would be difficult, if not impossible, to fake his death without a body. Really, the only way is if he drowns in the ocean or a lake and is never found. But there would be doubt. And to make it halfway plausible, we would need someone credible to tell the story."

"Like Naomi," Millicent says.

"And what are the chances of letting Naomi do that?"

"In the negative."

"Then maybe Owen doesn't die. Maybe he just leaves." I pause here, waiting for a reaction. When she doesn't say anything, I keep talking. "Owen has such a big ego he wrote to a reporter so everyone knew he was back and knew exactly when he would grab his next victim. So why wouldn't he tell everyone he is going to leave? He's the type that would brag about what he did. He would say, 'I told you exactly what I was going to do and when I was going to do it, and you still couldn't catch me. Now you'll never find me.'"

Millicent nods a little, like she's thinking about it.

"I know it's not ideal," I say. "But if Owen's gone, everyone will stop talking about him and maybe Jenna won't be scared anymore."

"The timing has to be right," she says. "They need to find Naomi before you send another letter."

"Oh, absolutely."

"I'll take care of that first."

"Maybe we should do it together."

She looks at me, her head tilted to one side. For a moment, I think she is going to smile, but she doesn't. This is too serious now. We have moved beyond using this as foreplay.

"I can take care of Naomi," she says. "You concentrate on the letter. You have to make everyone believe Owen has left."

I want to argue and go with my idea, but instead I nod. Her idea makes sense.

She sighs a little. "I hope this works."

"Me too."

I reach over and slip my hand into hers. We sit like this until she picks up what's left of my éclair and takes a bite. I take hers and do the same. A tiny smile appears on her face. I squeeze her hand.

"We'll be fine," I say.

Millicent has said this before. She said it when we were young and broke with one baby and another on the way. She said it when we bought our first house and then the second, bigger one.

She also said it after Holly, when her body was lying in our family room, her head smashed by the tennis racket.

WHILE I STOOD over Holly, coming to grips with what I had just done, Millicent went straight to work.

"Do we still have that tarp in the garage?" she said.

It took me a second to process. "Tarp?"

"From when we had that leak."

"I think so."

"Get it."

I paused, thinking we should call the police. Because that's what you do when you kill someone out of self-defense. You call the police and explain what happened, because you did nothing wrong.

Millicent read my mind.

"You think the police will believe Holly was a threat to *you*?" she said.

Me, the athlete. Me, with the broken tennis racket.

Holly, with no weapon at all.

I did not argue. I went out to the garage and dug through the shelves and plastic containers until I found the rolled-up blue tarp. When I returned to the living room, Holly's body had been readjusted; her legs were straightened, and her arms flat at her side.

We spread the tarp out on the floor, and together Millicent and I wrapped the body like a mummy.

"Let's move her into the garage," Millicent said.

It was almost like she didn't have to think about it.

I did what she said, and Holly ended up in the trunk of my car. I took her out to the woods and buried her while Millicent cleaned up the blood. By the time the kids got home from school, every sign of Holly had been scrubbed out.

We did the same thing with Robin, only she didn't get buried in the ground. Her body and her little red car ended up at the bottom of a lake.

Millicent is right. We have always been fine.

Now it's my turn to make sure of it.

BOTH HALVES OF the éclair are gone, and Millicent brushes the crumbs into a wastebasket. We stand up to go, walking back through the dark office and out to the car. It's late. Even the Chinese restaurant is closed, but the gym is available twenty-four hours. It stands out like a single halogen star in a dark sky.

Before starting the car, I turn to Millicent. She is checking her phone. I reach over and put my hand against her cheek, the same way she has touched me so many times. It makes her look up in surprise.

"So do we have a plan?" I say.

She smiles all the way up to her eyes. "Definitely."

Forty-five

THE NOISE IS gone. For the first time, as improbable as it seems, clarity comes all at once. Until I saw Jenna hit that boy, I never realized Millicent and I have been doing more than we realized. We have been destroying our own family.

Owen's final letter is the easiest one to write. I have a goal now—to get rid of Owen—and it feels like I know how to achieve it.

Though I will send it to Josh, as I always do, the letter is really addressed to the public. I tell them they are stupid.

I gave this to you. I tried to help you catch me by letting you know when, the exact day, I would take my next victim. I even gave you two weeks to prepare, to plan. Yet you failed. You didn't stop me, couldn't catch me, and because of you, Naomi is dead. Let there be no mistake: Her death isn't my fault. It's yours.

She knew it. Naomi had seen the same reports, had read my earlier letter, yet she was still out alone on that Friday the 13th. Naomi knew she had been stupid. She had faith, though. Faith that you were looking for her, faith that you would find her. She was half-right.

If I had the time, I would tell you everything I did to her. Every mark, every cut, every bruise. But that would be redundant. You already have her body.

Really, there isn't anything else to say. We played a game, and you lost. Naomi lost. Everyone lost but me. And now I'm done. I came back and accomplished my goal. I have nothing left to prove. Not to you, not to myself.

Goodbye.

Finally.

Once the final version is done, I tell Millicent. She has come to the club to pick up Rory, who played golf after school and is done before I am. Millicent stops by the tennis court, where I am waiting for my next client. Her flesh-colored heels thump against the cement as she walks toward me with a smile.

Days have passed since our late-night conversation. Now that Jane Doe has gone public she has been giving interviews to anyone who asks. She was impossible to avoid until Jane Doe #2 arrived last night.

Instead of having a press conference, she livestreamed her story on the Internet, and the local news rebroadcast it. The woman is younger than the others, maybe still in college, and she has jet-black hair, pale skin, and lips that look painted with blood. Jane #2 is almost the opposite of Owen's typical victims, but she told almost the same story as Jane #1. Only the parking lot was different, along with a few dramatic tweaks. This Jane claimed Owen hit her in the face, and she showed off a purplish bruise on her cheek.

As soon as the livestream ended, my old friend Josh appeared on TV. Of late, Josh has been very serious, but last night he sounded almost sarcastic. He did not come right out and say he thought Jane Doe #2 was a liar, but he may as well have. I cannot imagine anyone believed her. I know I didn't.

The problem is that women like her are keeping Owen as the lead story on the news. I do not have to remind Millicent of this as she walks onto the tennis court.

"I'm ready whenever you are," I say.

Her dark sunglasses hide her eyes, both from the sun and from me, but she nods. "Hello to you, too."

"Sorry." I lean over and kiss her on the cheek. She smells like citrus. "Hello."

"Hello. The letter is ready?"

"Do you want to read it?" I want her to say yes, I want to watch her read it, but she shakes her head.

"I don't need to. I trust you."

"Oh, I know. Just asking."

She smiles and kisses me on the cheek. "See you at home. Dinner at six."

"Always."

I watch her walk away.

She does not go to Joe's Deli today. Today is all work, either at the office or open houses.

I still watch the tracker, still check where she is going, but it is not because I want to know about Naomi. I already do. If she is not already dead, she will be soon.

I watch the tracker because I like to watch Millicent.

ANOTHER DAY GOES by, then another, and Josh is back to counting down how many days have passed since Naomi went missing. I watch him on my phone all the time, waiting for the breaking-news announcement about her body. Even when I wake up in the middle of the night, I feel an urge to see if anything is happening. On the Internet, news can break at any time. Normally, this is not a problem. But now that I am waiting for news to break, it is infuriating. And inconvenient.

I go downstairs and out to the backyard, where I check my phone. The news is the same as when I went to bed. Nothing is breaking, nothing is happening; it is like a boring rerun.

But I'm not tired. At two in the morning, the air is still, and so is our neighborhood. No one in Hidden Oaks throws late-night parties or even plays loud music. I don't even see a light on in any of our almost-mansions.

I wish I could say this was our dream home, that we took one look at it and knew it was the place we wanted to be, the place we had worked so hard to get. It isn't true. Our dream home is a bit deeper into Hidden Oaks, where the houses become real mansions. The inner circle is for hedge funders and surgeons.

We live in the middle circle, but only because of a nasty divorce, which led to frozen assets followed by a bank foreclosure. Because Millicent had sent that bank a lot of mortgage business, we were able to buy a house we should not have been able to afford. This is why we live in the middle of Hidden Oaks. We should be in the outer circle, but once again, I found my way into the middle.

The sound of rustling bushes makes me jump. There is no wind tonight.

The noise comes from the side of the house. If we had a dog, I would assume it made the noise, but we don't. We don't even have deer in this area.

The rustle comes again, followed by a creaking sound.

With my phone in hand, I get up to investigate. Our back porch is about half the length of the house, from the kitchen to the corner. In the dark, I walk over to the far railing. The path along the side of the house is partially lit by a street lamp, and it's empty. No animals, no burglars, no serial killers.

A soft scraping noise comes from above. I look up just in time to see Rory sneaking back into the house.

I had no idea he'd snuck out.

Forty-six

PARTYING, DRUGS, GIRLS. Or just because.

These are the reasons Rory sneaks out of the house. They are the same for all teenage boys. I first snuck out to smoke weed. Next, I snuck out because it worked the first time. Eventually, it was because of Lily. My parents never knew. Or more likely, they never cared.

And yet, even when Rory saw *me* sneaking out, it still did not occur to me that he was doing the same thing. This is how oblivious I have been.

Instead of confronting Rory when I see him, I wait until the next day. This gives me a chance to see if there is anything I missed, anything I should know before having this conversation with him.

His room is messy, as always, except for his desk. It is almost obsessive-compulsive but not officially, because he isn't particular about anything else. He doesn't care if his clothes are piled up or his books are all over the floor, but his desk is always orderly. Maybe because he never uses it.

Normally, I would never search through his room. I have never done it before. But then, I've never seen him sneak out before. My son has secrets, and, in my book, that warrants a search.

Rory is at school. He has his phone with him, and he is not allowed to keep a computer in his room, so my search takes place in the analog world. The nightstand comes first, then his desk, the dresser, and the closet. I even look under the bed, under the dresser, and in the back of his sock drawer.

It is the most disappointing search.

No porn, because he looks at it online. No notes from girls, because they text. No pictures, because they are on his phone. No drugs or alcohol, because if he is using them he isn't stupid enough to hide them in his room. That's something, I suppose. My son is not an idiot.

I do not tell Millicent, because she has enough to do.

She does not know. If she did, Rory would already be grounded for life. But she doesn't know because she would never hear him. Millicent sleeps like a rock. I am not even sure the fire alarm would wake her up.

It's almost lunchtime when I'm done with that pointless search, so I head to the school. The office administrator sends a text to his teacher, who sends him to the office. Even though Rory and Jenna attend a private school, uniforms aren't required. They do have a dress code, so every day Rory wears khakis and a button-up. Today the shirt is white. His backpack hangs on one shoulder, and his red hair needs to be trimmed. As soon as he sees me, he brushes the bangs off his forehead.

"Everything okay?" he says.

"Everything's great. Just thought we might spend the afternoon together."

His eyebrows lift, but he does not argue. For now, being with me is still better than his afternoon classes.

Lunch is at Rory's favorite restaurant, where he orders the steak Millicent never cooks for him. He does not question it until the waitress brings a soda, which we do not keep in the house. He knows something is up, so it is no surprise when he says, "What's up, Dad?"

But it is a shock when he follows it up with, "Are you and Mom getting divorced?"

"Divorced? Why would you even ask such a thing?"

He shrugs. "Because this is the kind of thing you do when you have to say something like that."

"Is that right?"

"Yeah." He says this like everyone knows it.

"Your mother and I are not getting a divorce."

"Okay."

"Really, we're not."

"I heard you."

I take a long sip of my iced tea, and he does the same with his soda. He says nothing else, forcing me to begin.

"How is everything?"

"Fine, Dad. How is everything with you?"

"It's great. Anything new going on?"

Rory hesitates. Our food arrives, giving him more time to think about what I am really asking.

When the waitress leaves, he shakes his head a little. "Not really."

"Not really?"

"Dad."

"Hmmm?" I take a bite of my steak.

"Just tell me why we're here."

"I just want to know what new and exciting things are going on in your life," I say. "Because it must be new and exciting if it's dragging you out of the house in the middle of the night."

Rory's hands freeze midway through cutting his steak. I can almost see the options running through his mind.

"It was just once," he says.

I say nothing.

Rory sighs and puts down his silverware. "Daniel and I both did it. We wanted to see if we could get away with it."

"Did he?"

"As far as I know."

"And what did you two do?"

"Nothing, really. Went down to the field, kicked around a soccer ball. Wandered around."

Plausible. At fourteen, it was thrilling just to be out of the house at midnight. But that didn't look like the first time he had climbed up to the window.

HE DOES NOT sneak out that night or the next. Not surprising now that he has been caught. But I am not only paying attention at night; I am paying attention to everything that has been ignored.

In the evening, I watch him when he is texting, when his phone vibrates and he checks to see who it is, and when he is on the computer. On movie night, I watch as he keeps his phone hidden but checks it a lot. One time, it rings, but the sound isn't rock music or a video-game beep. It is a song I do not recognize, but the voice is a raspy female, who sings as if she is standing on the edge of a cliff.

When picking the kids up from school, I get there early enough for a front-row view of the doors. This is when I see the girl who is obviously driving my son crazy.

She is a tiny blonde with rosy lips, milky skin, and hair that falls straight to her chin. She pushes it back while they talk and shifts her weight from one foot to the other. The girl is as nervous as he is.

How long, I wonder. How long has he had this girlfriend, or this almost-girlfriend? If I had not caught him the other night, I would have missed it altogether. Maybe I would have lived my whole life without knowing about this little blond girl that my son likes.

Have there been other girls—blondes or brunettes or redheads—who have made my son as crazy as this girl has? Did I miss the first, the second, and the third? At this point, I have no way of knowing.

He would not tell me if I asked. He did not even tell me about the current one.

And I did not notice, didn't have a clue, until I made the effort. Otherwise, it would have slipped right past me.

I wonder if this is what happened with my parents. They never made an effort, and I slipped right by them.

Forty-seven

During dinner, all of our phones are lined up on the counter behind Millicent. We are eating mushroom risotto, with leeks and baby carrots on the side, when my phone honks like a horn.

Breaking news.

Millicent reaches behind her and silences my phone.

"Sorry," I say. "Sports app."

She gives me a hard look. Phones are supposed to be silenced during dinner.

The breaking news could be anything, but I know it isn't. My news app is filtered for Naomi's name and Owen Oliver and the words *body has been found*. Technology is an amazing thing.

It is also a horrible thing, because now I have to sit through dinner until I can know more. This is worse than being completely ignorant for twenty minutes.

When we are finally done, I grab my phone as the kids clear the table.

BODY OF WOMAN FOUND

I look up at Millicent. She is standing in front of the sink, wearing an old sweatshirt and black leggings and a pair of my socks. I catch her eye, pointing at my phone.

She gives me a tiny nod with a smile.

I DO NOT see the rest of the story until the dishes are done and the kids sit down to watch TV. At that point, I go upstairs, into the bathroom, and watch the news.

It is perfect.

Naomi's body was found inside a Dumpster behind the Lancaster Hotel. She was last seen in that parking lot, not far from the same Dumpster, after she got off work on that Friday the 13th. The last image of Naomi was on a security camera as she walked across the lot to her car. The cameras only covered part of the lot. Naomi's car and the Dumpster were both in blind spots.

Josh is standing across the street from the hotel, right where I used to park and watch Naomi. He looks buzzed on caffeine or adrenaline or both, and it's good to see him like this again. The Jane Doe women, especially the second one, seemed to depress him.

Now, he is energetic, all full of innuendo and speculation, because not many real facts have been released. All we really know is that a dead woman who looks like the missing Naomi was found in the Dumpster when it was being emptied by a waste disposal company. The police were called, the whole area was blocked off, and a press conference may or may not happen tonight, but he thinks it will.

The one thing that does not come up is Naomi's past. Now that she is dead instead of missing, it would be unkind to say bad things about her.

Josh does note that it has been weeks since he last heard from Owen Oliver Riley.

I smile.

The letter is addressed to the TV station, and it is marked *Personal and Confidential for Josh*. I imagine that when it arrives, the look on his face will be orgasmic, though he will not be happy to learn that this is his final letter from Owen. The letters have made Josh a star, at least locally, and there is a rumor he has been approached by a cable station. He would do well on a station like that. He is so serious and earnest it is hard not to believe him.

Josh is one of the few who will have a better life because of this.

Trista will not.

Poor, dead Trista will never even be recognized as a victim. And she was, even if she did take her own life. I do feel bad about her, mainly because she felt so bad about the others. It is hard to dislike someone so empathetic.

The best we can do now is to prevent it from happening again.

I go downstairs, where the kids are arguing about what to watch next. Millicent threatens to send them upstairs to read if they don't agree on something, and suddenly the room goes quiet. The opening music of a teenage drama starts; it's Jenna's favorite, and somehow Rory manages not to groan. I suspect this is also because of the little blonde. She probably watches the same shows as Jenna.

Millicent motions to me, and we walk through the kitchen, into the formal dining room that we use only for holidays and dinner parties.

"They found her?" she whispers.

I nod. "They did. Waiting for official confirmation."

"Now you—"

"I'll mail it tomorrow."

"Perfect."

I smile. She kisses me on the tip of my nose.

We go back into the family room and join the kids, but since we are watching live TV, we cannot help but hear about Naomi. The news is announced during a commercial break, and it is so quick there is no time to turn the channel.

Rory's phone lights up. He picks it up and starts texting.

Jenna does not react. She stares at the TV as if she were still watching her show, not news about a dead woman.

"Who wants ice cream?" Millicent says.

Rory raises a finger. "Me."

"Jenna?"

"Sure."

"One scoop?"

"Three."

"Sure, honey," I say, getting up from the couch.

Millicent raises her eyebrow at me and follows me into the kitchen. I get four bowls, and everyone gets three scoops. She starts to say something, and I cut her off.

"Let's not talk about sugar content tonight. It's going to get worse before it gets better." And it's true. Naomi will be on the news every night, and they will go over every detail of how she was found and how she was killed. It will get even worse when Josh receives my letter, because then they will spend hours debating if Owen is really gone or if he is just waiting for all of us to get complacent again.

Eventually, it will fade. Something else will take its place, and Owen will be gone for good.

But until then, three scoops of ice cream.

We go back into the family room, and the teenage drama has ended. Rory changes the channel, and we watch the end of one show in anticipation of the next. In between, there is a newsbreak. Before Millicent has a chance to grab the remote, Josh is on our TV. He repeats the same information we heard on the other channel.

When he is done talking about the discovery of Naomi's body, Rory turns to his sister. "You think she was tortured?"

"Yeah."

"More or less than the last one?"

"Hey," I say. Because I do not know what else to say.

"More," Jenna says.

"Wanna bet?"

She shrugs. They shake on it.

Millicent gets up and leaves the room.

I take my ice-cream bowl into the kitchen. My phone is about to die, and I root through our junk drawer in search of a charger. They're always lying around, but never when I need one, and there isn't one in the drawer. Next, I try the pantry, because weird things end up in there. When Jenna was younger, I used to find her stuffed animals sitting around the cookies, protecting them. Now, I find electronic gadgets.

Tonight, I don't. But on the bottom shelf, behind some cans of soup, I find a small bottle of eye drops.

The kind Millicent is allergic to.

Forty-eight

WHEN I SEE the eye drops, I think of Rory. If Millicent used them to cover up the fact that she was stoned, then surely other teenagers have thought of the same idea. Maybe that's what he does when he sneaks out at night. Maybe he and his little girlfriend smoke weed.

There are worse things. Much worse things.

The pantry is not a logical place for eye drops, but I imagine he just stashed them there. Perhaps he had come home high and put them in at the last minute. Or maybe he thought no one would look on the bottom shelf behind the soup.

Then again, it could be Jenna. Maybe she's the one who has been smoking.

No, that doesn't seem right. Jenna wouldn't ruin her lungs. Soccer is too important to her for that.

I take the bottle. On my way to the club, I wonder what would cause red eyes other than smoke or dirt or some other irritant. Allergies and fatigue, though neither is something to hide. Maybe hangovers. Maybe some new drug I've never even heard of.

When Kekona arrives for her lesson, I am sitting on a bench staring at that bottle of eye drops.

Kekona is so amped on gossip she bounces up and down on the balls of her feet like she is six instead of sixty. As soon as she walks onto the court, she starts talking, because she has to get it all out before leaving town. Every year, Kekona goes back to Hawaii for a month, and her trip is coming up fast. She is afraid of all she will miss, now that Naomi's body has been found.

"Strangled," she says. "Like the others."

"I know."

"And the torture. All those damn paper cuts."

My heart skips. "Paper cuts?"

"Police said she was covered with them. They were even on her eyelids." She shivers like it's cold outside.

Paper cuts.

I close my eyes, trying not to imagine Millicent doing this. Trying to erase the idea that she has turned our private joke into something so sick.

It is only eleven o'clock in the morning. Earlier, they said her fingerprints had been filed off, but the police had Naomi's dental records ready. It was her.

"The police said this about the cuts?" I say.

"Not officially. Just unnamed sources," Kekona says. "But if you ask me, the weird thing is the timing." She pauses.

So I ask, "What about it?"

"Well, the last woman was held for a year. But Naomi? A month and a half."

"Maybe Owen got tired of waiting for the police to find him."

Kekona smiles at me. "Kind of cheeky today, aren't you?"

I shrug and hold up a tennis ball, indicating that we should play, since that's what she pays me to do. Kekona stretches a little and swings her racket around.

"If this were a movie, the timing difference would mean something," she says.

She is right, but for all the wrong reasons. "Aren't you the one who said life isn't a horror movie?"

Kekona does not answer.

"Serve," I say.

She serves the ball twice. I don't return her serves, because she still doesn't want to volley. She wants to serve an ace.

"They also said she was burned," Kekona says.

"Burned?"

"That's what they said. She had burns all over her, like she had been scalded."

I cringe at the thought of being scalded on accident. Yet Millicent did it on purpose.

"I know, it makes me sick, too," Kekona says. She serves again and stops. "This morning, they said he might be re-creating his old crimes. He burned another one of his victims, Bianca or Brianna. Something like that. They showed a picture of her this morning, and she looks a lot like Naomi."

I missed all of this. Not being able to watch the news at home can be a problem. "That's odd," I say. "Serve."

She does, and I count nine of them before she stops again, except this time she does not talk about Owen.

She talks about Jenna.

"I heard about your daughter," she says.

It does not surprise me that Kekona heard about the incident at Krav Maga. This used to be exactly the sort of thing we gossiped about. It just didn't involve my family.

"Yeah," I say, trying to think of how to explain, how to excuse my daughter for hitting a kid with a rock. She had a bad day, flunked a test, forgot to take her medication? They all sound bad. They all sound like my daughter cannot control herself.

Kekona walks over and pats me on the arm. "Not to worry," she says. "Your daughter is going to be a badass."

I laugh. And I hope she is right. I would rather Jenna be a badass than any of the other options.

* * *

WHEN KEKONA'S LESSON is over, I finally get to check the news. She is right about this former victim. Bianca and Naomi do look alike; both had dark hair and that wholesome girl-next-door look. Bianca had also been scalded, though not with water.

Oil.

This similarity makes the media go back and look at Lindsay again, and now they have come up with an earlier victim who also had straight blond hair.

I think it is all a stretch. The media just needs something to talk about, and, without any real information, they have made connections that do not exist. If Millicent wanted to re-create a crime, the details wouldn't be similar. They would be exact.

This news upsets me a little. On the way to work, I mailed the letter to Josh. It was early enough that the post office parking lot was empty, so no one saw the surgical gloves on my hands as I slipped the letter into the slot. But if I had seen the news, I would have changed the letter. I would have told Josh the media is wrong, and, as usual, they're just making things up. The old victims are not being re-created, so stop talking about all the various ways they were tortured.

My daughter does not need to hear it.

But I did not see the news, did not hear about Bianca, and now it is too late.

In the clubhouse, Josh is on multiple screens, looking exhausted but wired. He is still standing across from the Lancaster Hotel. The daylight makes the building almost look gaudy.

"While we know Naomi George was the woman found in a Dumpster behind this hotel, none of the other reports out there have been confirmed. However, our sources are telling us that Naomi had only been dead for one day before she was found . . ."

The GPS data for Millicent does not show anything unusual on that day. She didn't even go to Joe's Deli—only the school when she dropped off the kids, the office, several houses for sale, the grocery store, and a gas station. No indication of where Naomi had been held. Not unless it was inside one of the open houses. That seems unlikely, given that people go in and out of them all day long.

Not that it mattered at this point, because Naomi has been found. And tomorrow, Josh will get my letter.

He won't wait to get it on the air. Last time, I had expected the police to spend more time examining it, but the news about it came out almost right away. This one should be the same. It looks exactly the same, smells the same, and even the paper comes from the same ream. There will be no doubt it came from the same person as the others. If I were a gambling man, I would bet the letter will be all over the news before I even get home from work.

But I am not a gambler. In thirty-nine years, I have turned into a planner. Maybe even a pretty good one.

Forty-nine

HARD TO TELL if I won or lost my imaginary bet. It is a matter of degrees, or in this case a matter of hours.

My thought was that Josh would go live with the letter just before the evening news, so it would be on every channel by the time people sat down for dinner. Instead, it comes hours earlier, while Jenna and I are at Dr. Beige's office. He thinks she needs therapy more often. I think she needs a new doctor. Since Jenna started seeing him, she has gone from cutting off her hair to making herself sick to hitting someone with a rock.

Millicent and I divide up the appointments now. We both cannot take off from work three times a week, which is what Dr. Beige recommends after the Krav Maga incident. Today is my turn in the waiting room, where my options are therapeutic comic books, educational magazines, or TV. No one else is around, except a stern-looking receptionist who wears a jet-black wig and ignores everyone. I turn on a game show and play along in my head.

The story breaks about ten minutes into Jenna's appointment. Josh appears on the screen, and after a brief introduction, he starts reading Owen's letter out loud.

The receptionist looks up.

As Josh reads the words I wrote, a chill runs up my back. When he gets to the end, to Owen's final goodbye, I have to stop myself from smiling. Owen really sounds like a cocky bastard in that letter.

Goodbye.
  Finally.

Josh rereads the letter two more times before Jenna comes out of Dr. Beige's office. She looks bored.

The doctor is behind her. He looks pleased.

"Switch," she says. It is my turn to go into the office, so Dr. Beige can feed me a bowl of his oatmeal-colored nonsense.

Today, I refuse. "I apologize, but we just don't have the time. Would you be available for a call later?"

The good doctor does not look pleased with me.

I do not care.

"That would be fine," he says. "If I'm unable to take the call, just leave a—"

"Sounds great. Thank you so much."

I offer my hand, and it takes him a second to shake it. "Well, then. Goodbye."

"Bye."

As soon as we walk into the parking lot, Jenna looks at me sideways.

"You're being weird," she says.

"I thought I was always weird."

"Weirder than usual."

"That's pretty weird."

"Dad." She crosses her arms over her chest and stares at me.

"Want a hot dog?"

Jenna looks at me like I'd suggested we have a drink. "A *hot dog*?"

"Yeah. You know, a little tube of meat or whatever, in a bun with mustard and—"

"Mom doesn't allow hot dogs."

"I'll tell her to join us."

I think Jenna's head explodes a little at this thought, but she gets into the car without another word.

TOP DOG SERVES thirty-five varieties of hot dogs, including tofu. This is what Millicent orders. And she does not say a word when Rory orders two all-beef chili dogs. It feels like a celebration, because it is. Owen is gone for good. The news is all over the TV screens mounted above our heads. Today, everything has gone according to plan and everyone seems to feel it.

"Can home go back to normal now?" Rory asks.

Millicent smiles. "Define 'normal.'"

"Not on blackout. Back in civilization."

"You want to watch the news?" I say.

"I don't want to be banned from watching the news."

Jenna rolls her eyes. "You just want to impress Faith."

And just like that, I know Rory's blond friend is named Faith.

"Who's Faith?" Millicent says.

"No one," Rory says.

Jenna giggles. Rory pinches her, and she squeaks.

"Stop it," she says.

"Shut up."

"You shut up."

"Wait, are you talking about Faith Hammond?" Millicent says.

Rory does not answer, which means yes. It also means Millicent knows Faith's parents, likely because she sold the Hammonds their house.

"Why didn't they catch him?" Jenna says. She is staring up at the TV.

Maybe we are not quite back to normal.

"They caught him before," Rory says. "And he got out."

"So they can't catch him?"

"They will. People like him don't stay free forever," I say.

Rory opens his mouth to say something, and Millicent shuts him up with a look.

Everything I think of to say sounds stupid in my head, so I keep my mouth shut. Not even Rory speaks. No one does until Jenna says something.

"I don't feel so good." She rubs her stomach. Jenna had the barbecue-and-onion dog, which was almost as large as my chili cheese dog. I do not think it's the stress that has upset her stomach today.

Millicent gives me the look.

I nod. Yes, this is my fault for suggesting the hot dogs.

Millicent grabs her bag and motions for us to go. She has been a good sport about the hot-dog thing, considering we did not discuss it beforehand, and I take her hand in mine. We follow the kids out to the parking lot.

"And how's your stomach?" she says.

"Perfect. Yours?"

"Never better."

I lean over and try to kiss her. She turns away.

"Your breath is disgusting."

"And yours smells like tofu."

She laughs and I laugh, and my stomach does not feel nearly as good as I claimed. As soon as we get home, both Jenna and I are sick. She goes upstairs to the bathroom, but I can't make it. I end up using the one in the hall.

Millicent runs between the two, bringing us ginger ale and cold compresses.

"Sick as dogs!" Rory yells. He laughs, and inside I am laughing with him.

Tonight, everything is funny, even while I am sick on the bathroom floor. Tonight, it feels like I have exhaled.

I didn't even realize I'd been holding my breath.

Fifty

THAT HOT DOG kept me up at night, so I sleep in a little the next morning. By the time I get out of the house, it's too late to stop at the EZ-Go. Instead, I go to a coffee shop just outside the Hidden Oaks gate. It's the kind with five-dollar coffee and a male barista who has an obnoxious beard and stares at the TV. He shakes his head at it as he pours me a plain cup of coffee.

"I gotta stop watching the news," he says.

I nod, understanding this more than he knows. "It'll only depress you."

"Word."

I did not know people still said "Word" in a real way, but this big bearded fellow says it like he means it.

I leave without asking about the news. They are still talking about whether or not Owen is really gone, but there is no real news. No updates. Just new ways of repeating the old.

And already, Owen is starting to fade. He is still the lead story but no longer dominates the entire broadcast.

Just as I thought.

And now, my thoughts revolve around my family, my kids. About Rory's girlfriend, whom I still haven't met. I did figure out the Hammonds live on the next block. It would take Rory all of sixty seconds to get from our house to theirs if he cut through the middle of the block. I should have known this already, should have known Rory was sneaking out, but I was too busy doing it myself. Now I am making up for lost time.

Jenna has a new fascination with makeup. This has just started in the past week, perhaps because she is no longer trying to hide from Owen. I caught her putting lip gloss on before we left for school one morning, and Millicent said it looked like someone had been in our bathroom.

And she still has that knife under her mattress. I am starting to wonder if she forgot it was there.

These are all things I would miss if I were still distracted by Owen, by Naomi and Annabelle and Petra. I cannot remember the last time I charged the disposable phone.

And Millicent. We have talked about having a real date night. It has not happened yet, but when it does, we will not talk about Holly or Owen or anything of the sort. In the meantime, she has started an anti–hot dog crusade on the Internet.

I took the tracker off her car. Now, I want to look at my *wife*, not the blue dot representing my wife.

Even work has been booming, I have two new clients, because my schedule is no longer as erratic. Most of my day is at the club, and so when I'm not teaching, I have time to network.

Andy. I haven't spoken to him since he moved out of Hidden Oaks. He left right after Trista died; he put the house up for sale, and I haven't seen him since. He no longer comes to the clubhouse. It doesn't seem right that I have let him disappear out of my life. In part, that's been because of my own schedule. But it is also because of Trista.

I call him to see how he is. Andy does not answer and does not call back. I make a half-hearted attempt to search for him online, to try and figure out where he is living now, but I give up after a few minutes.

I still have that bottle of eye drops, though I have seen no evidence that Rory, or anyone, is using drugs of any kind. It doesn't make sense why they are in the house, much less in the pantry. Eye drops don't need to be hidden.

KEKONA HAS GONE back to Hawaii for a month, so my first client is Mrs. Leland. She does not like to talk about crime or Owen or anything of the sort. Mrs. Leland is a serious player, who only talks about tennis.

After her lesson is over, I have a minute between clients, just long enough to see a text from Millicent.

?

I do not know what it means or what she is asking, so I text back:

What?

Midway through my lesson with a retiree named Arthur, Millicent sends me a link to a news story. The headline does not make sense.

OWEN IS DEAD

I read the story once, then again, and the third time it becomes more unbelievable than the first.

Fifteen years ago, Owen Oliver Riley was charged with murder and let go on a technicality. He vanished without a trace until recently, when the body of a young woman was found and someone claiming to be Riley sent a letter to a local reporter, taking responsibility for the murder and promising to kill another woman, even naming the day she would disappear. When a second woman's body was found, it seemed he had made good on his promise. The next letter claimed that he was done and would now leave for good. But was he ever here at all?

"No," says Jennifer Riley. Owen's sister contacted the local police last week and subsequently issued a statement.

In a twist so shocking it hardly seems real, she claims that fifteen years ago, after Owen Riley was released, both she and her brother moved to Europe. Neither returned to the United States, not even for a visit, her statement says, and they changed their first names and lived in anonymity.

Five years ago, her brother was diagnosed with pancreatic cancer, she told police, and after several rounds of radiation, he finally succumbed to his illness and passed away. His body was cremated, her statement says.

Owen Riley's obituary did not appear in any U.S. newspaper. It was announced only in a U.K. paper under his pseudonym, Jennifer Riley claims. She provided a copy of it to police, along with a death certificate. Authorities are currently working to verify the information.

Until recently, Jennifer Riley told police, she had no idea her brother had "returned" to the area where they grew up. She went on to say, "I wanted nothing to do with this. After leaving the area so many years ago, I wanted nothing to do with it. However, an old friend of mine reached out and convinced me to say something, because the police were convinced it was Owen.

"I will state this as clearly as possible: The recent murders of two young women are tragic and heartbreaking. However, I need to make it clear that my brother had nothing to do with them."

Fifty-one

MY PHONE IS lying on the cement court, the screen shattered. I do not remember dropping it. Or maybe I threw it.

A hand is on my arm. Arthur, my client, is staring at me. His eyes are hidden under thick grey brows, and they are crinkled up. Worried. "Are you okay?" he says.

No. Okay is not what I am. "I'm sorry. I have to go. It's a family—"

"Of course. Go."

I pick up my phone and bag and leave the court. On the way to the parking lot, I hear people say hello but do not see their faces. All I can see is that headline:

OWEN IS DEAD

In the car, with the engine running, it occurs to me I have no idea where Millicent is. Not without that tracker on her car.

Through the broken screen, I send her a text.

Date night

Her reply:

Date lunch. Now.

I am already pulling out of the parking lot.

The kids are at school, so we meet at home. Her car is out front, and she is inside, pacing the length of the family room. Today her shoes are navy blue, and they do not make a sound when she walks. Her hair is shorter, cut above her shoulders, because she didn't want Jenna to be the only girl in the family with short hair.

When I walk in, she stops pacing and we look at each other. Nothing to say.

Other than we screwed up.

She smiles a little. Not a happy smile. "Didn't see this coming."

"We couldn't have."

I reach out to her, and she comes to me, into my arms. My heart is beating faster than normal, and she leans her head against it.

"They'll start looking for the real killer," I say.

"Yes." She leans her head back and looks up at me.

"We could just leave."

"Leave?"

"Move away. We don't have to live here. We don't even have to live in this state. I can teach tennis anywhere. You can sell real estate anywhere." The idea has just come to me, as I am standing here with Millicent. "Pick a place."

"You aren't serious."

"Why not?"

She moves away from me and starts to pace again. I can see her building lists in her mind, trying to figure out everything that needs to be done. "It's the middle of the school year."

"I know."

"I wouldn't even know where to pick."

"We can figure it out together."

She goes silent.

I repeat the obvious. "They're going to look for the real killer."

This was never a problem before. No bodies had been found, not until Lindsay. Up until then, no one even knew there was a killer. They weren't looking for anyone.

Now they are. And they know it was someone pretending to be Owen.

"They'll never know it was us," she says.

"Never?"

Millicent shakes her head. "I don't know how. We basically split everything up. I never touched the letters—"

"But wherever you kept Naomi—"

"You never even saw it. What about you? Did anyone see you with—"

"No. I never spoke to Naomi," I say.

"Never?" Millicent is silent for a moment. "That's good, then. No one saw you with her."

"No."

"And Lindsay?"

I shake my head. Lindsay and I spoke while hiking. "No one saw us."

"Good."

"Jenna," I say. "I almost think we should move because of—"

"Let's at least wait and make sure this is real. That it isn't some kind of hoax."

I smile. The irony is too thick not to. "Like Owen's letters. A hoax."

"Yes. Like that."

The reminder on my phone beeps. My next client is in fifteen minutes. Either I leave or I cancel.

"Go," she says. "There's nothing we can do now except wait."

"If it's real—"

"We'll discuss it again."

I walk over and kiss her on the forehead.

She puts her hand on my cheek. "We'll be fine."

"We always are."

"Yes."

THE KIDS HAVE already heard the news. We had planned to tell them together that evening, at dinner, but they already knew. The Internet and their friends are faster than us.

If Rory cares, he does not show it. His hand is clasped around his phone, the lifeline to his girlfriend.

Jenna's face is still as stone. Her eyes, normally so expressive, look right through us. She is not listening, not even here in the room with us. I do not know where she is. She does not speak until Millicent and I are done telling her what we have told her for weeks: You are safe.

I don't think she believes us. I'm not even sure I believe us. Everything she thought was true is turning out to be wrong. Owen was never here. It was always someone else, and no one has any idea who.

I cannot blame her for shutting down. I want to do the same thing.

When we are done talking, Rory jumps up and heads for the stairs. Already texting.

Jenna keeps staring.

"Baby?" I say, reaching over to touch her hand. "You okay?"

She turns to me, her eyes focusing. "So it's all a lie. The killer may not even be gone."

"We don't know that yet," Millicent says.

"But maybe."

I nod. "Maybe."

A minute passed, then another.

"Okay," she says, slipping her hand out from under mine. She stands up. "I'm going upstairs."

"Are you feeling—"

"I'm fine."

Millicent and I watch her go.

The rest of my evening is spent on the Internet, researching a new place for us to live. I flip between sites about weather, schools, cost of living, and the news.

It feels strange to not know what is coming next. Ever since I wrote that first letter to Josh, most of the news has not surprised me. I already knew what the letters would say and could guess how the pundits would analyze them. Not even Naomi's body was a surprise. I didn't know the details, but I knew it would be found.

The only thing that surprised me was the paper cuts.

Now, nothing is familiar, nothing is expected. I do not like it.

Fifty-two

I WATCH THE STORY unfold on TV as if I am not involved. As if I'm just another spectator. And, because I have no power to change the course of this story, I hope. Every time I turn on the news, I hope Owen's sister is a liar. But one night, I am outside on the back porch, watching the eleven o'clock broadcast, and this is not what Josh says.

He is in the studio tonight, wearing a jacket and tie, and his face looks like it was shaved minutes before the show started. Josh sounds like a serious reporter when he says that Jennifer Riley is coming back into the country. She wants to clear her brother's name.

The urge to throw my phone, again, is stopped by a scraping sound on the side of the house. I get up and look.

Rory.

Only he would continue to sneak out after getting caught sneaking out.

Or rather, only he could continue to get away with sneaking out after he was caught sneaking out. I wonder how many times I've missed him.

He sees me just as his feet hit the ground. Rory was on his way out, not back in.

"Oh," he says. "Hey."

"Going out for a little night air?"

He shrugs, admitting nothing.

"Come sit down," I say.

Instead of sitting on the porch, we go out farther into the yard. We have a picnic table with an umbrella on the far side, in between the big oak tree and the dismantled playset.

Rory says, "You don't have a lot of room to talk about sneaking out."

Days ago, when Owen was supposed to be gone forever, that comment might not have bothered me. I had been looking forward to talking with my son about his first girlfriend. Now, it just feels like a chore.

I point to one of the benches. "Sit. Your. Ass. Down."

He does.

"First," I say, "you may have noticed your sister has been having a difficult time. And I am sure you, her only brother, do not want to make her feel worse?"

He shakes his head.

"Of course you don't. So I know you won't tell her this little theory of yours about how I'm cheating on your mother."

"Theory?"

I stare at him.

He shakes his head again. "No. I'm not going to say anything."

"And I know you are not about to compare me to you and the fact that you are sneaking out late at night. Because you are less than half my age. You are not even close to being an adult. You do not get to sneak out."

He nods.

"What?" I say.

"No. I wasn't going to compare us."

"And I also know that if I ask you why you were sneaking out, you are not going to say it was to hang out with Daniel. Because that's not what you're doing, is it?"

"No."

"You're sneaking out to see Faith Hammond."

"Yes."

"Perfect. I'm glad we cleared that up."

Rory's phone buzzes. His eyes go back and forth, between the phone and me, but he does not look at it.

"Go ahead," I say.

"It's okay."

"Don't keep Faith waiting."

He checks the phone and sends a text while pushing that red hair out of his eyes. Faith answers right away, and he sends another. The conversation continues, and I wait until he puts the phone down on the table. Faceup.

"Sorry," he says.

I sigh.

I am not angry at Rory. He is just a kid who has discovered girls aren't so bad after all. He used to say girls were "heinous and foul and, most especially, ugly." The quote is from a book he'd read, and it always made me laugh. I would turn to Millicent and say, "You're the one who brought them to the library every week." If we happened to be in the kitchen, she would snap the dish towel at me. Once, she snapped it so hard it cut my arm. The wound was just superficial, barely breaking the skin, but Rory was impressed with his mother. Less so with me.

And now, he is leaving late at night to see a little blonde named Faith.

"Does she sneak out, too?" I say. "Do you meet somewhere?"

"Sometimes. But I can get up to her room, too."

I want to ban him from doing this, put a lock on his window, and call Faith's parents and say they are too young and it's too dangerous. Owen is dead, and a killer is on the loose.

Except it isn't true. I just have to pretend it is. Just like I have to pretend I don't remember my first girlfriend.

"You have to stop," I say. "You've seen the news. It's too dangerous for both of you to be out alone at night."

"Yeah, I know, but—"

"And you shouldn't be sneaking out at all. If I told your mother, she would lock your window and put cameras all over the house."

Rory's eyebrows shoot up. "She doesn't know?"

"If she did, you'd be grounded until college. And so would your girlfriend."

"Okay. We'll stop."

I take a deep breath. Just because I'm angry does not mean I am irresponsible. "And since you have a girlfriend, do you have protect—"

"Dad, I know how to buy condoms."

"Good, good. So just text her at night, okay? See her during the day?"

He nods and gets up quick, as if he is scared I might change my mind.

"One more thing," I say. "And answer me straight."

"Okay."

"Are you taking any drugs?"

"No."

"You don't smoke pot?"

He shakes his head. "I swear I don't."

I let him go. Right now, I don't have time to figure out if he is lying.

When I'm not watching the news, all I can think about is what else we might have missed. All the ways we might get caught, all the forensic data I have learned about on TV. The DNA, trace evidence, fibers—it all runs through my mind like it makes sense to me, which it does not, but I know it will not point to me. I never said a word to Naomi, much less touched her. Any evidence they find will lead to Millicent.

* * *

THE FIRST TIME I see Owen's sister is on TV. Owen was in his thirties when he was killing; now, he would have been about fifty. Jennifer looks a little younger, midforties. She has the same blue eyes, but her hair is a dirtier shade of blond. She is so thin her collarbone sticks out, as do the veins on her neck. They say the camera puts on ten pounds, and if that's true, Jennifer must look sickly in real life.

She is on every screen in the clubhouse, where the lunch crowd has stuck around for another cocktail so they can watch the press conference. This is the first time the public has seen Owen's sister.

The police chief is on one side of her; the medical examiner is on the other. One has hair, the other doesn't, and their paunches are the same size.

Jennifer says that she is Owen Oliver Riley's sister and that we are all wrong about these murders.

"I can prove Owen has not killed anyone in the last five years. I came all the way back here to make sure everyone understands that my brother is dead." Jennifer holds up a piece of paper and says it is Owen's death certificate, signed by a coroner in Great Britain and stamped with an official seal. She says it again. *"Dead."*

The medical examiner steps to the microphone and confirms what Jennifer has said.

Dead.

Next comes the chief of police, who goes on and on about how it was unavoidable that his police department had zeroed in on Owen, but they had been misled. He also confirms Jennifer's claim.

Dead.

We are all clear now. We believe her. Owen is dead, and the police are going back to the evidence to see what they missed.

But first, Jennifer has one more thing to say. *"I am sorry for the families. Sorry that so much time has been wasted focusing on my brother instead of looking for the real killer. An old friend contacted me about what was going on here in Woodview. When she begged me to come back, I knew I had to do the right thing."*

Jennifer motions to someone behind her, and the medical examiner steps to the side. The camera zooms in on the friend.

My head spins so fast I almost lose consciousness.

The woman who called Jennifer Riley is plump and blond, and has a smile that lights up the screen.

Denise. The woman from behind the counter at Joe's Deli.

Fifty-three

THE GPS TRACKER sits on the dashboard of my car. I flip it over on one side, then the other, and start all over again. It is the same thing I have been doing in my mind after the woman from Joe's Deli, Millicent's new favorite lunch spot, appeared on TV.

Denise. The same woman who served Jenna and me.

This is a coincidence. It must be. The fact that Owen is dead does not help Millicent and me. It hurts us.

And if Joe's was an organic bistro serving roast beef from cows raised on organic grass, it would never occur to me that this is not a coincidence. But Joe's is not. It is a deli where *organic* is a word from another language.

If I could ask Millicent about this new affection for cheap deli sandwiches, I would. But I am not supposed to know. This is information I acquired by spying on my wife.

I'd never done it before. Thought about it, but never did it. Not even back when Millicent was working with a man who liked her as more than a colleague. It was obvious from the moment I met him.

Cooper. The one-time frat boy who never married and didn't want to. What he wanted to do was sleep with Millicent.

Cooper was the one who went with Millicent to the conference in Miami. The weekend Crystal kissed me.

I was convinced Cooper had done the same thing to Millicent.

When they came back, that belief almost made me spy on both of them. I did not. At least not on her. But Cooper, I watched him long enough to figure out he wanted to sleep with every woman. It wasn't just Millicent.

And as far as I could tell, they had not slept together.

Now that I have spied on my wife, I see the problem with it. I cannot do anything with the information. The tracker is on my dashboard, and I am sitting in the parking lot of the club staring at the gadget, because spying only leads to more spying. If I had known it was such a vicious circle, I would never have done it.

As I go back and forth, Millicent texts me.

Chicken pho for dinner?

Sounds good.

I wait for another text, one that says *date night* or has some reference to the news today, but my phone stays dark.

WHEN I GET home, Millicent's car is already in the garage. I think about putting the tracker on it again but don't.

She is making chicken pho in the kitchen. I start to help her, slicing vegetables while she adds fresh onion and ginger to the broth.

The kids are not around.

"Upstairs," she says before I ask. "Homework."

"Did you see the news?"

She purses her lips and nods. "He's dead."

"They only said it a thousand times."

I smile a little. She does, too. We cannot change the fact that Owen is dead.

We are silent for a few minutes, working on dinner, and I try to come up with a way to mention Denise. The kids show up before an idea does.

I reiterate that they shouldn't pay any attention to everything going on in the news. "Nothing is going to happen to you."

This directly contradicts what I told Rory the other night, when I said it was too dangerous for him to sneak out, but Rory is not beating up kids with rocks. Jenna is.

Still, he notices. He rolls his eyes at me. We haven't said a lot to each other since our talk in the backyard. I am not sure if he is angry because he was caught sneaking out or angry because I asked if he used drugs. Probably both.

When no one has anything else to say about Owen, the conversation turns to Saturday. Rory is playing golf. Jenna has a soccer game, and it is Millicent's turn to go. I am working. We will all meet for lunch.

Owen does not come up again until later, after dinner is over and the dishes are done and the kids have gone to sleep. Millicent is in our bathroom, getting ready for bed, while I watch the news and wait for her. She comes out wearing one of my T-shirts from the club and a pair of sweats, her face shiny with lotion. She rubs it on her hands while staring at the TV.

Josh is standing in front of the Lancaster Hotel, where Jennifer Riley is staying. He talks about the press conference, then cuts to the video.

"I haven't seen this," Millicent says.

"No?"

"No. I saw the story online."

I turn up the volume. They show snippets from the press conference, including every time someone said the word *dead*. No one said Owen had passed away, not even his sister.

When Denise comes on the screen, I look at Millicent.

She tilts her head to the side.

I wait.

When the clip ends, she says, "That's weird."

"What's weird?"

"I know that woman. She's a client."

"Really?"

"She owns a deli. A pretty successful one, too. She's looking for a house."

Millicent walks back into the bathroom.

Inside, I exhale. Denise is a client. It had never occurred to me that she'd have enough money to buy a house—at least not the kind of houses Millicent sells—and yet she does.

I am so stupid.

Though I am relieved to know this has all been a weird coincidence, wholly caused by my own spying, our problem has not gone away. It's worse. Owen is dead, and the police are looking for the real killer.

The chief said a new detective has been assigned to the case. The detective is coming in from another precinct and will review the whole case with fresh eyes. I should have looked at Denise with fresh eyes.

When Millicent comes out of the bathroom, the TV and lights are off. She gets into bed, and I turn over to face her, even though it's too dark to see anything.

"I don't want to move away," she says.

"I know."

She slips her hand into mine. "I'm worried."

"About Jenna? Or about the police?"

"Both."

"What if we go out of town?" I say.

"But I just said—"

"I mean take a vacation."

She is quiet. In my mind, I run through all the reasons we cannot go. The kids would miss school. We don't have extra money. She has several deals pending. I should not cancel on my clients again. The same reasons must be running through her mind.

"I'll think about it," she says. "Let's see how things go."

"Okay."

"Good."

"The chicken pho was great," I say.

"You're silly."

"Even if we don't go on vacation now, we should when this is all over."

"We will."

"Promise."

"I promise," she says. "Now go to sleep."

Fifty-four

THE NEW DETECTIVE is a woman. Her full name is Claire Wellington, a name that sounds like her family dates back to the *Mayflower*, but I bet it doesn't. Not that it matters.

Claire is a severe-looking woman with short brown hair, pale skin, and brown lipstick. She wears no-nonsense pantsuits, all in dark colors, and never smiles. I know this because she is on TV all the time. Her idea of detective work is asking the public for help.

"I know someone in this community saw something, even if they don't realize it. Maybe it was the night Naomi disappeared. Everyone was on guard that night, and everyone knew something was going to happen. Or maybe it was when Naomi George's body was dumped behind the Lancaster Hotel. Please, think back to that night, think about what you were doing, who you were with, and what you saw. You may have seen something and not even realized it."

A website has been set up for people to send in information. Or they can stay anonymous and call a special tip line for anything related to Lindsay and Naomi.

I do not like this development. All sorts of new information might be dredged up because of Claire's public relations tour on TV. Josh is already reporting that the police have dozens of new leads.

"The police have also made use of an innovative computer program developed at UF Sarasota, where students have written an algorithm that can sort through the tips and match words used repeatedly. The tips are then ranked in order from the most useful to the least."

This all happens within days of Claire's arrival. It is bad enough that I have to see her on television. All. The. Time. Now I also have to listen about how innovative and effective she is. Even at home she is unavoidable. Millicent has been insisting that we don't watch TV in the evenings, because Claire always pops up during the commercials. The local stations have started running public service announcements about the tip line.

Instead of TV, we play games together. Millicent digs up a deck of cards and a rack of plastic chips, and we teach the kids how to play poker, because this is preferable to watching Claire.

Rory already knows how to play. He has a poker app on his phone.

Jenna picks it up fast, because she picks up everything fast. She also has the best poker face. I think it's even better than Millicent's.

My poker face is terrible, and I lose every hand.

While we are playing, Rory mentions that there will be an assembly at school tomorrow. Millicent furrows her brow and then unfurrows it. She is trying to furrow less because of wrinkles.

"I didn't get a notice about an assembly," she says.

"That detective is coming to school," Jenna says.

"The chick," Rory says.

Millicent's brow furrows again.

"Why is the *female* detective coming to your school?" I say.

Rory shrugs. "Probably to ask us if we saw anything. Same thing she's been doing on TV. Daniel said she's going to all the schools."

Jenna nods as if she'd heard the same thing.

"She's annoying," Rory says. "But at least we get out of a class."

Millicent gives him a look. He pretends not to see it and studies his cards.

"Well, I like her," Jenna says.

"You like the detective?" I say.

She nods. "She seems tough. Like she's really going to get him."

"Oh, I'd agree with that," Rory says. "It's like she's obsessed or something."

It figures that the woman who might catch us also makes Jenna feel better. "Everyone has a lot of confidence in her," I say.

"I hope I'll get to talk to her," Jenna says.

"I'm sure she is very busy."

"Obviously. I'm just saying."

JENNA AND RORY'S school does not hold assemblies in the gymnasium. It has a special hall, and it is named after the donor who paid for it. When I arrive, the hall is packed with kids, faculty, and parents. With as much as Claire has been in the news, she is almost a celebrity.

She is taller than expected, and even in a crowded room she is intimidating. Claire does not want to talk about herself, her past, or her experience. She begins by telling the kids that they are all safe.

"Whoever killed these women is not looking for you. He is looking for women who are older than all of you. Chances are you will never cross paths with the person who killed Naomi and Lindsay."

Jenna is sitting with her friends just to the right of the stage. Even from the back, I can see her leaning forward, trying to hear and see everything.

Rory is the middle, sitting with his girlfriend, and he may or may not be paying attention. Hard to tell.

"However," Claire says, "if you have crossed paths with this killer, you may not even know it. You may have seen something that you don't even know is important. Anything that you think is unusual, or that stands out, could be important."

She says the same things she said on TV but with smaller words and shorter sentences. She ends by saying she will be available afterward if anyone wants to talk. This is why I am here. First, to make sure Jenna has a chance to meet Claire. Second, to meet her for myself.

Jenna's friends are around, so she does not give me a hug. Together, we wait to speak to Claire. A jumbled line of people has formed in front of her, and when our turn comes I step up to Claire and introduce myself. She is tall enough that we stand eye to eye. On TV, her eyes look plain brown. Up close, I see flecks of gold.

"This is my daughter, Jenna," I say.

Instead of asking Jenna how old she is or what grade she's in, Claire asks her if she wants to be a detective.

"I would love it!" Jenna says.

"Then the first thing you need to know is that everything matters. Even the small things that seem like nothing."

Jenna nods. Her eyes are so bright. "I can do that."

"I'm sure you can." Claire turns to me. "Your daughter is going to be a fine detective."

"She already is, I think."

We smile at each other.

She moves on to the next person, turning her back to us.

Jenna is bouncing up and down on her toes. "You think I can really be a detective?"

"You can be anything you want to be."

She stops bouncing. "Dad, you sound like a commercial."

"I'm sorry. But it's true. And I think you'd be a great detective."

She sighs and turns back to her friends, who are waving at her. She brushes me off when I try to give her a hug. "I gotta go."

I watch her run over to her friends, who react to her news with more enthusiasm than I did.

Dad failure number 79,402, and she's only thirteen.

I am grateful for Claire, who is so careful about making the kids feel safe. She has made Jenna happier than I have seen her in a while.

That still does not make me like Claire. In fact, now that I've met her, I hate her.

Fifty-five

B EFORE I HAVE a chance to research our new detective, Jenna does. At dinner, we are treated to the life story of Claire Wellington, as per the Internet. Born in Chicago, college in New York, first job with the NYPD. She moved to the rural Midwest, where she became a detective and was part of a drug task force. Claire left the small towns for a bigger one, eventually getting promoted to homicide detective. She was part of a team that investigated a group of killings known as the River Park Murders. They arrested the killer within two months of starting their investigation.

Claire went on to become one of the most successful homicide detectives in her department. Her average clearance rate was 5 percent higher than everyone else's.

She is as formidable as she looks.

The kids and I are not the only ones who meet Claire. Millicent does as well. Claire needed a place to rent, because staying in a hotel is too expensive for the police budget, so she called the real estate office looking for a rental. Small, simple, and furnished, with a monthly lease. Millicent does not handle rentals, but she was in the office when Claire stopped by.

Early Sunday morning, when we are alone in the kitchen and the kids are still asleep, I ask Millicent what she thinks of Claire Wellington.

"She's very tall."

"She's smart," I say.

"And we aren't?"

We exchange a smile.

Millicent has just returned from a run. She stands at the sink, in her spandex, and I admire the view. She catches me and raises an eyebrow.

"Want to go back to bed?" I say.

"You want to show me how smart you are?"

"I do."

"But I need a shower."

"Want company?"

She does.

WE START IN the shower and move to the bed. Our sex is cozy and familiar, rather than passionate and furtive. Not a bad thing.

When Rory wakes up, we are still in bed. I know it's Rory, because he cannot shut a door without slamming it and his footsteps are heavy when he goes down to the kitchen. Not long after, Jenna gets up and follows the same routine—bathroom and then kitchen—but everything is softer.

Millicent is curled up beside me. She is naked and warm.

"The coffee is still on," she says. "They'll wonder where we are."

"Let them." I have no intention of getting out of bed until I have to. I stretch out and close my eyes.

The TV turns on, the volume loud. The kids are probably glad we aren't downstairs. Normally, we do not watch TV on Sunday mornings, so for them this is a treat. They flip between cartoons and a movie with explosions.

"I bet they're eating cereal," Millicent says.

"We have cereal?"

"Organic. No sugar."

"We have milk?"

"Soy."

I do not say "yuck" out loud, but I think it. "That's not bad, then."

"I guess not."

She snuggles a little closer.

This is what life was like before Holly. Everything moved a bit slower, less frantically, without much excitement.

The days blended together, punctuated only by big events. Our first house was so tiny, but it felt huge, at least until we outgrew it— followed by Millicent's first huge sale, Jenna's first day of school, our bigger house and bigger mortgage. The paper cut on Rory's hand.

When Jenna was four, she got sick with a cold that turned into bronchitis. She could sleep for only an hour or so before the coughing would wake her up. Millicent and I spent three nights sleeping in her room, me on the floor and Millicent in Jenna's little bed. Between the two of us, we helped Jenna get more sleep than us.

I taught Rory how to ride a bike. He would never admit it, but he used training wheels for an extended period of time. Balance was not his thing. Still isn't.

None of this was exciting, not at the time. They were routines and responsibilities, with an occasional smile or even a laugh. Moments of happiness followed by long stretches of blurry, repetitive days.

Now, I want it all back. Maybe I have had too much excitement, or this is too exciting, but either way it is not what I want.

"Hey," Millicent says. She sits up in bed, covered by the sheet. Her red hair is tangled. "You hear that?"

Downstairs, the breaking-news music blares out of the TV. It cuts off when one of the kids changes the channel to a cartoon.

I roll my eyes. "News breaks every five minutes." I pull Millicent back down on the bed, into my arms, with no intention of moving unless the police break down our door. "Probably some celebrity got arrested."

"Or died."

"Or a politician got caught cheating," I say.

"That's not even newsworthy."

I laugh and bury myself deeper under the covers.

My hope is that they have arrested someone for the murders. It would not be Naomi and Lindsay's killer, but it would be someone who has done other bad things. Someone who deserves to be locked up before he hurts someone. I imagine him as a disheveled, slovenly man who has crazy eyes.

"Okay, that's it," Millicent says. "I'm getting up." She throws off the covers all at once, like the old Band-Aid trick. It works. The bed isn't cozy without her.

She throws on a robe and heads downstairs. I jump in the shower first.

The kids are on the couch, watching a teenage show about aliens. Their empty cereal bowls are on the coffee table, and I am surprised Millicent has let them stay there. I find her in the kitchen, standing next to the coffee maker. Her cup is tipped over, and the coffee is running off the side of the counter, onto the floor. She isn't even looking at it. Her eyes are focused on the little TV set she keeps in the kitchen.

Josh is on the screen. He is standing in front of a woodsy area so thick with bushes I cannot see the building behind him, just the steeple high above the trees. I do not know the place or where it's located. The wooden sign in front of the church is weather-beaten and faded. Josh's mouth is moving, but no sound comes out. The volume is too low.

I do not need it anyway. The news is plastered across the bottom of the screen, in red.

HOUSE OF GOD OR HOUSE OF HORRORS?

UNDERGROUND DUNGEON FOUND IN ABANDONED CHURCH

Fifty-six

FOR A SECOND, I believed Millicent was upset because the news was horrific, because it was shocking, because it had nothing to do with us. Or I like to think I believed that.

Within another second, I knew it was her. The church was where she'd brought Lindsay and Naomi.

"A *church*?"

We are back upstairs, in our bedroom, but the mood could not be more different. There is nothing sexy about a dungeon in a church.

Our family does not go to church, and never has. Millicent was raised agnostic; I was raised Catholic and lapsed early. Church is where we attend weddings, funerals, and bake sales. And even I think this location is one of the most disturbing choices Millicent could have made. The only place worse would have been a preschool.

Millicent is no longer shocked by the discovery, nor is she scared. She has turned defensive. "I needed a place. Somewhere they wouldn't even search."

"Keep your voice down." The kids are downstairs watching TV, but I am still afraid they will hear.

"No one found it, did they? Not when they were still alive."

"No. No one found the church until Claire came to town." According to Josh, they found the church because of a tip. Someone had seen a car in what used to be the parking lot but was now full of weeds.

Millicent stood in front of me, hands on hips. She is still wearing her robe.

Behind her, the TV is on in our bedroom. The press has not been let into the church, nor have any pictures been released, so Josh is repeating what his unnamed sources have said.

"A vile scene . . . chains attached to the walls . . . iron cuffs drenched in blood . . . even a veteran police officer was brought to tears . . . like something out of a movie."

Millicent flipped her hand, brushing the words away. "It is not drenched with blood. That room isn't a vault. It's a basement. And the church has to be a hundred years old. Who knows what's taken place in there?"

"But you cleaned it?"

Her eyes narrow. "Are you really asking me that?"

I throw up my hands as an answer.

Millicent walks up to me, her face closer to mine than when we were still in bed, but there is nothing cozy or warm about her. "Don't you dare second-guess me. Not now."

"I'm not—"

"You are. Stop."

Her robe swishes as she turns around and disappears into the bathroom.

I can understand her anger. She is angry the church was discovered and angry I am questioning her. But I would not have left that basement with a speck of blood in it. The whole thing would have been doused in ammonia or bleach or whatever gets rid of blood and fluids and DNA of any kind. Maybe I would have left behind a lit cigarette inside and let it burn, making it look like an accident.

I never got the chance to do any of that, because I did not know about the church. I could never bring myself to ask.

MILLICENT DECIDES WE should all go to the movies this afternoon. Given the circumstances, the suggestion is absurd, but I tell myself it has to be better than watching the news all day. Yes, it's a good idea to get out of the house. Out of my head. Away from Josh. I repeat this as I get dressed, trying to shove aside that church and its basement. It almost works.

"I'm not feeling very well." For emphasis, I hold my stomach.

Millicent gives me the look. "Maybe some popcorn would help."

"No, no, you guys go ahead. Have a good time."

They leave without me.

I do not turn on the news. Instead, I drive out to the church.

The TV is not good enough. I want to see it for myself, this place where Millicent kept Lindsay and Naomi alive.

It is out on a lonely road between nowhere and nothing. The only buildings along the way are a boarded-up bar, a run-down gas station, and an empty ranch at the end of a private road. This is why I never spotted the church on the GPS. The ranch is up for sale, and the address showed up on the tracker several times. She could walk out the back door of the ranch and be at the church in minutes. No one from the road would be able to see her.

The area is flooded with cars, TV vans, and lookie-loos. I put on a jacket and baseball cap, and try to blend in with the crowd.

Reporters are spread out in front of the church, and the steeple rises up behind all of them. They stand right in front of the yellow tape, which is protected by uniformed cops. Some are baby-faced. Others are bloated and on the verge of retirement.

I have never been this close to Josh, never seen him anywhere other than on TV. He is shorter and thinner than he looks on-screen.

An older woman is beside me, her eyes shifting between all three reporters.

"Excuse me, do you know if they've said anything new?" I ask.

"Since when?" Her voice has a smoker's rasp. She has a thick head of white hair and yellowy eyes.

"About half an hour."

"No, you haven't missed anything."

Through a thick block of trees, the top of a white tent is visible. It looks like the same kind used at weddings and kids' parties. "What's that?"

"The police set it up first thing. They call it 'home base.'"

"The chief's back there," says a man standing behind me. He is large everywhere, standing a good four inches taller than me and at least a foot wider.

"They want to make sure," he says.

"Make sure of what?"

"Make sure it was just those two women," he says. "And not more."

"God forbid," the woman says.

There were two others of course—Holly and Robin—but neither was kept in the basement.

Not that I know of, anyway.

A bright light flashes on as Josh goes live. Once again, he mentions his sources, none of whom have names.

They have given him more information about the underground room beneath the church, and he says they found something. On the wall, hidden in a corner, it looks like someone who was held captive tried to leave a message.

Fifty-seven

FOR A SECOND, I think about asking Josh if he has any further information. We have never spoken, I have never communicated with him outside of the letters, but this rumor about a hidden message makes me panic. Almost.

Instead of doing something stupid, like I have so often in the past, I step back. Consider. Evaluate. And I reach a conclusion: Nonsense. The story is all nonsense.

Josh's sources are wrong. If it took the police less than a day to find this so-called message, there is no chance Millicent would have missed it. She may not know her son is sneaking out at night, but she can spot dust from two rooms away. She would not miss a message on the wall.

And what kind of message would Naomi or Lindsay leave? *Help? I'm trapped?*

It is unfathomable that Millicent told them her real name, so they wouldn't have been able to leave behind their abductor's identity.

The hidden message must be a lie planted by Claire, no doubt to try and draw us out. Anyone who watches TV knows the police lie. This is likely enough to make me walk away. Go home. Talk to Millicent.

When I arrive, the house is empty. I turn on the TV and surf through the news. Josh is still talking about this possible message but has no further details. A reporter on another channel repeats what Josh has said. The third reporter talks about the church.

The Bread of Life Christian Church began with a single family and grew to a congregation of about fifty. Old pictures show a stern-looking group with worn faces and tattered clothing. In later years, the group appeared to have prospered, with a lot more bread; they were heavier, and a few even smiled. They peaked in the fifties and then declined into nothing by the eighties. As far as anyone knew, the building has been empty for at least twenty years. Because it is Sunday, the blueprints from the city planning office are not available, but local historians suspect the basement was part of the original building. It may have been a room for cold storage.

I surf between the channels, waiting for something new to happen. Millicent and the kids don't get home until about five. They spent the afternoon at the movies and the mall, where Jenna got yet another pair of shoes and Rory got a new hoodie. Both run upstairs, leaving Millicent and me alone.

"Feeling better?" she asks. It sounds sarcastic.

"Not really."

She raises an eyebrow.

The TV is off. I have no idea how much news she has heard. "They're talking about a message," I say.

"A what?" Millicent walks into the kitchen to start dinner. I follow her.

"A message on the wall. Left by someone held captive."

"Impossible."

I stare at her. She is ripping up lettuce to make a salad. "Yeah, that's what I figured," I say.

"Here, finish this." She slides the bowl and lettuce over to me. "I was thinking of tuna melts tonight."

"I ate the tuna for lunch."

"All of it?"

"Most."

Behind me, the refrigerator door bangs open. She does not say anything, but I can hear her anger.

The door slams shut.

"I suppose I can throw together an eggplant casserole or something," she says.

"Sounds perfect."

We work side by side; she slices the eggplant, and I grate cheese for the top of the casserole. When it finally goes into the oven, Millicent turns to me. The circles under her eyes are darker than ever.

"I'm sorry about earlier," she says.

"It's okay. We're both on edge, with Claire and this church and all."

"Are you scared?"

"No."

"Really?" She sounds surprised.

"Are you?"

"No."

"Then we're good, right?"

She slides her arms around my neck. "We're great."

It feels like we are.

I GO UP to say good night to the kids. Rory's light is off, but he is awake and using his phone.

Before I can say a word, he says, "Yes, I'm texting with Faith. And Daniel. And I'm playing a game, too."

"Are you doing any of them well?"

He lowers the phone and gives me that look. It is the same as Millicent's. "And I'm not smoking weed."

As expected, he's still angry.

"So how is the girlfriend?" I ask.

"Faith."

"How is Faith?"

He sighs. "Still my girlfriend."

"Not sneaking out tonight, are you?"

"Only if you don't."

"Rory."

"Yes, Father?" His voice drips with smart-ass. "What lesson do you want to teach me tonight?"

"Good night."

I shut the door before he can answer. I do not want to hear it. Not tonight.

Jenna is just getting into bed, and I sit down to talk to her. Both the kids already know about the church and the basement under it, the same way they know about everything faster than light. I wish there were a way to stop it, because she is just so young. Not young enough to still sleep with stuffed animals, but young enough to keep them around. But she still knows too much about this kind of thing. Girls are abducted and locked up in books, movies, TV shows, and in real life. It would be impossible for her to have missed that, and she hasn't.

"They were chained up down there, weren't they?" she asks.

I shake my head. "We don't know yet."

"Don't lie."

"Probably they were."

She nods and turns over on her side, toward the nightstand. The light on top has a flower-shaped lampshade. Orange, of course.

"How's your stomach been?" I ask.

"It's fine."

"Good."

"Why would someone hurt people like that?"

I shrug. "Some people are just wired wrong. They think bad is good."

"I bet Claire catches him."

"I bet you're right."

She smiles a little.

I hope she is wrong.

Fifty-eight

THE FIRST PICTURES of the basement are surprising. It does not look like the medieval dungeon I have built up in my head.

Instead, it looks like the unfinished basement of an old building. Dirt floor, wooden shelves on the wall, an old staircase. Only the wall farthest from the stairs is different, because it is the only one that indicates what may have happened in that basement. The wall has been bricked over and covered in stucco. A jumble of chains and cuffs lie on the ground beside it.

Claire introduces the pictures at an evening press conference, and I watch it from inside a bar. It is the same bar I was in when Lindsay's body was found.

I nurse a beer and sit where I have a view of a front window. Across the street is the First Street Bar & Grill, where they make giant hamburgers to eat with their giant microbrews, and everything is cheaper than it sounds. Millicent is not a fan of burgers or beer, so we go there only to meet clients or attend a party.

Claire goes through each picture and describes the details. There are close-ups of stains on the walls and the dirt floor. They look like rust, but she says they are blood.

The bartender shakes his head. No one makes a sound. They are too busy drinking and watching.

I cannot imagine Millicent leaving so much blood behind, if that's what it is. Claire might be lying. Her eyes stare right into the camera, so it appears she is looking right at me. Or at the guy next to me. Or at the bartender. It is unnerving.

I hate Claire's pantsuits. Tonight, it is navy blue paired with a dark grey blouse. She always looks like she is going to a funeral.

Claire stands at a podium near the church, although it isn't close enough to see anything but trees. Not even the steeple is visible. The police chief and the mayor are on one side of her, and an easel is set up on the other. Large copies of the pictures are stacked on it, and a couple of uniformed cops flip through each one as Claire speaks.

"We are already running tests on the blood, comparing it to both Naomi and Lindsay. We also discovered traces of saliva, and those are being tested as well."

She does not take questions. The whole press conference lasts about twenty minutes, which gives the newscasters and pundits time to dissect it. Claire didn't say anything about a message left on the wall, nor was there a photo of one.

The bartender turns the channel to sports news. I order another beer and hardly touch it.

Forty minutes later, I see him. Across the street, Josh walks into the First Street Bar & Grill. It is his favorite restaurant.

I came across this information by accident while driving down First Street a couple of nights ago. While stuck at a red light, I watched Josh get out of his car and head into the restaurant. The next night, I drove by again and saw his car parked out front. The third night, the same thing. On that evening, I walked by and saw him sitting at the bar, alone, drinking a beer while watching TV.

I go across the street and sit a few barstools away from Josh. Since I have already eaten dinner, I order a shot and a beer. Same as he does.

I look at him and look away. Then I look back, as if I recognize him.

Without even glancing in my direction, he says, "Yes. I'm that guy from the news."

"I thought that was you. I see you on TV almost every night," I say. Josh looks a lot different in real life. His face does not look as smooth. The texture of his skin is uneven. His nose is red, and so are his eyes. Too bad I didn't bring the eye drops.

He sighs and finally turns to me. "Thanks for watching."

"No, thank you for your reporting. You've really been the go-to guy on that big case, right? The women who were killed?"

"I was."

"You still are. You seem to know everything first."

Josh drinks a third of his beer in one gulp. "Are you one of those true-crime freaks?"

"Not at all. Just someone who wants this asshole caught."

"Cool."

I motion to the bartender for another shot. "Hey, man," I say to Josh. "Let me buy one."

"No offense, but I'm not gay."

"None taken. Neither am I."

Josh accepts the shot. The bartender brings a couple more beers with it.

Together, we watch the sports channel, talking back and forth about this team or that one. I buy a couple more shots but pour mine into a peanut bowl when he is not looking. Josh drinks his and orders two more.

When a soccer game starts, he nods to it. "I bet on the Blazers. You?"

"Same." Lie.

"You play? You look like you play."

I shrug. "Not really."

He gulps down the rest of his beer and motions for two more. "I used to play for this soccer team called the Marauders. We sucked, but people were still afraid of us. That was kind of awesome."

"Sounds like it."

During a commercial break, an ad for the local news shows today's press conference. Claire Wellington is once again on the screen.

Josh shakes his head and looks over at me. His eyes are not as clear as they were when I walked in. "You want some inside information?" he says.

"Sure."

He points to the TV. "She's a bitch."

"Really?"

"It's not because she's a woman. Really, that's got nothing to do with it. But the problem with having a woman in charge is that they have to change everything. Prove themselves, you know? And it's not their fault they have to do that—I get it. I just wish they didn't screw everything up."

"Is that right?"

"That's a million percent right."

The young, earnest reporter I have been watching is not the person he is on TV. I don't know why I expected him to be.

I order a couple more shots. Josh drinks his and slams the glass on the bar.

"A couple days ago, I reported something a source told me. The next day, he calls and says I can't talk about it anymore. Technically, the police can get fired for talking to the press. She's just decided to enforce the rule." He throws up his hands, as if this is an abomination. "Even if they talk to *me*. And I *worked with the police* when I got those letters from Owen. Or whoever sent them. I didn't have to do that. I could have just read them on the air without telling the police at all."

"What does that mean?" I ask. "Your sources won't tell you anything?"

"Oh, they still tell me stuff. I'm just not allowed to report it on the air. Well, I guess I could, but I'm a nice guy. I don't want anyone to get fired, especially not someone I need. That bitch won't be here forever."

Before I can answer, his phone buzzes. He glances at it and rolls his eyes. "See, this is what I'm talking about. I get a tip from a source, the second time I've heard this information, but I can't do anything with it. Y-E-O, it says. 'Your Eyes Only.'" He lets out a big, noisy sigh. "Worst acronym ever."

"That sucks."

"No shit."

I wait. I stare at the TV, not saying a word, hoping to convey that none of this matters to me. Because the less I care, the better chance he will tell me.

It takes him one more shot.

"Okay, I have to tell someone," he slurs. "But if you tell anyone, I'll deny I showed you this. At least until they make it public."

"You think they will?"

"They don't have a choice."

Josh slides the phone over to me. The text is on the screen, sent by someone named J. The whole thing reminds me a little of being Tobias.

Until I read the text.

YEO: There are bodies buried under the church.

Fifty-nine

I THOUGHT THE TEXT was going to be about the supposed message on the wall. Instead, it is about buried bodies. "So what?" I say.

"So what?" Josh says.

"That church is over a hundred years old. There's probably a whole graveyard of people buried there."

"I'm sure there is. But that's not what he's talking about." Josh leans in and lowers his voice a little. The smell of all that alcohol hits me in the face. "Have you been out there?"

I almost say yes, but then remember I am not a true-crime freak. "No."

"They have this big tent set up, but it's behind a bunch of trees. That's where they're taking the bodies."

"You keep saying that. What bodies?"

"The bodies in the basement aren't from a hundred years ago," he says. "They're women who have been killed recently."

"No."

"Yes. And I can't go on the air with it."

Josh rambles on, complaining all over again about Claire and his sources. I am not listening anymore.

Naomi and Lindsay have already been found, which leaves Holly and Robin. Holly was killed at our house, then we took her body out to the woods and buried her.

Robin was killed in our kitchen. Her car and body are at the bottom of a nearby lake.

I interrupt Josh. "Do you know when this information will be released?"

"Soon, I'm sure. They can't hide those bodies forever."

He keeps talking, but I think only of Claire Wellington. It will take her about a minute to show up at our door, asking about Millicent's sister, Holly.

And why she was never reported missing.

Because we thought she just moved away.

Because we didn't care.

Because she used to torture my wife.

Because she was crazy.

I text Millicent.

We need a date night.

She turns me down.

No date night. I'm at the hospital.

I read it three times before throwing money on the bar and leaving First Street Bar & Grill without saying another word to Josh. Or maybe I say I have to go. I'm not sure.

Millicent calls me as I'm trying to call her. She is talking fast, and I've been drinking, so all I catch are the highlights.

Rory. Emergency room. Fell from the window.

I don't bother with the car, because I'm close enough to run. The hospital is three blocks away, and I arrive to find Millicent pacing in the hall.

As soon as I see her, I know.

Rory is okay. Or will be.

Millicent's fists are clenched, lips pursed, and it feels like an electric current is shooting out of her. If Rory was really hurt, she would be worried, crying, or in shock. But she isn't. She is bursting with anger.

She grabs me and hugs me. It is quick and violent, and then she pulls back to sniff my breath.

"Beer," I say. "What happened?"

"Our son snuck out of the house to see his girlfriend. He fell climbing up to her window."

"But he's okay?"

"He is. We thought his wrist was broken, but it's a bad sprain. He'll have to wear a sling—"

"Why didn't you call me when it happened?" I ask.

"I did. I texted you."

I pull out my phone. There it is, right on the cracked screen. Depending on the angle, it can be difficult to read. "Oh god, I'm sorry—"

"Forget it. You're here now. The important thing is he's okay." Millicent's anger is back, if it had ever really left. "He's just grounded for a century."

Someone giggles.

Around the corner, Jenna is sitting in a waiting room. She waves. I wave back. Millicent directs me to a vending machine for coffee. It is bitter and burns my tongue, and is exactly what I need. It settles me down instead of the opposite, because my heart is beating too fast, from the sprint over, and the alcohol, and my son in the hospital.

Millicent disappears into the examining room to be with Rory. When they come out, Rory has a brace on his wrist and a sling on his arm. Millicent's anger has softened, at least for now.

He does not look me in the eye. Maybe he is still angry at me, or maybe he knows he is in trouble. Hard to tell, because right now I am torn between knocking him upside the head and hugging him. I ruffle his hair.

"If you don't want to play golf, you should have just said so," I say.

He doesn't smile. He loves golfing.

We get home after midnight. I check on Rory a few minutes after he goes to bed. Even he falls asleep right away.

I sit down on my bed, exhausted.

My car is still at the First Street Bar & Grill.

And there are bodies buried under the church.

"Millicent," I say.

She comes out of the bathroom, halfway through her nighttime routine. "What?"

"I was drinking beer tonight with Josh. The reporter."

"Why would you—"

"He told me there are bodies buried in that church basement."

"Bodies?"

I nod, watching her. Her surprise looks genuine. "Did he say whose bodies?" she asks.

"I assume Holly and Robin."

"They aren't anywhere near that church. You know that." She walks away, back into the bathroom.

I follow her. "You really don't know anything about the bodies buried down there?"

"Absolutely not."

"There's just a pile of random bodies in a church basement."

"Jesus, I don't know. This is the same reporter who claimed there was a message on the wall. Where's that?"

She has a point.

Maybe Josh has it wrong. Or maybe someone is feeding him lies to keep him from the truth.

Fictional police do that all the time. And Claire might be just as smart as they are.

Sixty

NOW THAT MILLICENT has discovered that Rory has a girlfriend and has been sneaking out to see her, she wants to meet with Faith's parents to discuss the situation. The Hammonds are clients of hers, and they readily agree that we should all meet for dinner. Neither Rory nor Faith is invited.

We are on the way to the restaurant, a traditional place with white tablecloths and a menu of comfort foods. Their choice, not Millicent's.

"They're reasonable people," Millicent says.

"I'm sure they are," I say.

When we arrive, the Hammonds are already waiting at the table. Hank Hammond is small and blond, like his daughter. Corinne Hammond is not small and not a natural blonde. Both wear classic clothes and polite smiles. We get straight to the food. No one orders wine.

Hank's voice is twice as big as his body.

"Faith is a good girl. She never snuck out until she met your son," he says.

I can almost see the ball swing over to our court. Millicent smiles, polite and syrupy. "I could say the same about your daughter, but blame isn't going to get us anywhere."

"I'm not talking about blame. I'm talking about keeping them away from each other."

"You want to ban Rory and Faith from seeing each other?"

"Faith is already banned from seeing your son anywhere but at school," Hank says. "I suppose *that's* impossible to avoid."

"You could homeschool her," Millicent says. "That way they would never see each other."

I put my hand on Millicent's arm. She shakes it off.

"Perhaps your son is the one who needs homeschooling," Hank says.

Corinne nods.

"You really think that forbidding them to see each other will make them . . . stop seeing each other?" Millicent says.

"Our daughter will do as she's told," Hank says.

I can feel Millicent biting her tongue, because I'm doing the same thing.

Corinne breaks the tension. Her voice is stronger than expected. "It's for the best," she says.

Millicent shifts her eyes to Corinne and pauses before saying, "I don't make it a habit of just banning my kids from doing something."

Lie.

"I guess that's where we differ," Hank says.

"Perhaps we should get back to the subject at hand," I say. "I don't think we need to get into our parenting philosophies."

"Fine," Hank says. "You keep your son away from my daughter, and that's the end of it."

The check arrives, and Millicent grabs it before Hank can. She hands it to me and says, "We've got it."

The dinner ends with a terse goodbye.

Millicent is silent on the way home.

Rory is waiting at the door when we walk into the house. He has a sprained wrist, cannot play golf, and he is grounded. Faith is the only thing he has, or thought he had. I am not looking forward to telling him he has lost her, too.

Except we don't. Millicent walks over to Rory and places her hand on his cheek. "All good," she says.

"All good? Really?"

"Just don't ever sneak out again."

"I promise."

Rory scampers off with his phone to call Faith, who will get a different message from her parents.

Millicent winks at me.

I wonder if this is how some girls learn to be so sneaky. From someone else's mother.

THE NEXT DAY, we get a call from the school. Jenna, not Rory. And this time, it is not about a weapon or her stomach. Now, it's her grades.

She has always been an honor student, but her grades have fallen over the past month. Today, she neglected to turn in a paper that was due. Jenna didn't even give her teacher an excuse.

Neither Millicent nor I had a clue. Jenna has been such a good student I don't even check the weekly reports posted online. After a flurry of texts and calls, we decide to talk to her after dinner.

Millicent begins by telling her about the phone call from school and then says, "Tell us what's going on."

Jenna has no real answer, other than some hems and haws and a shake of her head.

"I don't understand," Millicent says. "You've always been an excellent student."

"What's the point?" Jenna says. She stands up from the bed and walks across the room. "If someone can just lock me up in a basement and torture me, what's the point?"

"No one will do that to you," I say.

"Bet those dead women believed that."

Another punch to the gut. This one feels like an ice pick.

Millicent takes a deep breath.

Ever since meeting Claire, Jenna seemed to be better. She talked about being a detective all the time. But it all stopped when we found out about the church.

We go around in circles with her, trying to use logic to take away her fear. It does not really work. All we get is a promise that she will not flunk any of her classes.

As we walk out of Jenna's room, I see a notebook lying open on her bed. She has been researching how many women are abducted and murdered each year.

Millicent gets on the phone, trying to find another therapist.

This is on the third day without new information about the church. Claire holds a press conference every evening to repeat what we already know.

DAY FOUR BEGINS with a barking dog. We have several in the neighborhood, so there's no telling which one wakes me up at five in the morning, but it will not stop barking.

I sit up in bed, wondering why it never hit me before.

A dog.

One big enough to make Jenna feel safe, and protective enough to bark when someone is outside. Like Rory, when he tries to sneak in and out.

I could kick myself for not thinking of it sooner. A dog would solve so many of our problems.

For once, I am up before Millicent. When she comes downstairs in her running clothes, I am drinking coffee and researching dogs on the Internet. She freezes when she sees me.

"Do I want to know why you're—"

"Look," I say, pointing at the screen. "He's at the shelter, a rottweiler-boxer mix."

Millicent takes the coffee out of my hand and helps herself to a sip. "You want a dog."

"For the kids. To protect Jenna, and to keep Rory from sneaking out."

She looks at me and nods. "That's kind of brilliant."

"I have my moments."

"You'll take care of this dog?"

"The kids will."

She smiles. "If you say so."

I take that as a yes.

On a break between lessons, I stop by the shelter. A nice woman gives me a tour while I explain what we are looking for. She recommends a few different dogs, and one is the rottweiler-boxer mix. His name is Digger. She checks the paperwork and says he would be a good family dog, but the kids have to come to the shelter and meet him before they'll allow us to adopt. I promise the woman I will be back.

The dog makes me feel a little optimistic.

I stop at a drive-through for an iced coffee and a panini. As I sit at the pickup window waiting for my lunch, the TV inside is visible. Claire Wellington is having another press conference. The words at the bottom of the screen make my heart jump:

ADDITIONAL BODIES DISCOVERED IN CHURCH

When the cashier slides the window open to hand me the food, I hear Claire's voice.

". . . *the bodies of three young women have been found buried in the basement.*"

I listen to the rest of the press conference in the parking lot, on my car radio.

Three women. All were murdered recently.

The police have to be wrong about the timing. There is no way someone buried bodies while Lindsay was—

"*At least two of the three were recent enough for investigators to identify how they were murdered. Like the others, they were strangled. There are also signs of torture.*"

I cannot catch my breath because Claire does not stop talking.

"We also found words written on the wall of the basement, behind a shelf. While we do not have the DNA tests back yet, the blood type matches Naomi's."

When Claire says the words on the wall, my heart stops.

Tobias.

Deaf.

Sixty-one

NAOMI COULD NOT have written Tobias's name. She had never met him.

I turn this over in my mind, trying to figure out how it happened. Lindsay knew Tobias. She knew he was deaf.

But her body was found before Naomi disappeared. They could not have spoken, could not have exchanged information like that.

Millicent was the only one.

It does not make sense. None of this does.

As I get my food and drive out, I turn on the radio to hear the end of the press conference. When it's over, the announcers keep talking. They say those words on the wall again and again.

Tobias.

Deaf.

Naomi didn't know about Tobias.

Lindsay did.

And Millicent.

I pull over to the side of the road. My mind is so muddled I cannot think and drive at the same time.

Tobias.

Deaf.

I turn the radio off and close my eyes. All I see is Naomi in the basement of the church, chained up on that wall. I try to force it from my mind, to think clearly. But I still see her, huddled in a corner, dirty and covered in blood.

It makes me sick. Bile rises in my throat; I taste it in my mouth. I step out of the car, feeling nauseous, and the phone rings.

Millicent.

She is already talking when I answer the call.

"Flat tire?" she says.

"Excuse me?"

"You're sitting on the side of the road."

I look up, as if a drone or a camera is looking down on me, but the sky is clear. Not even a bird. "How do you know where I am?"

She sighs. A big, exasperated sigh, and I hate when she does that. "Look under the car," she says.

"What?"

"Under. The. Car."

I kneel down and look. A tracker. Just like the one I'd put on her car.

That's why I never knew about the church.

She knew I was tracking her.

THE REALIZATION OF what is happening explodes like a bomb in my head.

There is only one person who could have written that message using Naomi's blood. I knew this when I heard about it—I've just been looking for another explanation.

There isn't one.

"You set me up," I say. "For all of them. Lindsay, Naomi—"

"And the other three. Don't forget about them."

My mind is flooded with images of Millicent killing women alone, framing me for the murders.

Now, I know what she has been doing while I was at home with Jenna all those days and nights when she was sick.

The future rolls out in front of me like a bloody red carpet.

I close my eyes, lean my head back, and think of all the ways Millicent could set me up. All the DNA she has access to. Everything she could plant, could give to the police. That does not even include the people who knew me as a deaf man named Tobias.

Annabelle. Petra. Even the bartenders.

They will remember.

Everything will point to me.

My mind fights against this idea. Around in circles I go, mapping out an idea, following it to the end, realizing it will never work. Every path is blocked, every idea already thought of by Millicent. It feels like a giant maze with no exit. I'm not a planner after all, not like my wife.

I pace up and down the length of the car. My head feels like it's being shocked again and again.

"Millicent, why would you do this?"

She laughs. It sounds like a bite. "Open your trunk."

"What?"

"Your trunk," she says. "Open it."

I hesitate, imagining what could be inside. Wondering how much worse it could get.

"Do it," she says.

I open the trunk.

Nothing inside except my tennis equipment. Not a single racket out of place. "What are you—"

"The spare tire," she says.

My phone, the disposable one. The one with messages from Lindsay and Annabelle. I reach inside the rim of the tire, but I don't find it. Instead, I find something else.

Pixy Stix.

Lindsay.

The first one I slept with.

It happened after that second hike.

You're cute. That's what Lindsay had said.

No, you're the cute one.

Millicent's voice brings me back to now. "You know, it's amazing what people will tell you when they're locked up for a year."

"What are you—"

"She saw you the night we took her. Lindsay was waking up before you left. She was pretty surprised you weren't deaf, actually."

A wave of nausea hits. Because of what I did. Because of what my wife has done.

"The funny thing," she says, "is that Lindsay thought I was torturing her because she slept with you. I tried to tell her it wasn't like that, not at first anyway, but I don't think she ever believed me."

"Millicent, what have you done?"

"*I* didn't do anything," Millicent says. "You did. You did all of this."

"I don't know what you think happened—"

"Do not patronize me with a denial."

I bite my tongue until I taste blood. "How long have you been planning this?"

"Does it matter?"

No. Not anymore.

"Can I explain?" I ask.

"No."

"Millicent—"

"What? You're sorry, it just happened, and it didn't mean anything?"

I bite my tongue. Literally.

"So what are you going to do?" she says. "Run and hide, or stay and fight?"

Neither. Both. "Please don't do this."

"See, this is your problem."

"What?"

"You always focus on the wrong things."

I start to ask her about what the wrong things are but stop myself. I am making her point.

She laughs.

The line goes dead.

Sixty-two

I SHOULD GET SICK. I should vomit up whatever is in my stomach, because when my wife of fifteen years has set me up for murdering multiple women, this should make me sick to my stomach. Instead, it feels like my whole body has been injected with Novocain.

Not a bad thing, because I can think instead of feel.

Run and hide. Stay and fight.

Neither is appealing. Nor is prison, the death penalty, lethal injection.

Run.

First, I take stock. Car, half a tank of gas, panini, partial iced coffee, and about two hundred in cash. Credit cards I cannot use, because Millicent will be watching.

I wonder if there is time to make a cash withdrawal at the bank.

Beyond that, my options narrow considerably. Can't keep the car for long unless I get rid of the license plate, and then there is the issue of where to go. Canada is too far. By the time I make it there, my picture will be all over the news.

Mexico is the only driving option, and even that would be a stretch. It depends on how quickly this all plays out. My name and picture could be out within hours.

I could fly out of the country, but then I would definitely need to use my passport. They would know where I landed. At no time did I prepare for this kind of escape.

Millicent knows this.

Running will get me caught.

It also means leaving my kids. With Millicent.

Now, I get sick. On the side of the road, behind my car, I empty my stomach. I do not stop until there is nothing left.

Run and hide. Stay and fight.

I start to consider a third option. What if I just walk into a police station and tell them everything?

No. Millicent might be arrested, but so would I. Claiming innocence is not an option, because it is not true.

There has to be a way, though. A way to implicate *her* instead of me, because I never killed anyone. A deal could be made with the right lawyer, the right prosecutor, the right proof. Except I don't have any. Unlike Millicent, I have not been setting up my spouse for murder.

You always focus on the wrong things.

Maybe she is right; maybe the why does not matter. But it will. The why is what will haunt me, what I will think about at night when I am lying in bed. If I am in a bed. Maybe it will be a prison cot. She is right about the why. It's the wrong thing to think about.

Run and hide. Stay and fight.

The options repeat over and over, like those words written on the wall of the basement. Millicent stated these options as if they were the only ones that existed. As if it were an either-or choice.

She is wrong. The options are wrong.

First, I will stay. Leaving my kids isn't going to happen.

And if I stay, I have to hide. At least until I can find a way to make the police believe me about Millicent.

That means I have to fight.

Stay, hide, fight. The first is easy. No running.

The police. I could go to the police and tell them everything, tell them . . .

No. Cannot do that. I have real blood on my hands, and even a rookie will figure that out. And if I cannot go to the police, I will have to avoid them.

Money. I have two hundred dollars in my wallet, and that will not last long. I head straight to the bank and withdraw as much cash as I can without triggering an alert to the IRS. Millicent will know about it, because the tracker is still on my car.

Millicent. How long did she know? How long has she been tracking me? When did she start to plan this? The questions are endless, unanswerable.

With all we have been through, with all we have done together, it is unfathomable to me that she did not talk to me, ask me about it, even give me the benefit of the doubt. Instead, I had no chance, no opportunity to explain.

It seems a little bit crazy.

And heartbreaking.

But I do not have time to think about either one. In less than an hour, my life has been reduced to its most base level: survival.

So far, I am not very good at it. Millicent knows where I am, and I have no idea what to do next.

HOME. IT IS still where I always go.

I grab what I can—clothes, toiletries, my laptop. The one we used to search for the women is gone, probably destroyed, but I find Millicent's tablet and take it. And photographs. I take a couple of pictures of the kids right off the walls. I also send them a text.

Don't believe everything you hear. I love you.

Before leaving, I turn off the GPS tracker but keep it with me. For a while, she will wonder if I am just sitting in our house. Maybe. But that is assuming I know my wife at all.

I pull out of the driveway and drive down the street, having no idea where to go next.

An empty building, a roadside motel, a parking lot? The swamp, the woods, the hiking trails? I have no idea, but it does not seem smart to be in a place I am unfamiliar with. I need somewhere quiet, somewhere I can think. Somewhere no one will bother me for a few hours.

A complete lack of options and originality sends me to the country club.

As an employee, I have a key to the office, which I never use, along with the equipment rooms and the courts. I make a quick stop at the store for a bag of food, mostly junk, and stay out of sight until after nine o'clock. That's when the lights are shut down on the tennis courts, and security locks them up for the night.

This is where I go. The club has cameras inside the building. There are none on the courts.

Sixty-three

EVERYTHING ABOUT THE tennis courts is familiar. I grew up here, on these courts. This is where I learned to play tennis, but that wasn't all I did. My coach made me run around these courts endless times to get into shape. I won trophies here and had my butt whipped, sometimes on the same day.

This was my escape; this is where I came to get away from my friends, school, and especially my parents. At first, I came here to see if they would look for me. When they never did, I used it as a hideout. I even had my first kiss here.

Lily. She was a year older than me and far more experienced, or so it seemed. On Halloween night, about a million years ago, my friends and I dressed up as pirates. She and her friends dressed up as baby dolls. We all ran into each other somewhere in the Oaks, while trick-or-treating, and Lily told me I was kind of cute. I assumed that meant she loved me, and I think she did.

One comment led to another, and it wasn't long before I asked if she wanted to go somewhere cool. She said yes.

"Cool" might have been an exaggeration, but when I was thirteen I thought it was cool to be outside the house, at night, with a girl. Lily didn't think it was too bad, either, because she kissed me. She tasted like chocolate and licorice, and I loved it.

For a second, I am so enveloped by this memory that everything seems okay. It is not. I am on this tennis court because the police are after me and I cannot go home.

But thinking about Lily makes me realize I do have somewhere to go.

THE ALARM ON my phone wakes me up at five. I jump up, gather my things, and get into my car. Trying to sleep on a courtside bench gave me plenty of time to come up with a plan. The Internet on my phone helped make it a good one. Turns out there are dozens of websites that explain how to disappear, how to go off the grid, how to elude the police, your boss, or your angry wife. Everyone wants to escape something.

I drive out of town, down the interstate, and do not stop for at least an hour. Eventually, I pull into a gas station, turn on the GPS tracker, and attach it to the bottom of a semi. After taking the battery out of my phone, I stop at a convenience store and buy a cheap disposable.

Then I head back to Hidden Oaks.

The Internet does not recommend this part, but the Internet does not have children. If I didn't, I would keep driving, change the license plate on my car or get rid of it altogether. Take a Greyhound from state to state and eventually end up in Mexico.

Not an option. Not when Jenna and Rory are still with my wife.

Halfway back, I stop and buy a trunk full of groceries. I check all the papers, looking for my own face, but I do not see it anywhere. The headlines are just those two words.

TOBIAS DEAF

As I drive back toward home, I wonder if I am being stupid all over again.

THERE ARE TWO gates at the Oaks. The front gate is where the guards are; you have to pass them to get in.

But Hidden Oaks is quite large, given that it has an entire golf course as well as hundreds of homes, so there is a back gate. Or rather, two of them. One requires a code; the second, an opener like the kind used for a garage, but there are no guards. This is where I enter.

Once inside, I drive past the less expensive homes, through the midrange development, and finally arrive at a house twice as large as mine. It has six bedrooms, at least that many bathrooms, and a pool in the back. Kekona's house is empty, because she is still in Hawaii.

This is the most brilliant part of my plan. Or the stupidest. I will not know until I try to get in.

This is where Lily lived. On that Halloween night, she became my first girlfriend. So many nights, I snuck out of my house and into hers. Just like my son does with his girlfriend now.

It has been many years since I have done it, and the house has been repainted, remodeled, and updated. The locks have probably changed several times. But that's the thing about real estate. People always change the locks on the front and back doors. I am betting the lock on the French doors around back, on the second-story widow's walk, has never been changed. The lock on those doors never closed properly. It did not need a key.

Climbing up is not as easy at my age as it was back then, but I am not worried about being seen. Kekona's house is deep in the middle of the Oaks, in the expensive area where everyone has more land than they need. The closest neighbors are barely visible from the front, let alone the back.

Somehow, I make it up without falling, and, sure enough, I know before I even try. The doors have been painted, maybe even resealed, but the lock is the same. I smile for the first time in twenty-four hours.

Minutes later, I am inside and then back out through the garage. Kekona has one car, an SUV, which leaves an extra space in her garage for mine.

I bring in the groceries, take a shower, and get settled. For the first time, I feel like I have a chance. A chance at what, I am not sure, but at least I am no longer sleeping on a tennis court.

When I open my laptop, problem number one hits: the wireless password.

Kekona has removed the code sticker from the bottom of the modem, so the password does not come easily. It takes me far too long to realize the sticker is right on the refrigerator door.

Once online, I search for a way into Millicent's tablet. It requires a four-digit PIN. I know without trying that she would never use a generic birth date or anniversary. I need a better way.

On the news, they won't stop talking about the press conference, about Tobias, and about the three women in the basement.

I try to figure out who they are, who Millicent would have chosen. Women from our list? Women I had rejected, like Annabelle or Petra? I hope it is not Annabelle. She didn't do anything to deserve Millicent.

No, that wouldn't make sense. Someone has to be alive to identify a deaf man named Tobias. She couldn't have killed everyone who has seen him.

Maybe Millicent chose strangers, women I have never even seen or spoken to. Or maybe that would be too random for her.

I tell myself to stop. My mind is going in circles and getting nowhere.

I keep working on the tablet, hoping to find answers. By the time the sun goes down, I am no closer to getting into it.

It is six o'clock, and I should be at home eating dinner. Tonight is movie night, and I am not there. If my text didn't let Rory and Jenna know something is wrong, my absence will.

* * *

I WAKE UP thinking I am at home. I listen for Millicent downstairs, back from her run, making breakfast. Today's schedule runs through my mind; my first lesson is at nine. I roll over and hit the floor with a thud.

Not at home. I slept on the couch in Kekona's great room. Her seafoam green sectional is huge, but I still roll right off it. Reality hits with the wood floor.

The TV goes on, the single-serve coffee brews, the computer boots up. I spent the previous night making lists. What I know, what I don't know, what I need to know. How to get the info I need. The last list is a little short, because I am neither a hacker nor a detective. What I do know is that there are two ways to go about this: prove she killed those women or prove I didn't kill them. Ideally both.

On the night Naomi went missing, I went home and stayed with the kids, leaving Millicent alone with her. Same with Lindsay; I was with Jenna, because she was sick. The kids are my alibi, and they're not a good one. Once they were asleep, they cannot verify anything.

But can I prove Millicent did it? Not any more than I can prove I didn't.

Millicent's tablet is a larger problem than I thought. Although there is software available to reset a PIN, it can be done only if I am signed into the e-mail address on the tablet. Another password I do not have and can't even guess. In the middle of the night, I resorted to reading hacker message boards populated by teenagers looking for the same thing I was.

There could be another way. Maybe. But only if I can convince someone to help me.

I spend half the morning wondering if it is better to ask now, before my face is all over the news, or after I am a wanted man. I try to imagine someone coming to me for help, someone who may or may not be a psychopath. Would I help them, or slam the door and call the police?

The answer is the same. It depends.

And my options are limited. My friends are Millicent's friends; we share them. I have many clients, but most are just that. Just one possibility comes to mind—the only person who might be both willing and able to help.

If Andy will agree.

Sixty-four

THE GOLDEN WOK is a Chinese buffet thirty minutes outside Hidden Oaks. I have been there once, on my way to somewhere else, and it is like every other Chinese buffet I've seen. I arrive early and fill up my plate with Mongolian beef, sweet-and-sour pork, chicken chow mein, and fried spring rolls. Halfway through the meal, Andy Preston walks in and joins me.

I stand up and offer my hand. He pushes it aside and gives me a hug.

Andy is not the same man I knew before Trista killed herself. He is not even the same man I saw at her funeral. The extra weight he carried is gone; now he is almost too thin. Not healthy. I tell him to grab a plate.

The Chinese buffet was his choice. He left Hidden Oaks after Trista died, and Kekona told me he quit his job and spends his days on the Internet, encouraging strangers not to kill themselves. I believe it.

Andy sits down at the table and gives me a smile. It looks hollow. "So what's going on?" I say. "How are you?"

"Not great, but it could be worse. It could always be worse."

I nod, impressed he can say something like that after what has happened to him. "You're right, it can."

"What about you? How's Millicent?"

I clear my throat.

"Uh-oh," he says.

"I need help."

He nods. Doesn't ask a single question—because he is still my friend, even if I haven't been much of one to him.

All morning, I have gone back and forth about how much to tell Andy about my situation. First, the tablet. I take it out of my gym bag and slide it across the laminate table. "Can you help me get into this? It has a PIN code, and I have no idea what it is."

Andy looks at the tablet and then at me. His eyes look a bit more alert. "Any eight-year-old could get into this thing."

"I can't ask my kids to do it."

"So this is Millicent's."

I nod. "But it's not what you think."

"No?"

"No." I gesture to his plate. "Finish eating. Then I'll tell you everything."

I say "everything," but I do not mean it.

After we are done, we go sit in his truck. It's an old pickup and nothing like the sports car he used to drive.

"What did you do?" he says.

"What makes you think I've done something?"

He side-eyes me. "You look like hell, you have a new phone number, and you want to get into your wife's computer."

As much as I want to tell someone *everything*, I cannot. No matter how far we go back, there are limits to friendship. Murder is one of them. So is keeping secrets about a friend's wife.

"I cheated on Millicent," I say.

He does not look surprised. "Not a good move, I'm guessing."

"That's an understatement."

"So she kicked you out and wants everything? The house, the 401(k), the kids' college fund?"

I wish that was all she wanted. "Not exactly," I say. "Millicent wants more than that."

"Can't say I'm surprised." He pauses for a second, shaking his head. "Now that you've gone and screwed it all up, I can tell you the truth."

"What truth?"

"I never liked Millicent. She's always seemed a little cold."

I feel the urge to laugh, but that seems inappropriate. "She's setting me up for things I didn't do. Some very bad things."

"Illegal things?" he says.

"Yes. Very much yes."

He holds up a hand, as if to stop me from saying more. "So I was right. She is cold."

"You were right."

He doesn't say anything for a few minutes. He runs his hand around the steering wheel, the type of thing someone does without thinking, because they're too busy thinking. It's all I can do to keep my mouth shut, to let him decide how insane I am.

"If all you needed was to get into that tablet, why tell me the rest?" he says.

"Because you and I go way back. I owe you the truth."

"And?"

"And because I'll probably be in the news soon."

"The news? What the hell is she doing to you?"

"You're the first one who has seen me since yesterday," I say. "Please don't tell anyone."

He stares out the window, at the neon Golden Wok sign. "I don't want to know more, do I?"

I shake my head no.

"That's the real favor then," he says. "Keep my mouth shut."

"Sort of. Yes. But I do need to get into that," I say, pointing to Millicent's tablet. It is sitting on Andy's dashboard. "Will you help me?"

Again, he is quiet.

Andy is going to do it. He may not know it, but he has already decided to help. Otherwise, he would have been gone by now. And by the way he looks, he may need this as much as I do.

"You've always been a pain in the ass," he says. "And for the record, your tennis lessons are way too expensive."

I smile a little. "Noted. But you accused me of sleeping with your wife. You owe me."

He nods. "Give it to me."

I give him the tablet.

THE WAITING IS the worst. Like knowing a bomb will go off but not when or where. Or who. I spend the next day in Kekona's theater room. It has a screen as wide as the wall, and distressed leather recliners. I watch Josh talk about Tobias nonstop. He even speaks to experts about what it is like to be deaf.

I have to admit some of the information is interesting. It would have been useful to have back when I needed it.

The breaking-news music interrupts my musings. The picture on the screen makes my heart jump.

Annabelle.

Sweet Annabelle, the meter maid whose boyfriend was killed by a drunk driver.

She is alive.

And she is still cute as ever, with her short hair and delicate features, but she is not smiling. She does not look happy at all when Josh introduces her as a "woman who has encountered the deaf man named Tobias."

It is not surprising that she is the first to come forward. She could not save her boyfriend, so she wants to save everyone else.

Annabelle tells our story, as she knows it, beginning with the moment she almost ticketed the car I claimed was mine. She explains how we bumped into each other on the street and I invited her to join me for a drink. She even names the bar. If Eric, the bartender, has not already come forward, he will.

Annabelle leaves out nothing, not even the text she sent me. The police will now have that phone number.

I wonder if Millicent will answer when they call.

Last but not least, Annabelle says she spent the morning with a sketch artist. The drawing is released right after the interview ends.

It looks exactly like me and, at the same time, nothing like me.

I imagine Millicent watching this and critiquing the drawing, saying that the nose is a bit too big and maybe the eyes are too small. She would say they missed the mole by my ear, or the shade of my skin is different. She would see everything, because she always does.

It will not be long before I am identified, although people must already be looking for me. My employer, for one. Millicent must be acting frantic, pretending I have just vanished without a reason.

Jenna and Rory—who knows what they think?

I spend the rest of the day inside, afraid to go out while it is still light.

It makes me think back to the day I married Millicent, at her parents' home in the middle of nowhere. I can see her in that simple dress, with her hair up and sprinkled with tiny flowers, like she was some kind fairy or nymph that came from another world. She was like that, everything about her was otherworldly. Still is, I suppose.

I also think of what she said that day, because it is so appropriate now.

Here we go.

THE NEWS STARTS to break faster, which is no surprise. The public has been given just enough information to provide more of it.

The second person who claims to know Tobias is a bartender, but not Eric. This young man works at the bar where I met Petra. Josh, while overexcited about all the news, seemed rather disappointed in this young man, because he does not remember the exact day, nor time, he met Tobias. He remembers so little it is almost embarrassing, at least for him. To top it all off, he gets the drink wrong. Tobias never ordered a vodka tonic.

I am almost offended by this. I always believed Tobias was more memorable than that.

Or maybe this bartender is just a moron.

When nothing new is happening, everything is repeated. I see Annabelle's interview over and over; they repeat the best parts until I have them memorized. During commercial breaks, I wonder if my kids are watching the same channel.

I know Millicent is. I can just see her sitting on the couch, watching Annabelle on our big TV. In my mind, Millicent is smiling. Or scowling. Both.

By the evening news, Eric shows up, but on another channel. Josh does not get this interview. The reporter who interviews him is a middle-aged woman, one of our more famous local personalities. Up until now, I have not seen her covering anything about this case—not when Owen was back and not when he turned out to be dead. The fact that she has become involved worries me. A serious manhunt is about to begin, or already has, and they are all looking for me.

Eric remembers more than the last bartender, beginning with the drink: gin and tonic. He describes my suit, right down to the type of tie I had been wearing. He remembers the color of my eyes, my tan, even the length of my hair.

Each new revelation makes my stomach turn. Somehow, I managed to find the only bartender in town with a photographic memory.

Within minutes, the other stations repeat what Eric said. It makes me a little sick to hear Josh repeat all those personal things about me. I wish I had known what a horrible person he really is. If I did, I never would have sent letters to him.

Though I suppose I am not one to judge who is horrible and who is not.

Hour after hour goes by, deep into the night, before the old movies and infomercials begin. I open my laptop and search the true-crime sites. The sketch is everywhere, along with all the same interviews I just watched, and I scan through all the message boards. My name is not there, nor should it be. Not yet, anyway.

Sixty-five

I DO NOT SLEEP for long. Within an hour of my waking up, the news stations have set up for a press conference by Claire Wellington. Coffee makes my stomach turn as I wait for it to start. Claire has not said anything good yet, and I know she will not this morning.

A podium is set up at the police station. It is flanked by the U.S. and state flags and surrounded by microphones, cameras, and lights. Ten minutes after the scheduled time, Claire walks to the podium. She is not wearing a pantsuit. Today, it a navy skirt and a matching jacket, which is similar to the type of suits Millicent wears, only not as tight. Somehow, I know this is a bad sign.

Claire begins with the sketch that has already been released, and she asks the community to post it at businesses, schools, and civic buildings, as well as on community websites. Although anyone who has not seen it by now doesn't have a TV or the Internet. Or is in a coma.

But this is not why Claire is having a press conference. This is just her opening act. The main event comes next.

"Now, I have an update on the three women we found in the church

basement. Trying to identify them is a painstaking process, given the vary-
ing amounts of decomposition. Their fingerprints have also been removed."

She pauses, takes a deep breath. *"Despite the difficulties, the Wood-*
view medical examiner and forensic investigators have done an amazing
job. The first of these women has been identified, and her family has been
contacted. Thanks to the hard work of a lot of people, this young woman can
finally be laid to rest."

Before she says the woman's name, a picture appears on the screen.

I know her.

Jessica.

The cashier at the EZ-Go where I get my coffee. She left not long
ago. The guy who took her place said she was going to school in another state. I am shocked Millicent knew who she was. Millicent does
not buy coffee or anything else at the EZ-Go.

She must have been following me for a lot longer than I realized.
Maybe Millicent has always kept track of what I do. And who I
speak to.

This idea makes my heart beat too fast. I put down the coffee.

On TV, a split screen has Jessica on one side and Claire on the
other. The detective is still talking, explaining that the other women
have not been identified.

Now, I know what Millicent has done. She has killed women I
know, who can be connected to me. Maybe this was part of her setup.

Or maybe she thinks I was sleeping with all of them.

Perhaps she has gone scorched-earth, destroying everyone who
could be a threat.

My mind spins with who the other two might be. Not any of my
clients. None have disappeared recently, and if they did, I would know.
Wealthy people don't just vanish without someone looking for them.

I run through all the women I know, particularly young women
who fit Owen's profile. A number of them work at the club as bartenders, waitresses, retail sales clerks. I know all of them by sight and
have said hello to most. Some have been there longer than others.
Most are *still* there; they aren't dead in a church basement.

Except one.

Beth.

Perky Beth from Alabama, a waitress at the club. We never had an affair; she was just a nice young woman, and sometimes we talked while I ate at the clubhouse. That was it.

Not long ago, she left because of a family emergency back in Mobile. The manager of the restaurant told me that. No one questioned this. No one suspected anything had happened to her. No one showed up looking for her.

If more time had passed, maybe her family would have.

I get up and start pacing—first, around the theater room, and then throughout the whole house. Upstairs, downstairs, into all the rooms and around in a circle.

One more.

Millicent killed a third woman. No one else has disappeared—not that I know of—so I wonder if it might be Petra. With Annabelle and the bartenders around to recognize Tobias, why not get rid of her?

A RINGING PHONE breaks through my panic. The only one who has my new number is Andy.

"It's you," he says. He does not mention the police sketch and does not have to.

I nod at the phone, as if he can see me. "This is what I was telling you," I say. "She's setting me up."

"Yeah, I got that part. But you failed to convey the magnitude of her anger."

"I said you didn't want to know. I told you."

"How is she even doing this?"

Again, I want to tell him, but I can't. I also do not have a good answer. "If I knew, I would tell the police."

He sighs. Right before he hangs up, he says, "Goddammit."

And he still has Millicent's tablet.

All day, I watch the news, scour my laptop, and look up my kids on the Internet. My search comes up with nothing new—just some old articles in the local paper from Jenna's soccer team or Rory in a golf tournament.

I look at the pictures I took from the house. They feel like they are from a hundred years ago, back when I had a life that now feels like a dream.

NIGHTTIME. I AM out by the pool, pacing around it. If Kekona had any neighbors, they would think I must be a madman, which I may be, but no one is close enough. Since no one is, I jump in the pool, clothes and all, and stay underwater until I can't. The air feels like a shock when I break the surface. It both wakes me up and calms me down.

I climb out and lie down on the patio, staring up at the sky, trying not to wonder how much worse it can get.

My life has just blown up, and I should feel angry. I think the anger is there, bubbling under the surface, all mixed in with the sadness and heartbreak, the guilt and shame and horror. It will all come, and it will all overwhelm me, but not yet. Not until I figure out how to get myself out of this mess.

And get my kids. I fall asleep thinking of them. Just us, not Millicent.

THE SUN AND the birds wake me up. It's so peaceful here at Kekona's, so easy to pretend the rest of the world doesn't exist. I understand why she rarely leaves the Oaks. Why would anyone willingly leave this for reality? I would not if I didn't have to.

Eventually, I do go back inside and turn on the TV.

Me.

I am on that wall, staring back at myself. My picture fills the screen, and my name appears at the bottom, along with a banner:

PERSON OF INTEREST

Even though I am expecting it, I still fall to my knees.

So fast. My whole life has fallen apart in less than a week. If it were not happening to me, I would not believe this is possible.

Josh's voice makes me look up. He is talking, always talking, but today he is not a reporter. Because we met at the First Street Bar & Grill, he is the subject of the interview. The star.

Most of what he says is a lie, and an abbreviated one at that. I approached him. I asked about the case. I begged him to give me the names of his sources. He skips the part about getting drunk, calling Claire Wellington a bitch, complaining about the information he had, and shared, but could not say on the air.

"I understand the police are calling this man a person of interest, and maybe that's all he is. I can only tell you what I felt. You know that feeling you get when something is just wrong? Like that little alarm goes off in your head, telling you to get away? That's how this guy made me feel."

His remark is creepy enough to make me sound guilty, even though Josh had been in no condition to feel anything when I met him.

I want to put the battery back in my real phone. To see if the kids texted me, if they're worried, if they believe what is being said about me. Or to see how many times the police have called.

Instead, I am alone, trapped in Kekona's beautiful house without anyone to talk to.

Until the phone rings. Andy.

I pick up but don't say a word. He is already talking.

"Those murders really upset Trista. I'm almost glad she can't see how many there are."

If Trista were still alive, she would know Owen didn't kill these women. And she would have no reason to kill herself. I do not mention this.

"I remember," I say. "She talked about it at the club."

"But you didn't do it."

"I did not kill those women." True. I only killed Holly, and no one found her.

"If I find out different—"

"Call the police," I say. "Turn me in."

"I was going to say I'll kill you myself."

I take a deep breath. "Deal."

"I got into this tablet. Can you tell me where you are?"

"For your own good, you—"

"Don't want to know," he says. "I got it."

WE MEET IN another parking lot, not the one outside Golden Wok. My disguise is a baseball cap and sunglasses, and I have not shaved for two days. It isn't much, but no one is looking for me inside Kekona's SUV. I drive out the back gate of Hidden Oaks to avoid the guards.

It is after dark, because I will not go out during the day. I also won't let Andy see the car or the license plate, so it's parked two blocks away and I walk down to the lot. He is standing outside his truck with Millicent's tablet in his hand. No other cars are around, no lights on. The lot belongs to a boarded-up car parts store.

Andy is standing a bit straighter than he was the last time I saw him. His chin is up.

"Whole damn county is looking for you," he says.

"Yeah, I got that."

Andy turns around and sets the tablet on the hood, keeping it propped up with his hand.

"If you tell me you failed, I'll stop believing you're a genius," I say.

"I never fail. But I don't know if any of this is helpful." He swipes the screen, which lights up with a keypad. "New code. Six-three-seven-four. First, the bad news. She must've known you took this, because she wiped out everything in the cloud."

"Of course she did."

"Not to worry—there is some good news. She did have some information stored on the hard drive. She couldn't get to that."

He shows me a few pictures. A couple of the kids, a few of open houses, and a snapshot of a grocery list.

I shake my head. It's all too mundane to be useful.

"She liked games," Andy says. He opens a few Match 3 games and crossword puzzles.

Any hope I have blows away like a dead leaf. Of course there is nothing on the tablet. Millicent would never be so stupid.

"Also found a few recipes," he says, bringing up some pdf files.

"Stuffed mushrooms, huh?"

"The spinach hummus dip sounds good."

I sigh. "You're an asshole."

"Hey, it's your wife," he says. "Last but not least, her Internet searches and the sites she visited. She cleared the history, but I recovered most of it, for what it's worth."

Not much. More recipes, medical websites about sprained wrists and upset stomachs, the school's online calendar, and a bunch of real estate websites.

"No smoking gun," I say.

"Doesn't look like it."

I sigh. "Not your fault. Thanks for trying."

"You owe me forever, you know," he says.

"If I don't go to jail for life."

He gives me a hug before driving away in his old truck.

I am alone again, in no hurry to get back to Kekona's. Even a big house can feel suffocating.

Instead, I go back to the tablet, looking through all those real estate websites she visited. No one is perfect, I tell myself. Not even Millicent. Somehow, somewhere, she made a mistake.

My eyes are almost bleeding when I find it.

Sixty-six

THE WEBSITE MILLICENT visited the most is a property database. She went to the site every day, researching sales records and real estate transfers, all of which were public information. Her browser recorded the addresses she researched.

One of them is a commercial building at 1121 Brownfield Avenue. Six months ago, a man named Donald J. Kendrick sold the building for $162,000. The building has been around for more than twenty years and has had one longtime tenant.

Joe's Deli.

Donald sold the building to an LLC owned by another LLC and then a third. Ultimately, the building is now owned by R. J. Enterprises, LLC.

Rory. Jenna.

This is Millicent being clever, because she would not see it as a mistake. Our children are never a mistake. This was on purpose.

I think back to six months ago, realizing that it was right after she sold three houses in a row. Plenty of cash for her to use.

Denise was never a client of Millicent's.

She is a tenant. A tenant who just happened to know Owen's sister.

Knowing Millicent, she spent hours researching Owen's history—his family, where they lived and went to school. She hunted until she discovered that Owen was actually dead, and then she found someone who could prove it. Like Owen's sister. She just needed to get her back in the country.

Who better than an old friend? Especially an old friend with a demanding landlord. Someone who contacted Jennifer Riley and begged her to speak up about Owen's death.

Millicent. All Millicent. And all within the past six months.

Now I understand her reaction about the Jane Doe victims in the news. Millicent was convinced they were lying; she'd insisted that the real Owen had not returned. She already knew he was dead.

Her dedication to ruining me would be admirable if it weren't so sick.

Yet I still have no proof. Just an LLC and a commercial building, which even a bad lawyer would argue was an investment, not a plot to frame someone for murder.

I drive back into Hidden Oaks through the back gate, using Kekona's remote to open it. Once inside, I have an urge to drive past my house. The sun is coming up, and I wonder if the kids are asleep. If they can sleep. If we lived anywhere else, they would be surrounded by reporters. Not here. The public does not have access.

But I don't drive by. That would be stupid.

Instead, I go back to Kekona's and turn on her giant screen.

Me. It is all about me.

Now that I have been identified, everyone has something to say about me, and they all say it on camera. Former clients, coworkers, acquaintances—all weigh in on the fact that I am a person of interest. A missing person of interest.

"Nice guy. A little too smooth maybe, but what do you expect from a tennis coach?"

"My daughter took lessons from him, and now I'm just glad she's alive."

"Used to see him at the club. Always hustling for clients."

"My wife and I have known them for years. Never would have guessed. Never."

"Right here in Hidden Oaks? This is unbelievable. Really."

"Terrifying."

Josh is now being interviewed by other reporters, because his talking to me makes him part of the story.

My boss says I was the best tennis pro he has ever employed, and it's too bad I'm a sicko.

And Millicent. She does not appear on camera, nor do they show a picture of her, but my wife releases a statement:

> My children and I ask that you respect our privacy during this unimaginably difficult time. I am cooperating fully with the police and have nothing further at this time.

Short, sweet, and written by Millicent. Probably dictated by a lawyer, perhaps one of her clients. Someone who used to be my friend.

Now I just have Andy, although if he knew the truth he would kill me.

I think of Kekona, wonder if she is my friend, if she would believe me if she were here. We've known each other for at least five years, and we have relaxed into an easy banter at our lessons. Even when she misses a lesson she still pays, and when she has a party she always invites us. Does this make her a friend? I don't know anymore.

I am not used to being this alone. For seventeen years, Millicent has been with me, and for most of that time so were the kids. I've had a family to worry about, to worry about me. After the first few years back in Hidden Oaks, my old friends started to get married, move away, start their own families. It didn't seem to matter that they weren't around. I was busy enough without them.

Now I see my mistake. Focusing only on my family has left me isolated and alone, except for one old friend who can never know the truth.

* * *

MY PITY PARTY is broken up by Claire Wellington, who I bet hates parties. She's that one who checks her watch, sips a glass of water, and waits for an escape. I have no idea if this is correct, but I believe it anyway.

She holds another news conference at five o'clock, just in time for the evening news. Today her suit is an ugly color of grey, like flannel, though it isn't, because this is Florida and that would be ridiculous. Her hair is dull, and so is her skin. Claire is not getting much sleep and should probably stop working so much.

"As everyone knows, we have a team of people working to identify the women found in the church basement. Twenty-three-year-old Jessica Sharpe was the first to be identified. Now we have identified the other two."

She takes a deep breath, and so do I.

Easels are set up on either side of her. Both pictures are covered, and a uniformed policeman reveals the first.

I am right. It's Beth.

She is wearing no makeup in the picture, and her hair is pulled back into a ponytail. This makes her look about twelve.

"Beth Randall was twenty-four, originally from Alabama, and she was most recently employed as a waitress at the Hidden Oaks Country Club. Not long ago, her parents received a letter they thought was from her. Whoever wrote it claimed Beth was moving up to Montana to work on a farm."

Millicent. I would know her sense of humor anywhere. The only thing she hated more than fishing boats was farms.

"At the same time, her employer received a letter saying that she had a family emergency and was returning home to Alabama to help. Neither knew their letter was a fake."

Claire pauses for a moment as the cameras zoom in on the photo of Beth. She then turns to the other easel. I still think it must be Petra. I cannot think of anyone else who has disappeared or moved away. And I haven't checked on Petra in a long time. If I could have left the house, I might have.

The policeman unveils the photo.

This time, I am wrong. It is not Petra.

Crystal.

The woman who used to work for us.

The one who kissed me.

I'D NEVER EVEN thought of her. Now that I think about it, I should have, but I haven't seen Crystal in more than a year. We haven't been in contact at all since she stopped working for us.

Did Millicent know about the kiss? Is that why she killed Crystal? Or was she just collateral damage, part of Millicent's bigger plan?

I may never know. Of all the questions I would ask Millicent, those would not be in the top ten.

But my guess is that Crystal told Millicent. She was tortured into it.

I do not want to think about that.

The press conference is still on, and Claire introduces a man whose name I recognize from a documentary about Owen. He is a rather famous profiler, now retired, who is now an independent consultant and has written several true-crime books. This man—this tall, thin, decrepit-looking man—steps up to the podium and says he has never encountered a killer like me.

"He kills women he knows in a peripheral way, such as this cashier, and he also has created a separate persona, a deaf man named Tobias, that he uses to find more victims. The variety of methods used may be what has kept him from being discovered for so long."

Or maybe it's all a lie. But no one says that.

Piece by piece, my life is destroyed, like it was never real at all. It was just a line of dominoes set up by Millicent. The faster they fall, the less likely it seems I can get myself out of this.

And still I watch.

I watch until my eyes blur and my head feels like it's crumbling into my neck.

Definitive proof. This is what I need. Something like DNA evidence on a murder weapon, or video of Millicent killing one of these women.

I just don't have it.

THE PHONE WAKES me up. In the middle of watching my personal apocalypse, I dozed off. Kekona's theater seats are just too comfortable.

I pick up my phone and hear Andy's voice.

"Still breathing?"

"Barely."

"I can't believe they haven't caught you."

"You underestimate my intelligence." On TV, they are showing a picture of me at my high school prom.

"More like dumb luck," he says.

On top of everything else, there is the guilt. Andy believes in me because he doesn't know the half of it.

Another profiler is on TV. He has a deep, twangy accent that makes me want to turn the channel. But I do not.

"The level of torture can be directly correlated to the level of anger the killer has for the victim. For example, the burns on Naomi indicate that the killer was furious with her for some reason. It's impossible to know if the rage came from something she did or someone she reminded him of. Likely, we won't know that until he is caught."

Now I turn the channel. And I see a ghost. My ghost.

Petra.

Sixty-seven

SHE IS NOT only alive; she looks different. Not as much makeup and less flash. More upscale, as if she has spent the past couple of days getting a makeover. Her blue eyes are sharp and focused, and her previously unremarkable hair is shiny and stylish.

I remember her apartment, her bed. The cat named Lionel. She likes lime green and French vanilla ice cream and she couldn't believe I like ham on my pizza. I don't.

I also remember the sound of Petra's voice when she asked if I was really deaf. The same voice she has now, on TV. Suspicious. Accusatory. A tiny bit hurt.

"I met Tobias in a bar."

When the reporter asks why she waited days to come forward, Petra hesitates before answering.

"Because I slept with him."

"You slept with him?"

She nods, hangs her head in shame. For having sex or for choosing me, I don't know which one. Maybe both.

At first the media portrayed me as just a sick, twisted psychopathic serial killer. Now I am a sick, twisted psychopathic serial killer who *cheats on his wife*.

As if people needed another reason to hate me.

If they knew where I was, they would be lined up with pitchforks. But they don't know, so I am still able to sit here, watch TV, eat junk food, and wait until they either find me or Kekona returns home. Whichever comes first.

Petra goes from being nowhere to everywhere. She lies about some things, tells the truth about others. With each interview, the story becomes a little more detailed and my depression digs in a little deeper.

I still have moments when I think I can do something, so for hours I go through that stupid tablet like something new will appear. Perhaps a video of Millicent in that basement or a list of the women to kill.

When I'm not doing something useless, I am useless. A lump of self-hate and pity, wondering why I ever got married in the first place. Wishing I had never seen Millicent, much less sat next to her on that airplane. I wouldn't have turned into who I am now without her.

And when I'm not sinking into the quicksand of depression, I stare at the TV. I pretend all of this is someone else's problem.

I wonder how much my kids hate me. And what Dr. Beige is saying about me. I bet he is telling Jenna I am the source of all her problems. It was never Millicent, never Owen, always me. Because it couldn't be her.

Andy calls again.

"I saw your wife," he says.

"You what?"

"Millicent. I went over to your house and saw her," he says.

"Why?"

"Look, I'm trying to help you out here. It's not like I want to be in the same room with that woman," he says. "So I called her. Millicent and I have a lot in common. We've both lost our spouses."

Except I'm not dead. "Were the kids there?"

"Yes, saw them both. They're fine. Maybe a little stir-crazy, because they're staying in the house. The media and all."

"Did they say anything about me?"

A pause. "No."

This is probably good news, but it still hurts.

"Listen, whatever you're going to do, you better do it fast," Andy says. "Millicent said she wants to take the kids and get out of here for a while."

This would be reasonable for a wife who'd discovered her husband is a serial killer. It would also be reasonable for a serial killer who'd framed her husband. "She didn't say where, did she?"

"No."

"Didn't think so."

"One more thing," he says.

"What's that?"

"If I hadn't talked to you before all this happened, I don't know if I'd believe you. Not after seeing Millicent like that."

"Like what?"

"Like she's devastated."

The last part is what worries me. No one is going to believe a word I say. Not without proof.

AS THE HOURS pass, I sink further into Kekona's chair. The images on the TV float past my eyes: Lindsay, Naomi, me, Petra, Josh. He is talking, always talking, and he repeats everything. *Autopsy. Strangled. Tortured.* He must have said that last one a million times.

At one million and one, I sit up straight.

I am up, racing around Kekona's house, throwing aside my clothes and garbage until I find it.

Millicent's tablet.

She had looked at medical websites for information about the kids' ailments, but maybe there was more. Maybe I had missed it.

If I was going to torture someone but not kill them, I would have to research it. And I would start by looking up various injuries on medical websites.

A long shot. A very, very long shot.

As stupid as I feel for thinking that this kind of evidence might be on the tablet, what keeps me going is imagining how stupid I would feel if I didn't look . . . and it was right there all along.

I find the tablet in Kekona's dining room, on a table large enough to seat sixteen. It seems like a perfect place to sit down and go through the tablet again. I check each site, looking for something about torture and strangulation. I look for hot water burns and oil burns and internal bleeding and cuts on eyelids. I even look for cigarette burns, which is absurd, because Millicent refuses to be near cigarettes.

And I find nothing.

She looked at how long it takes for a sprained wrist to heal. She also searched for a variety of information about upset stomachs—what caused them and what to do about them.

That was it.

Nothing about torture, nothing helpful. I should have known better.

I shove the tablet away, and it skids. My immediate reaction is to check and see if I scratched Kekona's dining room table. As if it matters, but I do it anyway. I stand up and look straight down at it, running my finger across the wood, when something on the tablet screen catches my eye.

It is still on the page about upset stomachs. On the right-hand side, there is a list of possible causes. One of them is purple instead of blue, because the link has been clicked.

Eye drops.

Sixty-eight

TETRAHYDROZOLINE IS THE active ingredient in eye drops that gets rid of red eyes. Swallowing a large amount can cause serious problems. The drops lower blood pressure and can put someone into a coma. Or kill them.

But swallowing a small amount causes an upset stomach and vomiting. No fever.

The eye drops belong to Millicent.

She has been giving them to Jenna.

No.

Impossible.

The thought makes me physically ill. Jenna is our child, our daughter. She is not Lindsay or Naomi. She is not someone to torture.

Or maybe she is. Maybe Jenna is no different. Not to Millicent.

My daughter does not have a recurring stomach problem.

She has a mother who is poisoning her.

* * *

I **WANT TO** kill Millicent. I want to go to my house, kill my wife, and be done with it. I am that angry.

This feeling is different. Before, I never actually thought, "I want to kill a woman" or even "I want to kill this particular woman." My desire wasn't that clear, that succinct. It was about Millicent, about the two of us, and what I wanted out of it was more complex.

Now it is simple. I want my wife to die.

I head for the front door without a hat or a disguise or a weapon of any kind. I am angry and disgusted, and I do not care if I have a plan. My hand is on the doorknob when I realize how stupid I am. How stupid I always am.

I could probably get across Hidden Oaks without being spotted. Most think I'm on the run, not hiding in my own neighborhood. And once I did get all the way to my house, I could get inside, because I have a key. That's assuming it's not under surveillance.

On the other side, my wife. Who I now know is a monster.

Just like the real Owen.

Also, my kids. They are in the house, and both believe it is me, not her. I am the monster. And now all I can see is their reaction when I kill their mother.

I do not open the door.

And I do not just need a plan. I need evidence. Because on TV, evidence of me is everywhere.

My DNA. Though it should not be a surprise, Millicent still astonishes me. I have been saying that since I met her.

She managed to get my DNA all over the Bread of Life Christian Church. My sweat is found on the door handle out front, on the lock down to the basement, even on the stair railing. It is like she had a vial of my sweat and dabbed it everywhere.

A spot of my blood is found on the shelves against the wall.

More sweat on the handcuffs.

Blood on the chains and dirt.

She makes it look as if I mostly cleaned up but missed a few spots.

Claire has a midday press conference to announce all of this. I am officially upgraded from person of interest to suspect. The only suspect.

She even says I am "probably armed and definitely dangerous."

After hours of watching the experts, reporters, and former friends crucify me, I finally leave the house. I drive right out of Hidden Oaks and out into the world, where someone may or may not recognize me.

Across town, I drive by the EZ-Go where I used to get coffee. Instead of stopping, I drive ten miles down the interstate to another EZ-Go, which has the same self-serve machine. With the baseball cap on my head and almost a full week's growth of facial hair, I go in and get myself a coffee.

The young guy behind the counter barely looks up from his phone. It is almost anticlimactic.

It also emboldens me a little. Every person in the world is not looking for me. I could probably eat in a restaurant, shop at the mall, and see a movie before someone recognizes me. I just don't want to do any of those things.

Once I am in Hidden Oaks, something makes me drive by my house. The lawn is clear of toys, and the welcome sign on the door is gone. The shades are drawn, and the curtains are closed.

I wonder if Millicent has bought another bottle of eye drops. Or if she even looked for the old one.

I also wonder if Jenna is the only one she poisoned.

I have been sick a few times as well. If Millicent can make her own daughter sick, she is capable of doing it to anyone.

But I do not go inside the house. Not yet. I go back to Kekona's. The police are not waiting for me, nor have I been followed. Everything inside looks the same.

I almost leave the TV off, to take a break, but I can't.

Just about everyone is talking about the DNA, and the only exception is Josh. He is back to being a reporter, and he is interviewing a criminal pathologist. This man's voice is not as irritating, but he is a little boring, like a professor, at least until he gets to the paper cuts on Naomi.

"*The locations of the paper cuts are important to determining what caused them. We say 'paper' because of the type of cut, but there are also different types of paper. For instance, Naomi had shallow paper cuts on tougher skin, like the bottoms of the feet, and deeper cuts in softer areas, like the underside of the upper arm. That indicates that the same item was used, but it couldn't have been a regular piece of paper. It had to be something that would cut through the heel of a foot.*"

I jump off the couch like I've been shocked. And in a way, I have. I know what Millicent used to make those cuts.

Sixty-nine

RARELY DOES MILLICENT do something by accident. She has a reason for everything, even if it's to amuse herself.

This is one of those times.

It began so many years ago, when she asked me how I would protect her from assholes on planes who try to pick her up.

I would force them into the center seat, hog the armrests, and give them paper cuts with the emergency information card.

The emergency information card. The one I gave to her on the first Christmas we spent together. She has always kept it.

In her old apartment, it was taped to the mirror in her bathroom.

Our first place together was the small house, a rental, and the card was stuck to the fridge with a googly-eyed face magnet.

When we bought our first house, she slipped it inside the frame of our full-length mirror.

And in our bigger, more expensive house, we have two kids who do not appreciate the emergency-card joke. They think it's corny. Millicent carries the card with her, stuck inside the visor in her car. When the sun is in her eyes and she flips it down, the card makes her laugh.

The card is what she used to make all those paper cuts. I am as sure of this as I have been about anything.

HIDDEN OAKS IS not an easy place in which to hide. People notice new cars, especially the ones that just show up and park. They do not notice runners or walkers. People are always starting and stopping exercise programs, so on any given day there could be ten people out or none. A few are always out, like Millicent, but most come and go.

With the same baseball cap, more facial hair, baggy sweatpants, and a big T-shirt—thanks to Kekona, who owns an extraordinary amount of oversize clothing—I leave out the back door of her house, jump the fence, and jog out to the road.

It has been only a week since I disappeared, and the press is still everywhere. It would be impossible for Millicent and the kids to live normal lives right now. She can't go to work and the kids can't go to school, but I want to know if Millicent ever leaves the house. It would be a lot easier to get that emergency card if she takes the car out of the garage and parks it somewhere I can access.

Just about anything can go wrong with this idea. Maybe she has thoroughly cleaned that card, so there's no DNA on it at all—not from her or any of the women. Or maybe she got rid of it, threw it away or burned it up.

For my sake, I hope not.

I may not know everything she does, or everything she has done, but I know who she is on the inside. She keeps that card to remind her of us. And to remind herself of what she did to those women. Millicent enjoys it. I know that now.

Will the police believe me if I bring them that card? If it has DNA from one or more of the dead women and from Millicent, but not mine? Probably not.

Will they believe me if I also tell them about the building Millicent bought with three LLCs, about Denise and Owen's sister, and if I showed them my schedule when all of these women disappeared? I was always home. And I have no idea what the kids will say about those nights.

No, they wouldn't believe me. With my DNA in the basement and multiple people identifying me as Tobias, not to mention Millicent's performance, they won't believe I'm innocent for a second. But they might believe Millicent and I killed those women together, which would keep my children safe.

It's the only chance I have. Not just to save myself but to put her where she belongs—in jail or in hell. Either one works for me, as long as it is nowhere near my children.

I jog down the block parallel to my house, watching for Millicent's car through the paths between the houses. On my second pass, I jog down the street she would turn on to go toward the school.

As expected, I never see her car.

Throughout the day, I check back but never see her leave. I just can't be sure. It would be so much easier if I had left the tracker on her car. Still, I try, because I have to. Jogging and walking have become my new hobby. Too bad I couldn't adopt that dog at the shelter. It would be handy to have one right now.

I call Andy. He sounds surprised to hear from me. Maybe surprised I am alive.

"I just have a question," I say.

"Hit me."

I ask if Millicent ever leaves the house. "I assume she isn't even going to work," I say.

He hesitates before answering. "I don't think so. Neighbors have been bringing food by every day. It's all over the place. I think they're hunkered down, avoiding the media."

"That's what I figured."

"Why?" he says.

"Doesn't matter. Thanks again. You have no idea how much I appreciate this."

He clears his throat.

"What?" I say.

"I have to ask you not to call again." When I say nothing, he keeps talking. "It's the DNA. This whole thing has just become so much bigger than—"

"I understand. Don't worry about it."

"I do believe you," he says. "I just can't keep—"

"I know. I won't call again."

He hangs up.

The only surprise is that he stayed by me as long as he did. I didn't deserve his friendship. Not after Trista.

The sun has started to set, and I decide to make one last pass by the house before trying to go in. All I have to do is get into the garage, to her car, but it has to be after Millicent is asleep.

And I have keys.

FIFTEEN MINUTES LATER, I pass by on the parallel block and look for anything unusual. Like an unmarked police car because they are waiting for me to do exactly what I am about to do. Nothing. No unusual cars, no work trucks. There is nothing I don't recognize in the neighborhood. Except me, the bearded guy who jogs too much. It's surprising no one has stopped me yet.

I head back to Kekona's using different streets. It's the long way, but I used the short way earlier. By the time I make it to the edge of the circular drive up to her house, I stop dead.

A town car is in front.

The driver pulls a suitcase out of the trunk.

I hear her voice. Kekona is home.

Seventy

SHE'LL KNOW. THEY will all know.

It will take Kekona seconds to realize someone has been staying in her house. The police will know it is me within another few seconds. My car is in the garage. My fingerprints are everywhere. So is my DNA, and Millicent's tablet is right on the kitchen table.

Oh, and my wallet. I did not take it with me on the jog. It's also on the kitchen table.

I go back the way I came and jog all the way out to the least expensive houses in the Oaks. Here, there is a small greenspace, away from the children's park, where I stop near a group of trees and pretend to stretch.

I've got nowhere to go. No Andy to call or phone to call him with. No money, no friends, and almost a total lack of hope. But I do have keys. They are the only thing in my pocket.

Tonight was going to be the night anyway, the night I go into the garage to get the emergency card. In that respect, nothing has changed. What has changed is that I need a place to hide until Millicent is asleep.

My first thought is the club. Plenty of small rooms and closets to hang out in until well after dark. Getting in and out is the problem. Too many cameras.

The golf course is empty at night, but it's filled with wide-open spaces visible from the road.

I'll never find an unlocked car, not in Hidden Oaks. Here, everyone has modern, expensive cars, the kind with computers that do everything, including lock the doors.

For a moment, I consider hiding under a car. I'm just afraid someone will get in and start it.

In the distance, sirens. They are coming this way, but not to me. To Kekona's.

My options are dwindling, and I have to move. I can't just stay in this little greenspace forever. Not unless I bury myself.

I even consider hiding in my own backyard. And then, I do.

EVERYTHING LOOKS DIFFERENT from above. The neighborhood, the cars, the sky. My house. My kitchen, where the light is on.

Millicent.

She is the one who convinced me to climb a tree. It was not something I thought I would do again, but here I am, hidden within the big oak tree at the back of our yard. Far enough from the house that no one heard the leaves rustling as I climbed up it.

Millicent is cleaning up in the kitchen. She is too far away for me to see any details other than her red hair and black clothing. I bet she wears black all the time these days, especially when the police come by. Mourning those women, her husband, and the breakup of her family.

I am both impressed and sickened.

Rory walks into the kitchen and goes straight to the refrigerator. He doesn't move his right arm, I assume because the sling is still on it. He grabs something and stays there for a few minutes, talking to Millicent.

Jenna never comes into the kitchen, but I have to believe she is okay. Not sick. Millicent has no reason to poison her today.

My legs start to cramp up, and I adjust a little, although there isn't anywhere to go. The kitchen light goes off, but the bedroom lights are on. Still too early for sleep.

Around me, the neighborhood goes quiet as everyone settles in. Very few cars are on the road. It's a Tuesday night, not a popular one for big outings. I lean my head back against the tree trunk and wait.

By ten o'clock, everyone should be in bed. At eleven, I almost climb down, but then I let another thirty minutes pass. At half past, I climb down and walk along the edge of the yard, next to the fence, all the way to the house.

As I head to the side door into the garage, I look up.

Rory's light is out, window closed.

We almost never use the side door to the garage. I am exposed a little, because it is in front of the backyard gate. I slip the key into the lock and click it open. The noise sounds much louder than it probably is, and I freeze for a second before stepping inside.

I stand in the garage, next to the door, and wait for my eyes to adjust so I don't have to turn on a light.

The outline of Millicent's car comes into focus. Her luxury crossover is parked in the center of the garage. No need to make room for me anymore. I walk around to the driver's side, thankful that the window is open. I don't even have to open the door. I just reach up and flip down the visor. Something falls out onto the seat.

I feel around but find no emergency card, nor anything that feels like one. I open the car door. All at once, the light comes on, and I see something lying on the beige leather seat.

A blue glass earring.

Petra.

She knew. Millicent knew about both of the women I slept with.

Rory never told Jenna. He told his mother.

* * *

I FALL TO my knees. Defeat does not describe it. Done. I am just done.

Eventually, I end up lying down on the cement floor, curled into the fetal position. No will to get up, much less run. It's easier to stay here and wait for them to find me.

I close my eyes. The ground feels so cool, almost cold, and the air is a combination of dust, oil, and a little exhaust. Not comforting, not pleasant. Still, I do not move.

An hour passes, or two. No idea. Maybe it's been only five minutes.

My kids are what get me up.

And what Millicent might do to them.

Seventy-one

THE HOUSE IS not quite pitch-black. Light from street lamps and the moon filters in through the windows, allowing me to see just enough to not trip. To not make any noise. Although I know I will be caught, and soon, it can't happen yet.

At the bottom of the steps, I pause to listen. No one upstairs is moving. I go up.

The fifth step creaks a little. Maybe I knew that, or maybe I never paid attention.

I keep moving.

Jenna's room is on the left, followed by Rory's room and, at the end of the hall, the master bedroom.

I start with my daughter.

She is lying on her side, facing the window, and her breathing is steady. Peaceful. Her big white comforter is bunched up around her, like she's inside a cloud. I want to touch her, but know it's a bad idea. I watch, memorizing everything. If they put me in prison forever, this is how I want to remember my little girl. Safe. Comfortable. Healthy.

After several minutes, I leave and close the door behind me.

Rory is spread out on his bed, limbs everywhere. Most of them, anyway. The arm he has in a sling is the only one by his side. He sleeps with his mouth open but does not snore; it's the strangest thing. I watch him the way I watched Jenna, memorizing everything. Hoping my little boy turns into a better man than his father. Hoping he never meets a woman like Millicent.

I cannot blame him for telling his mother everything. I blame myself. For Petra, for taking the earrings. For all of it.

I leave his room, close the door without making a sound, and start down the hall. I imagine Millicent in bed, curled up under the covers, her red hair spread out on the white pillow. I can hear the long breaths she takes when she is in a deep sleep. And I can see the shocked look in her eyes when she wakes up and feels my hands around her throat.

Because I am going to kill my wife.

When Millicent discovered I'd cheated on her, she found her breaking point.

Tonight, I found mine.

I reach the closed bedroom door and lean close, listening. No sound. When I open the door, the first thing I see is the bed.

Empty.

My first instinct is to check behind the door. Maybe because I know Millicent would stab me in the back.

Empty.

"It's about time."

Her voice comes from across the room. I see a shadow, her outline. Millicent is sitting next to the window, in the dark. Watching for me.

"I knew you'd come," she says.

I step forward. Not too far. "Is that right?"

"Of course. It's what you do."

"Come home?"

"You have nowhere else to go."

The truth hits like a slap. The worst part is I can hear her smile.

It's too dark to see it until she turns on the light and stands up. Millicent is wearing her long cotton nightgown. It's white and swirls around her feet. I was not prepared for her to be awake. I didn't even bring a weapon.

But she did.

The gun in her hand is at her side, facing down at the floor. She is not pointing it at me. She is also not hiding it.

"That's your plan?" I say, pointing to the gun. "To kill me in self-defense?"

"Isn't that what you're here to do? Kill me?"

I raise both my hands. Empty. "Not likely."

"You're lying."

"Am I? Maybe I just want to talk."

She chuckles. "You can't be that stupid. If you were, I wouldn't have married you."

The bed is between us. It's a king-size, and I wonder if I can leap over it before she can raise the gun and shoot.

Probably not.

"Didn't find that emergency card, did you?" she asks.

I say nothing.

"Rory gave me that cheap little earring," she says. "He thought you were cheating, but then realized you were sneaking out to kill women. Of course, I didn't tell him he was right the first time."

I shake my head, trying to understand. "Why—"

"I left that woman alive so everyone would find out what a cheating bastard you are," she says.

Petra.

Petra is still alive because she had sex with me. And she'll never even know it.

"Do you have any idea," Millicent says, "how much therapy our son is going to need?"

I cannot comprehend the madness of what she has done. The staggering amount of patience. Of discipline. "Why not just leave me?" I say. "Why do all of this?"

"Do what? Set up our home, take care of the kids, make sure everything runs smoothly? Keep track of the finances and cook dinner? Or are you referring to Owen? Because the original plan was to bring him back. *For us.*" She takes a step closer to the bed but not around it.

"No—"

"And you were so willing. I barely had to do anything. You killed Holly, not me."

"She threatened you. Threatened our family."

Millicent throws her head back and laughs. At me.

I stare at her, remembering all the stories she'd told me about Holly. The injuries, the accidents, the threats. The cut on her hand, between her thumb and forefinger. The pieces rearrange in my head, like a puzzle that had been put together wrong.

Millicent had done it all to herself. Holly just got the blame.

"Jesus," I say. "Holly was never a threat, was she?"

"My sister was nothing but a weak, sniveling girl who deserved everything I did to her."

"She crashed the car because you were torturing her," I say. "Not the other way around."

Millicent smiles.

Everything hits at once. It's hard enough to make me dizzy. Millicent set her sister up the same way she set me up.

She has always tortured people. Her sister. Lindsay. Naomi.

Jenna. Maybe she didn't just poison Jenna to keep me out of the way.

And me. Maybe all those times I was sick, she had done it.

Because Millicent likes to hurt people.

"You're a monster," I say.

"That's funny, because the police say the same thing about you."

The look on her face is triumphant, and, for the first time, I see how ugly she is. I cannot believe I ever thought she was beautiful.

"I found the eye drops," I say. "The ones in the pantry."

Her eyes flash.

"You've been poisoning our daughter," I say.

She was not expecting this. She didn't think I would figure it out.

"You really are crazy," she says. A bit less conviction now.

"I'm right. You've been making her sick all along."

She shakes her head. Out of the corner of my eye, something moves. I look toward the door.

Jenna.

Seventy-two

SHE IS STANDING in the doorway wearing her orange-and-white pajamas. Her hair is sticking out all over, and her eyes are wide. Awake. She is staring at her mother.

"You made me sick?" she says. Her voice is so small it makes her sound like a toddler. A heartbroken toddler.

"Absolutely not," Millicent says. "If anyone poisoned you, it was your father."

Jenna turns to me. Her eyes are filling with tears.

"Dad?"

"Baby, no. It wasn't me."

"He's lying," Millicent says. "He poisoned you, and he killed those women."

I stare at Millicent, not having any idea who I married. She stares back. I turn to my daughter. "She put eye drops in your food to make you sick."

"You're insane," Millicent says.

"Think back," I say to Jenna. "All those times you were sick, who cooked your food? How often do I cook at all?"

Jenna stares at me, and then her eyes shift to her mother.

"Baby, don't listen," Millicent says.

"What's going on?"

We are all startled by the new voice.

Rory.

HE WALKS UP behind Jenna. His eyes are bleary, and he rubs them while glancing from me to his mother to his sister, looking confused about everything. My kids have seen their own lives implode over the past week. Their father has been accused of being a serial killer; their mother has likely told them it is true. I do not know if they believe it.

"Dad?" he says. "Why are you here?"

"I didn't do what they say, Rory. You have to believe me."

"Stop lying," Millicent says.

Jenna looks at her brother. "Dad says Mom made me sick."

"She did," I say.

"He's lying," Millicent says. "All he does is lie."

Rory looks at her and says, "Did you call the police already?"

She shakes her head. "I haven't had a chance. He just walked into the bedroom."

"And you just happened to have that gun in your hand?" I say.

Rory's eyes widen as he sees the gun at Millicent's side. She still has not lifted her hand.

"She was waiting for me to show up," I say. "So she can kill me and claim I attacked her."

"Shut up," Millicent says.

"Mom?" Jenna says. "Is that true?"

"Your father came here to kill me."

I shake my head. "That's not true. I came here to get both of you away from your mother," I say. And I go even further, because they have to know. "Your mother set me up. I didn't kill those women."

"Wait a minute," Rory says. "I don't get—"

"What is happening?" Jenna yells.

"Enough," Millicent says. Her voice is low and hard.

We all shut up, just as we always do when she says that. It is quiet enough to hear everyone breathing.

"Kids," Millicent says, "get out of here. Go downstairs."

"What are you going to do?" Jenna says.

"Go."

"Dad doesn't have a weapon," Rory says.

Again, I raise my empty hands. "I don't even have a phone."

Rory and Jenna turn to their mother.

Millicent glares at me as she steps around them and raises her hand. She points the gun at me.

"Mom!" Jenna yells.

"Wait." Rory jumps forward, placing himself between the gun and me. He throws off his sling and holds out both arms.

Millicent does not lower her hand. She raises the other one and holds the gun with both hands. The gun is pointed at our son.

"Get out of the way," she says.

He shakes his head.

"Rory, you have to move," I say.

"No. Put the gun down."

Millicent takes a step forward. "Rory."

"No."

I can see the anger in her eyes, even on her face. It is turning an unnatural color of red.

"Rory," she says. "Move."

Her voice is a growl. I see Jenna jump a little.

Rory does not move. I hold my hand out, intending to grab his arm and pull him out of the way. Right then, Millicent shifts the gun and fires one shot. The bullet goes right into our bed.

Jenna screams.

Rory freezes.

Millicent takes a step toward him.

She has lost control. I can see it in her pitch-black eyes. If she has to, she will shoot Rory.

She will shoot all of us.

I jump forward and knock Rory down, covering his body with mine. Just as we hit the ground, I see a blur of orange-and-white polka dots. And a glint of metal.

Jenna. She has the knife from under her bed. I never even saw it in her hand.

She heads right for Millicent, the knife raised, and crashes into her. They both tumble backward onto the bed.

The gun fires a second time.

Another scream.

I jump up. Rory is right behind me. He grabs the gun, which has fallen out of Millicent's hand. I grab Jenna and pull her off. The knife comes with her. It slides right out of Millicent.

Blood.

So much blood.

Millicent is on the floor now, her hands clasped against her abdomen. The blood is coming from her.

Behind me, Jenna is screaming, and I turn to see if she's hurt. Rory shakes his head at me and points to the wall. The second bullet is lodged there, not inside my daughter.

"Get her out of here," I say.

Rory drags Jenna out of the room. She is hysterical and screams all the way down the hall, dropping the bloody knife as she goes.

I turn to Millicent.

She is lying on the floor, staring up at me. Her white nightgown is turning red, right before my eyes. She looks exactly like my wife and, at the same time, nothing like her.

She opens her mouth and tries to speak. Blood comes out. Millicent looks at me, her eyes wild. She does not have long. A few minutes, a few seconds, and she knows it. She keeps trying to say something.

I grab the knife and bring it down hard, plunging it right into her chest.

Millicent does not get the final word.

Epilogue

Three Years Later

THE MAP ON the wall showed the whole world, from Australia to the Americas, and the North Pole to the South. We didn't use darts, because we all have an aversion to metal objects with sharp edges. Instead, we pulled out an ancient Pin the Tail on the Donkey game and put new adhesive on the ribbon tails. Blindfolded, we each took a turn. Jenna went first, followed by Rory. I went last.

I breathed a sigh of relief when two of the first three tails landed in Europe. Neither the Arctic nor Antarctica sounded very inviting to me.

We tacked up a map of Europe and played again—wash, rinse, repeat—until we had found a new place to live: Aberdeen, Scotland.

Our choice was made.

That was two and half years ago, right after I was finally cleared by the police. I didn't think I would be. In fact, I thought Millicent would be named another one of my victims. No one knew Jenna stabbed her, not after I wiped off the knife and made sure the only prints were mine. I also confessed. I told the police I killed my wife in self-defense, because she was the real killer. It never occurred to me that anyone would believe it.

And they wouldn't have if it hadn't been for Andy, who said it couldn't be me. I couldn't even use a tablet computer, he told them, so how the hell could I kill so many women without getting caught?

Then there was Kekona, who said I was a terrible liar and could never be a serial killer. Although she did mention that I was a pretty good tennis coach.

And my kids. Jenna told the police that she overheard our argument and that her mother admitted to setting me up. Rory told them it was self-defense, because his mother was about to shoot him. Neither told the police what really happened. Those details do not matter.

I like to think the police believed everyone who stood up for me, that they knew I couldn't be a killer. But it was the DNA. All the evidence in the church basement underwent rigorous testing at the FBI lab in Quantico. The result confirmed what we already knew: The DNA was mine.

The samples came from two sources: sweat and blood. And they saved me. Or rather, Millicent's lack of knowledge saved me. The FBI tests revealed that all the samples of blood and sweat had the exact same amount of chemical decomposition. It looked like Millicent had collected my fluids just once and then sprinkled them around all at the same time. The report stated that I must have been in that basement only once, because the DNA had been left on the same day. An impossibility if I had killed those women at different times.

It's too bad Millicent never knew how badly she had screwed up.

As soon as I was cleared, we sold the house and left Hidden Oaks. The first thing I had to get used to was the cold. And the snow.

I've never lived where it snows before, but now it surrounds us. At first, it's light and fluffy, like hand-spun cotton candy. When it blankets the city, everything goes quiet. It's as if Aberdeen has been lifted right into the clouds.

The day after, it's slushy and dirty and the whole city looks covered in soot.

Our third winter is coming up, and I have grown a bit more used to it. Rory has not. Just last night, he showed me a website for a college in Georgia.

"Too far," I said.

"We're in Scotland. Everything is far."

He had a point. And that was *the* point, to get far away from our old life. We are doing okay. I can say that without crossing my fingers.

Jenna has a new therapist and a couple of prescriptions. I find it amazing that she functions at all, given what Millicent did to her. Rory has his own therapist, as do I. Once in a while, we have a group session, and we haven't hurt one another yet.

I do not tell them that I miss her. Sometimes. I miss the family she built, the structure, the way she kept us organized. But not all the time. Now, we don't have as many rules, but we still have some. It's all up to me, I can make a rule or not. Break it or not. No one is around to tell me if I am wrong or right.

Today I am in Edinburgh, a larger city than Aberdeen. I have come to see my tax attorney. Moving out of the country is complicated. Taxes must be paid in multiple places, depending on where money is kept. Our house in Hidden Oaks sold for a good amount; we are more than comfortable for the moment. I also coach tennis. It is a huge sport in Scotland, though much of the time we play on indoor courts.

When I am done with the tax lawyer, I find myself with a little time before the next train to Aberdeen. I stop in a pub near the station and motion to the bartender for an ale on tap. He fills a mug with a dark, syrupy liquid, unlike any beer I drank back home.

The woman next to me has dark hair and pale skin. She is dressed like someone who just got off work and is having a drink before heading home. I can sense her relief that the day is almost over.

After half a drink, she glances up at me and smiles.

I return the smile.

She looks away and looks back.

I take out my phone, type out a message, and slide it across the bar.

Hello. My name is Quentin.

Acknowledgments

When I sat down to write this, I realized I had no idea where to start. I've never written acknowledgments before, but what I do know is that many, many people worked very hard to get this book into your hands. I can never thank them all properly, but I'll give it a shot.

My agent, Barbara Poelle. Without her, *My Lovely Wife* would not be a published book. Turns out she is as disturbed as I am (maybe more so) and crazy enough to take a chance on a nobody like me.

My editor, Jen Monroe. She made this book better, caught all my mistakes, and refused to let me get away with anything. My heart jumps every time I see her name in my inbox, but that's a good thing.

My publicist, Lauren Burnstein, who has done things I never thought possible. I am pretty sure she has magical powers.

My marketing team, Fareeda Bullert and Jessica Mangicaro, who have gone above and beyond to make sure everyone has heard of *My Lovely Wife*.

Everyone at Berkley, I am so grateful you decided to publish this book, and grateful for all the time and resources you have dedicated to it.

My friends, critique partners and fellow writers, without whom I would be nowhere. Starting with Rebecca Vonier, who would not let me give up on this book. I never would have finished it without her, nor would it be a published book. Marti Dumas, who points out all the story and character problems and is always right. Laura Cherry, who notices every little thing and tells me about it. And Hoy Hughes, who started the original writer's group where I met all these wonderful people.

There are many, many others who have taken the time to read and offer opinions of my writing (most of it was bad). I won't even try to name every person, because I will forget someone, but you know who you are.

All the bloggers, writers, reviewers, and everyone who has found themselves with this book in their hands. First and foremost, I am a reader. I am grateful for the joy that books have brought me and grateful anyone would want to read my words.

I can't leave out my day-job boss and longtime friend, Andrea, who has always been supportive.

Last but definitely not least, my family. My mom, who is always there for me no matter what crazy adventure I'm on. And my brother, who made me tough.

My Lovely Wife

Samantha Downing

QUESTIONS FOR DISCUSSION

1. What is your first impression of the narrator and of Millicent?

2. How would you describe their marriage? Do you relate to it at all?

3. What is your first impression of their children, Rory and Jenna?

4. What was the first surprise in the story? Did it change your feelings about Millicent and/or her husband?

5. Who, if anyone, did you root for in the book? Did that change at any point?

6. What scenes did you most relate to, if any? Are there any conversations you have had with your own spouse?

7. The media has a large role in the story. How does it compare to your own life? What role does the media play, if any?

8. Are Andy and Trista real friends? If not, how would you categorize them?

9. What are your thoughts about Kekona? What role does she play in the narrator's life?

10. Do you consider the narrator unreliable? Why or why not?

11. Were you satisfied by the ending? Did it change anything for you?

BEHIND THE BOOK

One of the best things about having a book published is being able to talk to people who have read it. This is when I have a chance to share the "story behind the story." In other words, I can share my inspiration and thought behind many of the things that happen in the book.

For example, the country club where the husband works as a tennis pro. When I was growing up in California, my family belonged to a country club. My father played a lot of golf, so all of us kids also learned how to play. We spent a lot of time at that club, either taking lessons or hanging out in the clubhouse, where we drank Shirley Temples (a non-alcoholic drink) and ate all the bar snacks. When I wrote about Hidden Oaks Country Club in *My Lovely Wife*, the club from my childhood is the one I imagined. The same clubhouse, the same buildings, the same men's and women's locker rooms and lounges. That's the only country club I know, the only one I've ever belonged to, and it was my reference point for the club in the novel.

One of the questions I am most asked is about Millicent's name. How did I come up with it? Here in the U.S., it's an unusual name for a girl these days. Millie is rather common, but not Millicent. The name actually comes from *The Brady Bunch,* and I've seen every episode multiple times. The show was constantly on TV when I was a kid, and I remembered a girl named Millicent.

In case you don't remember or haven't seen the show, Millicent is the first girl Bobby Brady kissed—and she gave him the mumps! For some reason I always remembered her, so when it came time to choose a name for this novel, I decided it had to be Millicent. In fact . . . this almost makes me want to have someone named after a *Brady Bunch* character in all of my books. Stay tuned!

I also have to talk about the community of Hidden Oaks, Florida. Gated communities have become very popular in this country, and although I have never lived in one, I have visited friends and family who do. To be honest, the fictional community I created in the novel was to poke a little fun at those communities, at their lifestyle, and at the way they try to wall themselves off from the rest of society. Gated communities are considered *exclusive* and not *inclusive,* and I hope you get a few laughs from the portrayal of Hidden Oaks. It is certainly meant as tongue in cheek.

Oftentimes, writing comes from the subconscious and authors (definitely me!) don't always realize where an idea came from. For example, there is a street in the book called Danner Drive. It wasn't until after the book was published that one of my coworkers asked if the name was intentional. Only then did I realize that one of our offices is located on a street with the same name. I must have seen it sometime that day, and then used it in the book without making the connection. Somehow that made it all the way through edits and I *still* never caught it! I am usually so careful about not making any identifiable connections to my life, and yet there it is. As far as I know that's the only one in this book, and I'm trying hard not to make the same mistake in the next one!

I hope you enjoyed this inside look into some of the characters, locations, and ideas behind *My Lovely Wife,* and I really hope you enjoy the book as much as I enjoyed writing it! Please feel free to reach out to me on social media as well. I love hearing from people and getting their thoughts on the book. I've already received some questions about things even I didn't think about, and I love that!

FURTHER READING

A lot of people have asked why the narrator of *My Lovely Wife* doesn't have a name. The truth is, it never occurs to him to say it. He sees himself only in terms of his family—as a husband, and as a father. Without his family, he is nothing, just a man without a name.

I've always been intrigued by unnamed narrators, and writing one was certainly challenging. It's been done by many other writers—including in classics like *Invisible Man* by Ralph Ellison and *The Tell-Tale Heart* by Edgar Allan Poe. Here's of a list of my favorite books with unnamed narrators:

Bright Lights, Big City by Jay McInerney
This book was written in the '80s and takes place in New York, exemplifying all the "greed is good" era had to offer. It has the parties, the drugs, and all the yuppie angst . . . along with an unnamed narrator who tries to muddle through all of it.

Rebecca by Daphne Du Maurier
This novel was definitely an inspiration for *My Lovely Wife*. The unnamed narrator in this novel is the second wife. Rebecca was

the first; she is dead but still ever-present at Manderly, the couple's infamous home.

Fight Club by Chuck Palahniuk

Written in 1996, this post-80s book is a dark look at a society where everyone has become just a number, a consumer, another cog in the capitalistic world—in other words, the perfect scenario for an unnamed narrator.

When I Hit You by Meena Kandasamy

A brutal account of domestic abuse leaves the battered, bruised narrator without a name. Not an easy book to read, and it will stay with you for a long, long time.

The Yellow Wallpaper by Charlotte Perkins Gilman

This is a short story written in the nineteenth century and considered a classic. The narrator is a young woman locked away in a large, empty house, and with nothing else around, she becomes fixated on the yellow wallpaper.

Dept. of Speculation by Jenny Offill

A book about a marriage told by the unnamed wife, who tries to figure out how it all went wrong. This novel is unique, funny, and often right on point.

Blindness by Jose Saramago

Imagine a world where everyone goes blind all at once. That's the premise for this horrifying novel, where Saramago explores this terrible world through the eyes of an unnamed narrator. Not only does society break down fast, so does humanity.

Don't miss Samantha Downing's
thrillingly savage novel . . .

HE STARTED IT

About a family not unlike your own—just with a few
more violent tendencies thrown in.

14 DAYS LEFT

You want a heroine. Someone to root for, to identify with. She can't be perfect, though, because that'll just make you feel bad about yourself. A flawed heroine, then. Someone who may break the rules to protect her family but doesn't kill anyone unless it's self-defense. Not murder though, at least not the cold-blooded kind. That's the first deal breaker.

The second is cheating. Men can get away with that and still be the hero, but a cheating wife is unforgivable.

Which means I can't be your heroine.

I still have a story to tell.

It begins in a car. Rather, an SUV. We sit according to our rank, the oldest in the driver's seat. That's Eddie. His wife sits next to him, but I'll get to her.

The middle seat is for the middle child, and that's me. Beth. Not Elizabeth, just Beth. I'm two years younger than Eddie, and he never lets me forget it. I'm okay to look at, though not as young or thin as I used to be. My husband sits next to me. Again, later for that, because our spouses weren't supposed to be here.

One seat left, way in the back, and that's Portia. The surprise baby. She's six years younger than me and sometimes it feels like a hundred. With no spouse or significant other, she has the whole seat to herself.

In the very back, our luggage. Stacked side by side in a neat single row because that's the only way it fits. I told Eddie that the first time. Our handbags and computers bags go on top of the roller bags. You don't have to be a flight attendant to figure that out.

Under the bags, there's the trunk compartment. One side has the spare tire. In the other, a locked wooden box with brass fittings. This special little box in this special little place, all by itself with nothing else around, is to hold our grandfather. He's been cremated.

We aren't talking about him. We aren't really talking at all. The sun beams through the windows, landing on my leg and making it burn. The A/C dries out my eyes. Eddie plays music that is wordless and jazzy.

I look back at Portia. Her eyes are closed and she has headphones on, probably listening to music that is neither wordless nor jazzy. Her black hair is long and has fallen over one eye. It's dyed. We all have pale skin, and we were all born with blond hair and either blue or green eyes. My hair is even lighter now because I highlight it. Eddie's is darker because he doesn't. Portia's hair has been black for a while now. It matches her nails. She's not goth, though. Not anymore.

The music change is abrupt. I didn't even see Krista move. That's Eddie's wife. Krista, the one with olive skin, dark hair, and brown eyes with gold flecks. Krista, the one he married four months after meeting her. She used to be the receptionist at his office.

Pop music blares out of the speakers, a dance song from five years ago. It was bad then, too.

"The jazz was putting me to sleep," Krista says.

My husband's eyes flick up from his laptop. He probably didn't notice the change in music, but he heard Krista's voice.

Maybe she's the heroine.

"It's fine," Eddie says. I can hear the smile on his face.

I continue to stare out the window. Atlanta is long gone. We aren't even in Georgia. This is northern Alabama, past Birmingham, where the population is sparse and skeptical. If we were trying to rush, we'd be further along by now. Rushing isn't part of the equation.

"Food?"

That's Portia, her voice groggy from her nap. She's sitting up, headphones off, wide-eyed like a child.

She's been milking that baby-of-the-family shit for a long time.

"You want to stop?" Eddie says, turning down the music.

"Let's stop," Krista says.

My husband shrugs.

"Yes," Portia says.

Eddie looks at me in the rearview mirror, like I get a say in the matter. I'm already outnumbered.

"Great," I say. "Food is great."

We stop at a place called the Roundabout, which looks just as you imagine. Rustic in a fake way, with the lasso and goat on the sign, but naturally rundown with age. Authentic but not—like most of us.

We all climb out and Portia is first to the door; Krista isn't far behind. Eddie is the one who takes the most time. He stands outside the car, staring at the back. Hesitating.

It's our grandfather. This is our first stop of the trip, meaning it's the first time we have to leave him alone.

"You okay?" I say, tapping Eddie's arm.

He doesn't look at me, doesn't take his eyes off the back of the car because Grandpa's ashes are everything to us. Not for emotional reasons.

"You want to stay out here? I can bring you a doggie bag," I say. Sarcasm drips.

Eddie turns to me, his eyes wide. Oh, the shock. Like if I had just told him I was leaving my longtime partner for someone I met two months ago.

Oh wait, he did that. Eddie left his live-in girlfriend for the receptionist.

"I'm fine," he says. "You don't have to be so bitchy about it."

Yes. I'm the villain.

Inside the Roundabout, everyone is sitting in a semicircle booth. It's twice as big as it needs to be. The seats are wine-colored pleather. Krista and Portia have scooted all the way to the center of the booth, leaving Felix on one side. That's my husband, Felix, the pale one with the strong jaw and white-blond hair with matching eyebrows and lashes. In a certain light, he disappears.

"No," Portia says. "There's nothing vegan."

She isn't vegan but checks anyway. Portia also looks for wheelchair access and won't go in anywhere that doesn't have it because fairness is important.

"Should we leave?" I say.

No one answers. I sit.

The burgers are chargrilled, the fries are crisp, and the bacon is greasy. A fair deal, if you ask me. The only thing missing is decent coffee, but I drink their bitter version of it without complaint. I can be a good sport.

"We probably should get something settled," Eddie says. He looks like our father. "We're going to be driving for a while. A lot of gas, food, and motel rooms. I propose we take turns covering the expenses. More than anything else, let's not argue about it. The last thing we need to do is fight over a gas bill."

Before I can say a word, my husband does.

"Makes sense," Felix says. "Beth and I will pay our fair share."

Only a spouse can betray you like that. Or a sibling.

That leaves Portia. Given that she's doesn't really have a career, the deal isn't fair.

Oh, the irony.

She yawns. Nods. In Portia-speak, she's agreeing for now but reserves the right to disagree later.

"Great," Eddie says. "I'll get this one."

He takes the check up to the register, because that's the kind of place this is. Felix goes to the restroom and Portia steps out front to make a call. That leaves Krista and me, finishing those last sips of lukewarm coffee.

"I know this must be terrible for all of you," she says, placing her hand on mine. "But I hope we can have some good times, too. I'm sure your grandfather would've wanted that."

It's a nice enough thing for Krista to say, if a little generic. Given the circumstances, I expect nothing less and nothing more.

Still. If everything falls apart and we all start killing each other, she goes first.

You think I said that for shock value. I didn't.

No, I'm not a psychopath. That's always a convenient excuse, though. Someone who has no empathy and has to fake human emotions. Why do they do bad things? Shrug. Who knows? That's a psychopath for you. Or is it the word sociopath? You know what I'm saying.

This isn't that kind of story. This is about family. I love my siblings, all of them, I really do. I also hate them. That's how it goes—love, hate, love, hate, back and forth like a seesaw.

That's the thing about family. Despite what they say, it's not a single unit with a single goal. What *they* never tell us is that, more often than not, every member of the family has their own agenda. I know I do.

Author photo by Jacqueline Dallimore

Samantha Downing currently lives in New Orleans, where she is furiously typing away at her next thrilling novel.

Ready to find
your next great read?

Let us help.

Visit prh.com/nextread

Penguin
Random
House